CRITICS ~
AND *WED*

"Although the plot is ~ ed touch, and misaligned ~ , a deranged p~ ~ of real dange~ ~ y story put~ ~ e who like ~

~ *l*

"Once ag~ ~ a number o~ ~ e decent m~ ~ y romances.~

—*Romantic Times BOOKreviews*

"Ms. Craig delivers a well-paced and well-plotted mystery that will keep you guessing to the last page without compromising the happily-ever-after romantic ending."

—Fresh Fiction

"Humor runs rampant...Christie Craig takes the reader on a ride between laughter and fear. The pace is as quick as the quips. While the characters moan and complain about their various love dilemmas, they share humorous banter, making this trip to love a racy road."

—Romance Reviews Today

"If you want a sexy romance that will put a smile on your face, a Christie Craig book is the way to go!"

—Night Owl Romance

"A story that twines emotions and feelings with sizzle and steam, all wrapped around bits of humor...*Weddings Can Be Murder* combines passionate and intense characters with a plot that's well-balanced and fast-moving. It's edgy and fun."

—Once Upon a Romance Review

PRAISE FOR
DIVORCED, DESPERATE AND DELICIOUS!

"Christie Craig delivers humor, heat, and suspense in addictive doses. She's the newest addition to my list of have-to-read authors....Funny, hot, and suspenseful. Christie Craig's writing has it all. Warning: definitely addictive."
—*New York Times* Bestselling Author Nina Bangs

"Readers who enjoy Jennie Crusie and Janet Evanovich will fall head over heels for *Divorced, Desperate and Delicious*, a witty romantic adventure...filled with humorous wit, sexy romance and just enough danger to keep you up long past midnight."
—*New York Times* Bestselling Author Dianna Love Snell

"Suspense and romance that keeps you on the edge of your seat ...until you fall off laughing...a book you can't put down."
—RITA Finalist Gemma Halliday

"...an exceptionally funny, fast paced, snappy read with unusual humor that will make you laugh."
—Huntress Reviews

"I would compare this book to Janet Evanovich's Stephanie Plum series, but *Divorced, Desperate and Delicious* is even funnier and a thousand times sexier."
—Night Owl Romance

"This is an entertaining, fast-moving mystery and romance peopled with interesting, likable characters, as well as warm and cuddly animals. The main romance, as well as the secondary ones, are delightful, and the suspense is well done. This is an all-around enticing and fun story to read."
—*Romantic Times BOOKreviews*

"*Divorced, Desperate and Delicious* is funny, witty, suspenseful, and very entertaining....This is a wonderful book. The characters are charming, and there are enough twists and turns to keep the reader guessing. Christie Craig has a winner."
—Romance Reviews Today

BUSTED

"It was *one* kiss," he said.

Oh, yes. One kiss by a cop Sue couldn't forget.

"We have to stop avoiding each other. Let's go back inside and prove to each other, and to Chase and Lacy, we're adults."

She looked him in the eyes—blue eyes, long lashes. "Sorry, I'll have to be an adult another day. But if you start practicing now, you might succeed in a couple of years."

"Don't be silly." The wind blew again and the bow on her dress flew up to her Wonderbra cleavage. He jerked his fingers out of his pockets and tucked his hands beneath the opposite armpits like a child who'd been told not to touch.

"I'm not being silly. I'm meeting someone."

"You *aren't* meeting anyone. You're lying so you don't have to be in the same room with me." He rubbed his arm. "I happen to know that you don't date. You belong to that Divorced, Desperate and Delicious club that you, Lacy and Kathy started. Of course, Lacy jumped ship."

Sue gritted her teeth. Did everyone in town know she hadn't had sex in two years? "Well, throw me a landline, matey, because you can drop the desperate for me, too. I'm now divorced, delicious and dating."

Divorced, Desperate and Dating

CHRISTIE CRAIG

LOVE SPELL NEW YORK CITY

*To Jake, my canine office companion and muse, who gave
me the best years of his life.
I miss you, buddy.*

LOVE SPELL®

December 2008

Published by

Dorchester Publishing Co., Inc.
200 Madison Avenue
New York, NY 10016

ISBN 10: 0-505-52732-4
ISBN 13: 978-0-505-52732-5

The name "Love Spell" and its logo are trademarks of Dorchester
Publishing Co., Inc.

Printed in the United States of America.

10 9 8 7 6 5 4 3 2 1

Visit us on the web at www.dorchesterpub.com.

ACKNOWLEDGMENTS

I'd like to give credit where credit is due:

To the people who, at the last minute, helped me get this book out the door: Faye Hughes, my writing partner, personal publicist and computer guru who talks me down from my computer ledges; Suzan Harden, my cliché police—she's one in a million; Jody Payne, who stays up way past midnight to read my work and swears it's because I'm good and not because she likes me. Thank you all.

To my father, from whom I inherited his wacky sense of humor. (If you think I'm nuts, you should meet my dad.) To my mom, for passing on her ability to laugh at her own mistakes, as well as her love of telling a good joke. (Let's keep 'em laughing, Mom.) To my husband, who makes being married to me look easy, who never complains if I use him in my books or blogs, and who never whines when he has to share me with the characters living inside my head.

To Lieutenant D. R. "Duke" Atkins, Jr., with the Houston Police Department, who is finally going to get to read the gun/ tampon scene. Don't shoot me, Duke.

As always, thanks to my editor Chris Keeslar and agent Kim Lionetti for putting up with me. And finally, to Erin Galloway, Marketing Manager at Dorchester, who is always there to answer my questions and assist me on whatever crazy idea I get.

Divorced, Desperate and Dating

CHAPTER ONE

The worst part about murdering someone was planning exactly how to do it. Not that this was Sue Finley's first. She'd whacked at least ten people, but it never got any easier.

She bounced the toe of her strappy sandal against the kitchen island, the portable phone trapped between her shoulder and ear as she waited for the Poison Control Hotline. "How much poinsettia leaf would it take to kill someone?" she asked as soon as someone answered.

"Can ya hold?" the woman on the other end asked in a twangy voice, her Texas drawl as thick as the state's humidity.

"Sure." Sue reached for a magazine on the counter. The cover promised to make her a better lover and reduce the size of her thighs in ten minutes. Instead, she fanned damp air across equally damp skin with the glossy pages.

The heck with poinsettia; July in the South could kill. She heard the telltale humming of her central air just as her cell phone started chiming. Sue tossed away the magazine, rummaged beneath several loose tampons in her purse to find the phone, and pressed it against her other ear. "Hello?"

"Hey, it's me again," Melissa Covey, her agent, said. "I'm in the middle of downtown Houston. Am I taking—Oh, I'm getting another call. Hang on."

"Sure." Sue glanced at one silent phone and then the other. With a phone to each ear, she paced and watched

Hitchcock, her gray tabby, leap up on the table. The cat dipped his paw into Sue's coffee mug, testing the brew's temperature before lapping up his daily dose of caffeine. She really should start pouring him his own cup, but whenever the feline's green eyes gazed up at her with such adoration and unconditional love, Sue forgot about cat germs.

"Hey, baby." She bumped foreheads with her pet.

"Did ya say poinsettia?" the woman from Poison Control asked.

"Yes, poinsettia." Sue pulled away from the cat. "I'm a writer, and—"

"Can you hold again?"

"No problem." Sue bit down on her lip. *On hold.* The story of her life.

But no more. Her gaze caught on the black lace teddy stretched out on the butcher block countertop beside the Victoria's Secret bag. She only hoped sex was like riding a bicycle and one didn't forget how to do it. Then again, the last time she'd gotten on a bike she'd hit the right-hand brake instead of the left and nose-dived over the handlebars. Oh, Jiminy Cricket, she hoped sex *wasn't* like biking. Or at least she hoped it came with pedal brakes.

Doubts about the weekend started to fizz. She tried to visualize her and Paul doing the deed, but then she recalled last night's kiss. The kiss that had left her feeling . . . nothing. She'd even put her heart and soul into that kiss, hoping it would have the same earthshaking effect on her as The-Boyfriend-Who-Never-Was Jason Dodd's kiss had four months ago.

The earth hadn't moved. Not even a wiggle. Not with Paul.

For the hundredth time, she wondered if Jason had felt the earth shake that April night, too. Probably not. He'd never bothered calling her, even after he'd asked for her number. Not that it mattered now; she was *so* over him. Memories of how he'd tasted, of how hard his body had felt . . . Oh, brother. Well, she was almost over him.

With one phone pinned between her shoulder and ear, she skimmed her fingers over the slip of sexy fabric and tried not to hyperventilate at the thought of feeling nothing next weekend. She totally sucked at faking orgasms. Her *ooh*s and *aah*s never came out in the right pitch. Or at the right time.

Something at her entranceway window caught her attention—something tan and about the size of a horse. Her breath caught. Goliath, the English Mastiff. Her mother's drooling canine companion and one-dog destruction team had come to call. Unfortunately, the dog seldom traveled alone. Where Goliath went, so did Sue's mother.

Thoughts of her mother collided with previous thoughts of orgasms and sent Sue's brain into a Monday-morning blitz. Hit with a case of fight or flight, and always being more flighty than fighty, Sue grabbed the scrap of black lace and ducked behind the island.

Hitchcock, who was still nursing a grudge against Goliath for sticking a nose where it didn't belong, abandoned his coffee and darted under the living room sofa.

"You can't hide from me, Susie," her mother called out, shutting the front door. "And make your cat behave this time."

Sue dropped her new nightie on the floor, stood, then gave the sexy garment a toe-nudge into the corner. "My cat isn't the problem. You need to have that dog castrated. And I wasn't hiding. I was . . . counting dust bunnies."

"*Counting dust bunnies?*" her mom repeated.

The portable phone slipped down Sue's shoulder and she snagged it. "Sorry, I'm on hold . . . both phones. Kind of busy. But I love you." The last sentence came out with a touch of caring. Sue gave a wave with her pinky.

Her mother, juggling an orange purse, an armful of mail, and a gold-wrapped package, didn't leave. Sue's gaze shot to the package. Great. Her mother came bearing gifts. Now she would really feel guilty for trying to avoid her.

"Who's on the phones?"

"Poison Control." Sue tilted her head to the right. "And my agent." She leaned her head to the left and noticed her mother's low-cut tangerine-colored pantsuit. Lately her mother had seemed extra cheery, and her wardrobe . . . Fruit colors—apple red, lime green. And every time Sue saw her, the necklines got lower. It wasn't really indecent yet, but after a few more visits she'd be down to nipple exposure.

Sighing, Sue accepted that her feelings might stem from jealousy. Peggy Finley, at fifty-one years of age, had cleavage that Sue's size B's could only attain with a Wonderbra.

"What?" her mom asked. "Your agent get you a bad deal and you're planning on poisoning her?"

"No. My agent is in town and on her way here now. She phoned for directions."

"And Poison Control? Oh." Her mom's wide smile faded. "You didn't eat the casserole your grandmother sent over, did you?" Goliath sniffed at the gold package.

Sue studied her mother's suggestive neckline and decided to buy another Wonderbra.

"You didn't eat that casserole, did you?" her mom repeated.

"No. Since Grandpa had to have his stomach pumped, I flush everything. As for Poison Control, I'm trying to figure out how much poinsettia leaf it would take to kill a one hundred and fifty pound cross-dresser." Sue bounced her toe against the island. Then she paused before her mother told her to stop fidgeting. Sue knew she fidgeted, but her brain worked best when she moved.

Her mother's perfectly plucked eyebrows shot upward. "Taking out your ex, huh?"

"It's for my book." But her mother wasn't too far off target.

The panicked voice came back on the line. "This isn't good. How much poinsettia leaf was ingested?"

"It hasn't been ingested," Sue answered. "I just need to

know how much it would take to kill a medium-size man. I usually talk to Lisa. She always answers my—"

"You want to kill someone?" the voice squeaked through the line.

"Only on paper. I'm a"—the line went dead—"mystery writer. Great."

Her mother pitched the mail on the island and positioned the gold box on the counter. "This was on your doorstep." She scooted the stack of bills and the box closer.

Sue glanced at the Godiva Chocolatier sticker on the package. "Paul?" She got a funny feeling between her legs. Unfortunately, it wasn't a delayed reaction to Paul's kisses. It was Goliath's nose where it didn't belong.

Dropping the portable phone, she thrust the dog from her crotch. "You should train him not to do that."

"It's just his way of saying hello." Her mother set her purse on the island.

"I knew a guy in college who said that, and I trained *him* not to do it."

"Always the good girl." Her mom's gaze dropped to the floor, and the mama's-proud-of-you smile faded. "I don't like this Paul creature." Her mother scooped up the teddy.

"He's not a creature, and there's nothing wrong with him." Cell phone still held to her ear, Sue nudged the dog's nose from between her legs again.

"What happened to that cop you were so crazy about? Jason, wasn't it?"

Great. Now her mother was tossing Jason Dodd's name at her, too. It wasn't bad enough that she kept thinking about him and his kisses—or kiss, since, technically, that was really all there had been: one kiss. Not that it really mattered, anyway. She needed to stop thinking about Dodd altogether and start thinking about Paul. Paul, who had lots of great traits, even if kissing wasn't one of them.

"It didn't work out." She bounced her toe against the cab-inet. "Paul's smart, clean-cut, and sweet." She declined to mention that he was also dull, but four adjectives leaned toward purple prose. "You only met him that time we passed him on the road. You two never said more than three words to each other."

"Sweetie, I'd be the first one to tell you that you need to get on with your life. But I don't trust men who drive around wearing shower caps. And don't fidget, dear."

"It wasn't a shower cap." Sue forced herself to stand still. "He's a doctor, and he'd just come out of surgery and forgot to take off his surgical cap when—"

"Doctor?" Her mother's expression soured.

"Most mothers would be thrilled their daughter was dating a physician."

"Most mothers don't have my experience. Doctors think all women are hypochondriacs. And they're cheaters, blaming it on the fact that they have to look at naked bodies all day."

You are *a hypochondriac.* "Paul's a podiatrist. I don't think he's getting turned on by women's bunions." Then it occurred to Sue that Paul did spend an awful lot of time checking out her feet. Oh, great. Leave it to her mom to plant more insecurity. It wasn't as if Sue didn't already have a boatload of them. Boobs, thighs, turning men into wannabe women.

"He might. He has shifty eyes." Her mother dropped the nightie. "I don't want squinty-eyed grandchildren with foot fetishes."

"I'm not having his babies. I'm just . . ." Going cycling with him on a bike with pedal brakes. Her doubts resurfaced.

"You're sleeping with him?" Her mother's eyes narrowed.

"No. Not yet. I mean, I'm going to Mexico with him this weekend." At twenty-seven she should be able to tell her mother this, shouldn't she? So why was she getting that look? The same look she got when her mother found the gigantic hickey on her neck when she was fourteen.

"If he's good in bed, you'll marry him. You're that desperate."

Sue punched off her cell phone. It wouldn't do for

Melissa to hear her mother talking about how sexually deprived she was. Already Melissa complained about the lack of sexual content in her books.

"I'm not desperate." Desperate and horny were two completely separate emotions that involved two completely different parts of a woman's anatomy. "And as much as I would love to visit with you, I need to straighten my office before Melissa gets here."

"Melissa?" Her mom pushed Goliath's nose away from the gift-wrapped box, and Sue saw drool ooze from the creature's mouth.

"Melissa. My agent. Can I help you get Goliath back in the car?" She tossed her mom some paper towels.

"You're not offering me chocolate?" Her mother eyed the box before giving the dog and his drool the one-two swipe.

"Paul's scum but you'll eat his candy." Sue reached for the gold-wrapped package.

"It's Godiva." Her mom gave the dog a scratch behind his ears.

Sue understood. Even from scum, Godiva was . . . Godiva. Not that Paul was scum. And he'd noticed other parts of her body besides her feet, hadn't he? Either way, Sue was getting a new Wonderbra. After two years, her old one had lost its wonder.

"Have a truffle. Then go." Sue pulled at the box. The ribbon floated to the floor. The top came off, followed by the white tissue, and . . .

Sue's breath caught.

She froze.

It wasn't Godiva.

It wasn't even cheap chocolate.

Sue found her breath and the ability to move simultaneously. The package flew up. Air whooshed into her lungs, and the rat, with the word *die* written in red across its dead, hairy chest, went sailing up into the air.

Unfortunately, what went up must come down. The deceased rodent landed smack-dab in the middle of her mother's tangerine fabric-covered boobs. Her mother jumped, the C-cups boomeranging the rat across the room. Goliath, slobber now dripping from his jaws, lumbered after it, but Hitchcock dashed out from the sofa and beat him to the punch.

"I'm calling the police." Her mother grabbed Sue's cell phone. "That foot-fetish fiend sent you a rat! I hope you have wine."

With one hand over her heart, Sue watched Hitchcock rise up on his hind legs, his claws swatting left and right, his feline teeth buried deep into the dead rodent's head.

Thoughts swirled in Sue's own head, but of one thing she was certain: Unconditional love or not, tomorrow that cat was definitely getting his own coffee cup.

Her mom's voice vibrated through Sue's consciousness. "Someone just threatened to kill my daughter."

Right then, a bell rang. Sue's gaze darted toward the entryway.

"Oh, Hades!" Her mom pulled Sue against her. "That could be the killer now!"

Jason Dodd, a narcotics detective for the Houston Police Department, gazed at the leggy blonde strutting across the street in heels. Her tight red skirt jiggled back and forth with each step. He waited for the zing of pleasure.

Anticipated it. Wanted it.

But . . . no zing.

"You could always arrest her for jaywalking and get her number." His partner, Chase Kelly, tapped the steering wheel to the sound of a Dido CD, waiting for the light to change.

"She's not my type," Jason said, annoyed at his lack of interest. His lack of zing. Lately, no one fit the bill. For the last four months, he'd spent his weekends either held up in his apartment or helping his foster mom, Maggie, do odd jobs around the inn. He'd never gone this length of time without sex. Not voluntarily anyway.

Even Maggie had noticed. "I'm sixty-five years old and I've

never known a man who'd willingly come over to unstop a toilet on a Friday night. Why aren't you with a lady friend?"

His partner's hand-tapping jerked Jason back into the present.

"Something bothering you?" Chase asked. "You don't mind pet-sitting, do you?"

"I don't mind." Jason scrunched back against the seat. "But I thought Sue usually watched the menagerie."

"She's going on some trip." The light changed, and Chase started driving.

Jason stared out the window. "Probably another book signing."

"Maybe."

Something about Chase's tone made Jason turn around. A pink Cadillac, sporting a dented fender, darted in front of them. Chase slammed on the brakes.

"Pull him over," Jason said.

Chase sped up beside the car, and they both looked at the purple-haired old lady white-knuckling the steering wheel so she could peer over the dashboard.

"Or not," Jason said. "I'd drive like a bat out of hell if I was pushing ninety."

His partner chuckled and let off the gas. "You have a soft spot for old ladies."

"Do not." Jason glanced out the window again.

"You let that shoplifter go last week, even after you found that pot roast in her purse."

"She thought it was her wallet."

"Like hell," Chase said. "You paid for the pot roast and sent it home with her. I'm surprised you didn't throw in some baby carrots and pearl onions."

"She said she had those at home." Jason grinned. "So shoot me. I should have been a Boy Scout." Then he remembered he'd been too busy scouting for trouble to earn merit badges. People expected foster kids to be trouble, and he hadn't let anyone down. At least he hadn't until Maggie came along. But that had been different. Maggie needed him.

"You're going to come over for the Fourth, right? Lacy has the party all set."

"I'll be there," Jason answered.

"You bringing a victim?"

"Bringing a what?"

"A victim." Chase laughed. "That's what Lacy calls your girlfriends."

"They're not victims."

"Hey, she just means that you love 'em and leave 'em."

"I leave them happy. They needed some special TLC, and I'm good at it. What's wrong with that?"

"Hmm . . . maybe the leaving part?"

"They don't complain." Much. The fact that he hadn't made anyone, or himself, happy lately was another issue.

Chase's phone rang, and he looked at the caller ID. "Hey, Lace," he said before the receiver was anywhere near his mouth.

Jason dug into his jeans pocket for a piece of cinnamon candy and scanned the streets for his "type." When had he gotten so picky? Maybe he was just getting old. But thirty wasn't that old, damn it! According to that article in *Men's Health* even a married man should want sex at least three times a week. That meant he was forty-eight climaxes behind—and counting—because he had no prospects . . . and even worse, no real interest.

"What?" Chase's sharp tone brought Jason's gaze back around. "We'll be right there."

Jason waited until Chase hung up. "What's up?"

"Something about Sue getting a death threat."

Jason's shoulders stiffened. "Sue? What happened?"

Chase shook his head. "She's not making sense."

Jason got an image of Sue at her last autographing, wearing pink, bouncing in her chair, and smiling as she signed books. He'd seen the announcement of her signing in the paper. Having already bought her book, he didn't have a reason for showing up. Thankfully, he'd ducked out before she spotted him.

"Then let's move." Jason looked out at the traffic. "Is she okay?"

Chase punched the gas. "Lacy said she was." One of Chase's brows arched. "I thought you didn't like Sue."

"I don't *dislike* her. Just drive." Jason pointed at the road.

Thirty minutes later, Chase parked his Isuzu Rodeo across from Sue's house, located in Hoke's Bluff, one of the smaller towns outside Houston's city limits.

"Why's the media here?" Jason voiced his question aloud. Only a dead body could bring out this much press. The thought of Sue not moving or smiling gave him a jolt. Chase hadn't cut the engine off before Jason jumped out.

CHAPTER TWO

He sped past the television vans. Hurrying toward the house, Jason saw Chase jump out of the car and gravitate toward the side of the yard where a pack of women huddled together. Jason recognized one of the women as Lacy, Chase's wife, and he almost turned around to hear what she had to say. But he didn't see Sue, and he had a burning desire to make sure she wasn't lying facedown in a puddle of blood like one of the characters in her mystery novels.

He walked inside the house, only stopping when he saw a camera focused on Sue and a woman who sat beside her on the edge of an overstuffed red sofa. Relief melted through him as he scanned her for bruises or scrapes. She looked fine.

So fine, he inventoried her for reasons altogether different. She wore a skirt and had her legs crossed, revealing a creamy expanse of thigh.

"I don't think this is drug-related," a voice said nearby.

Jason glanced briefly over at Officer Donny Martin of the Hoke's Bluff PD. He had met the guy a couple of times at someone's barbecue but didn't much like him. Mostly because Martin thought of himself as a player and had mistaken Jason for someone who wanted to listen to him brag about his conquests.

"Sue's a friend of my partner's wife," he replied, then trained his gaze back on Sue. Something didn't look right. It took him a second to figure it out. Sue wasn't talking or moving. Sue always talked and moved. The woman was perpetual motion with a voice box. Jason had wondered how she sat still long enough to write a book. He'd also wondered how she'd be at other things. Constant movement could be a good thing when the clothes were off and—

Quashing that thought, he glanced at the brunette beside Sue. Dressed in a navy business suit, she spoke directly into the camera. Jason turned back to Martin. "What's going on?"

"If you ask me, it's a publicity stunt—but the view's nice." Martin pointed to the two women and then to a blonde reporter.

"There wasn't a death threat?" Jason asked.

"She says the dog and cat ate it." Martin chuckled.

"Ate what?"

"The rat someone sent the sexy little *New York Times* bestselling author."

Jason frowned. "She hasn't made that list yet. Who's the brunette?"

"Her agent/PR person from New Jersey. Kind of convenient her being here to help get the press out, wouldn't you say?"

The brunette placed a hand on Sue's shoulder. "Of course she's scared," she cooed into the microphone. "This is obviously the work of a stalker. Why, her next book, *Murder At Midnight* is due out in a few weeks. She'll be autographing copies at all the local bookstores. Her book received a glowing review from *Publishers Weekly*!"

"Yeah, it's convenient," Jason agreed.

He watched Sue lace her hands together and stare down at her lap. Along with that short khaki skirt, she wore a light blue polo shirt. Her shoulder-length blonde hair fell loose from where it was tucked behind her ear. She flipped it back with nervous fingers.

The reporter asked her a question, then shoved a microphone in her face. Sue's wide blue eyes blinked.

Jason flinched. Sue clearly wasn't up to being interviewed.

His gaze shot to Miss Navy-Suit, who appeared utterly prepared. "Yeah, it's a publicity stunt. But Sue's not in on it." He moved in. "Show's over." He glared at the woman in navy. "Police need to talk to Ms. Finley."

Sue's eyes grew round, and her vulnerability vanished. Jason took her by the forearm, lifting her off the couch.

"What are you doing?" Sue seethed as he pulled her away from the crowd.

"I'm trying to save you from making an ass out of yourself."

She jerked free of his hand. "What?"

"It's obvious that your PR guru set this whole thing up."

"Set what up?"

"Come on, Sue. Doesn't this look suspicious? Listen to her. She's done everything but give out a 1–800 number where they can order your book. She obviously devised this whole thing."

Sue latched her hands on her hips and gaped at her agent. She seemed to consider what he'd said, then met Jason's gaze. "No. She's taking advantage of the situation. I'll give you that. But she didn't send that rat."

"And I have some oceanfront property for sale in Iowa. For some reason I thought you were different from other blondes."

Sue's eyes squinted, her shoulders snapped back, and her chin tilted up. Not that it made any difference in her height. She barely measured chest high on his six-foot frame. Oddly enough, though, her petite body thrilled him.

As did the rest of her.

"What are you even doing here?" she demanded. "I don't need more police."

"What you need is your head examined if you're buying little Miss Priss's stunt."

Sue tapped the toe of her sandal against the wood floor. The sun spilling through the dining room window reflected off her blue eyes. Angry, but beautiful, eyes. He inhaled. Her fruity fragrance made him want to step closer and breathe deeper.

"Sorry to ruin your theory, Columbo," she said, "but when the rat was being delivered, Melissa was thirty miles from here filing a hit and run report on an old lady driving like a bat out of Disney World in a pink Cadillac." She hesitated. "Did Lacy call Chase?"

Jason stared at her moist lips, painted pink, and remembered the taste he'd gotten of them that night four months ago. Oh yeah, he remembered, all right. He'd been plagued with flashbacks. Desire stirred deep in his belly and spread lower. And lower. There was a very good reason why one taste had been more than enough, but with all that stirring going on in places that hadn't stirred in too long, he couldn't remember what it was. Then something really moved between his legs.

"Damn!" He removed a huge dog nose from his crotch.

"I think it's time you leave." Sue started the bouncing shoe routine. "You've outworn your welcome again."

Jason supposed he deserved that. After all, he'd expected something of a consequence for not calling her. It didn't matter that her number was tucked inside his wallet, the paper worn and faded from constantly taking it in and out. Still, her words made him flinch. Words he'd heard enough as a boy from caseworkers as they shuffled him from one home to another.

Right then he remembered why one taste of Sue's mouth had been more than enough. It went back to childhood lessons. Plain and simple. Jason Dodd never allowed himself to want anything too much—not a birthday cake, not a new bike for Christmas, not his mother to come back for him. Wanting things only led to disappointment. Even wanting a woman came with limits. And after one kiss, he'd wanted Sue Finley too damn much.

"Have it your way." He nearly tripped over a gray cat as he stormed out.

Walking straight to the Rodeo, he pulled his keys out of his pocket, found the spare key Chase had given him, got in, and drove away. Turning up the volume, he listened to

Chase's Three Doors Down CD and dug into his jeans for another cinnamon candy. By the time he got to I-45, he had forgotten about Sue. He was almost in Houston before he remembered something else he'd forgotten. His partner . . . and the owner of the car.

Sue knelt to loosen the straps of her sandals. They pinched her toes something terrible, but jeez, it had been a toe-pinching kind of day.

"Oh, that was good!" Melissa brushed a speck of dust off her navy jacket.

"Someone sent my daughter a dead rat, and you think that's good?" Sue's mother poured another glass of Merlot. Sue figured this to be about a four-glass problem, which meant she'd be driving her mom home.

Again.

"No, the rat wasn't good." Melissa wrinkled her nose, but her brown eyes glimmered. "But that free press was priceless. Now, if I could just catch Grandma in the Caddie. It's going to make her cost me a fortune to pay for that fender bender."

Sue dropped down on the sofa, feeling like a balloon with a slow leak. Everyone milled around the front section of her house. The reporters and police had left, except Chase, Lacy's husband, who stood next to his wife, absently toying with her dark curls as he stared out the window. Lacy looked over and offered Sue a supportive smile. Good ol' Lacy, as supportive as an underwire bra.

Sue forced a grin, then reached down to pull at the leather straps around her toe. Toe pain was the worst. Glancing up, Sue's gaze shifted and skidded to a halt on a newcomer: Lacy's mother.

"I picked it up at the Galleria last week," Karina Callahan said, dangling her bracelet at Melissa. Karina exhibited an Elizabeth Taylor charisma, and the woman had never met a shade of purple she didn't like. Purple suit, purple shoes. Sue had her earmarked to use as a character in a book, because Karina was, well, unforgettable.

"So, who was at the door?" Lacy asked, talking to Sue's mom.

"Just the good-looking FedEx guy," Sue's mom answered. "Before the police arrived, the cat and dog ate the evidence."

Sue fought back irritation. In spite of a request that she not, Lacy had called her husband, Chase. Which was how Jason Dodd had ended up here. Then there were the reporters, vultures for a story, and the other police. But it was Jason, his six-feet of male ego, that annoyed Sue most. Conversations bounced all around the room, and Sue wished everyone would leave. She'd had autograph parties that weren't as well attended. But give the crowd a dead rodent and—

She crossed her legs and swung her foot back and forth, counting the insults Jason had slung at her in the course of three minutes. It was bad enough for him to kiss her so completely that he checked out the back of her tonsils, ask for her number, and then never call, but for him to barge into her home, call her a dumb blonde, accuse her agent of planting a dead rat, and . . .

Why the heck hadn't he called? Had he found some tonsil defect? Maybe she'd better resist French kissing Paul this weekend.

At the thought of the weekend, her toes pinched again.

Lacy dropped down beside her. "Do you want to stay at our place for a few days?"

"No. I'm fine. This was just someone's idea of a prank."

"A dead rat with *die* written on it is not a prank." Her mother stepped closer to the sofa. Her tangerine outfit clashed with the red leather. "It was that doctor." She looked at Chase. "I want that foot quack checked out."

"Mom, why would Paul send me a dead rat?" she asked.

"Why would anyone send you a dead rat?" Chase gave Melissa a not-so-friendly look.

"I don't know." Sue pumped her foot back and forth. Jason must have told Chase his half-cocked suspicions about Melissa being involved, but Sue knew they were wrong. Melissa had worked at a Hollywood PR firm before moving east to start her literary/PR agency. Sure, the woman could be an opportunist—a talent that had gotten Sue all sorts of media coverage—but dead rats weren't her style. Melissa hated rats. She had freaked when she read Sue's chapter in which a victim received a dead rat.

Sue remembered the scene. The killer had sent the rat as a warning of what was to come. After tormenting the victim with hang-ups and threatening notes, the rat-recipient had been murdered. Coincidence, Sue told herself again.

"You okay?" Lacy asked.

"Fine." She considered telling Chase about the scene from her book, but how would it look? Melissa had been one of the few people who'd read it. If Chase suspected her agent now, what would he think then? It was just a coincidence. In her scene, the rat had been in the mailbox, and it hadn't had *die* written on it.

And it hadn't been disguised as chocolate.

A horn blew outside. Chase kissed Lacy good-bye. "Jason's back."

Lacy leaned into her husband for another kiss. All eyes turned to them. Lacy and Chase had been married almost a year but still gave each other looks that set off enough steam to carpet clean a Persian hotel.

"Okay, guys," Sue's mother said. "We're here for dead rats, not soft porn."

"Leave them alone," Karina Callahan chimed in. Somehow, even her voice sounded purple. "I want grandkids."

"You all need to get a life." Chase smiled. "That was just a kiss, not porn." With a confident gait he left.

"Sue needs to get a life." Melissa pulled at the edge of her jacket. "If she doesn't stop rewriting the same love scene, I'm going to hire her a gigolo."

Everyone giggled. Everyone except Sue.

"Sue's getting a life this weekend." Karina pressed a fingernail against her purple-tinted lips. "Or at least she's going to play 'One Little Piggy Went to Market' with her podiatrist."

"What?" Sue's mouth dropped open.

"Mom," Lacy said. "Going after *my* sex life is bad, but leave my friends' sex lives alone."

"You're finally dating?" Melissa got a this-is-news look about her.

"I swear," Sue growled. "If I read this in the paper, I'll fire you. And no—"

"I don't like Paul," her mother interrupted.

"You don't have to like him," Karina responded.

Lately, Sue had noticed Karina and her mom had been spending a lot of time together. She wondered if the six-times divorced Karina was behind her mother's fruity low-cut outfits. Perhaps Sue should just be glad her mom wasn't wearing purple.

"It's Sue who has to bump uglies with him," Karina continued.

"Mom." Lacy sent Sue a look of apology.

Melissa chuckled. "Bumping uglies? Now there's one I haven't heard. Real romantic."

Karina looked at Sue. "Your mom bumped uglies last week with Bill Delaney, the manager of the fruit stand by the highway."

Sue's brain went on the fritz.

Sex?

Her mom?

"Tell me this isn't true."

"I . . ." Her mom paused. "Bumping uglies? They are kind of ugly. I don't see how anyone can watch porn without cracking up." Everyone laughed except Sue, who was busy trying not to imagine her mom having sex with a fruit salesman.

Her mom shot her a get-real look. "Lighten up. It's just us girls. Besides, if you can play footsie with your podiatrist, I can talk bananas with my fruit stand owner."

"You did more than talk." Karina laughed. "You made juice."

Sue dropped her head back on the sofa. Her mother not only had better cleavage, but she had a better sex life. Not that Sue even had a sex life. Yet.

Unable to wrap her mind around her mom having sex, Sue tried to think of Paul and herself bumping uglies and making juice, but all she could think was that there had to be something wrong with her tonsils.

The bad vibes brought her focus back to her pinching shoes. She yanked off the sandals. Barefoot, she stomped over to the trash can and ceremoniously dumped the shoes. Everyone stared.

"Toe pain," she said. Everyone nodded in understanding. Then Sue's home phone rang, and her mother answered.

"Hello? . . . Fine, don't talk." She dropped the phone and downed the last of her wine.

"Was that a hang-up?" Sue asked.

When her mom nodded, Sue's heart missed a beat. Just a coincidence, she told herself. She got hang-ups all the time. Didn't she?

Two days later, Sue sat at Lacy's kitchen table on the Fourth of July and tried to figure out the best way to drop the bomb about having to miss the party. She had tried to persuade Paul, but . . .

"Did you find someone to pet sit?" she asked.

"Yes," Lacy said.

Chase sauntered into the room and gave Lacy a kiss on her neck. Sue tried to imagine Paul doing that this weekend. She couldn't.

"So, how are your plans for cha-cha-cha in Mexico?" Chase asked.

"Fine." Sue rubbed Lacy's dog, Fabio, with her foot.

"Just fine?" Chase asked. "You haven't had sex in years and all you can say is *fine*?"

Sue frowned at Lacy. "Do you tell your husband all my secrets?"

"I seduced it out of her." Chase wrapped his arm around his wife.

"Great," Sue said. "You two get it on while you talk about my nonsex life."

Lacy elbowed her laughing husband. He rubbed his side. "Speaking of your nonsex life, is this Paul guy going to show his face around here?"

Time to drop the bomb. "He's coming by to . . . pick me up." Sue winced at Lacy's frown. "Before I ever mentioned the party, he'd made reservations at a fancy restaurant by the Galleria."

"You think you'll get food better than mine?" Chase asked.

"No." Guilt started pulling tighter at the corner of Sue's heart. "I'm so sorry."

"What," Chase said, "the foot doctor's too high class to hang out with cops?"

"No." Sue met Lacy's eyes and pleaded for understanding. "He already had plans."

"Your mother seems to think he's behind the rat incident." Chase's brow pinched.

"He's not!" Sue snapped, and from the look on Chase's face she knew where the conversation was going. "And neither is my agent."

Sue's cell phone rang, and she grabbed it from the table. "Hello?" She prayed it wouldn't be a hang-up. She had only gotten two since Monday, but . . .

"I'm lost." Paul's voice echoed through the line as Sue watched Chase leave the room.

She gave Paul directions again, trying to find some flicker of warmth at the sound of his voice. But Paul had a wimpy voice. When she hung up, she met Lacy's eyes. "I hope you didn't cook steak for us. I should have called last night when Paul told me—"

"It's okay," Lacy said. "Jason will make up for it."

Sue's eyebrows shot up before she could fake a nonchalant expression. "He's coming?"

Suspicion filled her friend's eyes. "Is this why you and Paul are leaving? You're not still avoiding Jason?"

"I didn't even know he was coming," she said honestly. Yet who could blame her for wanting to leave? What girl wanted to spend time with a guy who found her tonsils defective?

The phone rang again. "You take a left on the dirt road," Sue explained when Paul said he was lost again. "It's a ranch-style house. I'll meet you out front."

Sue dropped the phone in her purse and went to hug Lacy.

"You're not going to bring him in at all?" her friend asked. "You're going to sleep with the guy and I haven't even met him. Isn't that against the girlfriend code of ethics? What if he's dog ugly and you just can't see it?"

"He's not ugly, and you slept with Chase before I met him."

"Yeah, but he had me handcuffed to the bed."

Sue chuckled, then asked, "Is Kathy coming?"

"Tommy's sick," Lacy explained. "I throw a party and neither of my two closest friends show up." She studied Sue as if using her all-powerful girlfriend radar. "It *is* about Jason, isn't it?" She pointed a finger at Sue. "Other than that day at your house, you two haven't been in the same room since the kiss."

"Pure luck," Sue said. Shoes in hand, she waved and headed out the door.

She hadn't gotten off the front porch when she realized her luck had run out. Jason's Mustang eased into the driveway.

CHAPTER THREE

Jason saw Sue's Honda. For a second, he considered leaving. But he'd spent a good part of the last two days telling himself he'd made more of this infatuation with Sue than existed.

So she tempted him. He wasn't going to act on it. She wasn't the first woman he'd chosen to avoid, and it wasn't as if she was some siren that drove a man to his knees. He'd had women with larger breasts and longer legs. Sue wasn't even his type. She talked too damn much, was too short, and . . .

"Crap!" All delicious five feet of her stepped out of Chase's front door.

Jason's gaze whispered over every inch of her, and his mouth went dry. For a woman who wasn't his type, she got his pulse rate going. She wore one of those loose-fitting, sleeveless summer dresses—the type of dress that led a man to think about how little was worn underneath. His mouth dryness increased, and he wished he had a beer. Hadn't he passed a convenience store a mile back?

"Don't be a fool." He crawled out of his car. *Or a bigger fool.* He'd already made a fool out of himself a couple days ago when he'd left her house, taken Chase's car, and forgotten to take Chase.

Jason pushed his door closed with more force than needed. He didn't like losing his head, especially over a woman he had no intention getting close to. But neither did he run from trouble. Best to face this problem head-on like any other.

Facing Sue, he first noted her frown, then the fact that dangling from her fingers were a pair of peach-colored sandals. But it was the frown that got to him, though the bare feet did a little something to his insides, too. Not to mention the low neckline that showed off her breasts, which in all fairness were perfectly proportioned.

Damn, she looked good.

"Where're you going?" Rearing back on his heels, he tried not to enjoy the view.

"Don't you know better than to ask a dumb blonde a question?" She skirted him.

Turning, he caught her by the arm. The feel of her skin sent his pulse to ticketing speeds. He told himself to ignore it. But he'd never been good at minding.

He ran his thumb over her elbow. "Don't you think this is silly?"

"What's silly?" She glared at his hand wrapped around her arm.

He let go, reluctantly. "This avoiding act you've been playing."

"I haven't been—"

"Don't lie. Every get-together I don't come to, you do. And when I'm here, you're not." If he were being honest, he'd done his share of avoiding, too. But this time his plan was to confront the problem head-on, and he couldn't let something like the truth get in his way.

"Pure luck." She glanced at the street—avoiding looking at him, probably.

"Pure stupidity." He decided to give her the same speech he'd given himself earlier. "It's not as if we're divorced or something. We didn't even date. We kissed. Once. Just once."

She moved from side to side, as if the sidewalk was too

hot on her bare feet. If her feet were as soft as her elbow . . .
He nudged her over to stand on the grass.

The grass felt better against the pads of her feet, though Sue
wouldn't give Jason the pleasure of such an admission.

"One kiss," he repeated.

But it was a *good* kiss, Sue thought, as the smell of smol-
dering charcoal and the hearty aroma of Chase's steaks
grilling in the backyard filled her nose. She stared down
the road and prayed Paul would magically appear.

If only Jason's kiss had been horrible. If only she hadn't
enjoyed having her tonsils strip-searched by a certain cop.

"I just don't get it," he said.

Neither did she. She had to bite her lip to keep from asking why he hadn't called. Another scented breeze caught
her hair. And she remembered the night and the kiss in
question. She'd forgotten her shoes on Lacy's patio and
stepped out to get them before heading off. He'd followed
her. They'd actually stood there and had a real conversation about the . . . stars. And—

"Look," he said, pulling her out of a memory that was
best forgotten.

"Gotta go." She tried to step around him.

"It was just a kiss." He moved in front of her. "I didn't even
touch . . . the merchandise."

Considering his eyes had gone to her newly acquired Wonderbra cleavage, she knew what merchandise he meant.

"For which I am very grateful!" she snapped. "Because I
don't like to be groped while some guy has his tongue
down my throat."

He muttered something under his breath and tucked
both hands into his jean pockets. The position made his biceps press against his white T-shirt. Not wanting to notice
things like muscles, or how good white cotton looked
stretched across his masculine chest, she pinched her toes
around the hot blades of grass.

"Look," he said. "Let's go inside and put this whole thing to bed." His voice rang baritone, and his hair, the shade of light wheat, whispered across his brow in the breeze.

"Sorry, but I don't intend to bed you." *But if you'd called four months ago I'm sure my life would have been off hold.* Yet somehow she knew sex with Jason Dodd would not come with pedal brakes. She'd be thrown over the handlebars for sure.

But you wouldn't have to fake it with him, a voice within chimed. A voice she ruthlessly ignored.

"You know what I mean," he said. "It's not fair to Lacy and Chase for us to keep this up. Let's go back inside and prove to each other, and to them, we're adults."

She looked him in the eyes—blue eyes, long lashes. "Sorry, I'll have to be an adult another day. But if you start practicing now, you might succeed in a couple of years." The wind blew again and the bow on her dress flew up to her Wonderbra cleavage.

"Don't be silly." He jerked his fingers out of his pockets and tucked his hands beneath the opposite armpits like a child who'd been told not to touch.

"I'm not being silly. I'm meeting someone." She noticed his gaze flickered to her chest every few seconds. So the Wonderbra was doing the trick, huh?

"This is what I mean." His gaze fell back to her breasts. "You aren't meeting anyone. You're lying just so you don't have to be in the same room with me."

Tension knitted Sue's brows, and she waved the sandals in front of him to get his gaze off her chest. The leather strap of one shoe caught him across his arm with a loud pop. "For your information, I have a date and—"

"Right." He rubbed his arm. "I happen to know that you don't date. You belong to that Divorced, Desperate and Delicious club that you, Lacy, and Kathy started. Of course, Lacy jumped ship."

Sue gritted her teeth. Did everyone in town know she hadn't had sex in two years? "Well, throw me a landline, mate, because you can drop the desperate from my title, too. I'm now divorced, delicious, and dating."

The sound of an engine buzzed in the summer air. "Sue?" Paul called from his car as he stopped in the driveway. His voice wasn't baritone, but she didn't mind because it blended perfectly with the purr of the Porsche's engine.

Victory tickled her insides, and she darted off, ducked inside Paul's window, and kissed him. She even put a little tongue in the kiss. "Perfect timing." Then she noticed he wore the surgeon's cap again over his short brown hair.

She yanked it off before backing up. Paul had to look good, just in case Jason checked him out. Not that she needed to worry. Paul could look like a dweeb, because his red Porsche had the power to mentally castrate any man who cared about cars. Jason might not care about Sue, or her tonsils, but she was almost certain he liked cars.

"What's this?" Paul leaned out the window, his gaze following her legs downward.

At first she thought he referred to her dress. Then he frowned. Had he somehow guessed that she'd found more sizzle standing on the same block with a certain egotistical cop than she had in the lip lock she'd planted on him?

He flicked the edge of her sandals with his index finger. "Never go barefoot!"

Barefoot? Here she'd worn a bra that pushed her boobs plum up to her nose and the man still only noticed her feet. Oh, goodness, in two days she would be having sex with this man.

Or not, whispered an internal voice. She could still tell him no. But her life might be on hold for eternity. She might never have sex again, and the whole world would know.

She shot a quick glance back at Jason, who stood, arms crossed, staring daggers at her. Then he bolted off to Lacy's front door.

"Who's the dude in the shower cap driving the Porsche?" Jason shoved Chase into the kitchen, away from the crowd.

"Oh, you must mean Paul, Sue's new squeeze. She said he drove a nice car. I wouldn't know about the shower cap." Chase shrugged. "Want a beer?"

"It's a tad more than nice. It's a Porsche, for Pete's sake. And why in the hell didn't you tell me Sue was dating?" Jason stalked to the fridge and grabbed a beer.

Chase studied him. "I didn't know you cared about Sue."

"I don't care." Giving the cap a vicious twist, he hurled it into the sink with such force that it pinged around the white porcelain. "But you could have told me."

"Hey, you made a play and said you weren't interested. In my book that means her dating status is off the record. I mean . . ." Chase smiled and snatched the cap from the sink. "If I got juicy details, I'd share them with you because you're my best friend, but—"

"I'm not interested. The woman can't stand still and never shuts up. When I kissed her she talked through the whole thing. Never stopped yapping. You know how hard it is to kiss a girl who's talking?"

"Well, excuse me!" Sue's voice brought Jason swinging around. She stood in the doorway, eyes narrowed, hands on her hips, and her peach-colored sandals now on her feet.

Jason went ahead and took a sip of beer, because from the look on her face he was going to need it. Hell, from the look on her face he might need a six-pack.

"Maybe I was telling you to get your tongue out of my larynx." She jerked a purse off the kitchen table then turned to Chase. "And if you share one tiny piece of my 'juicy details' with Mr. Deep Throat here, I swear you'll be singing soprano for at least a week." In a streak of peach, the woman stormed out.

Jason held the cold beer to his forehead and leaned against the counter. Chase waited until the front door slammed before bursting out in laughter.

"Cork it, would you?" Jason snapped.

"I'm sorry," Chase said. "But that was funny. You two got something good going. But you'd better move fast before the foot doctor gets her socks off. Her mother swears if he's good in bed, Sue will marry him."

Thursday night's weekly meeting with her longtime critique partners strained Sue's nerves to the breaking point. Hey, it had been a hard week. As if dead rats, bad-boy cops, and several more hang-ups weren't troubling enough, Benny Fritz, critique partner number three, was giving her the eye again.

She watched Mary and Frank walk out of the diner. Then her gaze darted to Benny, who still had his crooked smile in place.

"Have dessert with me." Benny eyes took on that glint again.

"Sorry, but Thursday nights I go for homemade cookies and hurricanes at my grandparents'. Weekly ritual. They're big on rituals." Sue looked at her bill.

"Isn't she the one whose cooking sends people to the hospital?"

"Yeah, but her cookies are safe. Burnt, but safe." Sue noted again the puppy-dog way Benny gazed at her. He looked as if he might roll over and offer his belly for her to scratch. She had no desire to scratch Benny's belly, stroke his ego or any other body part. Since his separation with his wife a month ago, the forty-year-old had been way too chummy.

Frankly, his interest surprised her. She'd seen Benny's wife, and she and the woman were complete opposites. Dark, light. Big, small. Sue fidgeted with her purse strap and tossed words at the awkward moment. "Your chapter had edge. The man-eating plant was a nice touch."

"You don't like sci-fi. I know that." He placed his hand over hers.

"But it's good writing." Sue slid her fingers from beneath his. "I sympathized with the donkey when that alien ate its baby." She liked Benny, appreciated his input on her own work, and admired his writing talent, if not his genre. Most of his one-eyed alien stories were published regularly.

"I'll take the compliment," he said. "When a beautiful woman says something nice, you shouldn't argue."

Sue half smiled. Benny wasn't half bad looking, but as soon as his wife forgave him for not noticing her new perm, or whatever stupid thing they had argued over, they'd be back together. All Sue had to do was discourage him until they rediscovered their twenty-year love affair, hopefully without damaging his ego or the dynamics of the critique group.

Benny winked at her. "Can I drop off my story at your place when I finish it?"

"Or you could e-mail it." She scooted out of the booth, dropped money on the table, and waved at the young pregnant waitress. Wondering about the girl's situation, Sue dropped another bill and glanced at Benny. "Later."

He followed her. Muggy July air greeted them as the door squeaked closed and sent one last wave of air-conditioning their way.

"Your hair smells good." His hand pressed against the small of her back; his head tilted downward until his breath, a little muggier than the night air, brushed across her temple.

He was going to try to kiss her. She couldn't deal with this now. She had bigger fish to gut—like if she was or wasn't going to go to Mexico and fake orgasms. Like why she'd spent all day fuming over yesterday's run-in with Jason Dodd instead of working on her new book. Add the two phone hang-ups she'd gotten today and trying to figure out if they had anything to do with the dead rat, and a kiss from Benny could be her breaking point. And when she broke, she was as bad as her mother. Tears and snot, snot and tears. It wasn't pretty.

Neither was the idea that someone really wanted to scare her, someone who had read her unpublished manuscript.

Like, someone in her critique group.

Hadn't it even been Benny's idea to use the rat? His hip brushed up against hers. Suspicion pricked her stomach.

Then evaporated.

The man spent his time imagining man-eating plants. Weird, yes, but he wasn't a rat-sending lunatic. Benny coached his son's Little League team and sold Bibles part-time to supplement his income.

He looked at her again, and his tongue brushed his bottom lip, reminding her of his alien before it devoured the baby donkey. Not a lunatic, but lonely enough to try to kiss her.

Two words shot through her head: *dead dog.*

She put on her brakes.

"Gross." She made a show of putting a finger in her mouth.

"What?" Benny asked.

"Nothing, I just found a piece of steak that has been stuck between my teeth for a week. Tastes like dead dog. I'm gonna have to floss better." Sue waved a hand in front of her face.

He backed away. "My car's over here. See you . . . later."

Sue bit back a smile. She hadn't used the dead dog trick in years. "Bye." Retrieving her keys from her bag, she cut into the restaurant's rear parking lot.

The night suddenly grew blacker, too quiet. With her heart drumming the music to the *Jaws* movies, she hurried like a woman wearing white in search of a tampon. She did have to hurry. Not a tampon hurry, but she had grandparents to see, and then she had to go home and pack or call Paul and cancel Mexico.

It was time to cook or get out of the kitchen. She'd sucked at cooking. But dang it, she was hungry for a little male companionship. Benny didn't count. Obviously, neither did Paul.

The click of her sandals on the pavement seemed to be soaked up by the darkness—a swarthiness cloaked by Texas humidity. The hair on the back of her neck began to rise at the same time her cell phone rang. Jerking it out of her purse, she hit the on button.

"Hello."

Nothing. Not a word. Then a click. She squinted to see the number of the caller. Restricted.

She took another step. Just like that, she remembered another scene in her book where a victim had been kidnapped in a parking lot. She tasted fear on her tongue.

Sue arrived at her car, her skin tight with goose bumps. "I'm being silly," she muttered . . . but then she heard it.

Footsteps.

Fumbling with her keys, she intended to hit the unlock button, but her hands shook. The keys clattered to the pavement. The footsteps drew closer. The *Jaws* music playing in her head increased in tempo.

Maybe she wasn't being silly. Breath hitched, she took off at a dead run away from her car.

CHAPTER FOUR

Sue had only made it past the trunk when she heard, "Ma'am!" The nonthreatening young female voice brought her to an embarrassed stop. She turned and faced the pregnant waitress standing about ten feet behind her.

"Someone forgot their papers." The waitress held a stack of manuscript pages to her round belly. "Didn't mean to scare you."

"You didn't. I ran because . . . I'm training for a marathon." She grinned at the obvious lie.

The waitress chuckled and, edging closer, handed Sue the papers. "I see you guys in here every week. Ask for me next time."

"We will, Tina," Sue told the girl, remembering her name. "Thanks."

Hand on her belly, the waitress wobbled away. She looked way too young to wobble. Sue wondered if she was wobbling through the pregnancy alone. She placed her fingers on her own flat stomach. There had been the time in her marriage when she'd thought she was pregnant. Collin had been thrilled, but it had been a false alarm. Shortly after she'd learned what else gave him thrills.

Shaking her head, Sue rattled the memory from her brain. She had outlawed all memories of her ex-husband, because even the good memories ultimately led to the bad ones. The bad ones brought on self-doubt. Self-doubt brought on fear. And fear made her want to verbally castrate every male that came within ten feet. She'd stopped mentally castrating men about four months ago, right after one blond cop started making her want something other than revenge.

Jason's face filled her mind. The memory of his kiss echoed: the way he'd tasted, the way he'd felt, all hard and solid against her.

"No!" She tossed his image, with the memories, into a mental Dumpster. "I should have used the dead dog trick on him, too."

Without haste, she found her keys and took off to enjoy her hurricane and cookies. Maybe her grandma hadn't burnt them this time.

Sue rose on her toes and kissed her grandfather's cheek in greeting. "Sorry. We had a lot to go over tonight. Where's Grandma?"

At eighty-three, the man had likely shrunk a few inches, but his thick, curly hair, growing coarser with age, now stood up by its roots and made up for any such loss. Sue often wondered why she couldn't have inherited his height or thick hair.

She glanced at the Lyle Lovett hairdo and decided she'd keep her own. However, bad hair and all, she loved every inch of this man. After she'd lost her father at age eight, her grandfather had filled his shoes. They were big shoes to fill.

He nudged her into the kitchen. "Your grandma's on the phone. Your mom's talking about your Mexican physician with a foot fetish."

Great! Her mother was tattling again. "He's not Mexican; I'm supposed to go to Ixtapa with him this weekend. And he's a podiatrist."

Her grandparents seldom watched the local news, so perhaps they'd missed the news segment about her receiving a dead rat. She wasn't about to tell them, and neither would her mom. At least Sue hoped. With her mom, one could never be sure. It depended on how much wine she'd consumed.

Her grandpa's bushy eyebrows knitted together. "That explains the foot fetish." He picked up a charred-around-the-edges cookie. "Oh, your grandma cooked her casserole. I mentioned sending it home with you. Don't eat it." He rubbed his stomach. "But if you'd take it, I'd be appreciative."

Clean-fridge casserole: Dump everything together, stir ten seconds, ignore smells and mold, bake at 400 for one hour.

Sue shook her head. "This is ridiculous. Tell her to throw the leftovers away."

"She went hungry as a child. Throwing food away is blasphemy to her. And it wasn't that bad this time. She added that mushroom soup."

Sue's stomach roiled. "You love her so much that you'd risk having your stomach pumped again before you'd tell her she's poisoning you?"

The wrinkles around his eyes softened. "Yup. That much. So why does your mother have her nose out of joint about this doctor?" He picked up the cookie plate.

"I'll give you one guess." Sue followed her grandpa to the kitchen table where a pitcher of Kool-Aid with rum waited. He placed the cookies beside a basket of fake fruit.

"The doctor thing, huh?" Grandpa answered.

"You got it."

Her grandpa filled a glass and handed it to her. "What do *you* think about the doc?"

"He's a nice guy." Sue picked up a cookie and looked at the edges.

"But?"

"I didn't say 'but.' All I said—"

"I heard the 'but.'" He poured himself a drink and his aged hand shook. Those shakes always got to her.

"I just want to move on with my life," she grumbled.

Her grandpa patted her wrist. "You will, Princess. You'll

meet someone who takes your breath away. Just like I met your grandma. But until then, don't settle."

The words reminded Sue of Jason's kiss. "Having the breath knocked out of you isn't all it's cracked up to be."

"Neither is settling. And we both know you settled when you married—"

"Collin just had issues." But why she continued defending him was a brain stumper. She tapped her foot on the floor. "Is it supposed to rain tomorrow?"

Sympathy creased her grandpa's mouth. "I forgot the no-talk-about-Collin rule." A frown pulled at his aged eyes. "The thing about washing mistakes from your mind is you have a tendency to repeat them. For example, does this doctor have issues?"

"Grandpa . . ."

He pointed a cookie at her. "You only seem to fall for guys with issues. Remember that high-school football player? Did he ever get out of prison?"

"You're never going to let me live that down, are you? I told you, he said he worked with his dad in the banking business. I didn't know they paired up to rob them." Sue sank into a chair. With no desire to rehash her romantic fiascos, she took a conversational turn. "Pretty weather today, wasn't it?"

"Okay, I'll change the subject." He eased into a chair. "Have you noticed anything strange about your mom lately?"

"You mean the wardrobe?" Sue started folding and unfolding a paper napkin. Some things one couldn't tell their grandpa. The fact that his daughter was bumping uglies with a fruit salesman definitely fell into that category.

"I hadn't noticed the wardrobe, but she hasn't come up with a new disease-of-the-week in a month. Yesterday, she said something about fruit juice keeping her healthy."

Sue started rearranging the plastic bananas in the bowl. "She does have a healthy glow about her." A forced smile in place, Sue attempted another conversational U-turn. "I started my new book."

"Susie Veronica!" Her grandma sashayed into the room and placed a kiss on Sue's cheek. "We need to talk, young lady. Your mom is concerned. Did you know . . . ?"

After her grandma's speech about the perils of not listening to her mother, her grandpa walked Sue to her car. He handed over the casserole and foil-wrapped pizza. "Don't eat the pizza either," he said. "Nearly broke a tooth on it a week ago. And don't be upset with your grandma or mother. They're trying to look out for you."

"They're both nuts. We are the only normal ones in the family." Sue opened her car door and glanced at her grandpa. "Take some Rolaids and Vitamin C before bed."

"Normal?" Her grandpa's hair, an inch high, bobbed from side to side. "Have you forgotten about my bug collection? We're all abnormal. You, too."

"Being a collector doesn't make you nuts. And I'm not a hypochondriac and I don't poison my loved ones with my cooking. But talking about doctor's appointments, your appointment is on Monday. I'll pick you guys up around nine."

He tilted his head. "They love you, Susie."

"I know." She kissed her grandpa again. "I'm just glad I took after you."

"Me? I don't kill people on paper, and I've never dated a bank robber."

Sue grinned. "Okay, *you're* the only normal one. I'll call in a few days."

"Does that mean you're not going to Mexico?"

"Nice weather, isn't it?"

Her grandpa laughed. "Let the fellow down easy."

Let the fellow down easy. Sue pulled up in her driveway and sat thinking how she'd give Paul the news. "I can't go because I've got to give my cat a bath." She dropped her head on the steering wheel. "I can't go because I'm terrible at faking orgasms and if your kisses are any indication, then . . ."

Whoever said that truth was the best policy had never dealt with her situation. Sue reached for the door and noted the darkness and the soft cries of the wind. Moonlit tree shadows danced on the ground. Creepy.

Grabbing the pizza and casserole, she darted across the yard. If someone attacked, she could whack them with the pizza. Weeks old, the thing could offer a lethal blow. She imagined the headline: *Mystery Writer Kills Stalker with Deep Dish, Extra Cheese Pie.* Her agent would love that. "Any press is good press," Melissa would say.

After scurrying inside and hitting the lock, Sue's surge of panic decreased. Kneeling, she set the dish and pizza on the floor, then petted Hitchcock, who sideswiped her ankles. Stroking his gray fur, her thoughts zapped back to Paul. "What do I tell him? Maybe you could cough up a few hairballs and I could tell him I'm afraid to leave you."

Hitchcock meowed but didn't offer up a convenient, excuse-laden hairball. Moving inside, Sue noted the light on her answering machine flashed. She thought of the hang-ups and, squaring her shoulders, hit the play button and went to dump the casserole down the disposal.

"Sue. It's Melissa. I'm back in New Jersey and got a copy of the book with the new cover. It looks good. The artist you met and didn't like did a fine job. But he put a dead rat in the corner of the cover, and that's when I remembered about the rat scene in your book. This is strange. You getting the rat. I want you to be careful. Your royalties are paying for my retirement." She chuckled nervously. "Seriously, do you have a gun?"

"No, but I have a pizza." Sue dropped the pizza in the trash. Hitchcock jumped up on the counter, rubbing his soft face against her cheek. "And I've got Hitchcock." Scratching the feline under his chin, Sue waited for the next message.

"Sue," Paul's voice came on the line. "My . . . ex called.

Our son broke his toe. We're going to have to postpone our trip."

What? Relief swirled along her rib cage. *Postponed?*

"Consider it postponed." Sue danced across the kitchen. Her dance petered out when she realized Paul had never told her he had a son. Or an ex-wife. Why would he have never told her? The realization that the trip wasn't the only thing that needed to be postponed rained down on her. The whole relationship needed to be put on the back burner or run down the disposal like a bad casserole. Her grandpa was right. Settling wasn't good enough. She wanted a guy without issues; she wanted the kind of love her grandparents had. A guy who'd eat her cooking and never complain. The thing was: her ex, Collin, had never complained.

You only fall for guys with issues. Her grandfather's words plowed through her mind. Problem was, she hadn't even known about Collin's issues when she married him—hadn't even known about them when she divorced him. But she had loved him, and his double dose of deception left her emotionally crippled.

Or had her grandpa nailed that one, too? Had she been settling when she agreed to marry Collin? Had she *really* loved him? More than once her mother had commented that Collin looked like her father. Had she been trying to fill the void of a missing dad?

Dear Lord, her father would die again if he knew she'd compared him to a man who . . .

What a nice day! She changed mental channels so fast her brain went on overload.

Her answering machine beeped. The third message clicked on. Silence. Then . . . "Sue, sweet Sue," the voice whispered.

Sue rose up, remembering similar words in her novel, "Sally, sweet Sally." Words spoken by a killer. Fear knotted her stomach. The machine clicked off. Who was doing this? And why?

The phone rang. Sue jumped. Then, bracing herself, she forced herself to answer. "Hello?" Her heart pumped, sending a gushing sound into her ears.

"Hey. You okay?" Lacy's voice blended with the gushing.

"Yeah."

"I wanted to say good luck this weekend. We're leaving tomorrow."

Sue almost told Lacy that her weekend had been canceled, but her heart hadn't stopped racing, and the voice of the caller kept ringing in her head. She half considered telling Chase about the calls and the rat scene in her book. But Lacy kept chirping about their vacation.

Telling Chase wouldn't help, but it might scare loyal Lacy enough to cancel their trip. And with Lacy looking forward to spending time with Chase's sister and niece, Sue couldn't do that, but what she could do . . .

Moving across the room as Lacy rattled on, Sue dug in her kitchen drawer until she found the card of the officer who had handled the rat incident. Officer Martin had made a point of telling her that he lived only five minutes away. He'd even written his home phone number on the back of the card and said if she needed anything to call him.

Sue had a feeling "anything" included swapping bodily fluids. Not that she'd go there, but calling him about the prank calls? Yup, she'd do that. And she'd also do as Melissa recommended and buy a gun.

"You okay?" Lacy asked. "You're quiet. You are never quiet."

"Well, after Dodd's comment, I've decided to turn over a new leaf."

"Don't pay attention to him. He's a great guy but . . . he has serious issues."

Well, that explained why Sue found him so dang attractive. "What kind of issues?"

"You name it. He failed relationship 101 and obviously French kissing, as well. Chase told me about the Mr. Deep

Throat comment. Good one." Lacy laughed but Sue couldn't return it.

Sue, sweet Sue. This was too much like her book. What if these weren't just prank calls? Okay, tomorrow she was *so* buying a gun.

But until then . . . Walking over to the trash, she retrieved the foil-wrapped package. Until then, the petrified pizza would have to do.

"You sure you're okay?" Lacy asked.

"Positive."

"We'll be back on Friday," Lacy said. "I'm still planning on being at Kathy's Friday night. Gosh, I'll miss you guys."

They chatted a few more minutes and said good-bye. Then with her cat in one hand and the pizza in another, Sue decided to call it a night.

Jason sat on his sofa, flipping Sue's card between his fingers. He owed her an apology, didn't he? Of course he did. He should have never opened his mouth to Chase. But seeing Sue plant one on the Porche-driving asshole had screwed with his head.

No. What had screwed with his head was that kiss four months ago. From the first time he'd caught sight of Sue Finley, she'd smelled and looked like trouble. Soft. Sweet. Sexy. Smart. Yup! Troubles each, with a capital S.

"It's not as if I haven't dated soft, sweet, sexy, smart women before," he told the orange feline staring up at him.

The cat cocked its head and twitched its right ear.

"Okay, so most of my girlfriends haven't been that smart. None of them were writers like Sue." He ran a hand over his jaw. "But it's not Sue's IQ that gets to me, it's . . ."

You've outworn your welcome again. He recalled Sue's words the day of the rat incident. Words that exemplified why he shouldn't have kissed her. Words he'd heard growing up. Words that still cut to the core.

Jason liked to believe that his past hadn't left any black

marks on his life. He'd learned how to cope after the third or fourth foster home: Never pick a fight with a guy twice your size unless the cause is worth taking a beating. Never reach out to someone whom you can't walk away from, or to someone you'd care about if they walk away from you. Because someone always walks away.

It wasn't as if he had the intimacy issues so many women accused him of having. No, he had all sorts of people in his life. People who counted on him, like Maggie, his foster mom. Hell, there wasn't anything he wouldn't do for her. Then there was Chase. He'd take a bullet for Chase. And his friends on the force, too. So what if he was selective of whom he let close?

His phone rang, and Jason answered it, eager to interrupt his thought process. "Yeah?"

"That was quick," Chase remarked.

"What's up?" The cat jumped into Jason's lap.

"Just making sure you're cool about everything. The food's in the cabinet. The vet's number is on the fridge. And don't feed Fabio too much—"

"He upchucks, you told me. You went over this today." *Twice.*

"These animals are Lacy's babies. So make sure you—"

Jason stroked the cat in his lap and listened—again. He knew Lacy wasn't the only one crazy about those damn pets. Chase was a total animal wuss. "I think I can take care of it."

"Fine." Chase sighed. "Can I get one more favor from you?"

"Depends." Jason kicked off his shoes and stared at the cat curled up in his lap. In spite of him telling the animal not to, the dang thing kept cozying up to him. And unlike Chase, Jason Dodd wasn't a wuss. To prove it, as soon as he found the time, he was taking the thing to a shelter. A good one, of course. He gave the cat's chin a scratch.

"Would you mind checking up on Sue when she gets back from Mexico? I—"

Jason's gaze zapped to the card beside his wallet. "Whoa. I'm not sure—"

"Just check in when she gets back on Sunday. Make sure nothing's going on with this rat freak."

Jason frowned. This wasn't good. Not good at all.

CHAPTER FIVE

"Hold it right there, or I swear I'll splatter your brains." Sue raised the gun, then lowered it. "Of course, you look half dead already," she told the down-on-its-luck ficus tree wilting by her back door.

Staring at her 60LS revolver made especially for a woman, Sue tightened her palm, adjusting to the feel of it. This baby was going to come in handy. Just holding it gave her all sorts of scene ideas.

Oh, goodness, she hoped a book was all she used it for. Yes, she'd bought some bullets, but she had no intention of loading the gun unless things got worse.

Remembering what she'd been doing before being distracted, she set the gun on her counter, grabbed the plant food in the plastic cup, and fed it to her sickly ficus. As she poured, another leaf cracked off and fell to its death.

She eyed the plant. "Hey, chin up. If someone breaks in and threatens you, I've got your back."

Hitchcock, in all his feline glory, lay on the arm of the sofa, staring at her as if she'd lost it. Which could be right. Face it. It had been a trying few days. A trying few years. Not that talking to her plant was insane. Nope.

Yesterday, after purchasing her gun, she'd stopped by the plant store to see if there was some miracle cure for a dying ficus. The clerk had sold her twenty bucks of plant food and then suggested Sue try talking.

Luckily, Sue excelled at talking.

"So," she said to the ficus. "How's your life? Mine sucks. I got two more hang-ups today. And then that rude caller who left the message called back. This time he used the word *die*. I don't like that word." She sighed. "And speaking of rude, did I mention Jason Dodd?"

She touched the plant, and three more leaves floated downward.

"Not that my life is worse than yours. You're almost down to your last leaf." She bit her lip. "I should have never brought you home. I'm much better at killing things than keeping them alive." She paused. "Relationships included. Not that I had a relationship with Dodd."

Sue dropped to the floor and picked up the brittle leaves. "Have you ever met someone who just fit like a good pair of jeans? As if they'd been made for you? After he kissed me . . ." She fought the swell of emotion in her chest. "Have you ever been so lonely that you spent your Saturday afternoon pouring your heart out to a plant? Probably not, huh? And axe the jeans question, too. As a plant, you probably can't relate to the whole jeans analogy. Besides, I've learned my lesson. He's not my pair of jeans."

She touched one of the plant's limbs. "If he showed up at my door now and begged for a second chance, I'd laugh myself silly. Not that I don't feel a little silly now, talking to a plant. And I do have friends. Got a whole club thing going. But both Kathy and Lacy are out of town—"

Sue's doorbell rang. She remembered who she was expecting. Getting up, she spotted her gun and hurriedly stuck the weapon in her purse. No use flaunting it in front of a cop.

"Hi." She waved Officer Martin inside. He'd already changed out of uniform, wore jeans and a short-sleeved button-down shirt, which bore the print of . . . smiley faces. Hmmm.

She'd called him this morning and told him she felt like she needed to report a few more things. He'd offered to stop by after work. The after-work comment bothered her, but she remembered he lived close and decided to go with the flow. And the flow right now dictated she offer him something to drink.

"Soda or tea?"

They sat at the kitchen table, sipping iced tea, and she spilled the beans. She told him about the rat scene in her book and the phone calls. He sat there looking at her, or rather, looking at her chest. She pulled the scoop-neck blouse up to a non-scooping level. When his eyes rose, she continued talking.

"It's just weird, things happening so close to how they happened in my book."

"And your PR person, she's read the book, right?" He scooted his chair closer.

"Yes." Sue inched her chair back. "But Melissa wouldn't be behind this."

He nodded. "And . . . you live here alone, right?"

"Yes." She waited for him to give her a piece of advice. Like "buy a gun," which she'd proudly announce she'd done.

Instead, he sent her one of those male, gotta-love-me smiles. The man could work on his smiles. "There's not a boyfriend who could come stay here?"

"Not really." She had spoken to Paul, said boyfriend, once since he'd left the message of the vacation cancellation. During the brief conversation, she'd arranged a Monday night dinner. A Monday night good-bye dinner. No more settling.

"How could that be?" Martin asked.

"How could what be?" Sue had lost track of the conversation.

"Someone like yourself being single."

Sue pasted a smile on her face, imitating the one on his shirt. "I kill people on paper. Excruciating deaths. Guys find that hard to deal with."

"I wouldn't," he said.

But maybe you should. "Look, about these calls . . ."

"Yeah," he said. "If she calls back . . ."

"She?"

"Whoever. If you get scared, need anything, day or night, call me. I can get here in minutes." He picked up her portable phone on the table, which he told her was exactly like the one he owned, and punched his number into her speed dial. "I'm one touch away."

She thanked him but explained that she thought she'd be okay. When he offered to take her out to dinner, she refused. When he offered to stop by later, she told him she didn't want him to go beyond his call of duty. Hint. Hint.

He didn't take that hint, and she was afraid she might have to bypass the polite I'll-never-date-you hints and go for the never-in-a-million-years bluntness. Then she spotted her ficus tree. She faced Martin, his gaze directed toward her chest, of course.

Okay, so the Wonderbra had its good points and bad.

She yanked up her top again. "You know, I'm sorry to do this but I have to cut this short. I have a sick friend to visit."

After Martin left, Sue donned a pair of pj's, drank one glass of Merlot—she needed to wipe the smiley faces from her mind—and chatted with Ms. Ficus and Hitchcock before going to bed.

She wasn't sure how long she'd slept when a paw, claws in, struck her face. Then Hitchcock howled. An ugly type of howl, too. Sue shot up. The cat jumped from the bed and paced in front of her huge bay window.

"What is it? A hairball? You don't have a cold, do you? Oh, Lordie, don't have a cold."

Hitchcock continued to pace. The blinds were up, and the backyard floodlight cast enough of a glow that the cat's fur shone silver. Sue watched. Not that she really cared to witness the hairball delivery, but it was good knowing where they were. Stepping on them was—

Then she saw it. It was not a hairball.

Oh God, someone was in her backyard! And they were

walking toward her window. The voice from the prank calls echoed in her head. *Die, sweet Sue, die.*

Unable to breathe, she grabbed her cat around the middle and darted out of the bedroom.

"Oh, God!" She started going in circles. Hitchcock, never fond of circles, leapt down. Sue accepted right then that everyone in their lives was faced with circumstances that proved what they were made of: strength, valor, courage. She owned not one of those qualities. No backbone, no nerve. She was one tiny muscle spasm away from wetting herself.

Focused on not peeing, it finally hit her to call for help. She spotted her cell phone on the table, grabbed it, and hit 911.

"Help me," she screamed as soon as the voice answered. "Someone is in my backyard. Someone's told me to die!" She rattled off her address. Then she remembered Martin telling her that he could arrive fast. She grabbed her portable phone. She started to look for his card, then remembered he'd put his number on speed dial. Three, wasn't it? Or four? "Crap, crap, crap!"

Hitchcock howled again. Sue's gaze shot up. She heard it. Her doorknob turned. It was locked, but the eerie clicking sounded like something out of a horror movie. Or a scary book! *Like one of my books. One where someone always died.*

A noise startled Jason awake. He forced his eyes open, his mind trying to process the noise and where the hell he was. Suddenly, he was nose to nose with something with bugged-out eyes and a short snout. In his youth, he'd woken up with some real dogs, but—

He remembered: Lacy's house, pet-sitting, Fabio. Pushing the ugly dog away, Jason heard the phone.

Grabbing his watch off the coffee table, he hit the light button to check the time. One A.M.? Who the hell would be calling at this hour? He vaguely remembered calling Maggie and leaving this number because his cell phone had run out of juice and he'd forgotten to bring his charger. Picking up the portable phone, he answered on the fourth ring. "Hello?"

"Someone's here. I saw him walk past my window. Oh, God, he's at my back door again! What do I do?"

Jason's foggy brain tried to place the panicked voice. It wasn't Maggie.

Recognition struck. "Sue?" But, wasn't she in Mexico doing the tango with the shower-capped Porsche driver? "Where are you?"

The line went dead.

The phone crackled under his intense grip. If she was in Mexico, she wouldn't be calling here. She had to be at home. The fear he'd heard in her voice ricocheted into his gut. He grabbed his jeans, his gun belt, swiped his keys from the coffee table, and ran to his car.

It was a ten-minute drive to her place. He made it in six.

A police car, lights flashing, sat in Sue's driveway. Jason parked on the curb, jerked his jeans up over his boxers, slipped on his shoes, and grabbed his gun. Jumping out of his car, he headed to the front door. Blue shadows danced across the yard. He made four steps when he heard, "Police! Hands up. Down on the ground. Now!"

"I'm Houston PD. Jason Dodd." He held up his hands, knowing the shape of the gun would be clearly visible. "I've got a gun. Sue Finley called me. I'm Houston PD," he repeated.

"Drop the weapon and get on the ground until I can see your badge," the man called.

Jason did as he was told even though it stung. A young man stepped from the shadows, his weapon aimed.

"Badge is in my back left pocket. Is Sue okay?"

The officer grabbed Jason's gun. Tossing it aside, he reached for Jason's wallet. A second later, he spoke again. "Sorry, Detective. You . . . surprised me. I'm Officer Tomas Poe. Hoke's Bluff police."

Jason pushed himself up. "Is Sue okay?" he asked again. After collecting his gun and wallet, he started toward the house.

"She's shook up." Officer Poe fell in step beside him. "But not hurt."

"What happened?" Jason asked.

"Donald Martin, one of our officers, asked me to drive by. I did. I noticed a car parked up the street. I thought it belonged next door."

Sirens screeched in the distance. "You get the license number?"

The young guy shrugged. "It looked like it belonged to the house next door." The kid had rookie written all over him.

"Then what happened?"

"I hadn't gotten but a mile away when I got the call of a break-in in progress. When I came around, the car was gone. I called for backup." He glanced back to the street as two patrol cars squealed to a halt. "After seeing she was okay, I did a sweep of the outside of the house, then you came up. I think what happened was the perpetrator saw me swing by and bailed. That is, if there was a perpetrator." Poe turned to the two officers and yelled, "It's clear."

"You're questioning the fact that there was a perpetrator after you spotted that car?" Jason's tone drew the man's attention back to him.

"I mean, a *real* perpetrator." Poe hesitated. "Donald thinks this is a publicity stunt by her PR agent. But since this lady called him about the phone calls—"

"What phone calls?" Jason snapped.

"All he said was she was getting prank calls, and to be safe he wanted me to swing by."

Two other officers walked up. The rookie introduced Jason as a Houston detective and explained he was an acquaintance of the victim.

"Isn't this the writer's house—the one Martin's got the hots for?" one of the newly arrived officers asked.

"Yeah." Officer Poe cut his gaze to Jason.

"Have you called him?" the larger newcomer asked. "He'll want to be here to comfort her, if you know what I mean. Or I could stand in for him if she's pretty enough." He laughed and attempted to suck in his gut. "Let her get a taste of a real man."

Poe shot Jason another look, as if questioning the relationship between Jason and Sue. Jason didn't care what the guy thought; he wanted to check on Sue.

"I called Martin," Poe stated. "He should be pulling up any minute."

Jason stalked toward the front door. As he walked, his mind started gnawing on what he'd learned. So, Sue had been getting disturbing phone calls. And she'd called Martin instead of Chase . . . or himself. Then he remembered the fiasco that had happened at Chase's on the Fourth, and he supposed he didn't blame her for not calling him. But Chase . . .

The door stood ajar, and Jason saw her on the sofa. Her knees pulled up to her chest, she had her arms wrapped around her calves, and her head rested facedown on top of her knees. Dressed in blue cotton pajamas, she looked small and so damn scared. Emotion kicked the inside of his ribs.

He stepped inside without knocking.

CHAPTER SIX

Sue couldn't stop shaking. Someone had attempted to break into her house. Someone had been calling and leaving weird messages or just hanging up. Someone had sent her a dead rat. Just like in her book. Someone really wanted to kill her.

She remembered seeing the shadow pass by her bedroom window. She remembered hearing someone at the back door, the knob turning. Thank goodness the police arrived so quickly. With her face hidden in the fold of her arms, she heard the officer talking to someone outside. Then she recalled hearing other sirens arriving. More police. She was safe. Safe but still shaking.

She buried her face deeper. This was grist for the mill. As a mystery writer, she should be taking notes of the emotional impact, but this wasn't fiction. She clenched her teeth and wished she had someone to call. But Lacy was in California, and Kathy in Dallas visiting her mom.

She thought of phoning her own mom but wasn't sure she had enough Merlot to keep her mother from hysterics.

Sue's mind turned to her grandpa. Her rock, her protector. But lately, their relationship had changed. Oh, his love had never faltered, but Sue found herself being the strong one. She envisioned the times he'd whispered, "It's gonna be okay, Princess." By golly, she could use hearing those words right now.

A tear squeezed its way through her closed lids. "Can't cry," she muttered. Any minute the officers would need to ask her some questions, and she couldn't be blubbering like a baby.

"It's going to be okay." The caring voice came out of nowhere, and so did the emotion in her throat. He hadn't called her princess, but it was close enough. The sofa shifted. He sat beside her. She kept her head down to hide her watery weakness.

The owner of the deep voice wrapped an arm around her shoulders. Probably the officer on duty—Tomas, if she remembered his name. Or was it Officer Martin? Probably him, because there was a familiar ring to the voice. He even smelled nice and familiar.

She started to raise her head, but the muscled arm pulled her against him, offering a shoulder—an offer she couldn't refuse. And it was a nice shoulder, masculine like his voice and his spicy scent. Oddly, she hadn't given Martin's shoulders, voice, or scent a second thought earlier. Nothing like a little panic to bring things home. She pillowed her cheek on the wall of muscle.

"You're safe." His arm tightened, and she felt safe.

The concerned tone, the warm touch, all made her throat ache and her sinuses sting. Her tears flowed. Knowing her nose ran like a floodgate when she cried, she inhaled a hiccupping breath and drew her face off his shirt. Any longer and he'd be wringing the garment out in her sink.

"Thank you." She sat up, pressing her hand over her face, hoping to collect any leakage without looking totally undignified. Only then did she look at . . .

"No." Could panic bring on hallucinations?

"No, what?" Dodd asked.

When she didn't answer, he rose and went into the kitchen. He came back, sat down beside her, and held a paper towel to her nose. "Blow," he said.

So much for looking dignified. She took the paper towel,

but when she felt the moisture collect between her nose and lip, she blew.

And she really wished she hadn't.

With one nasal cavity stopped, it made a honking noise that sounded like a mating call of a jungle bird. She wiped and wished she could slip between the sofa's cushions and disappear like an unwanted penny.

"What happened?" Jason's leg cozied up to hers.

"My nose is stopped. What do you think happened?"

He attempted not to smile, but humor danced in his eyes. "I mean tonight."

She leaned back into her leather sofa. "I . . ."

Officer Tomas and two more uniformed policemen walked inside. Sue looked at them and then back at Jason, who wore jeans and a white T-shirt. "How did . . ." She stared at the damp spot on his chest. Great, she'd snotted up his shirt. Maybe he wouldn't notice.

Jason glanced at his slimed shirt. Okay, he'd noticed. But she hadn't asked him for his shoulder.

"Do you think you could go over what happened again?" Officer Tomas asked.

Sue wadded the paper towel in her fist. Then, unable to help herself, she wiped at Jason's damp spot. "Hitchcock woke me up."

"Hitchcock?" One policeman, an Archie Bunker looka-like, stepped closer. Sue barely noticed him, because she was too busy noticing Dodd staring at her as she attempted to clean the snot off his shirt.

"My cat." She decided to leave Jason's shirt alone and looked up at the big cop. "He hit me with his paw. I think he saw the guy first. Then I saw him."

"A guard cat?" the same officer said. "I'm glad I don't have to write this one up."

"Did you get a look at him?" Jason's voice came out stern, and he stared at Archie.

Still uncertain how Jason had wound up here, she stared

at him. Remembering their confrontation at Lacy's, resid-
ual anger stirred in her chest. Then she recalled the tender
way he'd held her seconds ago.

She moved away from the warmth that his jean-covered
leg offered hers. "No, all I saw was a shape."

"Big or small?" Jason ran his hand down his leg, which
brought the backs of his fingers sliding against Sue's outer
thigh—an outer thigh covered only by a thin layer of cotton pj's. His touch sent her brain into sensory overload.
Nerve endings that hadn't been awake in a long time started
stretching and yawning to life.

"I . . . don't remember. But I assumed it was a man, so it
wasn't that small." She moved a couple more inches away
on the couch.

"Are you sure it wasn't just a shadow?" The larger officer
snickered.

"I'm sure." Sue's left foot tapped nervously against the
wood floor. "My backyard has a floodlight. And besides, I
ran in here and then I heard him at my back door. He was
turning the knob. Shadows can't do that, can they?"

The sofa shifted beside her. Jason got up and went to her
back door. He unlocked it and studied the doorknob on
the outside.

"Any damage?" Tomas asked.

"No, but dust it for prints." Jason's gaze returned to her.
"Then what happened?"

"I called for help and I . . ." *Hid,* she remembered but
didn't say so.

"Prints?" the bigger cop interrupted. "You're joking."

Jason met the man's gaze without flinching. "Do it, or I'll
call someone from my unit."

"Go ahead and call," Archie answered. "But you should
talk to Martin first. This whole thing is a sham."

"A sham?" Sue's left foot went still.

"I think it's more," Jason said.

"Sham?" Sue repeated.

Archie Bunker reared back on his heels, looking as if he might tumble backward. "Martin's just playing this up to get in her—"

"I don't give a damn what Martin's doing." Jason scowled.

"Wait!" Sue held up a hand. "What's a sham?"

The front door, left ajar, flew open. Officer Martin, wearing jeans and his unbuttoned, short-sleeved smiley shirt, rushed in. His light brown hair stuck up at an odd angle. He knelt between her knees and took her hands in his. "You okay?"

Sue glanced at their interlaced fingers, finding his affection too showy.

"Why didn't you call me?" Martin asked.

"I did." She tried to pull away. He held on. He leaned closer; she backed up. "Do you think this is a scam?"

Jason walked to the sofa and stared at Officer Martin crouched between her knees. Martin let go of her hands and stood. Both men's expressions grew pinched, and Sue got an image of two roosters clawing at the dirt, ready to spar. One rooster was wearing a smiley-face shirt.

"Why are you here?" Martin voiced the question she'd been dying to ask herself.

"Sue called me," Jason answered.

"I did not," Sue retorted.

Jason's pinched expression targeted her now. "You called Chase's. I'm pet-sitting."

"I . . ." Understanding dawned. "I must have misdialed. Lacy is three on my speed dial. Martin put his in as four."

"Yeah, I did that before I left tonight, didn't I?" Martin said. There was an insinuation in his tone that Sue didn't like.

Jason continued to scowl. "What phone were you on when you called?"

"My home phone. 911 said for me not to hang up. I called them on my cell."

"I don't think this is going to take two police forces," Martin said.

Without a word, Jason walked out the door. The fact that

it was the back door seemed a little odd. Odder still, Sue felt abandoned.

She looked at the four cops in her living room. If she broke down again, whom would she lean on?

No one.

She focused on Martin. "Why do they think this is a sham?"

He shuffled his feet. "It's nothing."

"Do you think I'm doing this for publicity?"

"No." He flushed. The man couldn't lie worth a diddly squat.

Sue crossed her arms and started swinging her foot. "I'm going to say this once more. My agent isn't doing this. I've been getting weird phone calls and someone sent me a dead rat. It doesn't matter that the evidence was eaten."

Martin knelt between her legs again and grabbed her hands. "You're upset."

Sue slammed her knees shut, blocking him from getting any closer, and jerked her hands from his. "When I said I didn't want you doing more than your call of duty, what I meant was . . . I'm not sleeping with you!"

The back door swung open. Jason stepped inside and his gaze homed in on Martin; then it turned to Officer Tomas. "You get someone here to dust for prints or I'll make a few calls and make it happen. And I want a detailed description of the car you saw."

"What car?" asked Martin.

"What car?" Sue echoed.

"Wait a damn minute!" the large cop spoke up. "The last time I checked the map, Hoke's Bluff is our jurisdiction. We call the shots here. Even if Martin is wrong, we don't dust for fingerprints for Peeping Toms. So just take your attitude and—"

"The phone line's been cut." Jason's tone could have etched glass. "Whoever was here wasn't just planning on peeping in the windows. Get the kit out here and dust for the prints."

Sue tried not to imagine what her stalker had intended to

do to her. She wouldn't let fear win. She could deal with this. Her gaze slid to her purse on the kitchen table. She was an adult, a gun-toting independent female. Okay, she was a gun-toting independent woman who'd forgotten all about the gun and hid in the pantry with her cat, but . . . she could handle this. She could handle anything.

A familiar dog bark sounded outside. Sue amended her last thought. She could handle anything as long as it didn't involve her mother. Sue sent up a serious, silent prayer. *Please, don't let it involve my mother.*

"Susie!" Peggy Finley scrambled inside, doing her best Scarlett O'Hara entrance without the staircase. She threw herself on the couch and hugged Sue against her low-cut grape-colored blouse. "Are you okay? Oh, God, why aren't you talking?"

"Because you're smothering me!" Sue pried herself free, frustrated until she saw the concern in her mother's eyes. "I'm fine." Sue held up hands and feet. "Got all my fingers and toes. No sore throat, either."

"She's not hurt, Mrs. Finley," Officer Martin said in an annoyingly in-charge tone. The man was *not* in charge. He didn't believe her, and he hadn't even arrived in time for her to leak snot on. No, she'd had the pleasure of doing that to the man who didn't like her tonsils.

"Oh, sweetie," her mother cried. "Bill and I were . . . playing checkers. We heard your address called out on his police radio that he listens to for entertainment. Tell me they caught the doctor."

Bill? Was this the fruit salesman? Glancing at her mom's disheveled clothing and mussed hair, Sue questioned the checkers story. Suddenly it all seemed too real—and she didn't mean that someone had tried to break in. She meant her mother. Her mom was having sex. A vision of her father flashed in Sue's mind.

Her mom straightened her blouse. "I hope they throw that foot doctor in jail for years."

"It's not Paul. But who's Bill?" Sue managed to say.

"Who's Paul?" Officer Martin asked.

Sue watched all two hundred pounds of Goliath lumber into her entranceway. Hitchcock zipped out of the room. Behind the dog, a middle-aged man with jet black hair appeared. Wearing tight leather pants and a silk shirt, he looked . . . familiar.

Recognition dawned.

"Get this beast away from me," Sue heard someone say, but she continued to glare at the leather pants–wearing man in blue suede shoes.

Great. Her mom was sleeping with a fruit-selling Elvis impersonator. Her father had hated Elvis. He hadn't been too keen on fruit, either.

"That's Bill," her mother said.

Sue opened her mouth but didn't have a clue what to say to a man who was, moments earlier, bumping uglies with her mother.

Before Sue could say anything, a masculine outcry arose. She turned her head just as Goliath jammed his nose into Archie Bunker's crotch and growled. The cop jerked out his gun. "You bite me there, you son of a bitch, and you're a dead dog!"

"No!" Her mother, a grape-colored streak, vaulted over the coffee table and latched her arms around her English Mastiff. Goliath, not used to being lunged at, jumped. All two hundred pounds of canine slammed into Archie Bunker. The cop tumbled backward. His hands, with one gun attached, flew up in the air. As he went down, the gun pointed in Sue's direction and exploded.

CHAPTER SEVEN

Sue pressed her hand over the bullet hole.

"It's not fatal." Jason walked closer, his expression softening.

She remembered him unleashing his anger on the officer who'd fired the gun. "I can't believe he shot my couch."

"It could've been worse." He looked at her, his blue eyes serious. "But if it makes you feel better, he'll be doing paperwork for hours. Explaining a misfired weapon is a bitch. And I'm sure you'll get a new sofa out of the deal, too."

"Yeah, it could have been worse," Sue repeated. "They could have arrested my mom. I don't think prison uniforms come in fruity colors."

The warmth of his smile worked its way into her chest. She returned the gesture, suddenly finding his presence a lot easier. Her gaze flickered over him—his wide chest, lean hips . . . It didn't feel so easy anymore.

Still smiling, he pulled a piece of red-wrapped hard candy from his pocket. "Want one?"

Sue's gaze shifted to the back door. The events of the last few days felt more like fiction than her life. Sure, she wrote about crazy things and murder, but she didn't want to live it. All that talk about grist for the mill was just talk. She could imagine all the grist she needed, thank you.

"I personally liked Elvis," Jason said. "But if that dog put his nose in my crotch one more time, I might have taken a shot at him, too."

Sue grinned. "He flunked obedience training four times."

A smile chased away the awkwardness again. How could Jason Dodd make her feel comfortable and then so uncomfortable in the next second?

"The dog or Elvis?" He stepped closer.

The humor helped, but reality crowded her mind. "Do you think they'll get a name from the fingerprint?"

"It was only a partial." He sat down in the chair across from her. Everyone else had left. Sue had insisted Mr. Delaney, a.k.a. Elvis, take her mother home before she finished off the bottle of wine.

Officer Tomas had gone back to the precinct and gotten the equipment to dust for prints, while Jason had taped the phone line back together.

Officer Martin had hung around long enough to ask her to go home with him. When she refused, he walked out in a huff. After Officer Tomas and Archie left, it was only her and Jason. And Hitchcock.

The cat jumped up in her lap. Sue stroked the feline and stared at the dancing penguins on her pajama bottoms. Her knees were still trembling.

"You okay?" Jason asked, bringing her gaze up.

"You can go, you know." She hoped she sounded more convincing than she felt. What if whoever had tried to break in came back? "I didn't mean to call you tonight, and I'm sorry about . . . your shirt."

"I haven't complained." He glanced at the door. Then they stared at each other for several suspended seconds before he stood up.

Thinking he meant to leave, she bit down on her lip to keep from asking him to stay. But instead of heading for the door, he moved to her DVDs shelf.

"You know, I haven't seen this movie in years." He held out the *Lonesome Dove* case. "Do you mind if I hang out a while?"

When she shook her head, he put the disc in, and because the only place to see the television was on her wounded sofa, he sat down beside her, keeping a good ten inches between them. The distance showed that he didn't intend to take advantage of her.

Of course he didn't. If he'd been interested in her, he'd have called four months ago. She petted Hitchcock and reminded herself that Jason Dodd wasn't her pair of jeans.

But, the smell of his cinnamon candy teased her senses. She knew Jason didn't want to see a movie. He obviously sensed she didn't want to be alone. But why did he care? The man didn't like her. She knew he didn't like her tonsils.

She looked back at the clock. When *Lonesome Dove* ended, it would be daylight. No reason to be afraid. Yup, tomorrow morning, she'd send Jason Dodd off with a big "Thank you" and a fond farewell. Tomorrow, she'd be fine.

She looked back at him. "I appreciate what you're doing. But after the movie, you should go."

Jason winked in response, but he didn't agree to anything, especially the leaving part. Thirty minutes later, Sue was out like a blown bulb. Her cheek rested against his arm, her mouth sagging open. Her breathing sounded heavy—not quite snoring, but serious rattling, as if her sinuses were still clogged. Not that they should be clogged. He'd never seen so much fluid come out of a woman. He smiled, recalling the look on her face when she'd seen his shirt.

Popping another piece of candy into his mouth, he watched her take even breaths and recalled another look on her face, the look when she'd thought he was about to leave. Sue Finley needed him. He could no more have left Sue than he could have left Maggie fourteen years ago.

Leaning his head back, he wasn't certain why that memory surged forward, but it did. He'd heard shouting as he let himself in the front door. Maggie sat in a ball in the corner of her kitchen, her eyes wet and swollen, her lip bleeding.

Jason had intended to walk into the house that night—

two hours after the curfew Maggie had set for him, the curfew he never kept—grab his things, and leave for good. At sixteen, he figured the foster system was as tired of him as he was it. But one look at Maggie that night and everything changed. Maggie needed him.

Sue's gray cat moved to his lap, ending his reverie. He wasn't a cat person, but damn if cats didn't realize that. The animal looked up at him, then back at Sue. Jason ran his hand over the feline's back and followed the cat's gaze.

"Pretty, isn't she?" he asked. Swallowing a wave of desire, he told himself there was nothing sexy about a woman wearing loose, penguin-printed pajamas buttoned up to her neck—a woman with a stopped-up nose. But tell that to the hardness growing between his legs.

Moving his hand from the cat, he reached up and touched a strand of Sue's hair. Soft. Leaning closer, he caught a whiff of the fruity scent. He'd smelled it the night he'd kissed her, and again the day of the rat incident.

Yeah, he'd noticed. So much so that yesterday at the drugstore he'd actually paused at the shampoo aisle and loosened lids trying to discover which she used. Very unlike him. He simply wasn't the type of man who cared what type of shampoo a woman used. But he cared about Sue.

His gut tightened when he remembered someone was trying to hurt her. He took a deep breath and swore that whoever had put that fear in Sue's eyes tonight would pay. Pay big.

For a second, he got that soul-wrenching feeling to run, the same feeling he'd gotten the night he'd kissed her. The one that said this could only lead to regret. But who would Sue turn to? She hadn't called the foot doctor tonight. She obviously hadn't gone to Mexico with him. Which meant she didn't care about him. An odd sense of relief flooded Jason's chest.

Sue nestled closer against him as if comfortable with his presence. He hoped that was the case. Because until he caught the stalker, he planned on staying right here.

Here, with Sue. With the woman he'd vowed not to get close to.

"I'm staying," he whispered, not loud enough to wake her but loud enough for her subconscious to hear. "So don't argue with me. Got that?"

She stirred again, her hand came to rest in his lap, and his sex stiffened. It felt good. He glanced at the rising bulge in his jeans. Realization hit. Things were back to normal. He smiled.

Ah, hell, since they were going to be together anyhow, he didn't see any reason they couldn't indulge in a few pleasurable pastimes. If she was up for it. He knew he was.

But why now and not last week, or last month? Because she needed him? Yeah, that was it; but there was also the whole no-dating rule she'd followed. Non-dating women were either too easily hurt or they were looking for more than the average man was offering. Jason was definitely the average man in the offerings department, and he hated the idea of hurting someone. But obviously Sue had moved past that. Now all he had to do was convince her that they could be good together.

Letting his gaze whisper over her, he shifted his arm so she rested closer against him. Nice. Real nice. Tilting his head down, he pressed his lips against her forehead and eyed the tiny buttons of her pajama top.

She let out another light rattle/almost a snore. He grinned and decided again that a little convincing was the only thing keeping him from exploring what was below those cotton pj's. Not tonight. But soon.

Knowing Sue, he expected her to try to talk him out of it. Luckily, he was good at convincing.

Light.
    Morning breath.
    A hard object.
    "Jiminy Cricket!" Sue snapped her eyes open, attempting to identify the hard object pressed against her hip.

She tried to dislodge herself, but her legs and arms were tangled with another pair of arms and legs. Pushing against a very masculine chest, she jerked up, lost her balance, and started falling off the couch. A pair of arms caught her and in one swoop she was once again against the warm, masculine chest . . . and the hard object.

"Relax." His voice sounded hoarse with sleep. "You're gonna fall."

His breath tickled her ear, and the hardness now pressed against her thigh. She pushed up, carefully.

Standing, she gazed at the large bulge between his legs. Yup, she'd been right. After two years, she should be proud she could recognize one. She might have been proud to have gotten Jason Dodd in the state, but she knew better. Men just naturally found lead in their pencils in the morning.

He followed her gaze. "Sorry. I was asleep. It has a mind of its own."

Yeah, because your other mind wasn't interested enough to call me! Sue looked at the silent television screen, then at the clock. It was almost ten.

"The movie's over." She marched across her breakfast room and into her hall. She opened her bedroom door, then called back, "Thanks for staying. You can see yourself out. And lock the door behind you."

Closing her eyes, she leaned against the wall. Perhaps it was normal for men to wake up to lead in their pencils, but it wasn't so normal for a woman to want to be used as stationery. Forcing herself to move, she headed to the bathroom and a cold shower. And then she needed to figure out what she was going to do about someone wanting to kill her.

Ten minutes later, dressed in a pair of cut-off jeans and a T-shirt, she stepped into the hall. When she didn't hear anything, she assumed he'd done as she'd asked and left. Later she'd call and thank him again. After all, it had been rude to send him off without offering him coffee, tea, or . . . *me.* She moaned at the wayward thought.

She got to the kitchen and froze when she heard the running shower in her guest bathroom. Dashing to the window, she peeked out to make sure Jason's car was still there. For all she knew, her stalker had come in and had decided to bathe before he did her in. Seeing the blue Mustang out front, she relaxed.

But as she reentered the kitchen, she got a mental picture of him naked, his pencil still ready to write, standing beneath a steamy spray of water.

Swallowing, she started coffee and made it strong. Jeepers! The man wasn't interested in her. The least she could do was return the feeling.

After calling her mom and leaving a short message that she was fine—not mentioning the whole Elvis situation, she would deal with that later—Sue phoned her grandparents to remind them of tomorrow's doctor's appointment. Her grandpa pointed out that she obviously hadn't gone to Mexico.

Sue told him the truth. "You were right. Settling isn't going to cut it. No more guys with issues." Then she reminded them both to take their vitamin C.

Hanging up, Sue poured herself a cup of vanilla java with milk and filled another cup for Hitchcock. "It's a little strong," she warned the cat waiting on the table.

Hearing footsteps, she darted to the fridge, opened it, and stared at some mayonnaise. The footsteps moved closer, then stopped.

Sue felt his gaze and pulled her cup to her lips, hoping to appear nonchalant, sophisticated, and totally uninterested. Suddenly not sure staring at mayonnaise said sophisticated, she focused the gorgonzola cheese. Much more sophisticated. Moldy cheese would always do the trick.

"Thanks," Jason said.

For what? She turned. He had on the same jeans and T-shirt, but his blond hair was wet and finger-combed. He held Hitchcock's coffee as if she'd poured it for him.

His gaze homed in on her as if she were something delectable. He sipped the brew before his delectable gaze shifted to the cup. "I usually take it black."

She glanced at an unhappy cat, tail twitching, staring up at Jason from a chair. "Yeah, but Hitchcock takes his with cream."

Jason eyed the cat, then the cup. "You serve him coffee?"

She nodded. "We used to share, but after he ate that dead rat, he gets his own cup. Nasty germs and all." Sue grinned at the look on Jason's face.

"Funny." He set Hitchcock's coffee on the table and opened a few cabinet doors until he found a new cup.

She should have gotten it for him, but the morning-after awkwardness had her in knots. Not that they'd had a night.

Then, feeling rude for staring, she refocused on the cheese. The cool air hitting her face felt good. She heard Jason pour coffee and felt his gaze on her again.

"Make yourself at home." Her tone bordered on sarcastic.

"I did." He either ignored her sarcasm or was deaf to it. "What are we having?"

"Having?" She refused to look at him. Safer to stare at the cheese.

"For breakfast." He nudged her over so he could share the fridge space and her much-needed cold air.

She looked at him.

He glanced into the fridge. "Eggs, milk, cheese." Still holding the coffee in one hand, he opened the vegetable drawer. Steam rose from his cup. A lock of wet hair fell to his brow. He looked at her and smiled. "You could make us omelets."

Yeah. She barely managed to scramble eggs.

Snatching the milk, she shut the fridge. Sue then retrieved a box of raisin bran and shoved it into his hand. "This is as good at gets around here." But why had she said that instead of asking him to leave?

"I'm a cereal man, myself." He carried the box to the table and then, bringing the cup to his lips, his slow gaze moved over her body. "Does the cat get his own bowl?"

His smile wrapped around her lungs making it hard to

breathe, and the unexplainable heat in his eyes made her heart drop. She grabbed bowls and spoons and, moving to the other side of the breakfast table, set them down.

"Look, I appreciate what you did last night. But I should be fine now. I mean, you're welcome to some cereal but—"

"Good, I'm starved." He opened the box and commenced to fill the two bowls.

Resigning herself to sharing a meal with him, she pulled one bowl closer. "Then you go."

He closed the top of the cereal. "No." He said the word so casually it surprised her. "After we eat, we talk."

"We don't need to talk."

"Yes, we do. I've got questions about the phone calls." He pointed to her bowl. "But now, let's eat."

She could have argued. Could have, but didn't. Instead she sat down, grabbed her vitamin bottle from the table, and poured out two for herself and two for him. Leaning over, she dropped his pills beside his bowl. "Vitamin C. Cold prevention." She'd answered his raised brow.

"I don't get colds."

"Anything that stays around here long enough starts dying." She motioned to Ms. Ficus. "Look at my plant." She swallowed her pills with a sip of coffee.

He smiled—one of those really nice smiles. Obviously, Jason thought she was too scared to be alone. Why else was he being nice? And why was she letting him?

"Look." She sighed. "As Officer Martin pointed out last night, this isn't your district, so it's not your problem."

He picked up his spoon and met her gaze. "Why? You want to call Martin again?"

"No." She leaned back in her chair.

"Good." He uncapped the milk and filled both bowls. "The guy's a jerk."

She propped her elbows on the table and watched him spoon bites of cereal into his mouth. Why was he still here? She understood the panicked phone call may have brought out his *to protect and serve* instincts, but to stay last night . . .

"Why are you being nice?"

He grinned. "I'm a nice guy."

"No, you're not."

He pointed to her bowl with his spoon. "Your cereal is getting soggy."

She hated soggy cereal, so she started eating. He refilled his bowl and finished before she did. Obviously not going back for thirds, he crossed his arms over his chest and watched her eat.

No longer hungry under his intense scrutiny, she pushed her bowl away. "Fine. Let's get this over with."

"Get what over with?" He smiled as if she'd secretly meant something sexual.

"The questions."

He settled back in his chair, and his smile melted away. "Okay. Why aren't you in Mexico with the foot doctor?"

CHAPTER EIGHT

"I . . ." Why did she get the feeling of déjà vu?

Oh, yeah. His smug tone reminded her of the conversation they'd had last week at Lacy's. The gratefulness she'd held for him for staying last night started to wane. "You know? I don't want to do this. You should—"

"Your mother thinks the doc is behind all this."

She wadded a paper napkin in her hand. "My mother is having sex with a fruit-selling Elvis. How much weight do you think you should put in what she thinks?" Sue shook her head. "Paul didn't do this."

"How can you be so sure?"

"I just know." She unwrinkled her napkin, flattened it, then ripped it in half.

His blue-eyed stare made her realize that the air conditioner hadn't come on. Hot, too hot. The memory of waking up on top of him did funny things to her stomach. She fidgeted with her napkin and tore it again.

"So, what happened to your plans for the weekend?"

Oh, I decided I couldn't fake orgasms. She ripped the napkin into tiny shreds. Realizing the mess she'd made, she swiped up the bits and closed them into her hand. "He had a medical emergency."

"Someone get an ingrown toenail?" Humor danced in Jason's eyes.

Sue stood and carried her bowl to the sink. "Paul's a doctor. He doesn't deserve to be ridiculed. Feet are important."

Jason turned in his chair. "So you broke up with him, huh?"

"I did not." She shot him her best go-to-Hades look. The fact that she planned to break up with Paul tomorrow night was none of Dodd's business.

"So, why didn't you call him last night to come rescue you? Isn't that what a girl does—calls her boyfriend during a crisis?"

She opened her mouth but couldn't answer. Truth was, she'd never considered calling Paul. Even before she'd decided to break up with him, she would never have counted on him. Didn't that say something about how little she really cared?

She bit into her lip. "How is that any of your business?" *Being that you're not interested in a woman who can't stand still and never shuts up,* she continued in her mind. But she didn't say it. Because to say it would make her sound hurt. And if she was hurt, then it meant she cared. Which she didn't, of course.

Sure, she had a bad case of you're-my-kind-of-jeans lust going on, but give her a break. It had been two years since she'd had sex and anything battery operated didn't count. Jason had all the right equipment, no batteries required. She'd probably be attracted to any man if he'd kissed her and discovered a never-before-found G spot in her throat.

Jason brought his bowl to the sink. His leg brushed against hers.

Zip.

Zing.

The thrill of his touch rushed through her again and sent liquid pleasure pooling in places that didn't need to be moist right now. Space. She needed space. She stepped to the side.

He edged closer. "You mom has a point. Stalkers usually turn out to be the boyfriend or the ex-husband."

"Not this time." She shifted to avoid touching him and opened the dishwasher.

"Why do you say that?" He leaned against the counter and watched her load the dishes. Wasn't that just like a man—to watch a woman clean and not offer to help?

When she rose up, she noticed his eyes on her butt. The words tumbled out before she could stop them: "Did I sit in something, or are you just enjoying the view?"

"It's definitely the view." He grinned, not at all admonished. She supposed she needed to work on her chastising voice.

His smile hit her again, pure sex appeal and a whole bunch of promises. She tugged on her shorts to make sure she wasn't truly giving him an eyeful.

He took her by the elbow and started to the living room. "Let's sit down. Tell me why you don't think this foot doctor or your ex is responsible for all this. Tell me about the phone calls."

His touch as he guided her to the sofa made it hard to think period, much less to think about Paul or her never-think-about-him ex-husband. Sitting down, the cool leather sofa pressed against her upper thighs and reminded her of the cut of her shorts. They weren't indecent. So they weren't Sunday school attire, but when she'd dressed she hadn't expected him to be here.

"Start with the phone calls. When did they begin?" He sat beside her.

The sofa gave way; a few pieces of foam shot out of the bullet hole. His weight brought Sue against him. She scooted over and considered telling him to go take a hike, but then she spotted the gunshot in her sofa again. While that bullet hadn't been intended for her, someone had wanted to do her harm last night.

She met his eyes. "I don't know. I got a few hang-ups. I don't know if they were part of it or not. I only started noticing them after I got the rat. By Lacy's party I'd gotten several. He never said anything, just hung up. And—"

"Why didn't you say something then?" Jason sounded annoyed.

She crossed her legs, her right foot swinging as she spoke. "I didn't know if they were connected. Everyone gets hang-ups when telemarketing computers—"

He held up his hand to silence her, reminding her of his comment about her talking too much and never standing still. She stopped fidgeting.

"But now he does more than just hang up?"

She nodded and accidentally kicked him as her foot began to swing again. Uncrossing her legs, she dropped her hands on her knees. "He says weird stuff. Things like, 'Die, Sue, die.'"

"Die?" Jason frowned.

"And what's scary . . . Yesterday he called my cell. Few people have that number."

He raised an eyebrow. "Does the doctor have your cell number? Your ex?"

"Yes, Paul has it, but he's not doing this, and I haven't seen my ex in two years. Neither of them is behind this."

Jason folded his arms across his chest. "How can you be so sure?"

She decided to just tell him. "Because neither of them has read the book."

"What . . . do you mean?"

She stood and walked around the coffee table. Bending, she straightened the bowl of wooden fruit. "My book, *Murder at Midnight*, isn't coming out for two weeks." Seeing his gaze travel again to her backside, she jerked upright and tugged at the bottom of her shorts. His gaze went back to her face.

"What does the book have to do with the phone calls?"

"My story has a serial killer who taunts his victims. He makes frightening calls, says strange things, and . . . once he sent a—"

"A dead rat!" Jason stood up. "Shit! Why the hell didn't you tell me this last week?"

"I didn't want to believe it. It wasn't exactly the same as my book. And you and Chase were already accusing Melissa. If you learned about the scene and knew she was one of the people who'd read it, you'd have probably taken her down for questioning."

"Well, hell yeah." He stepped in front of her. "Is she still in town?"

"No. And it's not her. Why would she do this?"

"Damn, Sue, you write about weirdos, but you haven't got the good sense to know that some people are just screwed up. I can't believe you'd keep something like this to yourself. Whoever is doing this is a real freak."

"I didn't keep it to myself. I told Officer Martin." She tried again with the chastising voice.

He scowled. "You told that jerk but you couldn't tell Chase or me?"

Okay, so she didn't have what it took to pull off chastisement, so she went with just plain old irritated. "If Lacy thought I was in danger she'd have canceled her vacation." She held out her hands. "And until he started saying things like 'die,' I didn't think I was in danger. As for not telling *you* . . . I had no reason to tell you anything. I still don't. You don't even like me. I talk and move too much. Remember?"

Guilt ran through his eyes. "I never said I didn't like you."

"The only reason you're here is . . . I don't even know why you're here. You're Chase's and Lacy's friend, not mine!"

And just like that she knew why he was here. "Chase asked you to watch out for me, didn't he?"

Jason's expression said it all.

"Great! Scoop poop and take care of Sue." She pointed toward her front door. "Go. I don't need a babysitter." She placed her hands on his chest to help him on his way. He didn't budge.

"I'm not leaving." He wrapped his arms around her waist. "I'm not going anywhere until this freak has been caught." He brought her closer. "You're stuck with me." There was a low, sexy growl to his tone.

She grew uncomfortably aware of how close their bodies were. And that perfect-fit feeling hit again. "You can't stay here."

"Why not?" His hands glided up to her shoulder blades, then slowly moved to circle her waist.

"Because I don't want you to." Her words sounded weak, not how she'd meant them.

"You need me." He lowered his face. His cheek, with day-old whiskers, brushed against hers. This close, she could definitely see the heat in his eyes.

"I don't need you."

She might want him badly, but she truly didn't need him. She'd learned during her financially lean days how to distinguish between a want and a need. A want made you temporarily happy but wasn't crucial to sustaining life. Some wants were even bad for you in the long run. Jason Dodd would definitely be bad for her. They would have over-the-handlebars, no-pedal-brakes sex and then what? He'd tire of her because he didn't really like her. Definitely a want, not a need.

"You need me." His pressed his forehead against hers. "Someone is trying to hurt you. I'm not going to let that happen."

His breath whispered across her lips, and she found it a little hard to breathe.

"No." She pulled her face back, away from his lips. "You've got to go." But she knew he made sense. She did need someone to protect her. She wrote about heroines who fought the bad guys and won, but she'd proven she wasn't one of them. Even with the gun in her purse, she'd—

"You need—"

"I'll find someone else to protect me." She couldn't allow Jason to needle his way into her life. She'd wind up broken and hurt. Lord knew she'd been hurt enough to last a lifetime. To have anything to do with Jason Dodd was like opening up her chest, handing him a hammer, and telling him to go for it.

She blinked at his unhappy expression. "I'll call the police and ask for some references." She stepped back, but he held on and moved in even closer. His thigh pressed between her legs.

Zip.

Zing.

His leg felt nice between hers.

"I am the police. Consider that a reference." His moist lips brushed her cheek. "You smell so good."

He smelled good, too. A little like coffee, with . . . the natural scent of how a man should smell: earthy but clean.

"Let me stay here until this blows over."

And then he'd be gone. "You can't." But she leaned against him, into him. *Just for a second,* she told herself.

"Then I'll just camp out on your doorstep." His lower body brushed up against her lower body. "Frankly, I like being close." His lips swept against her temple. "And I think you're finding it nice, too." He glanced down to where her breasts were pressed against his abdomen. She followed his gaze—and went on instant nipple alert.

He moved in, as if purposely brushing against the two sensitive points. Pleasure had her melting into her panties. Why was telling him no so hard? She swallowed and realized something else had become hard. It didn't belong to her, but it was pressed against her navel.

Good Gawd! What was she doing? Hadn't she discussed this very thing with her ficus tree last night?

"This has to stop." She pulled away. "And it has to stop right now." It really did.

He held up his hands. "You're right." The heat in his gaze faded. "Now isn't the time. I need a list of everyone who's read your book. I need names, phone numbers. I should probably read the book myself." His gaze moved down her legs and inched up again. "But first . . . you have to get out of those shorts. They're driving me crazy."

And just like that, the heat in his gaze flared back up. He reached out, his index finger hooked her belt loop and he tugged her closer. "Then again, maybe what we need to do is get this stuff out of the way."

"No stuff is happening." Pulling his finger out of her belt loop, she stepped back.

His gaze lowered to her chest, to her nipples pebbling through the thin cotton top. "Why not?"

"Because . . ." She pointed a finger at him. "You have issues, and I'm finished dealing with issues. And stop . . . stop staring at my boobs!"

His eyes shot up but he grinned. "What issues? Besides staring at your . . . boobs. Which, in my defense, are really nice to look at."

He stepped closer. His sexy, self-assured gait came off way too tempting. She stormed off to her bedroom to change clothes. Yet, even as she went, feeling slightly embarrassed and a lot cautious, the tickle of feminine power brushed over her. Jason Dodd might not have wanted her four months ago, but now was another story. Turnaround was fair play. And this time, she was the one who was going to turn him down.

"You're not staying," she called over her shoulder.

Her tone didn't even convince herself. Guess she needed to work on her convincing voice, too.

CHAPTER NINE

You're not staying.

Sue's words echoed inside Jason's head, but she hadn't convinced him. Not for a second. Not when someone was out to hurt her.

Stop staring at my boobs. A smile pulled at his lips. He hadn't lied; they were really nice to look at.

Then the image of her prancing down the hall replayed in his head. Damn, she had the cutest ass he'd ever seen. Why hadn't he ever noticed it before? Because she'd always been wearing dresses, skirts, or long shirts that hid the treasure.

The slamming door should have made him flinch, but nope. His smile held tight. In spite of being afraid for Sue, and madder than hell that someone was putting her through this, he still felt . . . happy. As if someone had just handed him a new lease on life.

He'd returned to the kitchen to see if Sue had any soda when the phone rang.

The phone. Shit! Realizing the call could be the stalker, he turned and snatched it off the counter. "Don't answer yet!" he yelled as he took off for the bedroom. "Don't answer." He got to her bedroom door. For a split second he considered knocking, but not wanting her to pick up before he got to her, he let himself in.

She shot him a quick look, but her concern appeared directed at the ringing phone. "It says it's restricted. All those calls are generally from *him*." Panic sounded in her voice.

"Sue?" Jason put his thumb on the talk button in case she snatched up the phone. "We're going to answer it at the same time so I can listen in. Okay?"

"It could be my mom, calling from Elvis's phone. Maybe he had his number placed on the restricted list." Her panicked gaze shot to him. "She calls a lot whenever she discovers her new disease. But I think sex with Elvis cured her."

Disease? Jason quit trying to understand and sat Sue down on the side of the bed. Then he sat beside her. "You ready?"

The phone rang a fourth time.

Her soft blue eyes had that frightened little girl look that made him want to wrap his arms around her. He resisted the urge and handed her the phone. They hit the buttons at the same time.

Sue brought the phone to her ear. "Hello?" Her voice sounded tight. Scared.

No one answered. Silence. And then . . . "Don't fight it."

Her scared gaze shot to Jason.

"The police can't protect you," the gravelly voice continued. It was raspy and low, but Jason couldn't tell the gender.

"Die sweetly," the voice continued. "Slowly. Die, sweet Sue. Die."

A shot of adrenaline hit Jason's gut. The line clicked silent.

The phone slipped from Sue's hands and crashed onto the wood floor. The batteries dislodged from the phone and rolled in different directions.

Because one of them needed to be calm, Jason fought back his own knee-to-the-gut reaction. "It's okay. We're going to catch this bastard." He pulled Sue close. Her face fit into the curve of his shoulder. He felt her trembling. Pressing a hand to her upper back, he expected her to start crying on his shirt again. Not pretty, but he didn't care.

Instead of leaking on his shirt, she pulled herself free. "Who does he think he is?"

"I don't know." Jason brushed her hair behind her ear

and felt an odd sense of rightness being there with her. In her house. In her bedroom. In her bed.

The scent of sleepy woman filled his nose. Just like that, the familiar tightness hit his lower abs again. He fought it. Right feeling, wrong time.

She popped off the bed. Jason watched her pace from one side of the room to the other. He recognized her reaction all too well; he'd seen it in a number of victims. Anger was always a short walk from fear and panic. And while most people could deal with being angry, fear gave people a run for their money. The problem was that anger took a lot of energy, and unless getting angry could solve the problem, a person generally ended smack dab back in fear, only they were exhausted from the emotional ride.

Not that she'd have to suffer exhaustion alone. He'd be there.

Die sweetly. Slowly. Die, sweet Sue. Die. The voice from the phone replayed in his head, and Jason gripped his hands together.

"We're going to get this guy," he said again, feeling helpless at fixing her emotional havoc but damn near certain he'd fix her other problem. He would catch this creep.

Sue continued to pace. And for the first time, he noticed what she wore. Or what she *didn't* wear. Her white T-shirt dangled mid-hip. Below, she wore . . . The tightening in his stomach came back threefold.

Below, she wore white bikini panties. Cotton, but they couldn't have been sexier. They fit her like a glove. And when she turned around he caught a glimpse of just how shapely her behind really was. Round. Perky. What he wouldn't give to remove that piece of white cotton.

For a second, he allowed himself to just enjoy the view, but then reality sneaked back in. Heightened emotions could easily lead to sexual arousal, but bedding a woman high on emotion was like bedding one who'd had too much liquor. The sex might be fantastic, but the awkward aftershock was considered by most females to be fatal to the relationship. To a male's way of thinking, it simply meant the chances of repeat sex were almost nil. And one time with Sue wasn't going to sate him.

Plus, he had to stay on her good side while he made sure some idiot didn't carry out this death threat. Yes, the sex between them was going to be great, but he had to do it right.

A pair of khaki shorts on the bed caught his attention. He'd probably regret this later, but he did it anyway. Picking them up, he handed them over. "Here, get dressed."

She yanked the khakis from his hands, unsnapped them, and slid her bare feet and slender legs into the shorts. "Who does he think he is?" she repeated.

"I don't know." Unable to resist, he gave her a quick kiss on the mouth. Very quick. Considering what he would like to do, he should win a medal for not doing more. A big gold one. "But we're going to find out."

He ran a finger over her lips, fought the desire to go back for seconds since she didn't seem to object to the first course. But he knew if she wasn't riding a wave of emotion right now, she'd be giving him hell.

Turning her around, and with only a slight amount of guilt, he put his hands on her backside, allowing himself the pleasure of touching her butt before giving it a gentle push toward the door. "Now let's get out of the bedroom before I forget my manners."

Moving down the hall, he knew he had to stop thinking like a man and start thinking like a cop. *Die sweetly. Slowly. Die, sweet Sue. Die.* The voice replayed in his head. And the cop inside him reared its head. He let out a hissing breath and accepted that Sue probably wasn't the only one riding that emotional high. Who was this asshole? His mind went back to the doctor. Then to Sue's agent. Jason replayed the voice again in his head. Sue had referred to the caller as a guy, and his gut agreed, but the voice had been so raspy, it could have been either gender.

Questions flipped through his mind. He needed answers. The sooner the better.

Something also told him they weren't finished discussing his staying here. He had no problem discussing it. He'd discuss it until the cows came home . . . but he wasn't leaving.

Sue found that being angry felt so much better than being afraid. Reaching down to her shorts' Velcroed pocket, she yanked it loose. The resultant sound, a crackling pop, felt good to her ears.

Jason led her to the wounded sofa and started firing questions at her.

Frustrated, she shot back, "No! I don't think Melissa would do this." She yanked the pocket loose again. *Rip*. "And no, I don't think my editor would do it."

"Then who?" he asked.

Rip.

"Well, if I knew that, I could just have Officer Martin arrest the guy for me."

Jason's brow pinched. "Martin's a jerk. Tell me about this critique group of yours."

Oh yeah. Anger won hands down over being afraid. But anger came with its own downside. No focus. She found herself getting mad at everyone. Officer Martin, for believing this was a scam. The fat cop, for shooting her sofa. Goliath for sniffing the man's crotch. And, oh yeah, her mom, for making juice with Elvis.

Rip.

Needing to spend some of the emotional energy zipping through her, she went to the kitchen to snag some coffee. Caffeine poured, she plopped down at the breakfast table. Jason took the chair beside her to continue his interrogation.

"So all three of these guys have read it?" he asked, taking notes.

"Well, yeah. That's what critique groups do. They read each other's work." She reached for the pocket, fingering the tab. Jason's suspicions of her critique group brought on another wave of anger.

Rip.

And when she thought about the critique group, she remembered Benny's crush on her, and she got mad at him for forcing her to use the dead-dog trick. Even if it saved her from bruising his ego, the man would always think she had bad breath. And by gosh, she flossed regularly. It was unhealthy not to.

Rip! Replace pocket. *Rip. Rip. Rip.*

She really liked that sound. So fitting to her mood.

Jason eyed her pocket, looking as if he was going to ask her to stop, but he didn't. Smart man.

But his questions continued, and so did her anger.

He wanted to know everything, from the names of the editors who'd read her novel to the art directors who'd been given the synopsis to help design the cover.

"I didn't like that guy." She figured that before her fury frenzy finished she'd be mad at everyone she'd ever met.

"Who? The copy editor or the artist?"

"Both. The artist wanted to take me to his place and show me his etchings, and the copy editor said I needed to take a grammar course. It's not my fault he doesn't speak or read Texan. He got insulted when I proved him right."

"I'll check them out. What about the book reviewers? Who has seen an early copy?"

"My publisher sent out ARCs—advance review copies. Lots of them. You'll have to get that list from them." She leaned her head back, emotionally strung out. No more anger to spend.

Then Jason suggested she whip up something for them to eat, and she got mad at her mom for never teaching her to cook. Which led to her getting mad at her grandmother, and her grandmother's mother. Sue came from a long line of women who couldn't cook. Ancestral anger ran deep.

Finally, she came to her senses and got mad at Jason for thinking it was the woman's place to cook.

"Sorry," he said. "I thought you loved to cook."

"Why? Because I'm a woman?" She reached for her pocket again. *Rip.* Replace.

"No. Because you said you loved to cook on that cooking show you were on."

She shook her head. "You saw that?"

He held up his hands, as though agreeing he'd been presumptuous. "I'll cook, you relax."

When he disappeared into the kitchen, Sue tried to do as he suggested: relax. But her skin tingled, and she remembered Jason pulling her against him before she'd gone to the bedroom. Remembered him staring at her breasts, and she hadn't even been wearing the Wonderbra. She remembered the way it had felt being close to him, the sensation of her tight nipples brushing up against his chest. Then she recalled that he'd kissed her in the bedroom. Not a hot and heavy kiss like four months ago, but a kiss. Sweet. Simple.

Sometimes simple was good. She'd certainly been too surprised to react.

Within ten minutes, Jason served her the best grilled cheese she'd ever eaten.

"These are really good." She savored the mouthful of sandwich.

"They should be; they're your recipe."

"*My* recipe?"

"From the cooking show. They posted several of your favorite recipes on their website."

She fought the light brushstroke of guilt. "Melissa sent those recipes in. She's always getting me spots on local shows or press in magazines. It sells books."

"Like that article in that dog magazine about you owning your mother's dog?" He laughed. "I asked Chase about that one."

"You read the dog magazine, too?" Sue frowned. She'd told her agent that somebody would find her out. But Melissa just kept saying, "It's press. Readers don't care if you can cook or if the dog isn't yours."

"You want more tea?" He grinned.

Realizing he was attempting to be nice, she got mad at Chase for lumping "Take care of Sue" into a list of chores for Jason that included cleaning up animal feces. That was when her anger once again became targeted toward Jason. Why hadn't he called her four months ago?

Still unwilling to admit she cared, she internalized that bit of anger. Immediately, the dangers of internalizing anger became clear. Because it opened up the Pandora's Box of angst. Angst at her ex, Collin. How could he take five years of total commitment and toss it aside? And her father. How could he die and leave her and her mother alone? If he had to die, why from something so common—why from the common cold? She leaned back on the sofa, emotionally drained.

Jason sat beside her. His hand sifted through her hair. "You want a blanket and pillow?"

She got a mental image of them together on the couch again. "No. I'm going to write."

"Fine, but we need to go feed Lacy's animals before too long."

She rolled her eyes at him. "It's broad daylight. My neighbors are home. I'm fine. And . . . and once you're at Lacy's . . . just stay. I don't need you."

He frowned. "Call the neighbors. If they're home, I'll run there and back."

She sat up. "You can't actually believe you're going to stay here."

"Until we catch this freak, I am." He said it with such conviction that she might have laughed if she wasn't an emotional wreck.

"And what about tomorrow?"

"What about it?" he asked.

"Now who's being a dumb blond? Tomorrow is Monday. I think you work. You know, the thing you do five days a week so you can pay your rent? I think it involves driving around in a car, playing like you're a macho guy, looking for people who sell drugs."

He smiled. "I love the way you simplify my job." His gaze settled on her lips. "I called and took off Monday and Tuesday. The first comp days I've taken in years. I've got four weeks of time saved up."

Sue dropped her head back and stared at the ceiling. "You can't . . ." She sat up again. "Why would you even want to? Look, I can understand you coming over when I called. And I can see that because Chase asked you to watch over me that you felt like you had to stay last night. But to take off work is . . . too much."

His gaze acquired a serious glint. "Last night you mentioned you'd hire a bodyguard. Well, hire me. I'm cheap."

"But . . ."

"No buts." He leaned in, bringing his face so close she could count his eyelashes. "You need me." He pressed his lips to hers. The kiss he'd given her in the bedroom earlier had happened so fast that she'd told herself he did it just to calm her—like someone slapping you, though in a nicer way. But right now she was calm. Calm and being kissed.

His tongue slipped inside her mouth. He tasted good: a little like coffee, a little like grilled cheese. But she had to stop him because . . . well, she didn't know why. Not exactly why; but if she had any wits about her, she would put an end to this. And she was going to end it. In just a few more seconds.

He reached up and threaded his fingers through her hair. The kiss deepened. She pulled back and took a deep, mind-cleansing breath. Then she looked up at him.

"Are you doing this because you think I'm going to sleep with you?"

Appearing genuinely offended, he held up a hand. "No, I'm not doing this because I think you're going to sleep with me. But . . . I wouldn't be disappointed if we found some pleasurable way to pass the time. We're adults. And I think—"

"I'm not sleeping with you." She scooted over.

He arched an eyebrow. "Why not?"

"Because I'm not settling." *Nope.* Her issue-dealing/settling days were long past. Her gaze shot to her dying houseplant. Plus, she'd already discussed this with her ficus tree. "Nope, not settling."

He ran a finger down her cheek. "Believe me, sweetheart. When I'm finished with you, you won't feel as if you've settled."

From that simple touch down her cheek, she knew he spoke the truth. Sex with him would be absolutely, totally, over-the-edge, purple-prose wonderful. Which was all the more reason she couldn't do it.

She stood. "Won't happen. Not in this lifetime." *But maybe in the next lifetime,* a voice deep inside her begged. She ignored that voice.

"Fine." He shot up and sounded frustrated but not mean, not accusing. "Don't sleep with me. We both lose, because it would be good. Really good. But I'm still not leaving."

"I'm on a deadline. I need to write." Why was he still being nice?

"So write. I can help. You know, critique like that group of yours."

"I only let people I trust read my unpublished work." It came out harsh, and she hadn't meant it to. Or maybe she had. Four months ago, she would have begged for a pinch of this niceness. But, oh no. He'd not given her the time of day, or a phone call.

He frowned. "Why wouldn't you trust me? I like your work."

As if he'd even read her books. "Don't lie to me."

"You think I'm lying?"

She ignored his question. Ignored that he sounded hurt. Ignored that she felt guilty for hurting him.

"And when I'm not writing, I'm not staying in the house behind lock and key. I have a life and I don't plan to let some scumbag turn me into a prairie dog who's scared of its own shadow."

"You mean groundhog?" A smile pulled at his too-sexy mouth that had moments ago been busy kissing her.

"No. I meant prairie dog. Groundhog is a cliché. I don't use clichés." She tried to not to use clichés. "And I don't like it when people interrupt me while I write. You'd have to entertain yourself."

Oh, damn! Was she accepting his help? She remembered last night, feeling like a sitting duck. Okay, a sitting duck hiding in the kitchen pantry, a can of peas in one hand and a can of pork-n-beans in the other. She remembered how safe she'd felt when Jason held her. A lot safer than the canned vegetables had made her feel.

Logically, he'd already asked for the time off anyway.

"I'm only agreeing to it for a day or two."

"Got it. No interrupting you. No sex—unless you change your mind. Which I maintain the right to try and change."

"I don't—"

He pressed a finger to her lips. "You can still say no and I'll respect it." When she didn't continue her argument he continued his. "You don't cook. I stay away from you while you work. I can't read your unpublished work, though I think that one is unfair. And you tell me where you need to go and we'll go. I got the rules down."

"Good," she said. "Because I have to take my grandfather to have his prostate checked in the morning, and I have a date tomorrow night." She turned and started toward her study.

"Whoa!" Jason caught her arm. "*That* I do have a problem with."

"Which one? The prostate check or my date?"

He ran a rough palm over his face. "Both. But mostly the date."

"Why?" For some reason she wanted to believe he was jealous. "Why do you have a problem with my seeing Paul?"

"Because, like I said earlier, usually the bad guys in crimes like this turn out to be a boyfriend or husband."

Okay, he wasn't jealous. That stung a little. "But Paul hasn't read the book. Remember?"

"He's the boyfriend. Meaning he's still a suspect," Jason growled.

"Well, he's about to move off the suspect list. I'm breaking up with him." She bit down into her lip, not certain she'd wanted Jason to know that.

He hesitated, as if digesting that piece of information. "That includes ex-boyfriends and ex-husbands." He studied her. "Why are you breaking up with him?"

"For the same reason I'm not sleeping with you. I'm not settling."

"Exactly what do you mean by settling?"

She walked away, toward her office, feeling his gaze follow her. Why had she agreed to let him stay?

The answer bolted back. *Because you're scared.*

But deep down she knew there were other reasons. Revenge came to mind. Yup, revenge was sweet. But there was more.

Stepping into her office, she shut the door with a solid thump, then unceremoniously dropped into her ergonomic office chair in front of her computer. The chair designed to prevent back aches and neck aches. It did little to help the pain in the butt that she'd left standing in her living room. If only that pain in the butt wasn't so darn sexy. If only his touch didn't set off other body parts aching. If only he'd called her four months ago.

She went for the Velcro again. *Rip.* Replace. Pat the pocket. *Rip* again.

Yup. She liked that noise.

Rip.

An icon on the bottom of her computer screen informed her she had e-mail. She clicked onto the envelope and . . . the screen turned red. Blood red.

Dots started swirling, making an image. Then a picture of a rat, a dead rat, and a poinsettia plant appeared before her. Then came the word *Die.*

"No!"

If that wasn't bad enough, one of those little fatal error

signs flashed across the dead rat image. Fatal error—as in, your computer is terminally ill. Fatal—as in, it has a cold from which it will never recover.

"No!" She tried to delete the message, but the computer froze. She hit more buttons. Nothing happened. Jumping up, she ran out the door and collided with Jason's chest.

"What?" He caught her.

She pointed into her study. "Threatening to kill me is one thing. But no one messes with my computer!"

Reaching down, she fingered her pocket.

The Velcro was really going to rip now.

CHAPTER TEN

After having a tizzy in front of Jason, Sue pulled out her old laptop—"old" meaning no Internet—shut Jason out of her office, and started on Chapter Two.

Well, the first hour she spent staring holes at her dead desktop computer. Of course she had back-up disks, but the nerve of the rat-obsessed lunatic made her mad enough to kill. Unfortunately, the only living things in the house were Hitchcock, her ficus tree, and a cop. She loved her cat, the ficus tree was too sickly to make it feel like a fair fight, and killing the cop would get her fifty to life. But the last was still tempting.

She finally found escape in her story and got at least seven good pages written. She was ending a scene when a tap came at the door.

"Come in," she called. As the door opened, she told herself she was prepared to face him.

Jason leaned his shoulder against the doorframe and crossed his bare feet at the ankles. "You okay?" His voice was husky, and his eyes were hooded as if he'd just awoken from a nap.

Six feet of sleepy bad-boy fantasy come to life.

Her heart hiccupped.

Her toes twitched.

Okay, so maybe she wasn't prepared to face him.

Her gaze moved up and down all six feet of him. It

should be a federal offense for a man to look so good while barefoot and dressed in a worn-yesterday pair of jeans and a T-shirt. No one was that perfect. So she looked harder, wanting to find his one flaw: the beginnings of a gut, a receding hairline, a hook nose, or perhaps beady eyes. Maybe he had a few extra toes.

Her gaze slipped back to his toes. She counted . . . all perfect ten of them.

Then her gaze rose up the denim-clad legs to the masculine package behind the fly, past the lean hips to the wide chest.

"Did I spill something on myself, or are you just enjoying the view?" Both a smile and masculine pride sounded in his voice.

Sue recognized that his words were similar to those she'd thrown at him this morning. She immediately went to work seeking a good excuse for staring at him like a yummy piece of chocolate.

Eureka. "You've got enough cat hair on you to weave sweaters for Houston's homeless."

He brushed off his shirt. "I fell asleep, and your cat parked his furry butt on my chest."

Sue recalled waking up to find herself parked on his chest this morning. She couldn't blame her cat. Jason's chest was so . . . parkable.

"There's a lint brush below the sink." She looked back at her laptop screen, away from temptation.

"Did you get some work done?" The husky quality of his voice breezed over her nerve endings.

She finished her last sentence—with three typos. The man could be the death of her writing career. "I got some done."

"Good. We should head over to Lacy's to feed the animals. And we need to make a run by my place. I thought we could get some dinner while we're out, too. I'm starving." He moved closer.

Had she really agreed to let him stay here? Yup, but for good reason. Someone wanted her dead. Maybe after some thought she would hire herself an ugly bodyguard, someone with a paunch, a big nose—someone who wasn't six-feet-plus of pure, unadulterated temptation.

"There're some granola bars in the pantry. I need to just tweak this," she said, still not looking at him.

"You look tense." He stepped behind her, pushing his hands between her and the chair, massaging her shoulders. With firm strokes, he rubbed the knotted muscles around her neck. "Why don't you take a break?"

His hands were magic, kneading with just the right amount of pressure. She bit her tongue to keep from purring. But even as the tightness eased in her shoulders, tension started pulling low in her belly—an ache that she knew he could make go away as well.

Reaching back, she grabbed his wrist to stop him. "Give me a minute." She felt him lean down behind her, felt the stubble of his beard against her cheek. How long had it been since she'd enjoyed the feel of a five o'clock shadow? Too long.

He brushed his lips against her temple. "Be thinking about what you want to eat." He rose up, got to the door, then turned back around. "Oh, yeah, I need a copy of your new book."

Her mind, stuck on how little things like beard stubble could be missed, took a while to compute his words. "I . . . don't have a copy yet. Just a disk. They misspelled my name on the first cover and had to have them redone."

"Then bring the disk, and I'll print it out at my house."

She watched him walk out, the backside of him just as nicely shaped as the front. Oh, Lordie, she had it bad. She dropped her head down on her desk and gave it one good thud.

Then she remembered. Just because he was perfect on the outside didn't make him perfect on the inside. The man had issues. She tried to remember everything she knew about him, surprised at how little she did know.

Rising up, she recalled Chase saying something about

Jason's mother living in Houston. Yet she'd never heard Jason speak of her. From bits and pieces of dialogue over the last year, she'd learned he'd never been married. Most importantly, she knew she had nail polish that lasted longer than some of his relationships. The man had brought one girl to Lacy's wedding shower and, two weeks later, he'd brought a different one to the wedding.

Oh, yeah, definite signs of issues.

And that's when Sue knew what she had to do. She'd spend the next two days getting under and past Jason's façade of perfect physical compatibility with her. Discovering his issues would temper the attraction. Then she might be able to stand to be in the same room with him. They could go back to the way things were before the kiss, to when the attraction had only been mildly irritating instead of mind-blowingly infuriating.

Armed with a plan and a surge of confidence, she stood. She glanced back at the unplugged computer. Fear settled in the pit of her stomach. She walked into her living room. But when she saw the big blond cop opening a granola bar, her fear took a hike. In her head, she heard him: *Someone is trying to hurt you, and I'm not going to let that happen.* She believed him. He wouldn't.

He saw her. His sexy-as-sin smile appeared in his eyes and she remembered something else he'd said. *No sex, unless you change your mind. Which I maintain the right to try and change.*

Jason Dodd would protect her from the stalker, but who was going to protect her from Jason Dodd?

Jason ate another granola bar while Sue freshened up. He'd made some calls while she worked. The phone company would put a trace on Sue's phone calls, though it would be tomorrow before they got it set up, and Bob, the go-to police computer forensic guy, who was off fishing in Galveston for the day, would be here at eight tomorrow morning to take Sue's computer in for analysis. Jason wanted to know if the jerk who'd sent the e-mail had also hacked into Sue's files. If so, the stalker wouldn't necessarily have to be someone Sue knew or someone who had personally been given an early copy of the book. It could be anyone, which meant finding him would be that much harder.

Jason had been forced to call in a few favors to get her hard drive looked at ASAP, but after years of collecting IOUs it wasn't a problem. He'd probably have a harder time convincing Sue to let Bob take her computer. Earlier she'd said something about taking the computer to her computer guru. After seeing Sue's antique laptop that she'd pulled out earlier, and hearing her complain about it not having Internet, Jason hoped loaning her his own laptop would appease her. And he'd have Bob fix her computer while studying the data.

Sue walked out wearing jeans that were slung low on her hips and a pink sleeveless top short enough to offer a smidgen of bare skin around the belly button. While the neckline offered no cleavage, the fabric outlined the soft swells of flesh in detail. Detail that told him she wasn't wearing a bra—or maybe it was one of those hardly-there bras.

Just like that, heavy wanting made his jeans tight. The granola wrapper slipped from his fingers and floated to the floor.

Stopping in front of him, she knelt.

Damn! A woman should never kneel down in front of a half-aroused man. Put a pretty face within a foot of a man's crotch, and a man's mind will take the image and run with it. Jason's mind was definitely running with it.

She looked up, thankfully past his bulging zipper and into his eyes. She'd pulled her blonde hair back with one of those cloth bands, but several strands danced down her neck. Her mouth looked wet, as if she'd just put on lipstick.

"You dropped this." She stood.

The erotic images faded, but he curled his hands into fists to keep from pulling her into his arms and kissing the pink color from her lips.

"I'm ready," she said.

So was he. Ready to quit pretending that there wasn't enough sexual tension between them to light up a city block. A big city block. Sue wanted him; that much he knew. But what the hell did "not settling" mean, anyway?

"What?" she asked.

Did she see the longing in his eyes, or had she noticed the bulge behind his fly? For four months his dick had hardly twitched, but it was making up for lost time now.

"I didn't say a word." He got up, moved to the door, and then stopped. "Did you get the disk to print your book?"

"Is that really necessary?" She grabbed her purse.

"Why would it be a problem?"

"It's just a lot of trouble when I can tell you what happens. You don't have to read it."

"First, I want to read it. Second, you might miss something." Was he detecting some issue with him reading her book? "And third, it's evidence, Sue."

She took off to the study. He followed. Standing in the doorway, he watched her fumble through a lower desk drawer. His gaze shifted to the soft sway of her breasts. The thin bra strap of her nothing bra—pink like her shirt—slipped off her bare shoulder.

Knowing it could be dangerous to start thinking about her underwear, he shifted his focus to the computer. He recalled the image of the rat and . . . "What did the poinsettia plant have to do with the book?"

Sue looked up, her eyes widened. "Oh my God!"

"What?" he asked.

"This freak is . . . he's reading the files from my computer. He has to be." She dropped into a chair and stared at the blank monitor.

Jason stepped closer. "How do you know that?"

"The poinsettia plant isn't in that book. It's in the book I'm working on now. No one has seen that book." She bit down on her lip. "Almost no one."

"Who's read it?" Jason's gut tightened.

Her eyes grew round. "My . . . critique group."

"The three people whose names you gave me earlier?" He mentally collected their names in his head and decided to get a background check on them as soon as he could.

She nodded. "But seriously, I've known these people for years. Whoever is doing this must have broken into my files." She looked back at her computer and fear filled her blue eyes.

Her vulnerability brought Jason closer. He twisted her chair and knelt in front of her. He was pretty certain women didn't have near the problem with kneeling men that men did with women. "Hey." He put his hand on her knees. "We're going to catch this guy."

"I just . . . If he's gone to the trouble to break into my computer, then . . . he's serious."

Jason thought cutting her phone line had rated the guy as serious, and the little *die* message earlier was also a big clue, but Sue didn't need to hear that. Instead, he pressed his forehead against hers and kissed her again. It wasn't the let's-go-to-the-bedroom kind of kiss he longed to give her, just a touch of lips against lips. But like all the kisses they'd shared, it held an emotional punch. Or maybe it was a pull.

A different kind of pull, too. His desire to protect her twisted in his chest alongside a knot of sexual want. Somewhere between those knots, fighting for space, was that ever-present voice from his childhood telling him that this wanting would lead to disappointment—the same voice that had kept him from calling.

He ignored the warning.

Ignored the nervous look she shot him when he drew back. Winking, he ran a finger down her cheek. "I'm not going to let anyone hurt you. Just believe that, okay?"

She nodded and dropped the disk into her purse.

He took her hands and pulled her upright, lowering his head to kiss her again. Just another taste. Because tasting her was addictive.

"Don't." She pressed a finger over his lips.

He caught her hand. "Your rules said no sex. They didn't forbid kissing." He pressed his mouth into her palm.

She pulled her hand away, but not before he caught a flicker of desire in her eyes. "But—"

"No altering the rules after they've been set." He hurried her out, determined not to agree to a no-kiss rule. How else was he going to change her mind about having sex with him? And he damn well intended to change her mind.

She stepped ahead of him. Her jeans fit her heart-shaped backside to perfection. Oh yeah, he fully intended to change her mind.

Sue sipped her iced tea. She and Jason had finished dishing out food and affection to Lacy's animals and were now at a small Mom and Pop restaurant a few miles from Jason's apartment. She bit into her chicken sandwich and tried not to look at him. He'd changed clothes at Lacy's and wore clean jeans and a dark blue, loose-fitting, button-down shirt.

Don't think about the shirt.

Okay, it wasn't the shirt but what was hidden beneath. She'd seen him raise his shirt to slip his gun in a shoulder holster. Not that the gun was the problem. It was his bare stomach, with a blond treasure trail whispering into his jeans.

"Try this." His voice brought her gaze up. He held his fork to her lips, a slice of steak on the end. "Come on. Try it."

Feeling awkward, she took the food into her mouth. The tender steak with melted Swiss cheese and spices had her taste buds singing. "Mmmm . . ."

As he pulled the fork away, he nabbed another of her fries. Sue watched him dip the fry in her ketchup and pop it into his mouth. It wasn't that she minded; it was just the ease with which he did it. She'd dated Paul for a month, and they hadn't gotten to the your-food-is-my-food stage. That stage meant something; it meant a relationship was . . . comfortable.

She hadn't been in that stage with anyone since her ex-husband. Well, except for sharing her coffee with Hitch-cock, and even that had come to an end.

"So, how long before you sold the second book?" Jason continued with his questions about her writing career. Sue wanted to accuse him of just chatting to fill the silence, but he appeared genuinely interested.

"A few months." She watched him take another of her fries. Then he cut another piece of steak and offered it to her.

"No. Thanks." She watched him eat with gusto. Impecca-ble manners, but he enjoyed eating. A lot.

"How many rejections did you get before you sold?"

Sue swirled a fry in her ketchup. "Lots." She eyed him. "You're not a wannabe writer, are you?"

"Me?" He laughed. "No. I'm more brawn than brains. It amazes me how you can just create plots and characters out of thin air. I'll bet you were always a straight A student from first grade through college."

"Hardly. I graduated in the second quarter of my high school, and after I failed college algebra three times, I quit."

She'd quit to marry Collin, but she left that part out.

Jason leaned back in his chair. "You don't have a degree in journalism or English?"

"No." Sue forked a fry, wishing she'd never told him. Not having a degree wasn't a sore spot, although she hated it when people acted as if a lack of a degree made her less of a writer.

"Now I'm really impressed. You're self-taught. So, were you writing stories as a child? Creating imaginary friends?"

"Yeah." Sue took a bite of her pickle and realized that Ja-son had managed to skirt around every personal question she'd asked him. How was she going to find his issues if he never told her anything? Maybe an inability to open up was one of his issues.

She swallowed. "How about you?"

"How about me, what?" He snatched another of her fries.

"Did you always want to be a cop?"

"Nah. I was more getting into trouble."

"You were a bad kid?" She watched him cut another piece of steak.

"Really bad." His grin was laced with sexual overtones.

"I didn't think they'd take you into the academy if you had a record."

"I said I was bad. I never said I got caught."

"Were you into drugs?" she asked.

"No." There was something adamant in his tone that said he didn't like to be misjudged.

"Stealing?" She didn't want to misjudge him, but she was mining for the truth.

"No." His answer and expression grew slightly defensive.

"Then how were you bad?" She fumbled with her napkin.

"I just was." He cut his eyes to her plate. "How's your chicken sandwich?"

"So, what made you want to be a cop?"

He hesitated. "I met one. He made an impression on me. End of story."

Not quite the end. "Did he catch you doing something bad?"

Jason's expression darkened. "Some people would say that."

"What were you doing?" She leaned in.

His pause heightened her curiosity.

"Fighting." Something that looked like pain filled his eyes.

Then the emotion evaporated so fast she felt certain she'd imagined it. But it left an imprint on Sue's mind. Sort of like that treasure trail.

"Was anyone hurt?" Her tone went soft.

He hesitated again. "Yeah, I beat the crap out of him."

Her breath caught. "Why?"

He shifted, as if uncomfortable. "Because I was a bad kid."

He snagged another of her fries. "Make sure you save room for dessert."

She tried to imagine Jason beating someone up for no reason at all. She couldn't. Not even in his youth.

"You're making all this up, aren't you?" She speared a fry with her fork.

"Making what up?"

She leaned her elbows on the table. "I don't believe that you were a bad kid. Or violent. Not without a cause." Even wishing it were true so she'd have found her fault, she didn't believe it was a possibility.

His gaze met hers and held it. "A lot of people would have disagreed with you."

"Well, I'm not a lot of people." Something about the way he looked at her gave her a glimpse of a younger Jason, a young boy who needed someone to believe in him. The emotion rooted in her chest. "Were your parents divorced?"

"Here's dessert." The waitress set down a small plate with a brownie topped with ice cream and hot fudge sauce. Sauce that still bubbled and crackled as the ice cream melted.

Jason appeared too happy at the waitress's timing. "Thanks." Pointing to the sundae, he looked at Sue. "I'd do time for *this* dessert." The waitress cleaned away their dishes and left.

The smell of warm chocolate moved into Sue's awareness. She eyed the plate. Jason picked up a spoon, carved out a perfect bite, and ran the utensil across the bottom of the plate to collect extra hot fudge sauce. Before she knew what he was doing, he'd moved to her side of the booth and held the spoon to her lips.

He scooted close. "This is heaven. They put whiskey in the sauce."

The spoon, chilled from the vanilla ice cream, slid cool against her lips. The warm brownie crumbled against her tongue—sweet, crusty yet soft. The coldness of melting ice cream and the heat of fudge brought a thousand taste buds to exquisite attention. Sue closed her eyes as she savored the hint of the whiskey warming her throat.

When she opened her eyelids, she stared right into Jason's blue gaze. He had gentle eyes, not the kind that would belong to anyone capable of violence.

He moved closer. His face lowered. The tip of his nose brushed hers. She closed her eyes again, expecting to feel his lips against hers. Okay, maybe she even wanted it.

Instead, she felt his tongue slide across her bottom lip. His tongue! His moist tongue, moving slowly.

A kiss she might have accepted; okay, wanted. Hey, his eating her fries had put her in the mood, but a tongue was . . . too intimate. Way too intimate. Her heart started to race. Had he really licked her in public?

She jerked back.

"You had . . . still have . . . fudge, right here." His mouth, soft and sexy, inched closer.

She slammed a palm against his chest. "Well, that's what napkins are for," she seethed and grabbed the scrap of cloth and wiped her mouth. "See! It works." She tossed the napkin at him and saw people at the next table snickering. Her face flushed. "I can't believe you did that."

"Did what?" he asked, totally clueless.

Clueless. The man was an idiot. *Add that to his issue list.*

Leaning in, she whispered, "The last time I checked, Miss Manners frowns upon licking someone in public."

Humor lit his eyes. "But in private it's okay, right?"

Images of his tongue running other places had her heart doubling its speed. She snatched the spoon from his hand, and helped herself to another bite. Then another. Then another. Deprived of sex she might be, but blast it if she couldn't have an orgasmic cocoa moment. And blast him if he thought she was going to stop asking questions because it made him uncomfortable.

She needed to know his issues. Seriously needed to know, because the next time he came at her with his tongue, she wanted to look him right in the eye and tell him she had no desire to be licked by him in public or in private.

And she really didn't want to have to lie when she told him.

It was eight when they left the restaurant. Dusk had turned the sky purple and the horizon a hazy gold. Jason gazed at Sue. "You're quiet."

"First I talk too much, and now I'm too quiet." She glanced out the car window as they pulled away. "You should really make up your mind about how you feel about me."

"I have." Glancing in his rearview mirror, Jason saw something surprising.

"Really? And what have you decided?"

"I think you're damn near perfect." He pulled off the road into a grocery store parking lot and watched in the rearview mirror as a car followed.

"You're lying."

"I don't lie." His focus stayed on the mirror and the gold Saturn.

The car's windows were tinted, and with the low light he couldn't get a look at the driver. He didn't think they were being tailed, not really, but he recalled seeing a gold Saturn like this one behind them earlier. He slowed down and parked. And just to be safe, as the Saturn rolled past, Jason read and memorized the license number. Officer Tomas had said the car parked on Sue's street last night had looked like a Chevy Cavalier. But a Saturn and Cavalier could be confused in the dark.

Jason reached over Sue's lap and pulled a pad and pencil from the glove compartment.

"What is it?" she asked.

"Nothing." He scribbled down the license number before meeting her gaze. "I need something from the store." No reason to alarm her when he wasn't sure.

She leaned over to read what he'd written. "Why don't I just wait here?"

"I'd rather you come in." He glanced in the direction the Saturn had disappeared.

"Why?" Her gaze shot out the window. "Was someone following us? Is that a license number?"

Right then Sue's cell phone started chiming.

CHAPTER ELEVEN

The hint of fear in her eyes had emotion pulling at Jason's gut. "Answer it," he said.

Sue pulled the cell out of her purse and checked the number. "It's my mom. I'll call her back." She tucked the phone back in her purse and refocused on the pad in his hand. "Was someone following us?"

"I'm not sure." It was the truth, and not one he was proud of. He should have been watching more carefully, but he'd been too busy watching her and that pink bra strap that kept slipping off her shoulder. "I noticed a Saturn earlier, so I wanted to get the license number just as a precaution." He leaned over her lap to put away the pad. While he was close, he considered kissing her again. But she seemed to expect it and bounced back in the seat.

"I'm pretty sure my face is clean," she snapped.

He loved sparring with her. "Damn shame." He grinned. "I hardly got to taste that dessert."

Her eyes narrowed. "I asked if you wanted any."

"But I could tell you didn't want to share." In truth, he'd have arrested anyone who'd tried to take it away from her. She'd practically made love to the spoon, running her tongue around it, causing all sorts of erotic images to flash in his mind. Another woman could have done that and he'd swear she'd done it intentionally. But not Sue. She'd seemed to forget he was even there.

He wondered if she became so lost in everything she enjoyed. He'd bet when she wrote she became totally submerged in her work. And when she made love, she'd probably be just as intense, focused on pleasure—giving and receiving it.

His next thought, totally unexpected, slammed against his brain. *Had Sue gotten intense with that doctor?* A few days ago the idea of Sue sleeping with the foot doc had chewed at his gut, but right now the idea seemed to gnaw straight to his backbone.

Jason remembered Chase's comment, which led him to believe Sue hadn't slept with the man. Jason hadn't believed it. Not when Chase said they'd been dating for almost a month. Men didn't see a woman as sexy as Sue for a month without taking things further. Hell, he himself had been with her for less than a day and he had zipper burns.

Sue licked her lips. "I would have shared."

She was talking about the dessert, but his mind stayed wrapped around the idea of her and the doctor. He didn't want to share Sue—didn't want to think about her sharing anything with another man. That instant possessiveness, not an emotion Jason usually experienced, rattled around his chest.

"Are we going inside?" she asked.

He watched her pull a lipstick from her purse and smooth some over her lips. A suggestion sprang to mind: "Or we could stay in the car and make out."

"You're crazy," she said.

"About you," he countered, realizing it was true. And that scared him, too.

Sue opened the car door and popped out.

Jason stepped out his door, and his gaze focused on her denim-covered bottom again. There wasn't a man alive who could date her for a month without . . .

He walked around to her side and locked her door.

"Sorry," she said. "I'm not used to manual locks."

And he wasn't used to having to work so hard to win a

woman's affection. Which could mean she hadn't slept with the doc, right?

But what had she meant by that "not settling" comment? And why had she lumped him in the same category as the foot doctor?

He guided her across the parking lot. Walking inside the store, he got that odd feeling of being . . . He spun around and stared out the glass doors. The gold Saturn sat outside the entrance.

"Wait here!" He bolted outside. Before his foot hit the pavement, the car spun off and skidded back onto the street.

"Fuck!" He reached for his phone only to realize it was in his car and out of juice. Turning around, he slammed right into Sue.

"Is that who was following us?" she asked.

He latched onto her elbow and hurried her into the store. "I told you to wait inside."

"I never was good at taking orders," she said. "You didn't answer my question. Do you think they were following us?"

He exhaled in frustration. "Anyone you know drive a gold Saturn?"

She gave it some thought. "No."

Once they were away from the glass doors, he stopped her. "Next time, when I tell you to do something, you listen to me!"

She rolled her eyes.

"Give me your phone," he insisted.

"Why?"

"Because I need it."

He called in to his precinct, and in the barest of sentences he had patrol cars in the area looking for the gold Saturn. "Yeah, call me back at this number if you find anything."

When he hung up, he handed her the phone. She dropped it in her purse and walked off in a huff.

Frustrated, he took after her. Yes, most of his frustration

was at himself, but what if that idiot had had a gun and taken a shot at her?

He caught up, took her by the elbow, and turned her around. "I'm serious, Sue. When I need to act on something, I can't worry if you will or won't do what I say."

Her eyes narrowed. Without saying a word, she darted off into the produce section.

He caught up with her beside the tomatoes. "You have to listen to me."

"All I did was step outside with you." Not looking at him, she bolted to the jalapeños.

Determined to make his point, he caught her by the arm and they came to a stop by the zucchini. "And all I did was ask you to wait inside. I can't do this if I can't trust you'll do what I say during a crisis."

She swung around. "Then don't do it." She blinked, and he could swear he saw the beginning of tears in her eyes.

He took a deep breath to settle his thoughts and cool his mood.

"I'll hire someone else," she said. "Someone who won't . . . eat off my plate."

Okay, the hire-someone-else statement fired his mood back to the pissed-off range. He passed a hand over his face and tried to make sense of what else she'd said. "What?"

Her chin inched up. An angry inch. "You ate my fries."

This conversation made about as much sense as tree hugging therapy for the emotionally unbalanced. Had they or had they not been talking about her listening to him during a crisis?

Her chin rose another notch. "You didn't even ask if you could have any."

He tried to wrap his head around the new subject of freaking French fries. "You weren't eating them."

"That's not the point." She put one hand on her hip.

"Then would you please explain the point? Because right now I'm clueless."

She blinked those scared, big baby blues at him. "Just because Chase asked you to watch out for me, that doesn't mean you have to babysit."

What happened to the discussion on fries? "I'm not babysitting. Someone is trying to kill you."

"I know." Her eyes grew rounded, brighter. Damn, she was going to cry.

She sniffled. "Don't get me wrong. I appreciate it. Last night I really needed you to stay, and maybe tonight, too. But tomorrow I'm hiring someone else."

Someone else? "Damn it! I'm not doing this because Chase asked me to. So quit . . . quit being ungrateful and—"

Her chin snapped up again. "I'm not being ungrateful."

"Yes, you are!" he bellowed. "I'm trying to help you, and instead of appreciating me or listening to me in a crisis, I'm getting yelled at in the middle of the produce section about . . . about eating your fries!"

"I just told you I appreciated you. And I'm not the one yelling. You are."

"Excuse me," someone said from behind them. "But she's right. You're the one yelling."

"Stay out—" When Jason turned and saw the purple-haired old lady holding a cucumber at him as if it was a weapon, his frustration shattered into disbelief.

He heard a snicker from Sue and saw laughter glittering in her eyes. His own laughter rose in his throat.

His gaze shot back to the woman and her cucumber, and he coughed to hold off his mirth. "You're right, I raised my voice and that wasn't good."

"You got that right, buster!" Wearing a navy dress and too-white tennis shoes, the granny stood a head shorter than Sue, and that included two inches of helmet hair. But even short and elderly, she had presence.

Maybe it was the size of her cucumber. Another laugh tickled his throat.

"I know it's none of my business." She shook the vegetable at him. "But I'm making it my business. You know why I'm making it my business?"

He didn't answer, thinking it was rhetorical.

"I asked you a question, young man!"

He nodded and heard Sue cough, which was really a laugh. "Why are you making it your business?" he asked.

"Because I lost Gerald a few weeks ago." Emotion tightened the woman's voice, and Jason's need to laugh vanished.

The woman continued. "He'd been with me for fifty years. *Fifty years.* I loved the man more than life itself."

"I'm sorry," Jason said.

"The man was the biggest pain in the rear I've ever known."

Sue let loose another snicker, but Jason dared not look at her or he'd lose it.

The cucumber waved onward. "But I still loved him," the granny continued, and a tear slipped down her aged cheek.

Jason frowned. "I'm really sorry for your loss."

"Me, too," Sue added in an honest voice.

The woman blinked back her emotion. "So . . . now I can't stand to listen to two lovebirds argue."

"You're right, and I'm really sorry. I—" Jason's apology and condolences were halted when the old lady walloped him in the abdomen with her cucumber. Sue coughed again.

The granny shook her vegetable. "I'm doing the talking now! And if you're going to apologize, you should be doing it to her, not me. Loving somebody isn't easy. But love isn't meant to be tossed away because it's hard. Love is to be cherished."

The cucumber suddenly took new aim, and Jason stepped between the two women. He'd take a vegetable beating but wouldn't allow the senile senior to swat Sue.

However, the granny kept her cucumber to herself and spoke in a more sympathetic voice. "Love is a gift, even when the loved ones are pains in the rear. And I can tell by looking at this tall drink of water that he's like my Gerald. The good-looking ones are the biggest pains in the rear. But it beats the hell out of being stuck with an ugly one."

The cucumber pointed back at Jason. "Now, tell her you're sorry."

When he didn't speak immediately, he got the cucumber poked into his ribs. "I'm sorry," he said, focusing on Sue, who had tears in her eyes, but he knew they were from laughter.

The old lady glanced back at Sue. "Now it's your turn. It's probably mostly his fault—it always is—but I'll bet you're not perfect, either. So come on, don't dilly-dally."

Sue looked up at Jason, and he knew she couldn't talk for fear she'd laugh. His own amusement bubbled up in his chest, making it hard to breathe.

"I'm sorry," Sue finally managed.

"Now, you know what you got to do, young man," the old woman said. "Do it."

Jason cut his eyes to the granny. "Do what?"

"Kiss her, you dimwit!"

Sue leaned forward. Jason wrapped his arm around her waist and pulled her close. Her lips tasted like chocolate and vanilla ice cream, and whiskey. Her mouth opened beneath his, and he slipped his tongue inside.

She tasted good. Felt good.

"Stop that!" the granny snapped.

Jason pulled back.

The woman hit his arm with the cucumber. "I didn't say French her! Pains in the rear, all of you. Maybe I don't miss Gerald, after all." She tossed her cucumber in her basket and rolled away.

Jason watched the woman cut the corner. Then Sue fell into his shoulder, buried her face in his shirt, and giggled quietly while silent laughter shook him as well.

There was something so right about Sue being close, laughing. It was so right that he got that feeling again—the one that had kept him away from her for the last few months. Sue pulled back. She must have read something in his eyes, because she stopped giggling.

"What do you need to buy?" she asked.

"This way." Taking her hand in his, he led her to the pet food aisle. While the uneasiness still bounced around his gut, holding her hand felt so damn right. Right, because Sue Finley needed him. For the moment, his desire was safe.

When he stopped in front of the cat food section, Sue pulled her hand from his. "There's plenty of food at Lacy's. Besides, she uses the food from the vet."

He grabbed the bag for tubby tabbies. "This isn't for Lacy's cats."

Sue cut him a questioning glance. "*You* have a cat?"

"Sort of." Why did her tone disturb him?

She blinked. "How do you 'sort of' have a cat?"

He shrugged. "When one sort of lives with you."

They started walking, and when he reached for her hand, she pulled back.

He stopped and turned to face her. "I won't eat any more of your fries. And . . . I'm not doing this because of Chase. I . . . I want to make sure you're okay."

Her cheeks turned pink. "It wasn't the fries."

He debated the wisdom of asking, but the words slipped out before he knew it. "Then what was it?"

"You made a big deal about my following you out and . . ." She shook her head. "I'm just scared."

He got the strangest sensation that she wasn't simply talking about the lunatic after her. But he shoved that thought aside. "You've got a reason to be scared. Which is why I'm here."

"For now," she said and looked at him almost as if in question.

"Until we catch the guy."

She nodded. "Right."

When they left the grocery store, Jason stayed on alert. He didn't spot a gold Saturn, but he did notice a pink Cadillac jumping a curb as it exited the parking lot. When the car passed under a streetlight, he recognized the football-helmeted hair as the cucumber woman from the store, and he also recognized the car as the one that had nearly hit him and Chase the day of the rat incident. As the Cadillac sped away, it nearly sideswiped another car, and Jason glanced at the tag.

Sue turned to him. "Oh, God. You know, Melissa said it was a pink Cadillac that hit her. You don't think she's . . . that it was the cucumber lady who hit her, do you?"

Jason remembered where Sue's agent said she'd been hit. "Could be. It happened in this area." He watched the old lady run a yellow light. "Damn, she's gonna kill herself or someone else."

He got Sue inside his car and unlocked his door. When he settled behind the wheel, he reached over to snag his pad again to jot down the Cadillac's license plate.

"What are you going to do?" Sue asked.

He shook his head. "Talk to her, I guess. If I report it, they'll take her license away. And that may have to happen. I don't know."

Sue didn't know, either. Didn't know why she kept thinking about a kiss that had happened in a grocery store produce section. And why she kept thinking about how Jason had treated the elderly woman. When the granny spoke of her deceased husband, Sue had seen emotion in Jason's eyes. And when the woman hit him with the cucumber, Sue half expected him to arrest her for assaulting him with a deadly vegetable.

But no, Jason had never lost his temper. And when he watched her driving erratically, he hadn't gone cop on her; he cared. He was a decent, caring man.

Dang it! Sue did not want him to be a decent, caring man. Did not want to like his kisses. She was supposed to be finding his flaws, not making out with him in the produce aisle. Not mentally awarding him the nice-guy-of-the-year award. Somehow she was going to have to get the no-kissing rule to stand. And she had to gain insight to his issues. He had to have issues, didn't he? Of course he did. As her grandpa had pointed out, she only fell for the guys with issues. And she'd fallen for Jason Dodd hard. Really hard.

So what if he was nice to old ladies? He went through women like they were potato chips. And he kissed girls, got phone numbers, and never called them.

They pulled into an apartment parking lot and stopped.

"You're quiet again," Jason said.

"Just thinking." Sue got out, remembering to lock the door this time.

"Care to share?" He grabbed the cat food from the backseat.

"Not really."

He set the bag on his shoulder. "Then it must be something good." His eyes twinkled in that bad-boy manner.

"Don't," she said.

He grinned. "Don't what?"

"Don't make this into something sexual."

"So that's where your mind is, huh? Come on, tell me what you're thinking about."

She couldn't. Because right now her thoughts again consisted of how he seemed to fit like a good pair of jeans. Feeling that way was dangerous. Letting him know it could be fatal.

When she didn't answer, he continued. "Hmm." He locked and shut the rear door. "I guess I'll let my imagination go wild. Let's see . . ." He curled an arm around her, his hand—accidentally, or not so accidentally—slipped under her T-shirt to touch skin. Naked skin. The pleasure of that touch whispered through her.

He shot her another devilish smile. "I know. You're hoping I'll take you up to my apartment and strip those clothes off of you."

She elbowed him when an older couple walked past.

Jason leaned his head down, and his next words were for her ears only. "Do some private licking. Make love to you. Slowly."

Sue swung around, took the four steps back to his car and

planted her butt on his trunk. He turned around, his bad-boy smile in place. A smile she wished she was immune to, but wasn't. On nipple alert again, she crossed her arms over her chest. "I'll just wait on you right here."

He laughed. "Come on, Sue."

"No."

"Why?" He closed the distance separating them.

She arched a brow at him. "I don't trust you."

Still grinning, he took her by the hand, giving her the lightest of tugs. "I think the person you don't trust is yourself."

As much as Sue hated admitting it, he was right.

Unwilling to admit it aloud, she followed him to his apartment. His apartment where nothing—*absolutely nothing*—was going to happen, she assured herself.

CHAPTER TWELVE

Watching him unlock his door, Sue realized this for what it was: an opportunity. Where better to find dirt on a playboy than in his personal domain?

When Jason pushed open the door, Sue entered the dark apartment. He had issues. After she uprooted them, surely even his melt-you-down-to-your-panties kisses would leave her underwear powder-puff dry.

As her eyes adjusted to the darkness, Sue prepared herself. She imagined garbage and half-eaten pizzas scattered across a coffee table. Maybe dirty underwear and smelly socks decorating the floor. God forbid she had to go to the bathroom while she was here.

And just like that, she had to go.

She pushed the need to pee back and swore she wouldn't start cleaning. She'd done that with a few college boyfriends, tried to clean up the man by cleaning his place. It hadn't worked. Once a slob, always a slob. She knew because she'd spent five years picking up after Collin. Trying to be the perfect wife. Planning the perfect life. Thinking she had the perfect man.

Then she'd discovered the red nightie. And his real mistress.

The lights flicked on. Sue blinked, and she got a look at Jason's place. The bad news was she wouldn't be able to tie the slob issue to him. The good news was she could probably go to the bathroom.

"You want something to drink?" He walked into the kitchen off the living room. "I've got cokes, beer, and red wine."

"I'm fine." She gazed around the room. She couldn't call him a neatnik. There were a few books on the sofa and a pair of shoes beside the coffee table. The decor was eclectic yet masculine. A toffee-colored sectional and leather chair filled one corner of the room, while a washed-oak entertainment cabinet with a plasma television and stereo equipment filled the other side. The pen and ink drawings on the wall were interesting.

"Bathroom?" She studied one framed print of a lone wolf.

"First door on the right." He motioned down the hall. "I forgot something in the car. I'll be right back."

She darted inside the bathroom. When she heard the front door shut, she shot straight to the medicine cabinet. Sure it was rude to nose around in a person's personal domain, but please, what woman hadn't done it? Besides, she was desperate. She needed dirt on this man, and she needed it fast.

She moved some headache meds around and frowned. No condoms, no weird rash medicines. A look under the cabinet and in the drawers proved just as boring. No porn or sex toys. Even the toilet looked reasonably clean. Which was good.

She unzipped her jeans while visually sizing up the room. No bathroom art. A green and white striped shower curtain, and a couple of well-used green towels.

Bladder happy, Sue zipped up, washed, and hurried out of the bathroom. She heard some sort of soft cry and stopped to listen. The sound faded. Maybe the tenants next door had a baby.

Moving down the hall, she walked to the entertainment case. She'd seen a framed photo on a shelf and wanted to check it out before Jason returned. The picture showed a younger Jason dressed in a police uniform with his arm around an older lady. Sue assumed it was his mother, although they looked nothing alike. Maybe he favored his father. The father who wasn't in the photograph.

Sue knew all about fatherless photographs. Her chest filled with sympathy. Had Jason's dad died, too?

She picked up the frame. Her heart clutched at the empty spot beside Jason in the picture.

The door opened. She dropped the frame back on the shelf and moved to the books. Checking out his reading material was less like snooping. Her gaze flitted over a couple of thrillers and a biography of one of Houston's well-known anchormen. Then her gaze stuck when it came across the spines of four familiar novels.

Her novels.

She looked back at him. "You bought my books?"

He fumbled through the notepad he'd tucked inside his glove compartment earlier. "Yeah." He glanced up. "You say that as if you're surprised."

"Why would you buy my books?"

He looked genuinely puzzled. "Why wouldn't I?"

"But . . . you never came to any of my signings."

She bit her lip, hoping he didn't think she'd been disappointed. She really hadn't been, but when she'd gotten his address from Lacy after the wedding to put him on her mail-out list, she had sort of expected he might tag along when Lacy and Chase had made their appearances.

Okay, so maybe she had been disappointed.

"Is that why you dropped me from your mailing list?" He raised an eyebrow. "Because I used to get these newsletters and notices about your books, and they stopped."

"I didn't drop you from my mailing list. Melissa takes care of all that."

And that was the truth. Well, partly. Melissa did take care of that; but yeah, after being kissed senseless and waiting two weeks for a phone call, she'd made her own decision.

"Axe Jason Dodd from the list," she'd told her agent. She hadn't given a reason.

Not that she didn't have a good reason. She'd had no desire to know he'd have the pleasure of receiving another invitation to a book signing that he wouldn't attend.

Jason studied her. Right then he looked more like a cop than she'd ever seen him.

"What?" She wished her eyelid would stop twitching.

He held up a hand. "I didn't say a word."

She glanced again at the books. "Did you read them or just buy them for show?" Turning back, she attempted to study him with the same polygraph-vision he'd used on her.

"The covers matched my decor." He made a face. "Of course I read them. I told you I liked your books." Tapping his finger against his notepad, he moved into the kitchen. A moment later he stuck his head out the door. "Maybe now you'll let me critique your work, huh? I could help you with police procedure information."

"I've got someone who does that." She moved to the kitchen door.

"Really?" Jason picked up the phone. There was just a bit too much surprise in his voice.

"What's that mean?"

He shrugged. "Nothing, it's just . . ."

"Just what?" she asked.

His brow creased, and he looked like a guy who'd just stepped in a pile of poo and couldn't figure out how to escape. But it was too late, he'd stepped in it.

"Out with it," Sue snapped.

He shook his head. "Okay, there were just a few incidents in your books that seemed a little more like fiction and less like fact. I thought a cop could give you the real low-down."

"What incidents?" She moved into the kitchen and stood across the table from him. "But before you start tossing out too many criticisms, you should know that my source is a real cop."

Jason frowned. "It's not Martin, is it?" He pointed the phone at her. "I told you, that man's a jerk."

"No. It's someone I respect and trust a lot more than Martin."

Jason studied her. "And a lot more than me, obviously."

She gave Jason a snarling smile. "He comes to my auto-graphings."

"Well, whoever it is, he's telling you only what you want to hear to impress you—probably to get in your pants. That or he's a crackerjack cop who doesn't—"

"I'm sure Chase would appreciate your opinion."

Jason's eyes grew round. "*Chase* helps you? He reads your work before it's published?"

"Yeah. Well, he doesn't read the book. I just go to him for advice."

Sue was about to fire a list of questions about the "too fictionalized" incidents when the phone in Jason's hands rang. He held up a finger as he answered.

"Jason Dodd," he said into the receiver, sounding like a cop again. "Hi." The cop tone vanished. "Yeah, I called you."

So he called *some* people. Just not Sue.

He stared away from her. "No, I'm house-sitting for Chase."

Sue walked out of the kitchen. Obviously he didn't want whomever he spoke with to know he was babysitting her, because he hadn't mentioned her. While being out of the room felt less intrusive, she continued to listen.

"I forgot my charger. Is everything okay?" He moved to the door and stared at her.

She feigned interest in his book collection again.

"No, I'll see you in a couple of days. Me, too." He hung up.

Me, too, what? Had someone said I love you?

Not wanting him to see the questions in her eyes, Sue didn't turn around. Not that she had a personal stake in knowing the caller's identity. However, as she expected, Dodd's issues were surfacing. The man apparently had a girl-friend but felt no remorse for making advances, kissing her, and playing sexual head games.

The realization stung, and she didn't quite understand the feeling. This was what she wanted, wasn't it—to discover all his dirty little secrets?

She heard him walk up behind her. "You sure you don't want something to drink?"

"I'm fine." She stared at the framed photograph. "Is this your mom?"

When he didn't answer, she glanced back at him. "Sort of," he said.

"Sort of? Like you sort of have a cat?" *Like you sort of have a girlfriend? And you sort of didn't tell her that you were hanging out and sort of kissing me all day?*

His brow wrinkled. "That's strange."

"What's strange? That you sort of have a mom and sort of have a cat? Yeah, I agree, it's kind of strange."

He shot her a puzzled look. "I'm talking about my cat not coming out to greet me." He stepped into the living room. "It usually greets me at the door."

"Kitty, kitty," Sue said, and then looked back at Jason. "What's its name?"

He gave her a blank stare. "I haven't named it."

Sue walked over to the curtains, one of Hitchcock's hiding spots, and peered behind them. Nothing. "So, it's just a kitten?"

"No."

"How long have you had it?"

"Six or seven months."

Sue's mouth dropped open. "And you haven't named it yet?"

He shot her another one of his looks, part guilt, part knowing he might have just stepped in another pile of poo. "I haven't named it because I'm not sure if I'm keeping it."

"Commitment-phobe," she muttered.

"What?"

"Nothing." She got on her knees and peered under the sofa. "Is it a boy or girl?" Jason didn't answer, and she glanced up him. "Don't tell me you don't know."

He shrugged. "That's personal information. I saw no need to investigate."

"Your vet didn't tell you if it was a boy or girl?"

"The cat hasn't been sick."

"And it hasn't had its shots either." She gave him a serious eye roll. *Bad pet owner.* She added to his list of issues.

"Shots? What kind of shots does a cat need?"

She didn't even look up. "You have a pet for six months, you don't take it to the vet, don't name it, don't know its sex, and you still haven't decided if you're going to keep it?" Oh yeah, his issues were rising to the surface all right. She got back to her feet and looked around. "Maybe you let it outside and it sort of found a better owner."

He frowned. "No, it's inside. I made sure before I left for Chase's."

"Is it nervous around strangers?" she asked. "Perhaps it just doesn't like me."

"No, it liked all the other girls."

"All of them." She shot him another look.

"You sound jealous."

"Please." She hoped that sounded convincing. Not that she was jealous. Nope. Not at all.

He looked at his watch. "I need to make a call or I'm going to miss someone. Can you look in my bedroom? It's probably asleep on my bed."

"You sleep with it but don't know its name. Just like a man."

He ignored her snide remark. "Look under the bed, too." He started punching in numbers.

Sue took several steps down the hall then hesitated. The idea of going into Jason's bedroom brought a new bout of flutters to her stomach. Sue heard him talking to someone about running a check on the tag number he'd called in earlier. She listened in.

"I didn't think you'd catch him."

So, they hadn't found the car that was possibly following them.

"Yeah, call me when you get something," Jason said. "Oh. I have another license number to run."

She continued down the hall to the last door on the right. It had been left ajar, and she could see the king-size, unmade bed with mussed black sheets.

Black? What kind of guy had black sheets?

The kind who sort of had a cat and didn't name it.

"Kitty?" She hit the light switch. Her gaze was searching . . . snooping . . . Though she didn't know why. She'd gotten all the dirt she needed. Jason Dodd was full of issues. So why hadn't the attraction vanished?

"Find it?" he called.

"Not yet." She got down on her hands and knees and poked her head under the bed. She found a few dust bunnies and . . . was that . . . ?

Sliding deeper beneath the bed, she confirmed her suspicions. Yup. A condom wrapper. Ribbed and . . . extra large?

Extra large.

Sue's mouth went dry. She put herself in reverse and bumped into something solid. That something solid turned out to be the owner of the extra large.

She looked over her shoulder at him, her eyes traveling to his zipper. Having never seen anything more than a medium, she couldn't help but be curious. She remembered feeling that hardness against her this morning but hadn't realized it'd been an extra large.

"Is it under there?" he asked.

"No." She forced her eyes upward. The temptation to tell him what she *had* found stirred, but wouldn't that sound as if she were jealous?

Suddenly, Sue heard that noise again: the soft whine. She got up and followed the cries to the closet door that stood ajar. Pulling it fully open, she peered inside. There, in the corner, between a couple pairs of shoes, she saw "it."

Sue looked back at Jason standing at the foot of the bed. "I found your cat."

"Good."

She smirked. "And I think I have the answer to that other question."

His brow crinkled. "What question?"

"It's a girl. And you could hold off giving her a name. She'll probably answer to Mama just fine."

Jason's eyes widened. "No!" He popped his head in the closet. "Fuck."

Sue grinned. "Guess this is one of the downsides of not investigating, huh?"

Twenty minutes after finding the cat, Jason sat at his desk in the second-bedroom-turned-study trying to figure out why his printer didn't want to print the copy of Sue's book. Sue sat on the floor, whispering to Mama and her five multicolored kittens. When the beast had kept leaving her young to join the two humans in the study, Jason had found a box and moved them in there, too.

What Jason would have liked was for Sue to join him and his cat in his bedroom. But Sue had been sending serious back-off messages. It didn't make a bit of sense, but he respected her wishes. For now. Jason Dodd wasn't a quitter. And he knew when a woman wanted him. Sue wanted him; she was just . . . fighting it for some reason.

The phone rang and, flustered about his printer, the overpopulation of felines, and being sexually frustrated, he hit the speakerphone and bit out a greeting. "Hello?"

"You're supposed to be at my place." Chase's voice boomed over the speakerphone.

Jason turned to Sue. Blue eyes wide, she mouthed the word, *No*.

The fact that she didn't want Chase to know she was here stung, but then Jason realized he wasn't quite ready to spill the beans yet either. God knew what Lacy would say. He loved Chase's wife and felt pretty certain she felt the same about him, but she didn't seem to care too much for his lifestyle.

Jason looked back at the phone. "I came home to feed my cat."

"Your cat?" Chase said. "You never told me you had a cat."

Jason focused his frown on Sue, who obviously enjoyed watching him getting called on the cat issue by someone else. "I didn't know I needed permission. What are you, the cat police?"

"No," Chase said. "Look, the reason I called is that I've already got a hysterical wife on my hands, and I'm getting a little concerned myself."

"What's wrong?" Jason unplugged and replugged in his printer.

"It's about Sue."

Jason stopped fiddling and looked at the woman in question. "What about her?"

"Well, after the rat incident, I made a few inquiries. This afternoon, I called and got my voice mail messages."

"And?" Jason held his breath.

"And I think I might know who sent her that dead rat."

CHAPTER THIRTEEN

"Who do you think sent the rat?" Jason asked.

Sue jumped to her feet.

"Sue's going to kill me for doing it, but her mother insisted," Chase said. "And—"

Sue bolted forward. "I'll kill you later! Right now tell me who you think sent the rat."

Jason saw the frightened look in her eyes, and he took her hand in his.

"Sue?" Chase's voice shot up an octave. "Jason, was—"

"Yes. It's me." Sue moved closer. "Tell me what you know."

"I . . . Where . . . Hot damn! I knew you two would be good together."

"We're not together." Sue jerked her hand from his and scowled at the speakerphone.

"Why didn't you go to Mexico?" Chase asked. "When you weren't at your hotel, Lacy had me calling every freaking hotel in Mexico trying to find you."

"The trip . . . I—" Sue closed her mouth.

"The doctor had an emergency," Jason answered for her. "Now, what's up?"

"If you weren't home tomorrow, I'd be in Mexico looking for your ass. Lacy's been—"

"Chase." Jason's frustration rang clear in his voice. "What do you have?" He caught Sue's hand again and ran his thumb over her knuckles.

Chase let out a frustrated sigh. "I did a background check on the foot doctor and something came up."

"What came up?" Jason wrapped an arm around Sue's waist.

"For starters, he has a record. He had a fetish for stealing nice cars back when he was younger. Did almost a year in the pen in the early nineties. Heck, you might want to check the plates on his Porsche. Anyway, he was also looked at for insurance fraud back in Georgia."

"Why do you think he sent the rat?" Jason knew neither of the two listed crimes would lead a good cop to presume the man guilty of stalking. And Chase was a good cop, even if he had given Sue some weak advice on her books.

"I don't think *he* sent the rat," Chase said. "His wife—"

"You mean ex-wife. Right?" Sue leaned against him. "Please tell me you meant ex-wife."

Hurt filled Sue's eyes. The emotion bounced around Jason's rib cage.

"Sorry. But according to what my guy uncovered, he's still married. Even has a four-year-old son. But you're not the only one he's lied to. He had an affair with a woman last year. Told her he was divorced. She believed it until his wife turned stalker. The lady had to get a restraining order against the wife after she purposely ran over the woman's dog."

"Shit," Sue said.

"Yup. Shit says it all," Chase agreed.

Jason ran his hand up from Sue's waist to her shoulder. "Chase, uhh . . . some things have happened since you left."

"What things?" Chase asked.

"Someone tried to break into Sue's house last night. Cut the phone line. She only got a glimpse of the person, but she thought it was a man."

"Maybe his wife is manly," Chase suggested.

"And someone has been leaving threatening phone messages." Jason tried to recall the voice. "I heard one of them.

If it's a woman's voice, she's disguising it. And it seems someone might have hacked into Sue's computer and has been reading her files." Jason explained about the rat scene in Sue's book.

"Why the hell didn't she tell me this was happening?" Chase snapped.

Sue shifted beside him. "*She* didn't tell you because you were leaving for L.A."

"You still should have told me."

Jason looked at Sue's pinched expression, and he didn't know if she was going to start leaking all over him or start pacing. He glanced at his shirt, prepared for either.

"Jason," Chase said. "Take me off the speakerphone."

Jason reached for the receiver, but Sue stopped him. "I have a right to hear this."

"Okay," Chase snapped. "It's just . . . I know you, Sue, and you're not going to take this seriously. But damn it, this sounds bad. Jason, don't let her do something to get herself killed."

Sue stared out the car window as Jason drove them back to her house. She'd heard him promise Chase and Lacy that he wouldn't leave her side until they got home on Friday. Lacy had also made her promise to accept Jason's protection.

There went her idea of hiring an ugly bodyguard. Sue might lie on occasion, but breaking a promise to a friend violated her code of ethics.

She closed her eyes and listened to the kittens mew in the backseat. Of course she'd have to keep Hitchcock and Mama and company apart until Jason got the cats their shots, but that wasn't too much of a pain. Mama didn't like the car ride, but there was no way Sue was leaving a mother and five kittens alone. "What if your apartment caught fire? Or if one of them gets sick and needs a vet?" she'd asked Jason.

Jason hadn't argued and had pulled out a never-used cat

carrier. The fact that he had a carrier surprised her. When she'd asked him about it, he'd shrugged and changed the subject. He was good at changing the subject.

The two glasses of red wine Sue consumed while Jason printed her book had left her with the energy of a slug on muscle relaxers. She might have even gone for a third glass but realized she was using her mother's Merlot-can-save-the-world theory. Which wasn't going to work, because she'd been drinking Cabernet.

But not even the best bottle of Merlot was going to make these problems disappear. Someone wanted her dead. And then there was this other itsy-bitsy problem that she'd been dating a married man. A married man who happened to be a car thief, and who was married to a psychopath who might be the person who wanted her dead.

Then there was Jason Dodd. Even after hearing him speak to someone who suspiciously sounded like a girl-friend; after finding an extra-large condom packet, which was proof of the girlfriend; after learning he had commit-ment issues to such an extreme that he wouldn't even name a pet or check out its genitalia—even after all this, she *still* wanted to curl up in his arms and let him protect her. Then she wanted him to help her catch up on two and a half years of missed orgasms.

Maybe she should have had that third glass of Cabernet after all.

"What were the plans for tomorrow night?" he asked.

Sue looked at him, her mind on wine and orgasms. "To-morrow night?"

"With the foot doctor?"

"Oh. I'm meeting him at a diner by the Westside movie theater. We'll have dinner, and right after he pays for the meal I'm going to shoot him in his kneecaps."

Jason grinned. "How about I shoot him for you?"

"Go find your own cheating lowlife to shoot. This one's mine."

Jason's soft chuckle had her closing her eyes again and

trying to ignore the fact that she liked his company. That, in spite of everything, she still saw him as a nice person.

Paul had been nice, too.

Now that Sue had given it some thought, she realized she should have known Paul had secrets. The man had never taken her to his apartment, never given her his home number. Oh yeah, she'd been played for a fool once again.

Jason's voice rang loud. "I'll probably get someone to come stay with you while I meet him."

Just like that, her wine-buzz buzzed off. She sat up. "*I'm* meeting him."

Their frowns met. "Sue, I don't want him or his wife anywhere near you. I'm going to meet him and then probably take him downtown for questioning."

"You can question him after I take out his right knee."

"I'm not joking." He pulled into her driveway. "It could be dangerous and—"

"You're not the one he made a fool of, or lied to. I want to face him myself." She jumped out of his car and took off to her front door where the porch light welcomed her. She dug for her keys in her purse. Her gaze shifted downward.

She froze.

"Crap!" On her front porch was an envelope, some flowers, and another gold box with a Godiva sticker.

CHAPTER FOURTEEN

Sue jumped back as if the package would bite and in the process slammed into Jason.

"What?" he said, steadying her with one hand while the other held the cat carrier full of felines. His gaze followed Sue's downward. "It's okay," he muttered.

Mama meowed.

Kneeling, he studied the card on the flowers. "It's signed, 'Benny.' Your critique partner, right?"

The tension rolled off her shoulders. "I forgot he threatened to bring his manuscript by."

"Threatened?" Jason asked.

"Told me," Sue corrected.

Jason's brows pinched. "You said threatened."

"It's an expression." She glanced at the envelope. "It's just his manuscript and some good chocolate. Which I could use now." She reached down—

"Don't." He caught her hand. "Open the door and show me where you want the cats, and then I'll get this."

"But it's from Benny," she said.

"And it could be Benny doing this. We're not certain the doctor's wife is behind everything."

"I trust my critique group."

"You just said he threatened you."

"No, I said he threatened to come by."

He zapped her again with that I'm-a-cop polygraph gaze.

"How come I get the feeling you're keeping something from me?"

Sue chose not to answer, and let herself inside.

Jason put Mama and the kittens in her study. Hitchcock went on immediate sensory overload and stalked indignantly around the room. Sue picked him up to assure him of her love and walked him back into the living room.

When Jason came back inside, he noticed her phone's flashing light. "You've got messages."

Benny had left one message, saying he was sorry he'd missed her and hoped she enjoyed the chocolate. The other three were from Lacy, her mother, and a panicked Kathy who mumbled something about Lacy leaving a message about the foot doctor. When the machine clicked off, Jason insisted she come clean about Benny.

Sue cratered. "He's separated from his wife, lonely, and he's a dog like every other living, breathing male on the earth, and he thinks we might get it on."

"Thank you." Sarcasm tightened Jason's voice. Then he retrieved some gloves from his car and opened the packages so as not to disturb any fingerprints.

"Duh, Benny signed his name. Why would you check for fingerprints?"

Carefully opening the items, Jason proved Sue right.

"See? I told you. It's just chocolate and a manuscript." She reached over to snatch one of the truffles.

Jason grabbed her hand again. "No."

"It's Godiva."

"I don't care. You don't eat candy from a person who might be trying to kill you."

She eyed the truffle. "You obviously haven't ever had Godiva. It's worth the risk."

"I'll get you some tomorrow." He dropped the flowers in the garbage. "You're not eating his candy."

"He's not behind this." She stared at the pansies decorating her trash.

"He's hitting on you. He's read both manuscripts. That

makes him a suspect. You don't accept flowers from a suspect. Plus . . . his writing stinks." Jason picked up the manuscript. "Is he really writing about man-eating plants?"

She grabbed Benny's manuscript away from him. "He sells just about everything he writes. Plus, someone has probably hacked into my computer. You even told Chase you thought so. That means Benny isn't any more of a suspect than anyone else. And he really isn't interested in me. He's just lonely. In a week or two he'll be back with his wife and he'll forget about me."

Jason's gaze brushed over her. "You're not that forgettable."

Really? You managed to do it for four months and not call. She grabbed the vitamin C tablets from the table and shook two out for her and two for him. "Take it." She watched him make a face, but he swallowed the tablets.

Stifling a yawn, she studied the clock. It was after ten. But she wasn't going to sleep until she got one thing clear. "I *am* going to meet Paul tomorrow night."

He frowned, but she saw defeat in his eyes. "Fine," he said. "I'm working on getting someone with Hoke's Bluff Police Force to pick him up for questioning. I haven't got it all worked out yet, but you'll do exactly what I say. I mean it. If I tell you to stay, you stay. If I tell you to run, you run. If I tell you to do the hokey pokey, you—"

"I do the hokey pokey." She started to sing, " 'I'll put my right foot out . . . ' " She walked into her hall closet, pulled out a flat sheet, a blanket, and pillow. Then she delivered the bundle. "Sleep well."

He glanced down. "You're putting me on the couch?"

"I don't have an extra bedroom."

His eyes twinkled. "You have a big bed . . ."

"Hitchcock and I like sleeping alone."

Two lies in one day, her conscience nagged. Even after two years, that was what she missed most about being married. It wasn't the sex. Sex with Collin hadn't been earth-shaking. But he'd been a cuddler and she missed—

"We slept together last night and you did okay."

"Not happening." She walked away but tossed over her shoulder, "We're getting up early. Remember my grandfather's prostate appointment."

"Thank you for that bedtime image," he called after her.

Jason checked on his cat and kittens. Mama slipped out of the open carrier and rubbed against his ankles.

"You could have told me." He knelt, scratched her chin, and gazed into the cat's eyes. "What are you going to do with all these guys? We can't keep 'em. I'm not even sure if I'm keeping you."

She meowed as if she understood.

From the first day he'd found the scrap of a kitten getting into the garbage on his back patio, he'd told himself that he would take the animal to a shelter. He'd bought the carrier to get it there and investigated which ones didn't euthanize. But he'd gotten so busy and . . .

Jason flinched at the lie. Truth was, every time he'd go to take the animal away, he remembered being taken away himself. First from his mother—she'd stood in the kitchen and watched as they'd pulled him kicking and screaming from the house. Then he'd been shifted from one foster home to another. Each one left its mark. Each one left him a little more jaded.

I don't believe you were a bad kid, Sue had said.

No, he hadn't ever done drugs, not after seeing what it did to his mom. He hadn't stolen anything. Nor had he ever started a fight. But hell, yeah, he'd finished many of them. He hadn't had to do anything wrong to be considered bad.

When people found out he was a foster kid, when foster parents found out his mother had abandoned him, he'd been stamped as Bad News. A bad kid. His only mistake, and it was one he continued to make, was that he'd never kiss someone's ass to win their hearts.

Uncomfortable where his thoughts had gone, he stood and moved his gaze around Sue's study. This was where she created her stories—where she wrote about bad things, murder and mayhem, but still managed to bring about happy endings and a lot of laughter along the way. On her bookshelf he spotted one of those hanging photo albums. The front picture portrayed a man holding a little girl. Jason drew closer and noted the child's white blond hair and sweet face. *Sue.*

He ran the tip of his finger along her image and smiled. Then he focused on the man in the photo. *Her father,* Jason thought, noticing the love with which the two- or three-year-old gazed up at the man. Jason flipped to the next image. In it, a year or so older, Sue posed by her father's side wearing an angel costume. A halo dangled above her head. In this image it was the father who gazed upon Sue with total love.

No doubt about it, Sue was a daddy's girl. Jason recalled Sue's mother was dating "Elvis," and he wondered when the parents had divorced.

Picking up the album, he flipped through the pages, marveling at Sue's picture-perfect world. Easters, Christmases, Halloweens, and birthdays. He could almost hear the laughter drifting from the snapshots. Love frozen in time on film.

Jason couldn't help but compare Sue's life to his own. About his second year in foster care, he had stopped expecting something magical to happen on holidays. More times than not, his birthday was overlooked, the presents under the tree were never what he'd asked for, but more importantly, his mother never showed up, never called. Yup, holidays pretty much sucked.

Shaking off those memories, he turned to the next page in Sue's happy life. His breath hitched. Instead of an image of smiling faces, there was a funeral notice. Above the writing was a headshot of Sue's father. *Robert Finley – 1953–1985.*

Damn.

Jason turned the page to the last image. As soon as he saw it, he wished he hadn't.

Double damn.

Standing with her shoulders square, her chin high but with tears in her eyes, was a young and heartbroken Sue standing next to a grave. Who the hell would have taken that picture?

Swallowing a knot, he exhaled, flipped the pages back to the beginning, and returned the hanging album to the shelf. Fifteen minutes later, dressed only in silk boxers, he stretched out on the sofa. He picked up his cell phone and put it on the coffee table. He stared at the ceiling a moment, then grabbed it again and dialed.

Sue's phone rang. He heard her open her bedroom door. "Should I answer it?" she called, a touch of panic in her voice.

"It's just me." He smiled, pleased she'd thought to ask him first. She needed him. The realization wound around his heart and made being here feel right.

"You?" Her door shut. He heard her footsteps; then the ringing stopped. Her voice came through the line. "What are you doing calling me?"

"I'm lonely."

"No," she said. "The answer is no!"

"No what?" His grin widened.

"I don't think you're that clueless."

Her mattress squeaked, and he envisioned her rolling over in bed. He recalled her white down comforter and matching pillow shams and tried to imagine her stretched out. "What are you wearing?"

"Is this an obscene phone call? Are you going to start with the heavy breathing?"

He laughed. "I was just wondering if you were wearing the dancing penguin pajamas."

"No. Tonight I'm wearing . . . bicycling teddy bears."

"I'm picking up a theme here. Exercising animals."

She didn't answer for several seconds. "My pajamas are none of your business."

"I liked the dancing penguins." He waited, but she didn't say anything. "I'm hungry. Can I have some cereal?"

"Help yourself."

He stood. "You want to join me?"

"No. Only chocolate will get me out of bed. And you think it's poisoned."

"I'll buy you some tomorrow." He walked to the fridge and pulled out the milk.

"I can buy my own chocolate."

"I sense an independent streak in you." He got out the cereal and a bowl.

"Because I can buy myself chocolate?"

"That, and because you balked when I paid for dinner tonight. Are you the type who refuses to let your date pay for you?"

"We're not dating."

"We could. How about if I take you out on a date tomorrow night? Someplace nice. Romantic. Quiet."

"I've got a date tomorrow night."

He fell into a chair. "You're breaking up with him, remember. I think you wanted to shoot him in the kneecaps for some reason. Oh yeah, for his being married."

"It's still a date."

That got to him. "Okay. How about Tuesday night?"

"I'm washing my hair." The mattress squeaked as if she'd rolled over.

He smiled. "Wednesday?"

"My cat needs a bath."

"Thursday?"

"Polishing my silver."

"Friday?" He bit his lip to stop from laughing.

"Toenails clipped and getting a tattoo."

His laugh slipped out. "Saturday?"

"Pap smear and, oh, then I have a meeting with the Pope, to show him my tattoo."

"I'm beginning to think you really don't want to date me."

"Hmm. It took you long enough. Most guys guess at the washing-hair stage."

He unscrewed the cap from the milk. "Well, I'm not most guys, Sue."

"Yeah, you're worse."

"How am I worse?" He opened the box of cereal.

"I don't know for certain, but when I figure it out you'll be the first one I tell."

"Come on. Spill it; why won't you date me?" He leaned back in the chair. "You don't have something against cops, do you?"

"Not particularly."

"So it's me, huh?" He picked up the spoon.

"You don't even *like* me," she said.

"I never said I didn't like you." He dropped the spoon.

"You didn't even . . . It's not important."

"It is to me. Come on. Be honest. You're not the type to play games."

The bed creaked again. "How do you know I don't play games? You don't know me."

"Yes, I do. I've read all four of your books and I've—"

"Just because you've read my work doesn't mean you know me. My work's fiction."

"I'm not just going by that. I'm good at pegging people."

She paused. "So how do you have me pegged?" she asked.

He moved his finger down the condensation running off the milk carton. "You're kindhearted to people and animals, but not to men who are attracted to you. You're a little chatty when you're happy, when you're at ease, and sometimes when you're nervous. But when you're scared or really worried, you get quiet. You fidget when you're nervous, but you're trying to stop. You look at life differently from most people. That's what makes you a good writer. And you're a good writer." He picked up the spoon again.

When she didn't say anything, he continued. "You're beautiful but you don't know it. Which makes you even more beautiful. You love chocolate way too much." A grin spread across his lips. "Your mother drives you crazy but you love her." The image of the last photograph in her album flashed in his mind's eye. "And your first heartbreak was . . . when your father died."

When she still didn't respond, he realized that he'd said too much. "Sue?"

"How did you know about my father?"

"I saw the photo album in your study."

"You were snooping," she accused.

"No. Well, yes, but I thought they were just photographs. You did the same at my place." He regretted the way that sounded, as if he was annoyed. But he was. Talking about the past wasn't something he did.

"It's late," she said. "I need my rest. Good night."

"No. Please." But the line went dead. He pushed up from the table and went down the hall. He knocked on her door.

"I'm going to sleep," she said. "It's late."

He leaned his forehead on her door. "Come out and talk to me. Please."

Suddenly, the doorbell chimed.

Jason swung around. "Stay in your room." Running to the living room, he grabbed his gun. As he cut the corner of the hall, he heard Sue's bedroom door swing open. He moved so he could stop her before she stormed out.

She appeared in the hall. Before he could insist she go back into her bedroom, he heard the front door opening.

"Police," Jason yelled and charged into the living room with his gun raised.

CHAPTER FIFTEEN

"Sue?" the female intruder yelled as she stumbled inside the door. "Lacy called . . ."

Her voice went straight to squeaky as her gaze alit on Jason standing in nothing but his silk boxers, legs slightly apart, gun held high.

She slung her purse down, and her hands flew up. "Don't shoot!"

Recognizing the redhead as Kathy, one of Sue's friends, he lowered his gun. "How did you get in?" Adrenaline still burned in his gut.

"The key under the fake poop." Her hands dropped.

Sue darted in and hugged her friend. "You scared the bejeebers out of me!"

"*You* were scared? I pulled in from Dallas just fifteen minutes ago and checked my messages. When I heard from Lacy that she still couldn't find you, I rushed over. Have you spoken with her? Your foot doctor is a married car thief, and his wife murders dogs for kicks!"

"I know," Sue said.

Jason's heart still hammered. A frown twisted his gut when he realized Sue had disobeyed him during a crisis. Then he remembered the fake poop comment.

Kathy glanced at him. "What's he doing here?"

Sue shot him a quick glance, too. "Lacy made me promise to let him stay. Personally, I think it's overkill."

"Overkill?" Jason repeated. "The freak cut your phone line."

Kathy ignored Jason and grinned at Sue. "Does he always run around like that?"

Sue frowned. "No. He normally wears clothes, but you know men. No shame."

"Total exhibitionists," Kathy agreed.

"I was in bed," Jason snapped.

Kathy continued, "But it's not their fault. The modesty gene's not in their DNA. That and toilet-lid-raising skills, and the ability to ask for directions, or . . ."

Jason scowled. "Funny."

"We weren't going for humor," Sue said. "We were hoping we'd embarrass you enough to get dressed."

He found his jeans and jerked them up his legs. Then he stormed outside and searched the flower bed until he found the fake dog shit. Walking inside, he went to the table shared by the two women and dropped the pile center stage. "This is stupid. You might as well put a sign out front that says, 'Hey, I'm a dumb blonde and just waiting for someone to take advantage of me!'" He pointed to Kathy. "If you have this at home, get rid of it."

He grabbed his cereal bowl and filled it with milk. Setting the milk back on the table, he headed to Sue's bedroom, calling back, "My faulty DNA will be in bed while you two visit."

"Grumpy, isn't he?" Kathy asked.

Sue watched Jason disappear into her room to eat cereal in her bed. "A pain in the rump."

Kathy grinned. "You're still carrying a torch for him."

Sue started to deny it, but with two lies down for the day she reconsidered. "Yeah, but I'm not going to do anything about it."

"Why? I thought you were ready to join the fornicating masses again." Kathy chuckled.

"Anyone tell you that you have a way with words?"

"No. I thought you were ready to date."

"I've decided to be particular."

Kathy pursed her lips. "How picky can you be? If I was going to fornicate, he'd be the one. Ooh-la-la!"

"I'm not fornicating with him. He has issues. I don't want . . . I want . . ."

"You want what Lacy has." Kathy relaxed back in her chair. "We all want what Lacy has. My grandma, heck, even my son's hamster wants what Lacy has: the gold ring and a direct path to the happily-ever-after." She put her elbows on the table and dropped her chin in her cupped hands. "Of course, we all know there's a lot more toads than white knights, and if we want to go for that gold ring we've got to risk kissing a toad. It's a corollary to Murphy's Law. I'm personally not willing to kiss toads. But many people are. They overlook the issues and risk it. And if you're going to be one of that crowd, well, you'd better get used to the risks."

"Why not just check for warts beforehand?" Sue said. "I checked." She pointed down the hall. "He's warty!"

"And the doctor wasn't?" Kathy asked. "Let's see. Married? *Wart.* Car thief? *Wart.* Married to a psychopath? *Wart.*"

"Okay, I overlooked Paul's warts," Sue snapped. "But I didn't fornicate with him."

"And it doesn't worry you that you didn't see the doctor's warts but you see Jason's?"

"What do you mean?" Sue asked.

"Well, you've had a thing for this guy for over a year, right? It was only after kissing him that you decided to go back to fornicating."

"I—"

Kathy held up a hand to silence her. "I'm just saying that maybe you're seeing warts that aren't there because you're scared. Let's face it. Kissing a toad is bad enough, but kissing a toad that you care about—that's risky."

"Which is why you don't use the same plumber?" Sue asked. Kathy had a run-in with her plumber when Lacy first met her husband. The plumber had done everything short of backward flips to get Kathy to go out with him. Of course, Kathy had handed him his tools and told him to find some other woman to plumb around with.

"Hey, I already admitted to my weakness. I'm emotionally okay with not risking kissing toads."

Sue picked up the fake poop. "You've been watching too much *Dr. Phil*."

"Yeah, but I watch *The Jerry Springer Show* to balance the effects." Kathy grinned and pulled her red braid over her shoulder. "Are we getting together Friday?"

"We'd better! I'm going to be a wreck by Friday. I'm down to having therapy sessions with my ficus tree. And . . ." Sue looked at what she held in her hands. "And fidgeting with fake dog crap."

They laughed and talked for another hour. After showing Kathy the kittens, Sue stood by the window and watched Kathy drive away. She locked the door and turned to face the situation. Jason was in her bed. She eyed the sofa and considered letting a sleeping dog lie.

Coward.

Willing herself to be strong, she slipped inside her room. Shirtless and stretched out atop her down comforter, Jason slept. A blond lock of hair fell across his brow, giving him that adorable little boy look.

Sue checked out his bare chest, where he didn't look so much like a little boy. Fanning out like eagle wings over his chest was a fine dusting of dark blond hair. Below his chest, a thin trail of hair swept downward. It parted around his navel, then disappeared into his jeans. The top button was undone, and in typical male fashion the tips of his fingers were tucked into his waistband. An inch beneath his fingers, Sue noted the way the denim fit his package.

Yup, extra-large.

She swallowed and let her gaze follow the length of his body. The sight of his muscled thighs and calves encased in denim brought on a sigh. His feet were at least size twelve, and beautifully sculpted. His second toe extended a bit longer than his big toe. Wasn't that a sign of a person being oversexed?

She wondered what it would be like to run her foot across his. Then she frowned. Paul's foot fetish tendencies must have been contagious.

Taking a deep breath, she gazed back up at his body. When she got past his chest, she saw a flutter of his pulse at the base of his throat. Looking up slowly, she admired the line of his jaw. But his lips were his best feature. Full and sensual. She knew how gentle they felt against her mouth. How would they feel other places? She let that thought warm her insides before she visually moved up to his blue eyes—

Oh, Hades. His eyes were open. She'd been caught ogling for sure, and from the heat in his gaze, he'd pretty much pegged her thoughts.

"You should . . . leave," she said.

"Or I could stay." His voice came out sleepy, husky, and so sexy.

He stretched out a hand for her. "Let me show you why I should stay."

CHAPTER SIXTEEN

When Sue placed one knee on the mattress, Jason's heart soared. When her hand hesitantly met his, he felt as if he'd been waiting on this moment all his life. He gave her a gentle tug and she came. Closer, then closer still. One of his hands went to her waist, the other to her shoulder. He gathered her beside him and pressed his lips to her closed eyelids.

Slowly, he kissed his way to her mouth. She tasted exotic, a bit like chocolate and a bit like wine—and entirely like Sue. Inhaling, he filled his senses with her fruity shampoo and her warm womanly scent.

Wanting to savor every touch, wanting to be the best she'd ever had, he brushed his tongue over her lips. She opened her mouth for him and he slipped his tongue inside.

While he made love to her with his lips, he slipped his hand inside her pajama top. She moaned when he cupped her breast. The soft weight filled his hand perfectly.

When she shifted in his arms, his first thought was he'd lost her, and he wanted to scream, No! He'd beg if he had to. But then her subtle shift brought her closer, and she pressed her palm against his chest to touch, to feel, to tempt.

As her soft hand moved over his pecs, over his abdomen, he passed his thumb over her tight nipple. Wanting to taste the bud, he shifted his kisses to her neck, lower to the V in her shirt. Her hands slipped around his back.

He slid his knee between her thighs. A soft feminine moan filled the room and played like music to his ears. Her hips rose from the mattress as she pressed the mound of her sex against his leg. Pulling his hand from under her shirt, he worked on unbuttoning her top. One, two, three.

His kisses moved to the opening in her shirt; his mouth watered to taste what his hands had touched. His breath caught as he gazed upon her breasts. Her nipples, a soft pink, puckered into tight little orbs that begged to be savored.

She arched her back, bringing her breasts closer to his lips. He gazed into her eyes, wanting to tell her how beautiful she was, wanting to tell her thank you for the precious gift she offered. Somehow he wanted to make right all the wrongs that had ever happened to her. He wanted to take the image of her standing beside the grave of her father and burn it. Never did he ever want to see her looking so hurt, so broken.

He lowered his lips to her left breast, took the tight nipple into his mouth and . . . and his freaking cell phone started ringing in the other room.

Sue stiffened. He felt her draw air into her lungs.

"Ignore it." He breathed the words against the roundness of her breasts. When she didn't, he raised his head to look at her. Her startled gaze met his.

Don't do this, a voice inside his head warned. *Don't risk it.*

"I want you, Sue. I want you more than anything. And I know you want me."

"I know. I want this. I just don't . . . I'm sorry," she said. She butt-scooted off the bed. Her pajama shirt remained open, her beautiful breasts a feast for his eyes. As she rose she said, "Your phone." She knotted her fingers in her loose, bicycling-bear pajamas and drew the cotton over her chest. Her next words came out in a barely audible whisper, "Please, go."

He opened his mouth to beg her to reconsider, but one look into her eyes and he knew it was too late. One look

into her eyes and the fear pooling in her baby blues ricocheted right into him.

"I want you, Sue," he repeated.

Wasn't this against everything he believed in, to want
something so much that he gave the person power over
him? Yes. And so he bounced off the bed and left.

His phone had stopped ringing, but it started again by
the time he reached the table. Snatching it from beside the
fake poop, Jason told himself to be civil. "This better be
fucking good." That was as civil as he could be.

"Did I interrupt something?" the familiar voice on the
line chuckled. "It's Langley at the precinct. Stewart said you
called in a couple of licenses?"

"Five hours ago."

"Sorry. Do you want the info or not?"

No, he didn't want it. His dick throbbed. His balls felt like
walnuts. His gaze shot to the bedroom door. What he
wanted was Sue.

He reached into his jeans to find a position less painful.
"Can I call you back?"

"Yeah, but I think you want to hear this."

He closed his eyes and pushed his desire back. "Spill it."

"The Caddy is registered to a Gerald Roberts." Langley
read the address.

"I thought this was supposed to be good?"

"Chill," Langley snapped. If the man had been standing
in front of him, Jason would have cold-cocked him. Instead, he took a deep breath, then turned around and dug
through a kitchen drawer until he found a pen and something to write on.

"Okay, give me the address again." Jason wrote Granny
Cucumber's address down, but he wasn't sure what he was
going to do with the information.

"And the Saturn?" He thumped his pen on the counter.

"This is the interesting one."

"Fuck it, Langley, just give it to me!"

"I must have really interrupted something good."

Jason drew in a sharp breath.

"Okay, the car was reported stolen around 6:00 tonight. It's registered to a Richard Andrews. Gomez and his partner took the report. The wife was raving mad, saying she thought her husband's long-lost buddy who'd borrowed the car had stolen it himself and was just saying it disappeared from some gallery's parking lot."

"Where did it come up stolen from?" Jason asked.

"Galleria area. Gomez spoke to the friend, some down-on-his-luck artist. Supposedly he went to the gallery trying to get the owner to take some of his paintings on consignment. While he was unloading, he left the keys in the trunk, and when he came back, the car was missing. According to Gomez, he seemed to be telling it straight."

Jason wrote down the name of the car's owners in case he wanted to talk to them. "Any leads on the car yet?"

"We were hoping you had some. Did you get a look at the driver?"

"No. It was almost dark, and the car has tinted windows. It seemed to be tailing me."

"You got some case going down that someone might be following you?"

"No. But I was with a friend who's picked up a stalker."

"A friend . . . or a good friend?" Langley asked.

"Just do your job."

"Ah, come on, Dodd. Throw a married guy a bone. You single guys get to have all the fun. The least you could do is share a little. Is she hot? Got a set of tits on her?"

"You tell me about your wife's tits and I'll tell you about my aunt Betty's." Of course, he didn't have an aunt Betty.

"You're a real pain in the ass, Dodd."

"Let me know if you get something on the car." Jason hung up.

His gaze shot to the hall that led to Sue's bedroom. What would they be doing right now if his phone hadn't rung? Would he be buried inside her? Holding her after the passion they'd spent? His pants were tight again.

Looking down at the paper in his hands, he turned it over, hoping it wasn't important. His gut clenched when he saw it was a receipt from Victoria's Secret.

Sue's animal-printed pajamas didn't look like anything that came from the sexy lingerie store. He checked the date and found the purchase was made a couple of weeks ago. Had Sue bought something to wear for the doctor? Had she worn it for him?

Great! Just the piece of information he needed to call this night a total screwup.

Sue's alarm went off at seven. She hit snooze twice. Last night she had tossed and turned enough to get an aerobic pulse rate going. If it wasn't for her grandfather's appointment, she'd pull the covers over her head.

Oh yeah, she needed a veg day, a whole twenty-four hours of breaking every rule in the book. Hibernating under the sheets until the smell of her own breath brought her out of a dead sleep. Eating chocolate for lunch and Cheetos for dinner. Looking at old albums with pictures of her and her dad, and having one of those cathartic crying jags. Maybe watching chick flicks, reading an entire romance novel. And depending on how good the novel was, getting out the electronic equipment that made her feel less deprived.

"Damn! Damn! Damn!" The fact she'd just broken her no cussing rule proved how badly she needed a veg day.

Had she really been going to give in last night? Yup, she had. And she'd been saved by the bell. Good old AT&T. If Jason hadn't gotten that call . . . as Kathy so poetically put it, Sue would have joined the fornicating masses. Forcing a deep breath, she felt her morning haze begin to defog.

Had the call last night been from his girlfriend—the one who'd called him at his house yesterday? She shook herself. What was wrong with her? She hadn't even broken up with her married boyfriend, and here she was considering getting involved with another guy who had a girlfriend.

Possibly had a girlfriend, she told herself, admitting she didn't know for sure.

She jerked back the covers and got up. Cracking open the door, she caught the smell of coffee wafting down the hall. Coffee?

She shouldn't be surprised, not after the killer grilled cheeses he'd whipped up for lunch yesterday. But this was another reason not to get involved with him. A woman should never date a man whose domestic skills outmatched her own. Of course, for her, that pretty much cut out 99 percent of the male population. Good thing she wasn't picky. Oh yeah, she'd go for just about anything: married car thieves, bank robbers, and then there was Collin.

Don't go there.

The smell of coffee filled her nose again. A hot cup before a shower would be heavenly. Listening and not sensing Jason's presence, she decided to go for it. If he got within a few feet of her, she could always breathe on him. Her morning breath would knock him cold.

She tiptoed down the hall. Hitchcock looked up from his spot on the table, where he sipped from a coffee cup.

Not believing it, Sue went over and, sure enough, the cup held a small amount of coffee with lots of cream. Jason had served Hitchcock his morning brew.

Sue gave her feline his morning ear rub, then filled a mug for herself, added cream, and was mid-hall when she heard footsteps. Was she ready to face him? Heck no. Did she have a choice? No.

Deep breath. She could do this. Just a quick hello and "I'll be ready in a snap."

Slowly she turned around, prepared to meet temptation. Prepared to have her pulse rushing at the sight of him, maybe without his shirt, maybe with his hair still damp from the shower. But—what the hell?

No temptation.

It wasn't Jason. Not unless his hair had grown dark,

shaggy, and he'd acquired that paunch she'd wanted to find on him yesterday.

Sue's frown grew.

It wasn't this man's extra thirty pounds or the missed hair appointment that unnerved her. It was the fact that he had her computer in his hands. And Mr. Needs-a-Haircut had his gaze on her front door. Was she being robbed?

"Stop right there!" She set her coffee down and ran across the room to barricade the door. Holding her arms out and her chin high, she attempted to look like a force not to be reckoned with. This was not easy to pull off when wearing pink bicycling-bear pajamas.

The man lowered her computer from the front of his face. "Excuse me, but I need to get this to my car." He seemed awfully calm for a robber.

"Jason?" Sue yelled, suspicious. She pointed a finger at the man holding her computer. "Who are you and what do you think you're doing with my computer?"

"I'm Bob. And this is kind of cumbersome."

"Sue. It's okay." Jason appeared behind the seeming computer thief. "I meant to talk to you about this last night."

"Talk to me about what?"

"We need to figure out who sent that e-mail."

"We *know* who sent it," Sue said. "The person who wants to kill me sent the e-mail."

Jason's grim expression darkened. "We need to know his name."

"Details. That's just details!" Her gaze slapped back on Bob. "Take it back in the study."

"Sue, we have to do this," Jason said. "I brought my laptop over last night. It's got all the bells and whistles. You can check your e-mail. You can use it until they finish. And Bob's going to fix your computer while he's checking it out."

Thinking with a caffeine-free brain so early in the morning wasn't easy, but Sue tried. "No one but Mr. Howard, my computer wizard, has ever touched my computer. It's old, it's temperamental, and requires TLC."

"Bob here will be tender. Won't you, Bob?" Jason said.

"Tender," the man repeated, his meat-hook hands curled around her PC. The unit slipped a few inches.

Sue and Jason lunged at the same time, bumping into each other. Mr. Tender caught the computer. Jason caught Sue. Held her practically chest to chest.

His hair appeared freshly-showered damp. He smelled of toothpaste and coffee, both of which she needed desperately. She stepped back.

"You want this freak caught, don't you?" he said.

"Yes, but—"

"Then let me do what I have to do." Jason held up his hands. "If something happens to your computer, I'll hold myself personally responsible. I'll buy you a new computer."

"I don't want a new computer."

"Sue." He took a step closer. "It's your safety I'm worried about. Computers are a dime a dozen, but I'm certain the Sue Finley mold was broken right after you graced the earth."

Even mad, she couldn't ignore the compliment.

"Please?" He straightened the collar of her pajama top. "I'll even buy you chocolate today."

"Excuse me," Bob muttered. "You two are mighty sweet, but this is heavy. And I'm trying to be tender."

Sue backed away from the door. Then she swung around on the balls of her feet, grabbed her coffee, and called over her shoulder, "My grandfather's appointment is in two hours. And if something happens to my computer, it'll be your prostate that needs to be checked!"

CHAPTER SEVENTEEN

"I'm not really superstitious, but I've written every book I've sold on that computer. Okay, I *am* superstitious. I went to a fortune-teller . . ."

Jason sat in the front seat of Sue's Honda, watching her drive as she chatted. Or rattled. This was more than a chat.

He wasn't sure what had her so uptight. Unless it was the same thing that tied him in knots? Her outfit didn't help. The light blue, snug-fitting capri pants and cotton sweater matched the color of her eyes and fit her body like shrink-wrap.

His gaze traveled up that masterpiece of a body to her face. She'd tried to cover the dark circles under her eyes with makeup. She hadn't slept any better than he had. If his phone hadn't interrupted them, they probably wouldn't have had any more sleep, but they'd have been a hell of a lot more relaxed.

"Anyway," she continued, "I didn't really believe it be-cause . . ." Today she wore her hair down and every few minutes pushed it behind her ears. She had nice ears. Small, dainty . . . sexy. Yeah, she had sexy ears.

Out of left field came a mental picture of the foot doctor running his tongue inside Sue's dainty, sexy ear. Grinding his teeth, Jason stared out the rearview mirror, checking for gold Saturns. He needed to forget about the foot doctor. Last night he'd spent hours chasing similar visions out of his head. Never had he suffered jealousy for the women he dated. Hell, he normally liked them experienced and well practiced. It was safer that way.

"Does that work for you?" she asked.

"Does what work for me?" If it had anything to do with himself and Sue naked, he felt certain it worked.

"The cover?"

"What cover?" He glanced out at the side-view mirror again.

"I said we'd tell them that you were just a friend of a friend. No. We probably should just say you're friends with Chase. Yeah, that's better."

He was both lost and disappointed that her plan didn't involve getting naked. "Tell who?"

"My grandparents." She shot him an annoyed look. "We'll say that you ran over a board with nails in it last night on the way to feed their animals. Or maybe you ran out for cat food and that's when you ran over it. Yeah, that sounds better."

She brushed her hair back again, giving him a peek at her right ear. He felt his arousal grow. Freaking hell, when had he gotten an ear fetish?

"And when you woke up this morning, you had a flat. Because you were staying at Lacy's house you called me. I agreed to take you to get a tire. But we'll say I didn't want to make two trips, so I insisted you come with me and after I take them home I'm taking you to get a tire." She finally took a breath, but it was a short one. "Where do you normally buy tires?"

Jason shook his head, finding her conversation harder and harder to follow. "Why?"

"Why what?" she asked.

He held out his hands. "Why are you making all this up?"

"They don't know about the rat, and I don't want them to. What size tires do you take?"

Laughing, he stared at her. "Why don't you just tell them I'm a friend? This isn't a novel; you don't need a whole plot."

She cut her gaze to him. "You don't know my grandparents. If I tell them you're just a friend they won't believe it. They'll think we're dating. And if we don't have our stories straight, they'll catch us in a lie. They're in their eighties but sharper than toothpicks."

He stared at the tiny, sexy, gold hoop earrings she wore. "What would be so bad about them thinking we're dating?"

"We're not." She refocused on the road.

Disappointment built in his chest. "I know. It's the whole tattoo-Pap smear-Pope schedule. But I was hoping after last night—"

"Last night didn't happen." She turned a corner too fast and frowned. "If they thought we were dating, you'd be interrogated. And not the nice kind of interrogation, but torture. And if you passed their tests, they'd bring out all my nude baby pictures to embarrass me."

Ha! He shouldered back in his seat. "How bad is the torture? Because the nude pictures might be worth it." The smile he shot her earned him one in return.

But it faded. "I'm serious." She pulled into a driveway of the white brick one-story home and then got out of her car. "Just remember, you're a friend of a friend and you had a flat."

A flat tire. But his memory scattered when she walked in front of him and his gaze caught the gentle sway of her backside.

He followed her to the door. He'd follow her anywhere.

She knocked. "Oh, and if you value your life, don't eat anything my grandmother offers."

"Why?" He ran his finger over the curve of her right ear, and she swatted his hand back.

"She poisons people."

"She what?"

"Accidentally, of course. And if my grandfather asks you to look at his roach collection, say no."

"His what?" Jason blinked. "Your grandfather smokes pot?"

Her mouth dropped open, and she laughed. Damn pretty laugh, too. He had the strongest desire to kiss her.

But then the door opened and a man who looked like an elderly version of Kramer on *Seinfeld* stood there. His light blue eyes, eyes that resembled Sue's, homed in on Jason like two sniper rifles taking aim.

"Hi." Sue stood on her tiptoes and kissed the man's cheek.

The sweetness with which Sue delivered that kiss made Jason jealous.

The feeling must have been mutual, for the man, whom Sue quickly introduced as Terrence White, her grandfather, seemed not so friendly.

Sue must have noticed the man's stern interest in Jason, because she began to fidget. And damn if Jason didn't feel a bit like fidgeting himself. He hadn't been checked out by a father figure in years. He hadn't missed this type of perusal, either. Father figures weren't keen on foster kids.

The tapping of Sue's sandal on the porch filled the silence. "Jason is a friend of Chase. He's pet-sitting, and he went out to get cat food and ran over a nail. After his coffee this morning, he discovered he had a flat tire and called me to take him to get a new tire."

The man's gaze still didn't ease up, but finally he looked at Sue. "Where were you going to buy this tire?"

Jason almost laughed.

Sue grew pale. Her mouth opened but nothing came out.

"Mmm," the old man said, and his keen gaze shot back to Jason. "So, you're dating my granddaughter, are you?"

Now Jason couldn't stop from laughing, though he got it under control when Mr. White didn't seem to appreciate the humor.

Jason offered his hand. "Nice to meet you, sir."

Sue finally spoke. "We're not dating."

"Yeah, and I'm not going in to have my prostate checked and be asked to cough, either." Grandpa eyed her.

Sue started to flush. "Where's Grandma?"

"In the bedroom. Her bra broke. She wants you to fix it. She also wants you to comb the back of her hair. She says there's a hole in it."

Sue moved past them and went into the house. Her grandfather's gaze scrubbed down Jason like sandpaper, ending and staying on Jason's shoes. Jason glanced down and wondered if the man had something against Reeboks.

Finally, Sue's grandpa raised his eyes. "You the foot doctor?"

That explained the shoe inspection. "No. I really am friends with Chase."

One of the old man's bushy eyebrows rose. "And I suppose you're really not dating my Susie, either?"

Jason considered how to answer. "Well, sir, I've asked, but she turned me down."

Surprise pulled at the man's eyes. "Must have stung like the dickens."

Jason fought back another chuckle. "Yes, sir. It did."

The man's gaze did another cross-examination. "You don't look much like a boy who gives up."

"I'm not," Jason admitted.

Mr. White moved away from the door, motioning for Jason to follow. "Susie turned you down, but she brought you today. Don't make much sense."

"Like you said. I don't give up."

The man stopped in the middle of the entryway. "I may look like an ol' buzzard, but I'm not about to let anyone hurt one of my girls."

Jason didn't flinch. "I wouldn't think of hurting Sue."

The man crossed his arms over his concave chest. "Chase is that cop fellow, right?"

"Yes, sir."

He stroked his chin between his thumb and forefinger. "You a cop, too?"

When Jason nodded, something changed in the man's expression. "What's going on?"

The directness of the question had Jason's neck itching. "What do you mean?"

"I just talked to Susie's mother. She let something slip.

Then she tried to cover it up, but she's as bad at lying as her daughter. Maybe you can clear things up for me."

Discomfort crawled around Jason's chest. Sue had asked him not to mention the rat. "What's that, sir?"

"Something about Susie receiving a threat."

Jason hesitated. "Maybe you should ask Sue."

"So that's why you're here, huh?" Worry filled the old man's eyes. "Is someone trying to hurt my girl?"

Jason shifted his shoulders. "I . . ."

The man held up his hand. "Don't say any more. Susie has obviously asked you not to. And I don't want her grandma to hear. But you take care of Susie. A more precious angel doesn't exist."

"I will." Jason decided right then that he liked the old man, even if the man didn't like him.

Sue's grandfather's gaze pinched. "You sleeping at her place?"

Jason considered his answer. "On the sofa."

"Stay on the sofa."

"Grandpa?" Sue called out. "Did you take your vitamin C this morning?"

"Yup!" Her grandpa stepped into the living room.

Jason followed, and something about the scent of bacon and Lemon Pledge made the house smell like a home. When Jason's gaze lit on Sue, his steps faltered. She stood behind an elderly woman, as if checking the zipper of the woman's dress. Sue's hands moved gently across the woman's back, the same gentleness reflected on Sue's expression. For some crazy reason the sight made Jason's chest ache.

"You should throw this one away." Sue patted her grandmother's shoulder.

"Nothing wrong with that bra," the lady said. "It's barely ten years old." She passed a hairbrush over her shoulder. "They don't make them like they used to." After Sue took the brush from her grandmother and ran it through the thin gray hair, Sue said, "Perfect."

A rush of emotion went straight to Jason's heart. Sue's devotion to these people was so alive it crowded the room.

Sue leaned over and kissed the woman's cheek. "You look beautiful." From Sue's tone, there was no doubt she meant it. The moment could have been filmed as a Hallmark commercial.

Which explained why he felt like an intruder. Hallmark moments weren't part of Jason's life.

Then, he wasn't sure why, he remembered being young and hearing his classmates talk about their grandparents. He'd always wondered what it might have been like to have had some older couple who cared about his sorry ass. Someone who took him fishing or cooked his favorite meals. That crowded feeling hit again. And a part of him wanted to turn and run.

Then he remembered Terrence saying, "Take care of my girl." Sue needed him.

Sue's grandmother looked up, studied Jason with the same intensity that her husband had used minutes earlier. "I guess that's your fellow."

"He's not my fellow," Sue said.

The woman nodded. "Name's Rose White. You dating my Susie?"

"I told you, he's a friend of Chase's. He had a flat tire." Sue's gaze met Jason's with an I-told-you-so glare if he'd ever seen one.

"Name's Jason Dodd." He nodded. "A pleasure to meet you."

"I'm gonna show him my roach collection." Sue's grandfather motioned Jason forward.

Jason glanced at Sue. The last guy who'd shown him his roach collection was spending two to five in Huntsville prison.

Sue laughed. "Cockroaches." Then she looked at her grandpa. "Can you show him when we get back? We should probably go."

"Cockroaches?" Jason whispered in Sue's ear as they walked to the car.

She nodded.

When they got to Sue's Honda, Mrs. White eyed him up and down. "You haven't robbed a bank, have you?"

Jason almost laughed, but oddly enough she seemed serious. "No, ma'am. Never."

He opened the door for the woman. She had one foot in the car when her wrinkled face gazed up at him. "You don't fancy ladies' underwear, do you?"

That had to be a trick question. He looked at Sue for help.

She moved between him and her grandmother. "Isn't it a nice day?"

It was two o'clock when they headed back to Sue's place. In a few minutes she'd be back home, where she'd hole up in her study. Away from Jason, away from temptation. He sat next to her, watching her drive, a pensive shimmer in his eyes.

She tapped her fingers against the wheel. "I wish you'd stop staring."

He stretched his arm out, his hand on the edge of her headrest as his fingers played with her ear. Yet, even as he took the time to touch her, to send her looks that could make panty hose unravel, he'd never stopped acting like a cop. His gaze continuously moved to the mirror to see if anyone followed them. Even when they'd waited in the doctor's office, he'd sat facing the door so he could see who came in.

Her hands tightened on the wheel, and she stared over her dash. She hadn't realized it until this morning, but subconsciously today had been some kind of a weird trial by fire: Throw Jason in the lion's den of her crazy family and see if he'd run for his life. The tactic had scared more boys away than Sue cared to admit.

Jason hadn't run. In fact, he'd seemed unaffected by the wacky morning. He'd even been sweet to her grandparents.

She, on the other hand, felt as if Jason had just been given a peek into her private world—a world that included prostate exams, dead roaches pinned to red velvet, and her naked baby pictures exposing the birthmark between her left thigh and buttock.

Which maybe explained her current resentment. The man kept his private world under lock and key. Had she gotten to see a naked baby picture of him? No.

That did it. The next time she visited her grandparents, she was confiscating that album. And Sue was super glad she'd managed to whisk Jason out of the house before he was in danger of getting his stomach pumped. Her grandma had just started to move toward the fridge when Sue jerked the album from his hands and dragged him to the door.

On the way home, they'd stopped off for fast food. While they ate, Sue had asked him about his mother. He'd changed the subject to the movies he enjoyed watching. Action-adventure. Who would have guessed?

When Sue asked him about where he'd gone to elementary school, he'd started talking about a drug case he'd worked a couple years ago. Interesting conversation, but it told her nothing about Jason Dodd.

"You're getting quiet again," he said.

"Long day," she muttered.

She glanced at him. He held a milk shake, running his fingers over the condensation on the cup. Then, as if he sensed her staring, he turned.

She jerked her gaze back to the road, where it belonged, especially considering she'd just missed her turn into her neighborhood.

"You still have that birthmark?" A smile sounded in his voice.

"I wouldn't know."

"I'd be happy to check."

"In your dreams."

"You got that right."

Silence hummed with her car's air conditioner. She saw him again checking the side mirror.

"You haven't seen anyone following us today, have you?"

"No."

"Good," she said.

"Your grandparents seem . . ." He looked from the mirror to her.

"Seem what?" Sue squared her shoulders, ready for a fight.

"That they appear very healthy for their age," he finished sincerely. "And I guess they know how lucky they are to have you."

Her spine relaxed. "I'm the lucky one."

"All of you are." There seemed to be some hidden emotion in his statement, and she was about to ask about it when he continued. "I should probably tell you that your grandfather knows about the rat incident."

Suddenly seeing the stop sign, Sue slammed on the brakes and then shot him an accusing look. "You told him?"

"No. You asked me not to. He said your mother let something slip and then tried to cover it up, but . . . but that she's as bad at lying as you are." He grinned when he said the last.

"I lie way better than my mom!" Sue gave a gulp of frustration and recommenced driving. "Now Grandpa is going to worry. I told her not to say a word. Dad burn it! Sometimes she . . ." She clamped her mouth shut. Jason wasn't interested in her mother's faults. And if he was, she wasn't so sure she'd tell him, not when he believed in a closed book policy for himself.

"She what?"

"Nothing." Silence returned to the car.

"He doesn't know everything." Jason fit his cup in a holder. "And I think the idea of my being around put him at ease."

"He'll still worry. I'll bet you a hundred bucks I have a message on my answering machine from him when we get home."

"I could talk to him again." He reached over, his fingers moving in her hair.

"No. It won't help," she said. "But thanks for offering."

Silence fell again. Sue toyed with the idea of turning on the radio and tried not to think about how Jason's touch was turning her on.

"Did your grandparents help raise you?" He gave the mirror another look.

"I always lived with my mother, but yeah, they were a big part of my life."

"Because of your dad's death?" He shifted, bumping his knee on the dash.

"You can adjust your seat," she said and realized he was doing it again. He was rummaging around her past when he wouldn't give even a hint about his own. Couldn't he share just a little bit?

He rubbed his knee. "How old were you when your dad died?"

Instead of answering, she tossed a question out herself. "Do you see your mother often?"

Her implication hung heavy, but she didn't care. If he wanted to know about her, he'd have to—

"I . . . uh . . ." He pulled his hand from her neck and hit his knee again on the dash. Then he reached down as if to adjust the seat.

Sure, she completely understood a reluctance to talk about painful memories, but he hadn't minded digging around in her painful memory bank. And she'd let him.

Pulling into her driveway, she cut off the engine and waited to see if he planned to answer her. Instantly, she remembered what Kathy had said last night. Kissing any toad was difficult, but kissing one you cared about was risky. Was that why dating Paul hadn't scared her? She knew she would never get hurt, because she hadn't cared?

Sue reached for her purse, wanting to run from the answer, run from the truth that would become evident if she let herself think about it. Jason caught her hand.

"She lives here in northwest Houston. I see her once a week."

He'd shared! Panic shot to her chest.

"That's what you asked, wasn't it? About Maggie."

"Yeah." And why had she wanted him to give, to share? Because then she could justify giving more of herself. Giving him her body, her soul.

Her heart.

The panic, already at an uncomfortable level, shot up past uncomfortable. Then her panicked mind shot to her ex-husband, the pain, the betrayal. Why had she thought she could start dating? She'd been much safer when she kept that door closed. Locked. Could she put on the brakes now? Lock Jason out?

CHAPTER EIGHTEEN

Jason watched Sue get out of the car as if she was running from something. And since he was the only thing she'd left in the car, that something had to be him.

He raked a palm over his face and crawled out of her Honda. "Are you going to lock it?"

She headed to the mailbox and, without looking at him, pointed her clicker and clicked.

She'd gotten quiet again as soon as they'd gotten to the hamburger joint, at which he'd purposely not eaten one of her fries. But had he said or done something else wrong? Was she upset about Bob taking her computer? Was she worried about breaking up with the foot doctor?

He didn't like her going. And he wasn't finished trying to talk her out of it, either. Frankly, he didn't want Sue within a mile of the man. The fact that she'd bought something slinky and sexy and had probably worn it for the jerk still chapped Jason's ass. The fact that the doc's psycho wife could be the one who was out to hurt Sue took that chapping to third-degree burns.

Opening and closing the mailbox as if it was empty, she headed toward the door.

Jason glanced at his watch. It was only two o'clock, and they weren't supposed to meet the doctor until seven. He had five hours to convince her not to go. And if they got that out of the way, maybe they could find something else to do. Something a lot more fun.

He watched her scoot across the driveway and wondered if her lapse into silence was due to the fact that she, like him, was thinking about last night. The memory of it had flickered through his mind a thousand or so times off and on during the day. Which meant he'd had an off and on problem all day. And at the most inopportune times, too! Like when he'd been sitting next to her in the doctor's waiting room and her leg had brushed up against his. That was all it took, and just like that he'd remembered unbuttoning her bicycling teddy bear pajamas and taking her breasts into his mouth. He'd remembered how she'd tasted, how she'd felt against him, how close she'd come to giving herself to him. Suddenly, bam! He'd had the problem. A noticeable problem, too. He'd had to snatch the one and only magazine from the table to hide the evidence.

Unfortunately, the magazine had been for lactating mothers.

Of course, the article about how to use a breast pump had taken care of his little problem right quick.

Seeing Sue at the front door, he hurried his steps to catch up with her. She fumbled with her keys. Was she nervous about their being alone? Nervous could be good. It meant she was thinking about them being together, which meant she thought it would happen.

She dropped the keys and reached down to snag them up.

Then again, nervous could be bad. Bad, because her nerves could be more than just the average first-time anxiety. Her "not settling" comment had jabbed at his curiosity off and on between his other issues. He'd considered talking to her about it, but talk was cheap; he'd rather just prove her wrong. If he could simply get her in bed, she'd see how good it could be. How good *they* would be.

Okay, he knew it wasn't just the sex that mattered. But they got along, laughed, and could talk about anything. On top of that, he genuinely liked her. Hell, he "got" Sue, understood her and respected her more than any woman he'd dated. Her quirkiness intrigued him: the way she tried to come across as tough as leftover steak but passed out vitamin C because she worried about everyone getting a cold. And he saw the goodness in her by the way she took time for her grandfather's prostate exams and to comb out the holes in her grandmother's hair.

When her second attempt to fit the key in the door didn't work, he took her keys and opened the door for her.

"Thanks." She hurried inside.

She scooped up her cat and headed straight to the counter to hit some buttons on her phone. Her gaze shot to him. "Three calls. The first one reads, 'Restricted.'"

Jason came up behind her and rested his hand on her shoulder. He wasn't sure if the phone company had started tracking her calls yet. "Play it."

The machine rewound. He felt her tense and pulled her and her cat closer.

"You've won a free vacation!"

"Thank God." Relaxing, Sue rubbed her face with her cat's.

The sales pitch ended and the next call came on. "Hey, it's Kathy. Just thought I'd see how the wart inspection is going." The redhead's laugh echoed from the machine. "Oh, he's not going to be listening to this is he? Oh shit."

Jason leaned over her shoulder, tilted his head down, and met her gaze. "Wart inspection?"

"Inside joke." Sue slipped out of reach.

"Anyway," Kathy continued. "If your ficus plant needs a break, call me. I promise not to quote Dr. Phil."

The line clicked off and then on again.

"Susie . . ." Her grandfather's voice came through the line. "Call your grandpa when you get home. Just want to make sure you're okay."

Sue looked at Jason. "Told you he'd call."

"And Sue," her grandfather continued in a lower voice,

"what's this your grandma's saying about Jason reading some breastfeeding magazine? Personally, I kind of liked the guy, but I could have misjudged him."

Sue grinned. Her smile, her first in a while, was almost worth being the butt of the joke.

"Hey, it was the only magazine available." No way was he going to explain his hard-on. From experience, women generally didn't understand.

Sue picked up the phone and called her grandfather. While she talked, Jason moved in front of her case of DVDs, but he didn't miss her defending him about the magazine.

"It was the only magazine available! He's not a weirdo."

Her defense of him felt really good.

When he heard her hang up, he looked back. "Why don't we watch a movie?" The thought of them cozying up on the sofa felt right.

Her gaze shot to the sofa, as if she thought the same thing he did, but from her expression he figured cozying up wasn't on her agenda.

She set her cat down. "I need to write."

"I need to feed my cat."

"I'll do it." She took off down the hall. "I don't need to be interrupted."

Definitely, she was running from him. He watched her go.

Disappointment burned in his chest, but he fought it. He needed to make a few more calls himself. He'd been on the phone off and on all day; he'd spoken with Steven, Chase's friend who'd done the background check on the foot doctor. But he still hadn't talked to his buddy, Carlos, a sergeant at the Hoke's Bluff division about bringing Paul in for questioning tonight after Sue—if he couldn't talk her out of going—met the married Toe Jerker. Because the case did come under Hoke's Bluff's jurisdiction, Jason's hands were pretty much tied. If he tried to bend the rules too much, he could get his ass in a crack. Jason preferred trying to keep his ass out of cracks. Mostly because he seemed to get it there without ever bending the rules.

Fifteen minutes later, he'd started to punch in Carlos's number when his phone rang.

"Dodd," he answered, without looking at the caller ID.

"What kind of crap are you up to?"

"Excuse me?" Jason tried to recognize the voice.

"It's Brian Peters."

Okay, Jason understood the hostile tone. He and Chase had butted heads last year with Brian about a case they'd all been assigned to work. Peters didn't like to be proven wrong. So much so that he'd left their department.

"I just heard you and your partner are butting into my case again."

"What case?" Jason asked.

"The Paul Everts case," Brian shot back.

"The foot doctor?"

"Yeah. I heard ya'll ran a background check on him."

"We did," Jason agreed. "What kind of case are you working?"

Peters's voice was grim. "Homicide."

Sue sat at her desk, iPod on, doing a trick that a writing buddy had recommended, the power of deletion. The writer types her thoughts, concerns, or fears into her computer and then gets rid of them from her life the way a good writer takes out poorly written sentences; she simply deletes them.

Sue's fingers started moving . . . *Jason Dodd still feels like the perfect pair of jeans.*

Highlight. Delete.

He's kind to elderly women bearing cucumbers and to my grandparents. He even pretended to be interested in cockroaches.

Highlight. Delete.

I just happen to have a sexy black nightie hidden in my underwear drawer that I've never worn. Should I go see what Jason thinks about it?

Highlight. Delete! Delete! Delete!

It wasn't working. Blast deletion therapy!

Sue yanked off her earphones when she heard a knock at the door. If she didn't answer him, would he go away? She watched the door.

Jason opened it. His gaze fell on her old, outdated laptop.

"I told you that you could use mine." He ran a palm over his face.

She'd seen this gesture enough to know that it was a nervous tick. Writers noticed traits like that because they could use them. Her newest book's hero had already picked up the little habit.

In response to his comment she said, "I'll use it to do Internet research, but I can write on this."

He nodded, and his palm made another pass over his face. Harder. What could Jason be nervous about?

Oh, yeah. The meeting with Paul. "You're not going to talk me out of going. I have the right to face him."

Jason stepped inside her room. "Sue—"

"I'm going." She grabbed her stress ball.

Jason stepped closer and put his hand on her shoulder, gave it a squeeze. A caring squeeze. She looked up. He was nervous, giving her caring squeezes? She suddenly became suspicious.

"Did I get another phone call from that freak?"

"No," Jason said. "But I . . . I just got a call from HPD, a homicide detective. They found your doctor in his office this morning. Someone . . . someone shot him. Twice."

CHAPTER NINETEEN

"Paul? Someone *shot* him?" Sue blinked. "Is he dead?"

"He's in surgery. But if Homicide has been called in, it's bad."

Emotions raced through Sue like rats in a maze. Her breath lodged in her throat as her thoughts slapped against each other. Paul may have been a jerk, but he had a four-year-old son. If he died, another kid would grow up without his daddy. Her gaze shot to her photo album.

Then another thought hit so hard tears stung her eyes. This could indeed be her fault. Had someone shot Paul because of her?

She glanced up at Jason. "Do they know who did it?"

"No one in custody yet. But I'm sure his wife is being looked at."

Sue stared at the wall. Had Paul's wife shot him because she'd found out about their relationship? Did the wife know that Sue hadn't realized he was married? Probably not.

She stood, not sure what she was going to do or where she needed to go. She didn't go anywhere; she just stood there, bombarded by emotions: Anger at Paul for not telling her he was married. Anger at herself for not figuring it out. Sympathy for a four-year-old who might grow up with the same emptiness she'd known.

Jason cupped her chin in his hand and turned it so he could look at her. "You okay?"

She blinked away the beginning of tears and swallowed a lump of guilt. "Guess I should hold off shooting him in the kneecaps, huh?" That lump grew larger.

Jason leaned down and pressed his lips against her cheek. He didn't say he understood how she felt, but the gentleness of his kiss said it all. And now his gaze held so much tenderness that she was going to cry for sure.

"Go ahead." He pulled her against his chest. "I've got a clean shirt this time."

"That's not nice." She sniffled into his warm chest, and the tears came.

"Holding you feels nice." He held her tighter, but it wasn't a sexual embrace, just a caring one.

That's when she started crying for real, and she cried for a good solid minute. When she was done, she came up on her toes and kissed him on the cheek.

His eyes widened. "What's that for?"

"For being here. You didn't have to do any of this."

He ran the back of his hand across her cheek. "I'll stay here as long as you need me."

She wanted to believe that was true with all of her being, even though she knew Jason Dodd wasn't the staying kind of guy.

That night, Sue lay in bed, staring at her swinging-monkey pajamas. Jason was right; she had a theme of exercising animals. What did that say about her? Maybe Kathy should ask Dr. Phil.

Closing her eyes, she tried to relax, but her mind kept jumping from one fact to another. Someone wanted her dead. Her car-thieving, adulterous boyfriend—whom she hadn't had an opportunity to break up with—was in intensive care, possibly shot by the same person who wanted her dead. Top all of that off with the fact that her grandfather had called three times frantic with worry and concerned about Jason's fetish for lactating women, that her mother had called saying she wanted to introduce Elvis to her grandparents, and that Kathy had called to remind her that every toad had a few warts.

Jiminy Cricket, but who could expect her to sleep? She should be working on her second bottle of Merlot by now.

Her phone rang, and Sue sat straight up in bed. Every time before, Jason had come hurrying to her side, giving her the same instructions: If it was the stalker, she was to keep calm, talk slow, keep him on the line. He had told her he'd arranged to have a trace put on her phone, but she had to keep the bastard on the line long enough for the trace to kick in.

The phone kept ringing. Sue stared at the door, waiting for Jason to barge in. He wasn't coming.

Taking a deep breath, she answered. "Hello?"

"It's me." Jason's voice, deep and sexy, sounded over the receiver. Sue dropped back against her pillows.

She should have remembered that he'd called her last night. "What do you want?"

"That's a loaded question." He laughed, low and husky. "But I thought you might like to . . . talk."

Warmth washed over her. "And here I thought you called because you wanted more cereal."

"Trust me. That's not what I'm hungry for."

"There's granola bars in the cabinet." Sue pretended to misunderstand, though the truth was she understood him perfectly . . . and she was loving the conversation. What woman didn't want to be wanted? "I don't see where you put all that food you eat." She petted Hitchcock.

"I'm a growing boy." She didn't miss the double entendre.

She cleared her throat, making the scolding scratchy sound her mother used, but Jason continued, "And somebody ate all my dessert again tonight."

They'd gone out to a local diner for dinner. "Yeah, but you ate half of my omelet." She stroked Hitchcock from neck to tail.

"Hey, I waited until you stopped eating it. And I asked first."

She remembered, and she'd felt bad because she knew he'd done it because of her comments about the fries. But that didn't stop her from teasing him now.

"You should have ordered two desserts." She watched Hitchcock stretch.

"And miss out on the right to complain? Never."

"So you're a complainer, huh?"

Jason hesitated. "No. I usually get what I want."

"And what do you want?" The question slipped out before Sue could stop it.

"You. Naked. Willing."

Yup. She really should have stopped it.

She swallowed. Her pharynx caught on her tonsils and made a gulping noise. "Why don't you have a bowl of cereal instead? I bought the kind with an extra scoop of raisins." She pressed a hand to her forehead. He wanted sex, and she was offering him breakfast?

His laugh flowed through the phone. "Can you tell me why?"

"Because I *like* raisins. They're sweet and a little chewy."

"I mean, why are you in there and I'm out here, when we both want to be together?"

"You don't know what I want," she said. It was a lie, but self-preservation justified it.

"So you're saying you're not attracted to me?"

If she thought she could make him believe it, she'd lie. "No. I'm not saying that."

"Then why won't you sleep with me?"

"You're asking the wrong question," she said.

"I am?" He sounded genuinely puzzled.

"The question isn't why I won't sleep with you. It's why *should* I sleep with you?"

"Give me three minutes and I'll show you," he whispered.

"Three minutes? Boy, you're quick," she blurted.

His laughter rumbled. "Oh, that's just to convince you to stay for the show. The curtain wouldn't fall until morning—though there'd be a couple of intermissions, a standing ovation, and several grand finales. If you know what I mean."

Oh, she knew. She closed her eyes and tried not to imagine. "It's late. I should—"

"No," he said quickly. "Talk to me."

"About what? I think you've covered all the similes for sex and theater."

His laugh came again. Then she heard him draw in a deep breath. "About anything. Just talk to me."

She traced the edge of her down comforter, determined to cool herself off. "Have you called the hospital again?"

"Just a few minutes ago. He's still in the ICU."

"Have the police found his wife and son?"

"No, but they're looking."

She sat up. "Do you think the fact that the stalker hasn't called is a sign that it's her? His wife?"

"It looks suspicious. But I managed to get a description of her. She's only an inch taller than you. Do you think it could have been her trying to break in Saturday night?"

Sue tried to remember exactly what she'd seen. The images were a blur. "I could have sworn it was a man, so I think he was bigger. But maybe . . . I guess I could have just seen what I expected to see. I'm sorry I don't know for sure."

"Don't be sorry. You were scared." Jason hesitated. "At least now that the shooting took place in Houston I can get information and see that things get done right. I don't have to step on so many toes trying to get info from another precinct."

"Did they say if Paul was any better?" she asked.

She heard Jason shift on the leather sofa. "It looks as if he'll pull through."

"Good." The guilt sitting on her chest lightened.

"Do you care about him?" he asked. He sounded a bit nervous, but if so, he quickly covered the emotion with a joke. "Or are you just wondering how long before he's well enough so you can take out his knees?"

Sue thought about Paul, about their phone calls that always felt awkward, their kisses that left her feeling as if she was eating something sinful but not enjoying it. The kind when your hips called out, *Don't waste the calories on this!* Jeepers! She'd come so close to running off to Mexico with him to have flavorless sex. But her lack of attraction wasn't his fault.

Then she recalled how he'd lied to her about his marital status, played her for a fool. He deserved this, didn't he?

But then she remembered he had a son. Paul might deserve it, but that boy didn't.

"I don't want him to die."

"How close were you?"

She stared at the ceiling. "Obviously not too close. I didn't even know he was married."

"Did you sleep with him?"

She hadn't expected that question. Her first instinct was to tell Jason the truth, but then it felt awkward. "How is that relevant to the case?"

"I'm curious."

She traced the outline of a swinging monkey with her fingernail. "Curiosity killed the cat, you know."

"I'm not a cat . . . Did you sleep with him?"

"I think I'd better hang up."

"No," Jason said. "Wait! I'll change the subject. Tell me about your grandparents."

"What about them?"

"What was it like having them around as a child?"

Sue leaned back. "I guess like all grandparents. They thought I was perfect. I thought they were old. But when things . . . got bad, they were there. Sort of like a safety net."

"Bad?" When she didn't answer, he tried a different tack. "Sounds as if you were all close."

"What about *your* grandparents?" Sue asked, turning the tables. She waited, and his pause told her he didn't like being on the opposite side of the question.

"I, uh, didn't know mine." He let out a breath. "What did

your grandmother mean when she asked if I'd robbed a bank and if I liked women's underwear?"

"Nothing." Determined to dance around that subject, Sue asked, "How old is your mom?"

The question drew a pensive silence. Then: "Maggie is sixty-five."

"Why do you call her Maggie instead of Mom?"

He inhaled. "Let's talk about something different, okay?"

"Why?" she asked.

"Because I don't like talking about myself."

There was a surprise. "Why not?"

"Because I didn't come from the Brady Bunch, like you did."

Sue sat up. "The Brady Bunch?"

"Yeah."

She resented his statement. "Life wasn't perfect for me."

His tone softened. "I know it wasn't. You lost your father. I didn't mean to downplay his death, I just . . . Let's drop it, okay?"

"It wasn't just my father." Sue suddenly wanted to tell him, hoping he'd confide in her as well. "My mom lost it when my dad died."

"Lost it?"

"Yeah. She went to bed and stayed there. Most weeks she wouldn't even go grocery shopping. I would get into her purse and get money and go to the small grocery store down the block. We lived off Beanie Weenies." She paused, finding it odd that she felt compelled to tell Jason something she'd never told anyone else. But she did want to tell him.

"It was six months before my grandparents got wind of things. They were living in Austin and visited twice a month, but Mom would put on an act for them because . . ." Her throat grew tight. "Because she said if anyone knew how sick she was, they'd take me away from her."

Sue hesitated. "I'd lost my father, and for almost seven months I was so scared that I was going to lose my mom that I chewed my nails off."

She swallowed the knot in her throat. Jason didn't speak, but she could hear him breathing, so she knew he was still there.

"Then my grandparents showed up unannounced. They saw how things really were. They bought a house a block away and took care of both of us. They got Mom in therapy, and she got . . . better."

"Better?" he repeated, obviously hearing something different in her voice.

"On bad days, instead of going to bed she'd just drink a bottle of wine."

"She's an alcoholic?"

"I wouldn't call her that. But she uses wine as a crutch."

"That's what alcoholics do," he said.

"But she's stopped before. And she does off and on." Sue suddenly felt guilty for discussing her mom's issue. "Did you know there's nothing in life that four and three-fourth glasses of Merlot can't solve?"

"I'm sorry." Jason's voice was tight. "She deserves to have her butt kicked."

Sue heard the anger in his tone, and her protective instincts took over. "No. She's not . . . she wasn't a bad mother. She was depressed and grieving. She never meant to hurt me. And after a few months of counseling, she was a great mother. I mean, the whole PTA-and-homeroom kind of mother. She was still kooky, but other than being a hypochondriac who used an occasional bottle of Merlot to compensate, she was perfect. Still is."

"She abandoned you, Sue."

"Never," Sue snapped.

"Emotionally, she abandoned you."

"Only until she got herself picked back up. And seriously, she doesn't really drink all the time. Just when . . . when something is bothering her."

"You didn't deserve that. You lost your father and—"

"She lost him, too." Sue paused. "We both were hurting."

Silence filled the line. Sue began to wish she'd never told

Jason. Then she remembered why she had. "See? My child-hood wasn't an episode of the *Brady Bunch*, either. So what is it you're not telling me about you?" She considered going into the living room, but something told her he'd be more inclined to open up over the phone.

"Hey," she said. "I told you my secrets."

The line was silent. Finally: "Maggie isn't my real mother."

"You're adopted?" Sue realized how hungry she was to know about him.

"No. I was . . . a foster kid. Moved from home to home."

A wave of pain gripped Sue's heart. "What happened to your real parents?"

Another silence. "No. No more depressing subjects. Tell me something wonderful about yourself."

Sue wanted to pry deeper, but something about Jason's tone warned her to let it go. For now. Tomorrow would be a new day.

"What do you want to know?"

"Break my heart and tell me about your first date," he suggested.

"Oh, you won't have your heart broken. It wasn't won-derful."

"What happened?"

"My grandpa happened. He showed the boy his roach collection and threatened to pin him to a piece of velvet if he didn't behave. The boy wouldn't even hold my hand."

Jason chuckled. "I knew I liked your grandfather."

"So did I. Which was why I cold-cocked the guy when he started telling people my granddad was a roach-loving freak."

Jason laughed. "What about other boyfriends?"

"There weren't many after that. The boys were afraid of me," she admitted. "I mean, I was almost fourteen, and all my friends had already gotten hickeys and gone to at least second base with a guy. Here I was, never been kissed. At the time, I was convinced that the reason I wasn't . . . uh . . . bigger up top was because I didn't have the experience other girls did."

"You're fine up top," he said. His voice was husky again.

"Right." She didn't want to start on *that* conversation. "Anyway, it was bad. In fact, I was so livid and humiliated at the thought of facing all my friends, to keep from being embarrassed I got my mother's vacuum cleaner and gave myself a real dandy of a hickey."

His laugh vibrated through the line. "Damn. I've *so* lost my touch."

"Your touch?" she echoed.

"You made out with a vacuum cleaner, and yet won't give me the time of day."

"Hey, that vacuum cleaner was a better kisser than—"

"Is this another slur against my kissing talents?" Jason interrupted.

"No. But for the record, I think you complained first about *my* kissing talents. Remember that little chat you had with Chase in his kitchen on the Fourth?"

Jason laughed. "You should never believe anything a man says when he's thinking about punching a foot doctor in the face."

"So, you were jealous of Paul. Interesting."

"I'm not admitting anything," Jason growled. "Besides, we're not talking about the foot doctor anymore. We're talking about kisses. And what I want to know is: Are you finally admitting that you like my kisses?"

"I'm not admitting anything, either," she replied. She snuggled deeper in her pillow and tried not to think about how much she loved the kisses in question.

"Aah, Sue. You're killing me."

"If I'm killing you, why . . . why didn't you call me four months ago?" Her stomach muscles tightened while she awaited his response.

"Maybe I lost your number." His tone had lost its playfulness and now sounded cautious.

"Maybe I'm not blonde enough to fall for that." She fought a wave of disappointment.

"Is this why you won't sleep with me?"

"No," she said.

But then it hit her. In the beginning, his not calling her was exactly why she'd fought against getting involved with him. He'd rejected her; she didn't fancy letting him do it again. But now . . . now she couldn't give herself over to this until she knew they had a fighting chance of making it work. If she made love to Jason and he just walked out . . . Heck, she might be like her mom and go to bed for a year. She'd barely managed to survive Collin's betrayal. How would she survive Jason's?

"It's late," she said.

"It's not too late." His tone was seductive again. "Talk to me."

"Only if you tell me honestly why you didn't call me."

He didn't speak. She counted to three.

"Good night."

She hung up. And while her body yearned to give Jason everything he wanted—yearned for several hours, right up until she fell asleep—she knew she'd done the right thing. No giving in until she knew this was real.

"Three minutes. Three minutes is all I ask," Jason said. He looked up at Detective Brian Peters, who was standing outside the door where the doctor's wife waited.

He had gotten a call at eight that morning from Detective Reyes, Peters's partner, telling him that they'd found the doc's wife and were bringing her in for questioning. Jason had contacted his friend Danny, a patrol cop, to stay with Sue while he headed to the precinct. But no sooner had he hung up, Sue had gotten another call from her stalker. And they'd gotten a trace. Unfortunately, the stalker was calling from what was probably one of the last existing pay phones in the city. Jason had a few cars check it out and, as soon as Danny arrived, rushed to check it out himself. Not that he'd expected to find anything. And they hadn't. However, the timing meant the caller couldn't be the doctor's wife.

Then again, maybe she'd hired someone to do it for her

and throw off suspicion. Jason wasn't going to leave any stone unturned. This freak stalking Sue had proven that he wouldn't stop at murder. Which meant Jason had to stop him . . . or her.

Detective Peters squared his shoulders. "This isn't your case, Dodd. Why do you want to question her?" The guy was being a hard-ass.

"Someone's stalking a friend, and I think that woman knows something. Besides, I've already done some research." Jason wasn't above bribery. "Let me talk to her, and I'll give you everything I've got."

The man folded his arms across his chest but gave a nod of acquiescence. "You owe me."

The two of them walked into the room where the doctor's wife sat waiting. "Mrs. Everts?" Jason said.

"When are you going to let me see my husband?" The woman shifted in her chair as she spoke. Jason noted her feminine voice. If she'd been doing the earlier calls, she'd done a damn good job at disguising it.

"You didn't know he'd been shot?"

"If I'd known he'd been shot, I'd have been at the hospital."

Jason turned a chair around and straddled it. "Where were you last night?"

"My son and I were at a hotel."

"And why were you at a hotel?"

The woman blinked. "My husband and I had an argument."

"About what?" Detective Peters asked from the corner of the room.

Her gaze shifted. "A silly argument."

"Humor me," Jason said.

The woman's lips went white around the edges. "It's none of your business."

Jason stood and moved closer. Leaning palms down on the table, he met her gaze. "It is if you want to convince us that you didn't shoot him."

"Me?" Her brown eyes widened. "If you want to find the guilty party, go talk to the little blonde bitch he's screwing!"

The muscle over Jason's left brow started to tick. "So, you argued about his girlfriend."

"Yes. My husband has a problem keeping his pants zipped."

"Is that why you shot him? You lost your head, and—"

"I didn't shoot him!"

Jason reared back. "I happen to know that this isn't the first time your husband has cheated on you." Jason saw Peters's eyes widen with interest.

The podiatrist's wife stiffened. "I didn't mean to run over that dog. And I didn't shoot my husband!"

"Dog?" Peters asked.

Jason continued. "He probably said something that set you off . . ."

"If you want to find out who shot my husband, talk to that whore he's seeing."

Jason flinched. "For your information, I was with Miss Finley all last night."

The woman's gaze grew wide. "Who is Miss Finley? I'm talking about his office nurse he's been screwing. Don't tell me he's seeing somebody else!"

CHAPTER TWENTY

Jason sat at his desk, rolling his pencil in his palms. Everything felt off kilter, as if he were on the wrong road, speeding toward a destination that he had no business going to. And he wasn't just talking about the case.

He couldn't believe he'd told Sue about being a foster kid. That morning, while he'd been waiting for Danny, Jason had waited to see the look in her eyes—the same look he'd gotten from his teachers and the parents of his classmates. It was the look that said, "Get away. You're not good enough." He hadn't gotten it. But there was always later.

He dropped the pencil. It had been an hour since he'd interviewed the doctor's wife, so he leaned back in his chair and snatched up the phone to call Danny. "How are things going?" he asked as soon as his friend answered.

"Nothing's changed since you called thirty minutes ago."

Jason scowled. "Anyone call her?"

"The phone's rung off the hook. Her grandfather called. Chase and his wife Lacy called from California. Miss Finley's agent called. And some Benny guy, a writing partner, called to ask her out on a date. I think you've got some competition." Danny sounded mildly amused passing on this information.

Jason's tension headache worsened. He said, "I'm going

to make some calls and run down a few leads. It'll be a few hours before I'm back." He closed his eyes. The truth was it wasn't the headache bothering him. He missed Sue.

But, no. He couldn't let himself get that cozy, at-home feeling with anyone. No matter how much he liked or wanted Sue, he couldn't let himself start feeling as if he belonged. She needed him, and it was okay to protect her, to enjoy being with her, and God knew he wanted to have sex with her. But to feel as if he belonged anywhere was . . . well, it was dangerous. He'd learned that lesson time and time again. He wasn't stupid.

"Hey, I've got all day," Danny said. "I owe you big-time for helping my nephew."

"I didn't do that much." Jason picked up the file he'd made for the case and stared at his list of suspects. Whether she'd shot her husband or not, it looked as if the doctor's wife wasn't involved in his case. She hadn't even known about Sue, which meant she wasn't Sue's stalker. Since the foot doctor was still in ICU, he pretty much was off the suspect list, too.

"Not true." Danny's voice brought Jason's attention back to the conversation. "He would have gone to prison if you hadn't gotten hold of him."

"He's a good kid." Jason eyed his list again and decided to visit Sue's critique partners before heading back. He didn't like this Benny Fritz. If Fritz was asking Sue out, that made him even more of a suspect.

Also, Jason had left the chocolate Fritz sent Sue at the lab with a buddy. Without the proper orders to do a serious lab test, his friend had agreed to check for needle marks and such. Maybe Jason would drop by and see if he'd found anything.

Then Jason recalled telling Sue that he'd buy her some chocolate. He should do that, too.

"Besides," Danny remarked. "Watching her isn't hard at all."

Jason went on full alert. "Keep your hands to yourself."

"Hey, I'm not touching. Just looking. But she seems like a keeper. Smart, funny, beautiful."

"I thought you said she'd been in the study all morning?"

"Not all morning. We spent about an hour talking. She told me about her new book. Asked my advice about how a cop would handle a few things. Maybe she'll mention me in her dedication. That'd be cool."

Sue had asked Danny questions? First Chase and now Danny. Why the hell wasn't she asking him? He'd even offered!

He passed a hand over his face. "I'll be back later. Meanwhile . . . if you touch, you die."

He hit the off button and started dialing Sue's home number, wanting to hear her voice. Realizing what he was doing, he hung up. What was he going to say? *Hey, I miss you. And why the hell are you asking Danny for advice about your books and not me? And why the hell won't you sleep with me so I can stop obsessing about you?*

Leaning back in his chair, he remembered his phone conversation with Sue from the previous night. He never shared his past with women. As a matter of fact, when they started asking, he started backing off. But he didn't want to back off with Sue; he hadn't even gotten started yet.

Gritting his teeth, he decided to channel his pent-up frustration into finding Sue's stalker. His first stop would be to see if Bob had made headway with Sue's computer; then he'd swing by the lab to check on the candy, then he'd see if they'd discovered anything on the names he'd called in yesterday. Maybe he'd check and see if the Saturn had been found, too.

Standing, he again looked at his list of suspects, which included a New York editor and an art director. His gaze paused on the name Melissa Covey. Sue's agent. While Sue seemed adamant that the woman wasn't involved, Jason had initially suspected her. Sometimes, first impressions were correct.

"Dodd?" Jason's sergeant popped his head into the office.

"Yeah."

"Thought you were taking some personal time."

"I am. Just stopped by to do a few things."

"Those things involve a Hoke's Bluff case? Got word from someone that you were invading their territory."

Jason frowned. *Martin*. "A friend's being stalked. I'm just making sure things are done right. Especially when one of the suspects just got shot last night. Our homicide team is on that case."

"Yeah, I got a call from Brian, too. Overstep your bounds and I'll have to rein you in."

"TCP/IP tapping." Bob said, standing over Sue's dismantled computer.

Jason ran a hand through his hair. Was everyone purposely trying to piss him off, or were they just getting lucky? "In English, Bob."

"Well, somebody was knocking on her door and they found it open," Bob said. "Did you know this thing is ten years old? The components are new. It's been rebuilt several times."

"What the hell does an open door mean?" Jason looked at the scattered parts. He hoped Bob knew how to put it all back together.

"It's called TCP/IP tapping."

"Lose the computer lingo. Did someone get into her computer, and do we know who it is?"

Bob smirked. "Yes, someone broke into her computer. And no, we won't be able to find out who it was. They used a local Internet source from a copy store. You might be able to go see if the hired help remembers anyone, but whoever did this knew how to cover their tracks."

Jason wrote down the information about the copy store. It was a long shot, but it seemed that long shots were all he was going to get. "When can you get the thing back together?"

"I'm going to have to reformat the hard drive. He sent her

a time-bomb virus, which wiped out everything. I made a note of her peripherals so I can replace the drivers, and I have a couple of her disks with her backup files, so I can probably replace her apps and files. But she's got to get antivirus protection and firewall this machine."

"Load anything you think she needs. I'll cover it. And hurry," Jason said.

"So you and her are . . ." Bob tapped his fists together.

"Yeah," Jason said. It wasn't really a lie. As soon as Sue came to her senses, they would be hitting the sheets. Maybe then some of his infatuation would wane.

"She's cute, but bad taste in lingerie." Bob laughed and shook his head.

Jason shrugged and headed for his car. There was nothing wrong with Sue's taste in lingerie; not as far as he could see. Besides, if he ever got close to any exercising-animal pajamas again, she wouldn't be wearing them that long anyway.

Sue plugged in Jason's laptop to research antique Welsh dressers. Her heroine in the new book had one in her kitchen, and Sue wanted to check her facts. Deep down she knew that whenever she went on the chase for minuscule details it meant she was just finding a reason not to write. But sometimes you just needed a reason to goof off.

It was almost two o'clock, and she'd pretty much goofed the day away. She hadn't even finished a scene. She could blame it on not having her computer to work on, and maybe on having a stranger in her house, though Danny seemed nice. For sure she could blame it on someone trying to kill her, or her concern over Paul's son losing his father. She could attribute it to the fact that she loved watching Jason's cat with the new kittens. But the truth of her inability to write sat in the pit of her stomach like one of her grandmother's casseroles. She missed Jason—missed his teasing, missed the heat in his blue eyes. She missed how he made her feel safe. Danny was nice, but . . . he wasn't Jason.

Today, Sue had actually brought her purse into her office. Her gun-concealing purse. Maybe this time, if she didn't have any cans of veggies available, she might remember she had a real weapon. Maybe.

Every time the phone rang, her heart pounded. And it wasn't because she feared it was the stalker, but because she wanted it to be from the man who hadn't bothered to call her four months ago. Making the whole thing worse was knowing that Jason had called Danny. Why hadn't he called her? Just to say hello. Just to . . . update her on things. It shouldn't hurt but it did. She grabbed her heart-shaped stress ball and squeezed.

How long would it take him to pick up the phone and dial her number?

Okay, logically, she knew he probably had good reasons for not calling today, but what about four months ago? He had yet to explain that.

Maybe it was just the time apart from him making her question things. Maybe it was remembering how rejected she'd felt when he hadn't called her four months ago.

Maybe she was scared of being rejected again.

Jason's computer blinked at her, and Sue pulled up the Internet. Once on his home page she noticed the favorite websites button. What was on Jason Dodd's favorites list? She moved the mouse, then stopped. What if he had porn sites listed? Was this snooping?

"Oh, Jiminy Cricket!"

She'd already gone through the man's medicine cabinet. If he had secrets lurking in his computer, he wouldn't have offered it to her. Right? Besides, most men checked out porn sites. But if he had all big bust websites listed, she'd know to give up. Size B breasts would never satisfy a man into double Ds.

Biting down on her lip, Sue wondered what she might have found if she'd done a search on Collin's computer. Delete thought! She didn't want to go there. As she'd explained to her ficus tree during their last horticulture therapy session, Collin was history. But Jason . . . there was still a chance she might decide the risk was worth taking with Jason Dodd.

She glanced back at his computer and hit the favorites button. The list appeared. Sue's mouth fell open. She blinked, not believing it. How could . . . ? Needing proof, she clicked on the first web address.

Jason knocked on Benny Fritz's apartment door.

Luke, Jason's buddy in the lab, had claimed the chocolate sent by Sue's critique partner appeared clean. To prove his point, he'd popped one in his mouth. But poison or no, a good cop followed his gut. Jason's gut told him to check out Fritz. So here he was. Checking.

His sergeant's warning rang in his ears, but it wasn't like talking to a few people could get his ass in trouble. And if it did? Well, his ass would just have to crawl out of trouble.

The door swung open. Jason stared at the young boy who appeared. "Is your father here?"

"He's writing. I'm not to interrupt unless there's blood."

Jason smiled. "Well, this is pretty important."

"Okay." The boy closed the door.

The information Jason had dug up on Fritz was hardly incriminating. One outstanding speeding ticket and two calls out to his house for a domestic situation.

The door swung open. "You better not be selling anything," came a man's voice.

Jason gave Benny Fritz the once-over. The author stood a few inches shorter than himself, and while fit, leaned more to the thin side. His brown hair was tinged with gray, and Jason supposed that some women liked the GQ/professor look. It was then that Jason realized he was surveying the man as his competition rather than Sue's possible stalker.

He slipped his hands in his pockets. "My name's Jason Dodd, Houston PD."

Fritz opened the door, offering a silent invitation and no

apparent worries. Jason entered, but the phone rang. "Excuse me." Fritz stepped into the study off the living room.

Jason took the opportunity to look around. The place appeared half empty. He remembered Sue telling him that Fritz had recently separated from his wife.

Inching closer to the door, Jason glanced inside and around the study. He heard Fritz on the phone: "Yes, but I'm serious. If they can't up my advance, I'll go with another house." Jason's gaze slid to the man's desk. And stopped. On top of a stack of papers was a dog magazine. A familiar dog magazine. The one that had the article and photographs of Sue. He knew because he had his own copy.

His attention shifted to a framed photograph on the desk. In the image, Fritz stood with his arm around Sue. The photograph appeared to have been taken at one of Sue's signings. There wasn't anything intimate in the pose, but the fact that the man had it on his desk said a lot.

"Sorry." Fritz hung up. "Sue said you'd be by."

She had? Jason managed to hide his surprise. He'd never told her not to tell her critique group, but he'd expected her to know better.

"So, you're aware I'm speaking to anyone around here who has read that manuscript." Jason's gaze fell back to Fritz's desk.

The writer picked up a few papers and dropped them on top of the dog magazine. He said, "Yes, but she also said you thought someone tapped into her computer. Probably did some TCP/IP tapping."

Jason recognized the lingo Bob had tossed at him. "You're familiar with computer tampering?" he asked.

"It's part of my business. I've warned Sue she should put up firewalls."

The phone rang again. Fritz grimaced. "Jimmy, can you grab that and take a message?"

As he heard the boy scamper to the phone, Jason nodded. "I'm getting Sue's computer taken care of."

"Really? That's funny. She just called me and asked me to load a firewall when the computer is returned."

"That won't be necessary." In relaying the information, Jason accidentally let his cop tone slip.

"Dad?" Fritz's son called. "It's Mom. She sounds upset."

Fritz frowned. "Tell her I'll call her back." Then he leaned back in his leather loafers and gave Jason a curious look very similar to the one Jason had given him when he'd opened the door.

Jason crossed his arms over his chest. What kind of guy wore leather loafers? The writer kind. The kind Sue would relate to. Jason's mood darkened even more.

"Maybe you should worry more about your wife and less about Sue," he suggested.

Fritz got a cocky smirk on his face. "I'm picking up a vibe. I could be wrong, but I think you're here about my interest in Sue and not because you suspect me of being a stalker."

"It's your interest in her that makes you more of a suspect." Jason didn't hide his frown.

"Then I must be high on your suspect list, Detective. Because I'm very interested in Sue Finley."

This was on Jason's favorites list?

She was on Jason's favorites list?

Sue pressed a thumbnail between her teeth and gave it a nip as she stared at her website. Designed by Melissa, the opening page had a picture of Sue with small images of the covers of all four—no, five—of Sue's books. Melissa had already downloaded the image of the newest cover.

Sue gave the new book cover a quick glance, then went back to Jason's list of favorites and clicked on the dog magazine in which she'd been featured. The link that Jason had saved took her directly to her story. And when Sue checked out the rest of his favorites, all but three of the twelve were about her. There was a link to a small Dallas newspaper that had written a feature about her, a link to the website of the cooking show where she'd appeared, and several on-line sites with either interviews or posted reviews.

Why had he gone to all these sites? Before that kiss, he hadn't even done a double take. He'd been nice at Lacy's get-togethers, but when she'd tried to catch his eye he'd seemed to purposely avoid her. And he'd always had a girl—some big-breasted model-type—attached to his arm. Which had led Sue to assume he wasn't interested.

Then he'd shown up at one of Chase's barbeque parties without a date. They had all been drinking beers and laughing. It had been late. She'd stepped out on the patio to get the shoes she'd left outside, and he'd followed. They'd started talking about the stars. She was trying to point out the Big Dipper when he'd . . . dipped down. The kiss had been seriously amazing. Her first kiss in two years.

True, she had tried to stop him and had started talking, but he'd swept his tongue around her mouth again and she'd lost all interest in whatever she was saying. When the kiss ended, he'd seemed as blown away as she. He'd asked for her number. She hadn't even played it cool but grabbed her purse and handed him her card, smiling like an idiot. He'd tucked it in his wallet, run his finger down her cheek and promised to call.

Which he hadn't.

And she'd waited.

She'd waited and waited, and fumed, and then she'd taken him off her mailing list. In spite of being upset, she'd accepted that she just wasn't his type. But a person didn't Google, bookmark, and practically research someone on the computer if he wasn't interested. Right? So, what . . . what did all this mean?

An hour later, painting her toenails, Sue heard her doorbell ring. Was it Jason? Would he ring the bell?

The fact that she'd missed him so much stung, but not enough to keep her from darting into the living room. Danny had his gun out and was making his way to the door.

"It's not Jason?" Sue asked.

"No. He just called. Stay back," the policeman warned.

Sue frowned, not wanting another incident like what had happened with Kathy. "Shouldn't you see who it is before you hold them at gunpoint?"

"That's what I was going to do," he said, clearly insulted.

"Sorry."

He peered through the side window. "Older woman, blonde, wearing bright green clothing, with nice, uh . . ."

"Cleavage," Sue finished with a grimace. Her mom. She recalled the woman telling her grandfather about the threat. She remembered the woman was sleeping with fruit-mongering Elvis. "Go ahead and shoot."

Danny's brow rose.

"I'm joking. It's my mom."

He blushed. "Oh, uh, sorry."

"Me, too." Sue glanced out the side window and confirmed what she'd suspected. Glancing back at Danny, she probably offered him the best tip he'd gotten in days. "Watch your crotch."

"Oh, Susie!" Her mom stumbled as the door opened and Goliath trampled past. The dog lumbered into the middle of the room, his big head darting left, darting right, looking for Hitchcock. He let out a soul-felt doggy whine, then immediately perked up when he saw something else of interest: Danny's unguarded crotch.

Five minutes after rescuing Danny, Sue and her mom went into her office. "We need to talk," her mom snapped.

Sue plopped down on the floor by the kittens. Her mom sat at the desk.

"So . . . ?" her mom asked, as if Sue knew what she wanted to discuss. She didn't. However, she had several questions bouncing around her head that might be up for discussion. Why had her mom told Grandpa about the rat? Why did her mom have to dress in only fruity colors? Why all of a sudden had her mom decided that showing her boobs to the world was a good thing? Why did her mom not worry at all about her alcohol consumption? Why was her mom cheating on her dad?

The minute the last question flipped around Sue's brain, she knew she was being unfair. Her mom wasn't cheating. You couldn't cheat on a dead man twenty years in the ground.

"Susie Veronica Finley," her mom said.

Susie Veronica Finley, who would have killed anyone else using her full name, stared down at the kittens. "That's my name."

Her mom went straight for the clearing of the throat, which Sue could never ignore. "What is it, Mom?"

"What *is* it?" Her mom threw the question back. "You've got a madman after you, sending you dead rats and trying to break into your house. You've got one man living with you, and now I find this . . . this new guy here? He's cute too, but that's not the point. Let's not forget that your ex, the married foot doctor, has been shot. And I learn most of this info secondhand and not from my own daughter!"

Sue almost snarled. Her mom's new best friend, Lacy's mother, had such a big mouth.

She drew her knees up to her chest, bouncing her heels against the floor. "I didn't want you to worry, that's why I didn't tell you about Paul. I didn't tell you I was dating a married man because he'd neglected to tell me himself. And I'm not living with anyone." She took a deep breath. "Lacy insisted I let Jason stay here until she got back in town, and Danny is a friend and coworker of Jason's. Basically, you don't need to worry." She wrapped her arms around her knees. "Any other issues you'd like me to clear up?"

"I'm your mother. Worrying is my right."

"Maybe," Sue said. "But Grandpa is too old to worry. Why did you tell him about the rat?"

Her mom blinked, and Sue saw a flicker of guilt touch her eyes. "Well, I accidentally let it slip. But I told him I was mixed up about something."

What you should have told him was that you were drinking. "Guess he didn't believe you."

Her mom stared. Concern added a soulful quality to her voice as she asked, "What else is wrong with you?"

Sue shook her head. "That's not enough?"

Her mom leaned forward. "It's Bill, isn't it?"

Sue hugged her knees tighter and lied. "Who's Bill?"

"He's my boyfriend, and you know it." Her mom hesitated. "You don't like him, do you?"

"I don't know anything about him." *Other than he's an Elvis freak and you're bumping uglies with him.*

"You think I'm too old to date?"

Sue looked up. "I think you're too old for . . ." Sue lost her nerve and simply stared at her mom's cleavage.

Wide-eyed, her mom glanced down at her breasts and gave them a two-handed lift. "You think I'm showing too much?" she asked.

"Maybe a little. Don't get me wrong. They look great. But you're not young enough to show the merchandise."

Her mom continued to stare at her boobs. "That's the problem. I feel young. I know I'm not." She blinked and considered her next words. "But for the first time in years, I feel as if I actually have a life. I feel sexy, and . . ." She lowered her voice. "Did you know it's possible for a woman to come twice?"

Sue's mouth dropped open. "Stop. Stop right there, Mom. I'm sorry, but I just can't talk to you about multiple orgasms."

"Why not?" her mom asked.

"Because . . ."

Her mom's eyes tightened. "Do you think I'm being disloyal to your dad?"

Sue couldn't lie. "I shouldn't feel that way, but yeah, it sort of feels like that."

"I loved him, Susie," her mom said. "But, he's gone. Been gone for years."

Yeah, people could just come and go in your life. People

you trusted to always be there. Her father. Collin. And then there were the people you couldn't even trust. People like Jason. People who may or may not call you.

Sue held up her hand. "You don't have to explain. I said I know I shouldn't feel that way. But I still don't want to hear about it or talk about sex with you."

"Why?"

Sue rolled her eyes. "It's gross!"

A smile widened her mom's mouth. "Sex is gross any way you look at it. It involves bodily fluids, and anything involving bodily fluids is gross. Take blowing your nose—"

"Stop! Do not compare blowing your nose to having sex. Anyway, I'm not even supposed to know you do it."

"Everyone does it," her mom said.

"Not everyone," she wanted to say. She didn't.

"It doesn't matter. I'll bet it's in some ancient rule book. Oh heck, I'll bet it was the eleventh commandment and just got chipped off. Thou shalt not tell your children you have sex."

Her mom's brow pinched. "You're not getting any, are you?"

Sue gritted her teeth. "The twelfth commandment that also got chipped off is, Children, thou shalt not tell your parents when you have sex."

"Fine." Her mom sighed. "We won't talk about sex. But we do have to talk." She cupped her hands together. "You got any Merlot?"

Sue sat up straighter. "You can't drink. I can't drive you home and—"

"It's not for me." A frown appeared on her mother's face. "I promised Bill that I'd cut back on the wine. It's for you."

"For me?" Sue asked.

"You might need it after hearing my news."

"Which size?" the salesclerk asked.

Jason leaned against the counter. "Large or extra large."

Jason had heard that, if given a choice, some women

would choose chocolate over sex, so why men bought them chocolate had always been a mystery. He'd never given a woman chocolate before. Frankly, he hadn't had to sweeten the pot. He usually got what he wanted on charm alone.

Until now. Sue seemed immune to his charm. But she liked chocolate, and he had thrown away the ones Fritz had bought her, so . . .

The clerk pointed to several boxes. "Large, extra large . . ."

"Extra large." Jason dropped two twenties on the counter. Inhaling, he found the scent of chocolate teased his empty stomach. He hoped Sue was ready to go grab a bite to eat when he got home. He'd barely eaten all day.

The clerk pointed to the biggest box and raised an eyebrow.

"That's fine."

Jason looked at his watch. Almost six. He'd only planned to be away a few hours but had been gone all day. He'd called Danny five or six—okay, ten—times, but he hadn't spoken to Sue.

Maybe on some level he'd done it on purpose, thinking the time apart would make him want her less. It hadn't worked. And his meeting with Mr. GQ Fritz had only made things worse. Still dealing with the fact that Sue had probably slept with the foot doctor, now he had to chew on the fact that another man had set his sights on her. And Benny Fritz had a determined air. Jason felt damn certain that as long as he was around, Fritz couldn't win Sue's affections. But whenever they were no longer an item, she'd probably fall for the guy. Fritz and Sue shared the same career, and they helped each other with their writing—something Sue didn't want Jason to do. Which explained why Jason hoped Benny turned out to be the stalker. Oh yeah, he wanted to keep Fritz away from her permanently.

"Any special type?" The salesclerk motioned to the display case.

"A mixture," Jason said and wondered why in hell he was

thinking about ending things with Sue when he hadn't even gotten started. So what if he wasn't Mr. Long-Term Commitment? They could be different. Hell, he could even see himself enjoying Christmas with her, them decorating a tree together, having one of those real relationships that he'd really never had. The kind that lasted more than a year.

"That'll be a hundred-thirty-six and forty-two cents," the clerk said.

Jason shook his head. "*What?*"

She repeated the amount.

"For chocolate?"

The woman's smile thinned. "It's Godiva."

"Do you know how many Snickers I can buy with a hundred and thirty-six bucks?"

She grinned. "Snickers won't impress a woman."

Jason pulled out his credit card. "I'd better get laid," he muttered.

The woman just chuckled.

The idea of Christmas returned to him. The idea of actually putting up stockings, of having someone to share Christmas with had his chest feeling full. Yeah, he still heard the voice of warning—Jason Dodd didn't do holidays—but he was too tired of listening to warnings to pay it any heed. Still, as he watched her scan his card, Jason decided one thing for sure: If this chocolate wasn't the best crap he'd ever eaten, Sue was getting Snickers in her stocking.

Jason's phone vibrated in his back pocket as the clerk handed him the bag. He flipped it open, one-handed. "Yeah?"

"Dodd, it's Peters. I don't have to tell you this, but I thought you might like to know. The foot doctor came to about an hour ago. We know who shot him."

CHAPTER TWENTY-ONE

Jason stood on Sue's porch and half expected Danny to jerk open the door. Danny didn't. Then he heard voices and . . . laughter.

"Oh," Sue squealed. "Do it again."

Danny's laugh came next. "No, you do it."

Just freaking fantastic. Instead of watching out for intruders, Danny was . . .

"Push it in," Danny said. "Now pull it out."

Just what the hell was Danny doing? Jason fit his key in the lock and pushed open the door. Danny was . . . playing the Nintendo Wii. Sue had a remote control in her hand. Danny sat beside her on the floor.

Pulling out the door key, Jason set his bag with the chocolates just inside. He spotted a pizza box on the coffee table, along with a couple of beer bottles.

"Hey," Danny said, never taking his eyes off Sue.

"So if I'd been the stalker, were you going to invite me in for a beer?"

Danny pointed to the window. "I saw your car pull up. I recognized your Mustang."

Jason recognized something, too. How close Danny sat next to Sue. He also noticed that Sue only gave him a quick glance before she refocused on the television screen. He didn't know what he expected from her, but hell, after spending over a hundred dollars on chocolate for the woman, he would hope she might be able to look him in the eyes.

His stomach growled at the smell of pizza. He walked over and flipped the lid of the box. Empty. His gaze moved back to Sue, who was wearing jeans that hugged every curve and a red tank top that outlined her breasts and even gave a hint of cleavage.

Danny must have read some of Jason's mood and stood up. "Well, I'd better leave." He smiled at Sue. "It's been fun."

Sue rose, too. "Thanks for babysitting me, and for the advice about that scene."

Jason inwardly flinched.

Danny started outside, and Jason walked with him. "Any more calls?" he asked, trying to hide his unfamiliar possessive feelings.

"Yeah, her agent and that Fritz guy again. You'd best watch him. He's coming on hard and heavy."

Like you were? He wanted to ask but didn't.

"Oh, Sue's mom came over." Danny frowned. "I probably should ask for her dog's hand in marriage. I had more intimate contact with that dog than I've had with women in the past six months."

Jason laughed then realized how silly his worries had been about Danny. "Sorry about my wisecrack when I came in. Long day."

Danny's smile faded. "Don't worry about it." His gaze shot back to Sue's house. "However, for the record, if you're stupid enough to let this girl go, I'll be here on her doorstep."

Jason flinched. Okay, maybe he hadn't been so silly. "What's that supposed to mean?"

Danny met his gaze. "It means you go through girls like popcorn. For once, try not to screw things up."

The younger cop didn't stay around to hear what Jason thought of his statement. It was a good thing, too. Letting out a sigh of frustration, Jason went to tell Sue about Paul Everts's shooter. She wasn't going to like it.

Sue wasn't in the living room. He found her sitting Indian-style on the study floor, petting his cat and kittens.

"They doing okay?" He sat down beside her, and the scent of her shampoo tempted him to move closer.

"Fine." She stroked a finger over a kitten. "Hitchcock came in here this morning. Mama needs to get her shots."

Silence followed. Sue was being quiet again.

"Did you eat?"

"Yeah, but there's another pizza in the oven. Danny said you liked it all the way." She still hadn't looked at him.

"I do. Thanks."

Taking a chance, Jason brushed a strand of hair from Sue's face. When she didn't push him away, he leaned over and pressed his lips to her cheek. She closed her eyes, and he ran two fingers under her chin to turn her face to his. Her lids opened. He gazed into her blue eyes, giving her every chance to pull away before he brushed his lips against hers. She didn't pull away.

He tasted her mouth, which was a little salty like pepperoni, a little malty like beer, and a lot of something natural that was Sue. Slipping his tongue between her lips he decided to hell with the pizza. To hell with talking about the damn foot doctor, too.

He brought her closer, and he heard her speak. Or rather, heard her try to speak.

"Yum go tut op." The mangled words seeped out the corner of her mouth.

He pulled back and brushed a finger over her lips. "You're talking again when I'm kissing you," he teased.

"I said you had to stop." Obviously not in a teasing mood, she rose and shot toward the door.

"Is something wrong?" he called.

"Wrong?" Sue replied over her shoulder, fleeing. "What could be wrong?"

She continued down the hall, heard Jason's footsteps behind her, and quickened her pace. As she darted past the coffee table, she snatched up the pizza box and took off for the kitchen. Slamming her foot on the lever to open the trash, she crunched the box into the garbage. Wrong? A knot tightened her throat. She had a wide array of "wrongs."

There was her mama's you-might-want-wine announcement about wanting to marry Elvis. Sue would be step-daughter to The King of Fruit Salesmen. Oh, and guess what? He wanted to take them all on a vacation to celebrate the engagement—a vacation to Graceland!

No way, Jose. Not in this lifetime.

And then there was Jason. Jason who hadn't called her all day. Not once. However . . . a few months ago, he'd taken the time to research every piece of information on the Internet about her. What did that mean?

Hearing him come closer, she hustled into the kitchen, picked up a sponge and attacked the counters.

She felt him staring at her.

"Okay," he said. "Spill it."

She looked at him. "Spill what?"

"Whatever it is that's making you clean countertops that don't need cleaning. When Maggie takes a sponge to clean counters, I'm usually about to get an earful."

Tossing the sponge in the sink, she started out of the kitchen. He grabbed her around the waist, swooped her up, and sat her down on the clean, freshly wiped and wet granite. "What's wrong?" He tilted her chin up to look at him. "Talk." He smiled. "I'll bet if I kiss you, you'll start talking." He leaned in.

"No!" She felt the counter's dampness seep into her jeans.

He pulled back. "Then tell me what's wrong."

"I used your laptop today." She studied his reaction.

He stared at her. "And?"

"And I just happened to stumble across a list of your favorite websites."

He didn't look concerned. "And?"

"And I just happened to notice that ten out of twelve were about me."

"And that's a problem because . . ." He motioned with his hands for her to finish his statement.

"It's weird."

"Weird? I read your books. Your books listed your website. I checked out your website, and then I checked out the links listed." He stepped back. "Isn't that why they're posted? To get people to read about you?"

"But you bookmarked them. And you had to have Googled me."

"Since when did Googling become a crime?"

Okay, now she felt as if she'd overreacted. Had she? She tried to think clearly. All of a sudden, every fear, every doubt she'd had about Jason Dodd came barreling back to her. If she hadn't been good enough for him four months ago, why was she good enough for him now? And if she wasn't good enough for him, why was he checking up on her on-line?

"But . . . but you could have asked me anything, talked to me and gotten that information from me personally. And you didn't. You didn't even come to my autographings."

The words rolled out of her and she decided to just let them flow. "You didn't give me the time of day until four months ago, and then you followed me outside on the patio and kissed me senseless. And then you asked for my phone number and . . . and never called."

He wrapped his hands around her waist. "I called you last night . . . and the night before. Don't those phone calls count?"

"You didn't call me *today*." She bit her tongue, hating that she sounded like a jealous girlfriend who'd been ignored. She wasn't his girlfriend, wasn't jealous. So why had she spent a good portion of the day envisioning Jason on the arm of some other woman?

She had almost been relieved when Benny called to say Jason had been by. At least she'd known he hadn't completely forgotten about her.

"I was working on the case," he offered.

"Yes, *my* case. And you don't call and tell me anything. Do you think I don't care?" Okay, that sounded legit.

He leaned forward until his forehead touched hers. "You're right. I should have called. I'm sorry." He moved flush against the counter until his waist fit between her inner thighs, until she had a close-up view of the heat simmering in his dark blue irises.

"Forgive me." The palms of his hands glided down over her hips to palm the tops of her thighs. He inched them lower on her legs and ever so slowly moved them up again. His thumbs came dangerously close to the V between her legs.

Sue's breath caught. Every muscle in her body clenched, including the muscles that created liquid warmth between her thighs. She managed to put her hands on top of his and push. She only moved them an inch, but her gesture sent the message. He removed them.

She studied him. "Did you bring my computer home?"

"It's not finished yet, but I spoke with Bob." When he saw her shift to get down, he caught her and helped.

"And?" she asked, stepping out of his hold around her waist.

"And we now know that someone broke into your files, but we can't trace it." Jason turned around to the oven. He opened the door, pulled out a slice of pizza and sank his teeth into it. "Thank you," he said, gesturing.

Sue drew out a plate and handed it to him. "Paul is doing better. They think he's going to make it now."

Jason dropped the pizza on the plate. "You called and checked on him?" He appeared annoyed.

"Chase called for me, after I called him. *My* investigator ran off." She offered him a beer from the fridge.

"I didn't run off. I was chasing leads!" he argued. He motioned for her to set the beer down.

Sue remembered another reason why she was upset, more things to add to her gone-wrong list. "Does working this case include accusing my friends of trying to hurt me? Calling—"

"That reminds me," he interrupted. His voice had changed to a deeper tone. "Why did you tell Fritz I was coming?"

"I told everyone in my critique group. They're my friends. I don't believe any of them did this, and I couldn't let you show up accusing them and think I suspected them."

"This Fritz guy wants to be a lot more than your friend, and I'm not so sure he isn't behind this. But I'll give you credit, the other two seem completely innocent."

"Benny just misses his wife." Sue picked up the beer she'd gotten Jason, opened it, and took a sip. "And he didn't do this. Neither did Melissa, and she said you called and accused her of setting all this up." Sue shot Jason another hard look. "And my editor called Melissa wanting to know about the cop who was calling and leaving messages. You can't go messing with my editor. That man has my career in his hands."

"All I wanted to do was ask a few questions about the assistant editor and the art guy, both who gave you the creeps. As for Melissa . . . she's still a suspect."

Sue shook her head. "That doesn't make sense. Those people are thousands of miles away. How could it be them trying to break into my house and following us around in a gold Saturn? Most people up east don't even drive."

"It's only a four-hour flight. And some Yankees drive. They just suck at it."

"Wait!" Sue held up her hand. "What happened to the theory that this was Paul's wife who was behind all this? That she shot Paul for the same reason?"

Jason frowned. "Well, that doesn't seem likely now."

"Why?"

He took the beer from her and had a long sip. "I interviewed her this morning."

"What? You interviewed her and didn't even call me?" She squared her shoulders, truly peeved. "Did it occur to you that I might like to hear?"

"Yeah, but I wasn't sure she was telling the truth."

Something about his expression said there was more. "And now you are?"

"Yes." He hesitated. "The detective assigned to Paul's shooting just called me before I came here."

"What happened?"

He took another long pull of beer. "Paul came to. He remembered who shot him."

Air hinged in Sue's lungs. "Who?"

He took his sweet time answering. "He said . . . his girlfriend."

That air came out of her lungs. "I did not shoot Paul!"

"His other girlfriend."

"Other . . . girlfriend?" Did she want to know?

Jason seemed a bit embarrassed to explain. "The doctor was a very busy man. It seems he was dating two different nurses at his office. One of the nurses didn't appreciate it."

"He was cheating on me?" Sue asked. "With two people?"

Jason picked up his plate and half-grinned. "Three, if you count the wife."

"Ohhh!" She started pacing. "How long before I can shoot him?"

He laughed for real. "Let's give him a few days."

Sue paced over to her breakfast table, slid down into a chair, and dropped her forehead on the table. Winners. Every man she felt an ounce of attraction for was a real winner.

Then she remembered she was attracted to Jason. Majorly attracted. Was he going to be an exception to the rule, or was he going to prove once again that she had a real knack for picking top-notch scum?

She shook her head and tried to get her head around what was important. "So, Paul getting shot has nothing to do with me or what's going on with me, right?"

Jason moved in. "It appears that way. We're going to look closely at the nurses, but it doesn't seem connected."

"Which means," she realized, "we don't have a clue who's doing this." It was a major downside.

"We're still looking."

"Where?" she asked.

"For starters, I tried to contact your ex-husband—"

Speaking of top-notch scum . . .

"No!" Sue jumped up. "And let me say it one more time, just in case you didn't get it. *No.*"

"No, what?" Jason asked.

"No, you are not going to contact my ex."

"You said your ex was a computer engineer. That means he knows how to work on computers, which means he would know how to break into your files."

"I don't care if he knows how to sprout wings and fly backward while doing the funky chicken. Leave Collin out of this!"

CHAPTER TWENTY-TWO

Jason lowered the manuscript pages he held to peek at Sue. They sat at opposite ends of the sofa, reading. He read Sue's new book and had her cat in his lap; Sue read Fritz's manuscript, occasionally scribbling something in the margins. The box of chocolate lay open on the coffee table before them. It was damn good chocolate—not hundred-dollar good, but almost. Sue had been grateful for the gift, and it had won him a smile. The *smile* was worth a hundred dollars, especially after she'd gotten so angry about him trying to contact her ex. In the end, Jason had agreed not to contact him unless they ran out of suspects. Needless to say, her outburst had given Jason something to think about. What had her ex done to her?

Hitchcock moved from his lap to Sue's. Jason finished chapter three and looked up to watch Sue shift to accommodate her feline. He wondered if she'd accommodate him.

Her red bra strap slipped down her shoulder. A red bra? He envisioned it came with matching panties. Staring at her bare shoulder, his body began to throb.

Sue looked up, and their eyes met. Jason set his pages down and picked up a piece of chocolate. He took a small bite; then, moving next to her, he placed the sweet morsel to her mouth. When she opened, he tucked the truffle inside and then kissed her.

The taste of Sue and chocolate sent him reeling. The fact that she was the first to slip her tongue into his mouth sent a flood of hope to his chest. Followed by some serious blood flow down south.

He pushed Fritz's manuscript off her lap, at the same time sending Sue's manuscripts pages raining to the floor. Unconcerned, he tucked his arm behind her and leaned her back on the sofa. Keeping most of his weight on his elbows, he settled atop her. Their bodies met in all the right places.

She arched up against him, a slow deliberate brush, and his body screamed to start shedding the layers of their clothes. But his head said he'd better not move too fast. Instead, he concentrated on their kiss. Using his tongue, he swirled the melting chocolate around her mouth.

Her fingers came around his back, then slipped into his hair. He moved his lips to the curve of her neck and traced a path of dampness to her shoulder. Encouraged by her response, he slid his hand beneath the red tank top. Her flat abdomen felt soft, firm, and he risked moving a bit higher. When the tips of his fingers touched the satin of her bra, he moaned.

The pebbled hardness of her nipple pressed against the slick material, and he rubbed his fingers over the tightness as the aroused skin grew tighter, harder. And he grew harder along with her. She sighed.

Thinking about how good her nipple had felt against his tongue, he pulled his hand away, capturing her red tank top and whisking it up and off, over her head. She let him. He soon gazed down at her red bra, her taut nipples straining against the flimsy material.

"You are so beautiful."

He moved back to her lips, savoring the passion and chocolate as he moved his fingers to her breast. Her hips shifted upward again, more demanding. Her boldness gave him permission to let his own hips press against hers.

Moving his lower body, he rubbed the hardness between his legs against the softness between hers. In high school, he'd heard this referred to as dry humping. Right now, he referred to it as heaven. A dress rehearsal to making love.

Her hips rose to meet his. Their bodies met, hungry for the contact. But as good as it felt, Jason wanted so much more.

He wanted to be inside her. He wanted her naked, him naked. He wanted to move his kisses down her, wanted to make her come with his tongue.

He leaned in for one more kiss before he started shedding clothes. She arched her sweet little pelvis up again. Held the contact.

"Om thin op oving." Her mangled words buried beneath his kiss sent pain straight to his groin.

"No." But he broke the kiss and waited to hear her say it.

"Something's moving." She stared down at where their bodies met.

He blinked as her words sank in. Or they tried to sink in.

His gaze caught on the bulge in his jeans, then shot back at her. "Er, you don't like it when it moves?"

A smile lit up her eyes. "I think it's your phone."

"Oh." He felt the vibration in his front pocket then. "Ignore it." He went back in for a kiss.

She dodged his lips. "No."

He dropped his face into the crook of her shoulder and moaned. "No, what?"

"I'm sorry. You probably think I'm just a . . . I didn't mean to let this happen again."

"What if I beg?" His phone stopped vibrating. He let his body rest against hers again.

She chuckled. "I'd love to see that, but it won't work." She brushed his hair from his forehead. "I'm really sorry."

He stared into her blue gaze and, in spite of being sexually frustrated to the hilt, he couldn't be mad at her. She hadn't started this; he had. "So, basically, my cell phone has ruined my sex life."

Her smile took his breath away. "It's vibrating again. Are you going to answer it?"

"No." He rested his forehead on her shoulder, loving the

smell of her skin. "I'm going to enjoy it. It's the closest thing to sex I've had in a long time."

She ran another hand through his hair. "Is this what you call vibrating phone sex?" she joked. Her laugh shook her body, which felt really good because his body was still pressed up against her.

He leaned up a bit, hopeful. "Phone sex? Would you have phone sex with me?"

"Probably not." Smiling, she scooted out from under him and sat up.

He studied her expression, humor and desire dancing in her eyes. Lowering his gaze, he saw her nipples pressing against her red bra. Sue followed his gaze and snagged her red top and slipped it back over her head.

Before he could sit up, he had to reach inside his jeans to readjust. Finally pressing his feet to the floor, he rested his elbows on his knees, dropped his head into his hands, and took several deep breaths. When he looked up again, she was on the floor, organizing the pages of the two manuscripts.

He touched the top of her head. "Sue?"

"No."

"I wasn't going to ask *that.*" He exhaled in frustration. "Look, it's not that I can't take no for an answer. I'm just curious. I know you want it. I want it and—"

She looked up. "When I was fourteen, I wanted my nose pierced. When I was sixteen, I wanted to kill my mom."

He stared at her. Women had always perplexed him, but Sue took that feeling to a whole new level.

"Okay, I'm biting. What does having your nose pierced and killing your mom have to do with us having sex?"

"Nothing, exactly, but now I'm kind of glad I didn't get an extra hole in my body. And I'm glad I didn't do my mom in." Still down on all fours, she paused. "Well, some days I'm glad. Today wasn't one of those days." She sat back on her bottom. "Anyway, the point is that you can't go through life simply doing whatever you want."

"You can't tell me that you've never followed your instincts, done something because it feels good or right!"

"I have lousy instincts," she muttered.

"So you don't listen to them ever?"

"Not when they're about piercings or killing people. And not about men. Not anymore at least."

Shit. A lightbulb went off. Why hadn't he realized sooner? "This isn't about me. It's about him."

"It's not about *Paul.* Yes, I'm mad that he made a fool out of me—"

"Not Paul. I mean your ex. What did he do, Sue? What did he do to you?"

Sue looked back at the window. "It looks like rain."

"What does rain have to do with your ex?" He struggled to follow Sue's logic.

"Nothing. It's a polite way of saying, 'Go jump off a cliff. I'm not talking about this.' "

"Okay, he hurt you really bad." He studied her. "And it was probably raining at the time. Now tell me the story."

The memory came on so strong that Sue could smell the rain and the sweaty scent of Collin's gym clothes. She saw herself at the grocery store parking lot, rain beating down as she attempted to put the soaked bags into the trunk of his car. His car, because he'd asked her to have his oil changed. Collin's gym bag had been left unzipped in the trunk, and red silk peeped from the faded leather.

Delete! She attempted to shake the image out of her head.

She looked at Jason. "I'm not talking about this." She stood and tried to step around him, but he blocked her.

"He cheated on you, didn't he?"

"Make that a really high cliff you're going to jump off."

"That's why this hurts so much with Paul."

"I'm not talking about this," she reiterated.

He tucked a strand of hair behind her ear. "But, Sue, don't you see? This isn't a problem with *us.* " His fingers lingered against her neck.

"It won't be a problem if you dive off that cliff right now." She pushed his hand away.

"It's not a problem, because I don't cheat."

"All men cheat." Collin had cheated her out of five years. She'd worked at being a good wife. Dreamed of babies. She'd even planned on taking cooking lessons.

"I don't cheat. I'm a one-woman man."

His words swam through her head. She focused on Jason instead of the past. She couldn't change her past, but she could change her future. She'd almost slept with Paul, almost been another notch on his bedpost. And now, twice she'd almost slept with Jason. She had to be careful. As Kathy would say, she had to be always on guard for men and their warts.

"You've never cheated on a girlfriend. Never?"

"Never," he said.

She didn't believe him. "What about the phone call you got while we were at your apartment? The one where you didn't tell the caller you were with me."

His brow wrinkled. "The only person that called that day was Maggie. And I didn't tell her because . . . I don't tell Maggie about everything I do. Do you tell your mom everything?"

She swallowed that bit of logic but refused to give up her point. "You've never had a relationship with one woman and then met another you liked better?"

"Yes, but I didn't cheat."

"So, let's say you're in a bar. You have a thing going with one woman but she's not there. Then you meet someone who's hot. What do you do, call the girlfriend and tell her it's over while you have your next bang toy hanging on your arm?"

The look on his face took her by surprise.

"You have! You've actually broken it off with a girl on a phone in a bar because you met someone else."

The guilt in his eyes intensified. "The relationship was practically over. It had dried out."

"Dried out?" she repeated.

"Gone stale."

"Stale? Like bread goes stale?"

"Yes," he said. "I mean, no."

She got a mental image of him trying to pull his foot from his mouth. But it was too late; he had to either choke or swallow.

She sighed. "Life's too short to eat day old bread, isn't it? So . . . how long does it take for a woman to go stale?"

He stared at her, then tried to change the subject like she had earlier. "You're right. It's going to rain."

"Oh, no. Tell me." She needed to know this. She needed to tattoo this information across her heart so the next time she even considered having sex with Jason Dodd, she'd know that to him she was nothing more than a leftover dinner roll waiting to be tossed out with the table scraps.

She eyed him from beneath her lashes. "What's the longest relationship you've ever had?"

He stared back. "Fine. I'll answer if you'll tell me why you divorced your husband."

It was a tough choice. She debated.

"He cheated, didn't he? Did you find him in your bed with a friend? Oh, God, not your mom?"

"No!" She started to walk away, but then again, she really wanted to know everything about Jason. Could she tell him the truth? Tit for tat? She would give him an answer for one of his own. It would be worth it.

She met his gaze. "Deal. I found some sexy underwear in his trunk and it didn't belong to me. And yes, it was pouring down rain at the time."

This wasn't a lie. Let him think what she herself had until two months after the divorce, when a drunk, vaguely familiar-looking woman who called herself Colleen had shown up on her doorstep wanting to explain. When Sue had found the teddy, she'd thought nothing could be worse than knowing the man you loved had turned to another woman for sex. But she'd been so wrong. Having your husband turn to a woman wasn't near as bad as having your husband want to turn *into* a woman.

I still love you. Collin had tried to explain how the woman trapped in his body was actually a lesbian. While he enjoyed flirting with men, it was just to prove he was feminine. He'd confessed that all his boys' nights out for the last year had really been a girl's night out. And while Sue had been home trying to figure out how they could afford to have a baby, worrying about her husband's hair loss, Collin, AKA Colleen, had been using hair-be-gone and was bar-hopping.

If that wasn't enough, that skinny excuse of a man had worn her clothes to do it. Well, everything except her lingerie.

Jason's touch to her arm brought Sue back to the present. "He was a fool to have cheated on you. Just like that freaking foot doctor. But I'm telling you, I wouldn't do that."

Sue glanced at Jason. At least he'd never fit into her clothes. Then again, she didn't suspect him of being a cross-dresser. He was one hundred percent playboy, a man who toyed with a woman until he found a better play toy. And obviously he'd found someone better four months ago or he'd have called her.

"So that's why you didn't call me. Because you'd met someone else," she said.

"No!" he protested.

"Then why?" she asked.

He shook his head, clearly not wanting to answer, but he'd agreed to answer her other question. Tit for tat.

"What's your record in relationship endurance?" she asked.

He hesitated.

"We had a deal. Come on, Jason. What is it—eight months? Less?"

His frown deepened. "Three months," he finally confessed. "But—"

"Three? I should have known!" She shook her head. "You didn't even name your cat or know its sex."

"I can guarantee you that I knew both the name and the sex of all the women I dated."

He might be surprised, Sue thought, remembering Colleen.

Jason passed a hand over his face. "This isn't fair. You can't judge what we might have by . . . the past. We don't know what could happen."

A little hope flourished. Was he trying to tell her that what he felt for her was different from the others?

"Why shouldn't I judge you by your past?" Part of her longed to hear something that would convince her to risk it all, to throw caution to the wind.

"Because," he said. "We don't know how things could go. We could last . . . for a long time."

It was the pause that did him in. And "a long time." Not forever. Forever wasn't in Jason's relationship dictionary.

"How long? How long might we last, Jason? Six months? Doubling your record? Maybe a year? How long before you decide I'm just not worth calling back?" Hell, Collin, who claimed to be a woman on the inside, had lasted five years. She turned to leave, then decided she wasn't finished and faced him again. "Wow. If we accidentally made it a year, I'd have mold growing on me."

"I didn't mean it like that!" he bellowed.

"I know exactly what you meant." And knowing, she took off down the hall, her loyal cat making the walk with her.

"We're not through talking!" he yelled. "Damn it, Sue, I'm calling you! You're going to talk to me. You can't—"

"No!" She got to the bedroom and was about to fall back on the bed when, dang it, true to his word, her phone rang.

"Not tonight, buddy," she seethed and grabbed up the receiver. "Listen to me and listen good. I'm not going to sleep with you. I won't have phone sex with you. Keep your tongue out of my throat. I don't care how good-looking you are, or how much I appreciate all you're doing for me. Or that you wear an extra-large condom. Sex is out. No sex. You got that, Buster Brown?"

That's when she saw Jason standing in her opened bed-room door. He didn't have a phone in his hand.

"Oh," a feminine voice echoed through the line. "I . . . uh, this is . . . Maggie. Jason's mom."

Oh, crappers! Sue felt her face turn red.

Maggie continued, "Jason gave me . . . this number and said if I couldn't reach him to try it."

Sue had heard that there were times to cut your losses and shut up. Being a writer, who made her living using words, she had never believed it.

"I didn't mean I wouldn't have sex with *you*," she said. "Not that there's anything wrong with you. I just . . ." Sue forced her mouth closed. Okay, *now* she believed it. She held the phone out to Jason and saw the question in his eyes. "It's your mom."

He laughed—one of those really hard belly laughs.

"Talk to her." Sue forced the phone into his hand.

Taking a deep breath, he pulled the phone up. But be-fore he started talking, his laughter exploded again.

It stopped at the sound of shattering glass in the other room. The noise was like an explosion. Jason took off to see what had happened.

Sue shot after him, coming to a dead stop when she saw the broken glass and still-wobbling rock on her dining room floor. Taped around the rock was a note. Just like in her book.

"Jason?" Maggie's voice rang from the phone.

"I'll call you back." He hung up.

Sue continued to stare at the rock. If it was really like her book, that note wasn't going to be an invitation to tea.

CHAPTER TWENTY-THREE

"It was straight out of another scene from her book, too," Jason told Chase.

"Get her ass out of there!" his friend replied.

Jason cradled the phone to his ear, leaned back on the sofa, and glanced down the hall to where Sue had retired for the night in her bedroom. "I suggested we go to my place, but she wouldn't hear it."

Chase growled. "You see? This is what I meant about her not taking things seriously. She has a freak threatening to kill her, and she wants to stay home and nest."

"She *is* taking it seriously," Jason said, feeling the need to defend Sue. The look on her face when she saw the words *You're dead, bitch*, on that note kept flashing through his mind.

"Not serious enough to get her ass out of there," Chase muttered.

"Would *you* leave?" Jason asked.

"That's different," Chase said.

"Not really. Besides, her leaving for a few days isn't going to do it. If he's really serious, and it damn sure looks like he is, he'll just show up again when she comes back."

Chase let go of a deep breath. "I don't want anything to happen to her. She's half nuts, but she's good people."

"I'm not going to let anything happen to her." Jason was almost offended that his friend thought he might.

"Maybe I should change our flights and we can head home tomorrow, instead of Friday," Chase suggested.

"Why? Don't spoil your trip. What can you do that I can't? I got this." Jason also remembered that Sue had only agreed to let him stay until Chase returned, and the idea of being pushed aside rubbed a raw spot in his chest. His grip on the phone tightened. "It's personal for me now. I'm going to catch this freak. Myself."

The next few seconds of silence told Jason that Chase was half picking up on what he really wanted to say.

"Sue's not driving you crazy?" he asked.

She was, but not how Chase meant. "No. We've got past that whole kiss thing."

"Got past it?" Chase sounded surprised. "How did you do that?"

"We moved on."

"What about the whole 'no call' thing? Lacy seems to believe that'll be the one to drive a nail in your coffin. You move past that one, too?" Jason didn't answer. Instead he said, "The Hoke's Bluff people took the rock and note. But they aren't going to get anything more."

His partner was quiet for a moment. "You still betting on that critique partner being behind this?"

"Yeah," Jason said. "I'm still waiting to hear if they come up with anything on the Saturn that was stolen, and I'm checking into some people who Sue mentioned might have a grudge about her success. And I still haven't ruled out her agent being behind it all. But it's turning into more than a damn PR stunt. So yeah, I got my money on him."

"Did they arrest the nurse that shot the doctor?"

"I hear they brought her in. Peters hasn't let me know anything else."

"That's because he hates your ass."

"Yeah, and he doesn't care too much for yours, either."

Chase chuckled. "True. The doc still doing okay?"

"Yeah, he's gonna live. But he got what was coming to him if you ask me."

"Yep. Hey," Chase said. "My sister is calling me, so I'd better head out. But . . . look, I don't want to get in your shit, but . . . just be careful where's Sue's concerned. You hurt her, and Lacy—"

"I hurt her and Lacy's going to have my nuts—I remember."

Chase laughed. "I don't think it was just your nuts."

"Funny." Why the hell did everyone assume he would hurt Sue? It was all very frustrating. "Go see to your sister," he said, and he hung up.

That night, Sue tiptoed out of her room. Silence filled the house. Unable to sleep, wondering which scene of her book the stalker would try to emulate next, she'd suddenly remembered she hadn't taken her vitamin C.

Determined to not even glance toward the sofa, she moved to the kitchen table and, trying not to rattle the container, lifted the bottle of pills.

"Hey."

Startled, she tossed up the pill bottle, which crashed against the ceiling before rocketing back to the floor. Jason chuckled, and the lamp beside the sofa came on. Sue's eyes adjusted to the light, but she wished they hadn't. Wearing nothing but silk boxers again, Jason rose from the couch and stepped toward her. Bare-chested. And oh, he looked good bare.

"I . . . forgot to take my vitamins." She got on her hands and knees, searching for the bottle, and while she was looking she hoped to find some willpower.

Appearing beside her was a pair of bare feet. Hair, dark blond hair, grew on his legs, on his calves, ankles, even a few strands on his big toes. If he ever went into cross-dressing, the stock in hair removal companies would shoot up.

She moaned. Why was she thinking about that? She'd managed not to think about Collin for a long time.

Spotting the vitamin bottle, she snagged it but didn't stand up.

"You going to stay under there?"

"Maybe." Putting it in reverse, she backed herself up. Standing, she opened the bottle. "Here." She dropped two tablets into his palm.

He smiled.

She really should have stayed under the table. The smile was sweet, sexy, and everything she didn't need. What she needed was vitamin C and the willpower she hadn't been able to find while on her hands and knees.

"Good night." She turned to go.

"Stay. Talk to me. Just talk."

She turned around. Her gaze went to his bare chest and her heart raced. "Every time we do that I end up losing my shirt."

He chuckled. "You could take it off now and save me the trouble."

She frowned.

"Fine. Talk to me on the phone, like you have before. Neither of us can sleep. What would it hurt?"

"The last time I spoke to you on the phone, I was insulting your mom."

He shook his head with amusement, then grinned fully as his gaze shifted to her pajamas. "Tightrope-walking elephants, huh?"

She walked into the kitchen and got a drink to swallow her pills. All vitamined up, she walked back and handed him the water. "Take your vitamins," she commanded.

He looked down at his hand. "Only if you'll talk to me. On the phone. Your shirt's safe."

"Then don't take the vitamins." She headed for her room. Alone. Shirt on. She was keeping things safe for herself.

"What if I get sick?" he called out. "Wouldn't you feel terrible knowing all it would have taken was talking to me, and you could have prevented it?"

She swung around. "That's emotional blackmail!"

"See what you're driving me to?" He held out the pills.

"Deal?" When she didn't answer, he baited her. "I swear I feel a sore throat coming on."

Jason gave Sue a minute alone in her bedroom before he called. He smiled the whole time. "Now, is this so bad?" he asked when she answered.

"What do you want to talk about?"

He lay back on the sofa. "You."

"I'm not that interesting."

"Not true. Maggie found you quite entertaining."

"Please. She thinks I'm nuts."

"No, she said you sounded like a good girl. Which is why I'm in trouble. She said I had to keep my tongue out of your mouth and stop pressuring you to go to bed with me."

"You told her that I thought it was you?"

"She asked, and Maggie always knows if I'm lying."

Sue paused. "She knows you that well, huh? When did you go to live with her?"

Jason didn't want to talk about himself. But Sue had made it clear that if he wanted her to open up he would have to do the same. "Almost sixteen."

"That old?" she asked. "How many foster homes did you live in?"

"It's my time to ask a question," he said.

"Oh. I didn't know we were taking turns."

"It's only fair. You play fair, don't you?"

"Okay. What do you want to know?"

He wanted to know about her ex but decided to start off small. He tried to think of a different question. Something lighter. "Why are you obsessive about not getting colds?" he asked. But when she didn't have a quick reply he got a bad feeling.

"My father," she finally said. "He died of complications from a cold."

Real good, Dodd! "I'm sorry. I didn't know."

"How could anyone know?" she said. "It was a damn cold. He shouldn't have died."

It was the first time he'd ever heard her use foul language. Pain echoed in her voice. "How old were you?" he asked.

"Eight."

Her ache wrapped around his heart and became his own. He pictured the photograph of her standing beside her father's grave. "Things like that just shouldn't happen to kids," he said.

"What happened to you? How did your parents die?"

Her question flipped around his head, landing like a dead fish on his heart. But he had to talk or she would shut up.

"I never knew my father. My mom had a drug problem. They put me into the foster program while she went to re-hab. She didn't come back."

He closed his eyes. He'd never told anyone. Not even Maggie. Oh, he was certain she knew, but she hadn't heard it from him. Things like that would have been in his file when Maggie first agreed to take him in. He still didn't understand why Maggie had done so.

He remembered Sue was on the phone. "Not the Brady Bunch, either."

"I'm so sorry." Her words came heavy.

"Don't be." He hated the pity he heard in her voice. It was as bad as the condemnation. "I did fine." He raked a hand over his face and shut his mind to the past. "My turn. Did you sleep with the foot doctor?"

"Maybe I'll take the dare," she said.

"The dare?" he asked.

"Aren't we playing truth or dare, where you either answer a question or take a dare?"

She'd asked the question lightly, but he could still hear pity in her voice. Jason tried to think about what he could say to make her forget about his pitiful past. "I dare you to come out here naked and spend the night in my arms."

"I never slept with him."

He ran a hand over his chest, surprised but pleased. And

he'd also gotten her to forget about him—which is what he'd truly wanted. "You dated him a whole month and never had sex?"

"We were going to Mexico to . . . make it a real relationship. Then he canceled. But I'd already made up my mind I wasn't going."

"Why?"

"Because I realized he had issues."

"So you knew he was married and dating his nursing staff?"

"No. He has a foot fetish."

Jason laughed. "Well, I hate to tell you this, but you do have sexy feet. And ears. I love your ears."

"So I'll add feet and ear fetishes to *your* issue list."

He waited a second before asking, "My issue list? What are my issues? Besides not naming or knowing the sex of my cat. Which I really don't think is a big deal."

"It's a big deal. Plus, you look at women as bread! According to you, we go stale. And the longest relationship you've ever had was two months."

He pushed his head back on his pillow. "I didn't mean stale like that and you know it. And it was three months. It isn't fair judging someone from their past. Damn! Why do women do this?"

Frustration built in his chest. For the first time, he accepted that Sue could really turn him away, really not let him get any closer. No making love. Worse, no Christmas. The realization brought a lump of regret into his stomach.

"Why do women do what?" she asked.

He sat up. "Try to see the future. What's wrong with living for today? Enjoying what is right now?"

"Now doesn't last very long," she replied. "See? It's already gone."

"But what are you missing by not living in that moment?" Jason's grip on his phone tightened. "Think about how many things you've enjoyed and experienced. How many of those things are still a part of your life?" He let out another sigh of frustration. "Things come and go, but to close your-self off because you can't look into the future and find writ-ten guarantees . . . well, it's fucking wrong. It's cheating yourself out of life. Because nothing in this life comes with guarantees."

"You've obviously never been in love," she said. "You've never had your heart ripped into tiny pieces. Had every-thing you thought was real suddenly be . . . not real." Her voice shook a little. "There are some things, Jason, that just aren't worth the risk."

He knew all about having his heart ripped out, and not by just any woman. "So I'm not worth the risk. Is that what you're saying?" His mother sure as hell hadn't thought so. He pushed a hand through his hair.

"No. I'm just not wanting to jump into something be-fore . . ."

"Before what?"

"Before I'm sure."

Hope and frustration fought for a spot in his chest. "How long before you're sure? Because I'm sure *right* now. I'm sure I want you beside me. I want . . ." *Christmases.*

"Sex, right? You want sex."

"That, too. But this isn't just about sex, Sue. It never has been."

He hung up, but as he did so, Jason realized the signifi-cance of what he'd said. Because it *had* always been about sex with him before. Always. It was a lot safer that way.

Looked like things just weren't safe anymore.

If it wasn't just about sex, what else was it about? That was the question that kept Sue up most of the night and even plagued her on Wednesday morning when they went to feed Lacy's animals. Upon returning, even though she doubted she had one creative sentence in her, Sue barri-caded herself in her office to write—though what she re-ally intended was to ponder just a bit more. What were she and Jason all about?

It took her almost an hour before she came to an all-important realization: To get the answer, she'd have to ask Jason. Frankly, she wasn't quite brave enough to do that.

She stepped out to find Jason on the sofa, reading her book. He was so focused that he didn't hear her. Sue tried to see the page number, wondering where he was in the story and trying to read his reactions.

Writer's insecurities, perhaps, but how could she not be insecure? He thought she wrote unrealistic plots. Even if it was his friend who'd given her information.

He chuckled and raised his eyes. "Hey." He sat up, the humor still reflecting in his gaze.

"What's so funny?"

"Your heroine jerked off the detective's wig and tossed it to her dog." He set the manuscript aside, stood, and a few steps later his lips were on hers. It happened so fast she never had a chance to argue.

And maybe she wouldn't have. Who knew anymore?

She leaned in and accepted his kiss as part of right now.

Of course, she couldn't help but wonder what else Jason's "right now" included. Great sex? A few weeks of great sex? Months? More? Did he want a real relationship? Did it matter? Was she going to miss something wonderful with Jason because she was afraid it wouldn't last? The saying, "Better to have loved and lost than never to have loved at all," whispered through her mind. Not that this was about love.

Yet, she knew what a short trip it could be from infatuation to love. And she was already knee-deep in infatuation with Jason Dodd.

He brushed a finger over her ear. "You get some work done?"

"Not much." She glanced at her window, which he'd covered with a piece of plywood he'd found in her garage. Then her thoughts went to the manuscript on the sofa. "So, are you finding more unrealistic scenes?"

He frowned. "If you are talking about what I said at my

apartment the other day, I didn't say they were unrealistic, I said they read a little more like fiction than fact."

She arched an eyebrow accusingly. "Which is the definition of unrealistic."

"Look, you don't write unrealistic scenes. You just go weak on facts to inject humor. And the humor is great."

"So what was it about the wig scene that bothered you?"

"That scene was perfect. I love your writing. I didn't even really mean that—"

"I'm a big girl, Jason. Stop pretending and tell me."

His expression changed from frustrated to something different. "Why should I tell you? You don't want my opinion. You've got Chase. And now you have Danny."

"I'm asking you, aren't I?" Was that jealousy she heard in his voice? "Tell me where I used humor for humor's sake. Come on."

He hesitated. "Okay, it's not a big deal, but the scene in the convenience store. When the heroine pulled out a tampon and passed it off as a gun. A true criminal would never buy that."

"I'll have you know, the medium extra absorbent HEB brand tampons are the same size as that gun I named in the book. I know this because I called a gun expert and got measurements. Then I bought an eon's supply of tampons until I found one that measured right."

He held up both hands. "You know, I don't know why we're even having this conversation. Because I told you, I thought it was funny. I liked it."

"But you didn't believe it, did you?"

He frowned. "Maybe not, but I wouldn't have changed it. I'm just saying as a cop, I couldn't see it happening."

He passed his hand over his face again. "A person who handles guns isn't going to be fooled by a tampon. But for your scene, I can see why—"

"Really?" Sue walked to the breakfast table, grabbed her purse, and walked behind him. He swung around to face her. "No," she said. "Let's do a little test."

"A test?"

"Turn around." She nudged him.

"What kind of test?"

She nudged him again. "Just do it. Don't you trust me?"

"It's not me with the trust issues." He swung around.

Ignoring his trust-issue comment, she pulled a tampon from her purse. Then she pulled out her gun.

She ripped the wrapper off the tampon, crinkling the paper to make sure he would hear it. Then, only giving the tampon so much pressure, she pressed it against his head.

"Now, Mr. Tough Guy, are you going to argue with me when I say, 'Drop the gun, you lowlife slime ball or I'll shoot?' Wouldn't you be scared?"

CHAPTER TWENTY-FOUR

She was a flake with trust issues, but the cutest flake he'd ever known.

"Of course I'd be scared. You're holding me up with a tampon. Nothing is scarier than a woman with PMS." He turned around and his heart stopped when he saw the gun.

On automatic, he caught her by the wrist and pushed the gun downward. "What the hell are you doing?"

He jerked the gun away.

"See? I was right," she said.

"Right?" He checked the gun for bullets and his blood pressure dropped a couple of points when he found it unloaded. But those couple of points didn't drop his temper below a boil.

"Are you fucking nuts? You *never* point a gun at anyone unless you plan to use it."

She smiled triumphantly. "I didn't. I used this." She held up the tampon. "But you weren't sure, were you?"

"Damn it, Sue. You don't play with guns."

"It's not loaded."

"I don't give a damn. Have you been carrying a weapon in your purse this whole time?"

"Someone is trying to kill me."

"Do you even have a permit?"

"I have a license." Annoyance edged her voice.

Jason didn't give a flip about her annoyance. The woman

had practically held a pistol to his head. "Having a license doesn't allow you to carry it in your purse."

"You're just mad because I'm right." She held up the tampon in one hand. "You thought I only had a tampon, and therefore you believed it was a tampon, but when you saw the gun you thought it was a gun."

"I'm mad because you think this is a fucking toy!" He shook the gun.

"My point is," she continued, "that if someone holds something to your head and says it's a gun, you're going to believe it."

"Do you know how many presumably unloaded guns have killed people when they were doing something stupid like just now?"

"But I knew it wasn't loaded."

"How long have you had this?"

"I got it last Friday."

"Have you ever even shot a gun?"

"Yes," she said. "Okay, just once, but—"

"Could you use it if you had to?" He darted to the kitchen and placed her gun in a drawer. Then he swung back to her.

She fidgeted under his intense stare. "I think I could scare someone enough to back off."

"It doesn't work that way. People get shot with their own guns because they don't intend to use them. And for God's sake, don't ever point it, or even pretend to point it, at someone!"

She got that really hurt, pissed-off look women get. Then she took off down the hall.

Shit. He'd been too hard on her. He took a step to go after her, then stopped. He hadn't been too hard. Guns weren't toys. She'd just have to be mad.

She swung around and came back to face him. Her pissed-off look had faded. Now she just looked hurt. Which made him feel terrible.

"Sue, I'm sorry—"

"You're right. I shouldn't have pretended to point the gun at you. I wasn't thinking. I probably shouldn't have the gun, but I . . ." He could see it—she was going to cry. "Someone is threatening to kill me. I find out my boyfriend is married and cheating on me at the same time."

"Ex-boyfriend," he corrected.

"You tell me I don't write realistically, and you . . . don't name your cat, and I know I'm eventually going to wind up being leftover toast."

He grinned. "Trust me, there would never be any left-overs where you're concerned." Then the expected sheen of tears appeared in her eyes, and his grin faded. He pulled her into his arms. "I'm sorry I got mad."

She fit against his chest as if she'd been made for it. He buried his face in her shampoo-scented hair. "You were right. I thought it was a tampon, but the moment I saw the gun I thought it was the gun." He ran his hand over her shoulders. "And I never meant to insult your writing. You're a great writer."

She raised her face. "You're just saying that because you want me to sleep with you."

"No, I'm saying it because it's true."

Her blue eyes bright with unshed tears met his. "Too bad. It was almost working."

"Really?" He lowered his face to kiss her, but the door-bell interrupted. He growled, "I'm going to kill whoever it is at the door."

"Here, use this." She dropped the tampon in his hand and stepped forward.

He caught her. "I answer the door, remember?" He tossed her the tampon and felt for his gun in his holster before looking out the side window.

"It's FedEx," he said. "Are you expecting something?"

"If he's a good-looking blond guy, looks like a weightlifter, then it's the real thing. It's Hunky."

Jason glared at her. "You got a thing for your FedEx man?"

"No, but he's fun to look at." Sue walked over and peered

out the window. "It's him." She slipped the tampon in Jason's shirt pocket and opened the door. Jason stood back and listened.

"Hi there, Beautiful," the FedEx man said.

"How are you, Hunky?"

"Still heartbroken, since you refuse to go out with me," the FedEx man said. "I could really help you on those . . . those sex scenes."

Jason stepped beside Sue in the doorway. Mr. FedEx's smile shrank a notch.

Yanking away his clipboard, Jason handed it to Sue. "Sign it so this guy can go try to pick up his next customer." He reached in his shirt pocket and pulled out a pen, forgetting the gizmo was an electronic board.

Sue stared at his hand and grinned. "I . . . think that one's out of ink."

Jason looked down at the tampon. The FedEx guy laughed. Jason tossed the tampon over his shoulder.

Sue signed the clipboard and handed it off. The FedEx guy gave a two-finger salute and left.

As Sue shut the door, Jason glared at her. "Does that asshole always hit on you?"

"I'll bet he's wondering if you always carry unwrapped tampons in your shirt pocket."

"Funny," Jason said.

"Yeah, it is kind of funny." Sue focused on the envelope. "It's from Melissa. It's probably a copy of my book's new cover. They misspelled my name and had to completely redo it. Melissa posted it on my website." She ripped open the envelope and gave it a quick glance. "Do you want to read the real thing instead of the manuscript?"

"Sure." Jason shot the door one more glare before taking the novel. He studied the cover, a dead rat in the forefront, but in the background there was a small blonde half hidden behind a door and staring out. "I like it." He stared at the book, then raised his gaze, realizing why he liked it. "It's you."

"What's me?" she asked.

"The girl on the cover. It's you. Well, it looks like you."

"No, it . . ." Sue pulled the book from him. "It's not." She frowned. "Crappers. It does look like me, doesn't it?"

"Is that bad?" he asked.

"Yes. I don't want people to think I'm so conceited that I want my own picture on the cover. And besides, my heroine in that story didn't look anything like me." Sue tapped her finger against the book. "I knew I didn't like that cover artist. I'll bet you fifty bucks he did this because I didn't want to bang him. I'm calling Melissa, and if she's behind this, I'm firing her."

Right then Jason decided that Sue's editor—who still hadn't returned his calls with contact information on the cover artist—would be hearing from him again.

Several hours later, Jason looked down the hall to where Sue was holed up again. He left his third phone message for Sue's editor, hung up, then redialed her agent. Both he and Sue had talked to the woman briefly. The agent/publicist vowed she hadn't known about the cover and said she'd check into it, and she'd promised to get back to Jason as soon as she knew more. Of course, her "soon" didn't match Jason's. The phone rang for the sixth time and Jason disconnected.

Hitchcock dashed from the sofa and did figure eights around Jason's legs. Jason closed his phone and leaned over to stroke him. The cat, knowing there were other felines in Sue's study, seemed pretty put out. Jason sympathized. He was feeling pretty put out himself.

Sighing, he picked up his case folder and stared at the names of suspects. His phone rang. "Jason Dodd," he answered.

"Yes. My name's Carl Jetton. I'm Sue Finley's editor."

At first the guy sounded annoyed, but when Jason explained there had been threats made, Carl changed his tune.

"Look, you can speak to my assistant editor," he said. "But I can tell you he didn't do any of this stuff. He could use a dose of tact with my authors, and I know he's gotten rude with Sue. However, when I called him on it, he did apologize. He's just young and arrogant."

"Has he been off from work any time this last week?" Jason asked.

"No. He's here from eight till almost six every day."

Jason reached for Sue's book and stared at the cover. "Were you aware that the cover artist—I believe Ms. Finley's agent said his name was Michael Braxton—put Miss Finley on the cover?"

"Look, I've already heard an earful about that from Sue's agent, and yes, it does sort of resemble her, but frankly I think it's just a coincidence."

Jason didn't believe in coincidences. "And what's Mr. Braxton saying?"

"I had my assistant try to reach him but couldn't. Honestly, I don't know him that well. He's contract and works out of his home. This is the first job he's done for us. But . . . the guy was recommended by someone we use. He wouldn't be stalking an author."

Jason frowned. "I heard he hit on Ms. Finley when she was up several weeks ago, and he seemed upset that she wasn't interested."

"Hey, have you met the author? She's gorgeous. The guy's single. Hitting on her isn't a crime."

It was to Jason. "I'd still like to talk to him."

"Fine. As soon as I get him, I'll have him call you."

Jason set Sue's book down. "How about giving me his number?"

"I don't have that on me, but I'll have someone get it for you."

"Great."

"It'll be tomorrow."

Jason frowned. Hitchcock jumped up, landing with a thud on the family jewels. Jason grimaced, resettled the cat in his lap, and started rubbing him behind his ear. "Just get it to me as soon as possible."

As Jason hung up, he looked down at his list of suspects. His gaze returned once again to the name Benny Fritz.

"What do you say?" he asked the cat. "Is Mr. Leather Loafers our guy?"

"I don't know about you, but I'm starving." Sue wiggled her toes. It was almost eight on Wednesday night. Jason had picked the restaurant last time, so tonight it was her choice. She'd chosen one of her old stomping grounds. Though why she'd chosen it still gave her pause.

"Yup, I'm starving, too." He stopped the car at a red light and looked at her.

She knew what he wanted wasn't just food. *How long am I going to have to wait?* he'd asked.

If this afternoon was any indication, not long. She'd already given in to his kisses, his touches . . . and was considering giving in to much, much more.

"There it is." Sue pointed to the flashing neon sign. She noticed Jason's gaze on the rearview mirror. "Are we being followed?"

"No, I'm just checking." He pulled into the parking lot and looked up at the sign. "We're eating at a dance hall called the Fuzzy Duck?"

"Don't judge a book by a title. I . . . I used to come here a lot."

A smile brightened his eyes. "You going to dance with me?"

She thought about being in his arms, moving against him as some slow song played in the background . . . and shook her head. "No, we're here for the food."

They walked in. The atmosphere was dark and honky-tonkish, but Sue remembered it fondly. A wave of old memories moved over her. Memories of her and Collin. Sue waited for the pain to follow, but amazingly, only nostalgia lingered.

"How did you find this place?" Jason asked after they were seated.

"I stumbled across it when I was writing my first book. My hero was a country-western singer, and Collin and I came here every Friday so I could soak up the ambience. Even when I finished the book, we kept coming for the food and music. We even got pretty good at line dancing."

Jason stared at her, an odd expression on his face.

"What?" she asked.

He shrugged. "It's the first time you've said anything about your ex to me."

"He's not my favorite subject."

"But it sounds like you were happy—for a while anyway."

The question tumbled around her head. "It wasn't all bad." Sue glanced at the menu, surprised by this truth.

"I think I liked it better when I thought it was," Jason grumbled.

She looked over the menu at him. "I didn't picture you as the jealous type."

"Neither did I." He frowned. "Which steak is it that you recommend?"

She and Jason devoured their dinners before the band started. The steaks were as good as ever. The house red wine complemented the beef's peppery seasoning, and Jason cleaned his plate and managed hers as well.

He asked if she'd be mad if he ate some of her fries. She laughed. "I told you it wasn't about the fries."

"Yeah, but the last time I ate them I ended up in all kinds of trouble. Got whacked by a grandma with a cucumber."

When their plates were cleared, he ordered a chocolate cream pie for dessert.

"Here." He handed her the spoon when the pie arrived.

Sue stared at the meringue and thought about the calories. "No, I've eaten way too much chocolate today."

He frowned. "I only ordered it to watch you eat it. What you do with a spoon and dessert is sinful."

The heat in his eyes told her he spoke the truth. It also told her he relished sinning.

"Okay, I'm adding dessert pervert to your list of issues."

"Hey." He shrugged. "You and chocolate do it for me."

"Well, you'll have to settle for just chocolate. I'm stuffed." Sue picked up her purse and placed her credit card on the table. "I'm paying, but I'm going to the restroom."

He caught her around the waist and pulled her close for a kiss. A soft, wet kiss. Then he pulled her down for another one. Realizing how easy it was to just let go and let this happen, she pulled back. What exactly was she willing to let happen?

Not "it." No, she was just flirting with the *possibility* of letting "it" happen. There was a huge difference.

But did he know the difference? She dropped back down in her chair.

"What is it?"

Sue bit down on her lip. "I'm having fun. This"—she waved a hand between them—"is fun. But . . ."

"But what?" he asked.

"I don't want you to think that I'm . . . that I've completely changed my mind about . . . you know. Us." She needed more time. "Us now," she continued. "Especially us tonight."

His brows knitted together. "Let me see if I can translate that." He paused. "You don't want me to think I'm getting lucky tonight."

She felt herself blush and looked around to see if anyone had heard. No one seemed to be listening. "Right."

"I was afraid that was what you meant." He leaned back and stared. Then he leaned back in. "I don't get what you're waiting on. I—"

"I shouldn't have ever let you kiss me. I—"

He caught her hand. "Can I finish?" When she closed her mouth, he studied her. "Answer me this. Am I closer to getting lucky than I was, say, last night?"

She couldn't lie. "Yes."

He smiled a warm, sexy smile. "Then I guess I'll have to be happy with that."

"You can accept it?" she whispered.

"I told you before—I'll always respect if you say no."

She sent him a questioning look through her lashes. "But you're still not going to stop trying?"

"Oh, hell no." He grinned. "Not when I know I'm getting closer."

She rolled her eyes, but deep down she felt a tiny thrill. "Well, it's not going to happen tonight."

"The night's young."

Her thrill faded a bit. "This isn't a joke. I'm trying to be serious. I don't want you to think I'm playing head games with you."

He caught her hand. "I know you're not playing head games." His hold on her hand tightened. "Look, what I mean is that . . . whenever it happens, I'm sure it will be worth the wait."

She nodded. Then, suddenly feeling awkward about talking sex with him, she pulled her hand free and got up. "I gotta pee!" She hurried away before he could stop her.

She was almost at the bathroom when she heard, "Susie?" A familiar voice. A voice from the past. A voice she would just as soon have never heard again. And, turning around, she saw him. Or, rather, her.

Sue's heart dropped. He/she leaned against the wall, watching her. As always, Collin looked impeccable. Not a hair out of place, even if it was a wig. A slob in the house he might have been, but personal hygiene he never lapsed on. Sue braced herself for the old feelings of betrayal, but instead she felt . . .

Her eyes lowered. Okay, she felt angry, but not because of the lies or the five years she'd given to their marriage, but because she recognized the skirt he wore. It was hers!

Collin smiled and took a very feminine step forward.

Wanting to be alone with her confused emotions, Sue darted into the bathroom. When Collin followed, she realized her mistake. The women's restroom wasn't off-limits to Collin, not when he was dressed as Colleen.

"That's my skirt!" she hissed.

"That's why it's my favorite. I had to let it out a size, though." He looked her up and down, the way one woman should never assess another. Okay, like no *heterosexual* woman should assess another. But Colleen wasn't heterosexual. She was lesbian.

"You look great," he said.

Sue's gaze moved from his long red wig to his body, physically redistributed to somehow look female. "I hate you."

"Because of this?" A sad note entered his voice. He waved a hand up and down. "You're not the only one. My family can't accept it, either."

Sue's heart toyed with some emotion almost like sympathy. "I didn't mean that. I hate you because my skirt looks better on you than it did me."

Collin grinned. "God, I've missed your sense of humor. Every time I've come here, I hoped I would see you."

Uncomfortable with her newfound emotion, Sue twisted the toe of her sandal into the tile floor. "This is the first time I've been here." And why exactly had she come?

"You seem happy." He stared into her eyes, and the awkwardness level inched up.

Sue took a deep breath. "I'm doing okay." And she realized it was true. It had taken her a long while, but she *was* okay.

"I bought your books. I buy the autographed copies you leave at your book signings. You've done great. Not that I ever doubted you. You always had enough spunk for both of us." He toyed with the scarf around his neck.

"Thanks." She remembered how Collin had always supported her dreams. She stared back into his bright green eyes, a bit emotionally baffled.

The sadness filled his gaze again. "I hated hurting you. But I couldn't have stopped doing this any more than you could have stopped writing. It's part of me."

She realized she'd been so angry that she'd never tried to see his side of things. "Then you did the right thing," she said. And she meant it. She didn't understand him being a lesbian trapped in a man's body, but she didn't need to—at least, not to wish him well.

He touched a strand of her hair. "If I'd told you in the beginning, do you think you could have accepted it? That we could have made it work? I really never wanted anyone but you. We were good together."

Had they been? She thought for a second, then offered the truth. "We weren't that good. And I'm sorry, but no, I couldn't have accepted it. Maybe that says something about me, or maybe it says something about what we had." She inhaled a deep breath. "You telling me the truth, however, would have been nice. Maybe before we got married."

"I thought it would go away, that getting married would cure me." He glanced down at Sue's left hand. "No rings. So . . . that guy who was all over you out there—is he someone special?"

Sue considered the question. "He could be. I'm not sure." Collin nodded.

They talked for a few more minutes, mostly about his job, and then Collin left her alone. Sue turned to the mirror and stared at her reflection. After a second she smiled. As crazy as it sounded, seeing Collin had been okay. She might even say the encounter felt a little like fate—a little like the closure she'd needed, an end of a very long chapter in her life. In the next chapter, she stopped being angry and stopped blaming herself for things out of her control.

But what else was in this new chapter? Great sex with a certain cop?

How about going to the potty? her bladder begged, and she hurled herself into a stall.

Three minutes later, she stepped out of the bathroom and back into the dark atmosphere of the restaurant. She came to an abrupt halt as she spotted Jason standing outside the door talking to . . . Collin. Jason's gaze swung to her.

"He's such a dear," Collin said in a high voice, reaching out to straighten Jason's collar. "He asked me to check on you."

"I'm fine." Sue cut a warning look at her ex-husband.

"Susie always took a long time in the ladies' room. Nervous bladder."

Jason glanced back at Collin. "You two know each other?"

"Why, we were *very* close at one time." Collin pursed his lips at Sue. "Weren't we?"

Sue eyed Jason. "We should go."

"Not without hugs." Collin wrapped his arms around an oblivious Jason, who froze, caught by complete surprise. Collin took advantage of the situation and pressed his lips to Jason's mouth for a quick kiss. When he pulled back, he looked at Sue. "If you get tired of him, send him my way. But if he ever hurts you, I'll kill him."

Sue stepped back. "Let's go." She grabbed Jason and led him back to their table, signed the credit-card receipt, then headed out of the club and into the hot, humid night.

They hadn't gotten to the car when Jason, holding her hand, slowed them down. "You're going to explain that, right?"

"You wouldn't want to know." She dropped his hand and headed to his car.

He caught up with her. "Maybe I would. Maybe I wouldn't. I'm not sure." There were all sorts of innuendos in his tone. He opened the passenger door for her. After crawling behind the wheel, he turned to her. "Who is she?"

"Someone I used to know." Sue stared out the windshield. *Someone I used to care about.* Only, she didn't hurt as much as she once would have. She took a deep breath and couldn't deny some emotional current still lingered, but not like before.

"Come on. Tell me," Jason pushed.

Sue looked at him. Maybe she'd found her closure tonight, but she didn't feel up to sharing it yet.

"How well did you know each other? You two weren't—"

"Oh, please." Sue leaned back. "Don't even go there."

"Go where?" He grinned knowingly.

"What is it with men and their lesbian fantasies? How

would you feel if the thought of you having sexual encounters with men turned me on?"

"Stop!" He held up a hand. "I've *never* had a sexual encounter with a man. Not that there's anything wrong with it, but . . ."

But you were just kissed by one. She wasn't sure if she wanted to laugh. Instead she replied, "How would you feel if I wanted you to have had an encounter just so I could hear about it?"

"I didn't say I wanted . . . that. I was just asking."

"If I'd slept with her, would you want to hear about it?"

He hesitated. "Okay, so somewhere in the male brain our wiring is off and it would probably turn me on. But that's not to say I'd really want it." He started the car. "Frankly, I'd like to think you're into men, because that's what I'm offering."

Sue leaned back. "Just drop it, okay?"

Twenty minutes later, they pulled into her drive, and Jason turned to her with a sigh. "I can't drop it. Were you two lovers? From what I saw . . ."

Sue exhaled. "You know what? I wanted to spare you, but . . . yes, we were lovers."

"Really?" He looked more shocked than turned on.

She unbuckled her seat belt and scooted close. Raising her hand, she brushed her fingers over the lipstick still smeared on his mouth. Colleen's lipstick. "I was married to that cute little redhead."

CHAPTER TWENTY-FIVE

"Married? You're joking!" Jason said.

Sue stared at him. "No. I'm serious."

"You were married to a woman?" He looked puzzled.

"No." She brushed her fingertips over his lips. "You, Jason Dodd, were kissed by a man."

He sank back into the seat and studied her. "That . . . that was your ex-husband?"

"Yes." She added a bit of sweetness to her tone. "Are you happy now?"

"Hell, no!" His shoulders stiffened.

She expected him to start ranting about being kissed, but nope. He went for a different rant.

"Why the hell didn't you tell me? He could be the one behind all this!"

She frowned. "He's not."

"Damn it!" He slammed his hand on the steering wheel. "You think it's a coincidence that he was there?"

"It wasn't a coincidence. I told you Collin and I used to go there. Well, he still does. But we weren't followed. You said so yourself." In fact, Sue was more suspicious of her own motives. She wondered if, deep down, maybe she hadn't gone there on purpose, knowing she needed to put the past to bed.

"How could you not tell me that he was your ex? I needed to ask him . . . her . . . him . . . some questions."

"What was I going to do, step out of the bathroom and say, 'Excuse me, that cute redhead rubbing herself all over you is my ex-husband'?"

His face paled. "Fuck! He kissed me."

She waggled her eyebrows. "How was it? I want details. So I can fantasize."

He wiped a hand over his mouth. Twice. Then he unbuckled his seat belt. "Come on." He dragged her out of the car and to the front door. "I'm going to brush my teeth and then you're going to kiss me until I can forget. And that may take all night."

He brushed his teeth so hard his gums stung. When he came out of the bathroom, he found Sue sitting on the sofa, the remote control in her hands, surfing channels but not looking at the television. Crap. How hard had her ex's betrayal been on her?

He sat next to her on the sofa, took the remote control, and cut off the television. "You want to tell me about it?"

"You know everything," she said.

"Not everything." He pulled her against him.

She rested her head on his chest. For the longest time, neither of them spoke. Then he heard her sniffle. "I wasted five years loving and believing in a man who was living a lie."

It all came out. She started talking, and he listened. Several times he wanted to get up and go back to the bar and beat the shit out of Collin Jacobs, and he didn't care if the man now wore a dress or looked better than some of the women he'd dated; hurting Sue made him despicable.

Sue batted at her eyes and tried to dry his shirt with some paper towel. Then she said something surprising: "But . . . believe it or not, I'm okay. Seeing him was closure for me. You know what I mean?"

Jason didn't, but he nodded anyway. After a moment, he pulled her into his arms and kissed her.

When the kisses got good, she pulled away. "We shouldn't. I just—"

"I know. You don't know if I'm worth the risk." It was his frustration talking, but when he looked at her it vanished. "It's okay."

But it wasn't. He saw a world of doubt and lingering pain in her big blue eyes, and damn, if he didn't wish he had the magic words to make it all go away. He recalled something she'd said several times when she'd talked about her ex earlier. *It was supposed to last forever.* Then he heard the numerous warnings he'd been issued over the past few days. From Sue's grandfather, from Danny, from Chase. Even Maggie had told him, "Jason, you treat that girl right. Don't you go hurting anyone." And while he could offer Sue a thousand promises, he knew the one thing he couldn't offer was forever.

Not that she'd asked for it, herself. Not exactly. Hell, most people didn't believe in forever anymore. One out of two marriages ended in divorce, didn't they?

Whoa! How had the word marriage come up?

"It's late," she said.

He nodded. "I'll call you." He watched her walk away, then headed straight for the bathroom.

He stayed in the shower for the longest time. As he leaned against the tiled wall, the water rolled down his body and ran down the drain. Its coldness chased away his arousal, but he kept waiting to lose the uneasy feeling in his chest.

The feeling didn't go away. So he did what he'd done for most of his life, shoved the emotions away and focused on something else. He focused on Sue's case, went over the facts and made himself a mental list of what to do next. And by the time he tossed his sheets on the shot-up sofa, he realized it was after midnight.

"Shit." He'd said he would call Sue. Grabbing his phone, he punched in her number. She finally answered.

"Were you asleep?" He imagined her softly tucked in, her curves draped in cotton animal pajamas.

"Almost. But don't sweat taking a long time—I'm used to you not calling."

He fought back annoyance. "Hey, I had to take a cold shower. Someone left me in a world of pain."

"I told you that you shouldn't be kissing me," she replied.

"How else am I going to convince you?" He lay back on the sofa and his frustration peaked again. "I could make you feel so good. Do you know what I'd do first?"

"You're going to talk yourself into another cold shower," she warned.

"Or you might have pity on me," he said.

"Remember, your mother said for you to stop pressuring me."

"I never minded very well. First, I'd slip my hand under your pajama top. Wait? What kind of animal are you wearing tonight?"

She hesitated. "Kittens."

"I'd slip my hand under your kitten pajamas, slowly move it up your stomach and higher. Your nipples would tighten and beg for me to taste them."

He wondered if this was turning her on. It was definitely arousing him.

He ran a hand over his own chest. "To do that, of course, I'd have to remove your shirt. I'd undo one button, then another. Like I did when I was in bed with you the other night. Do you remember what it felt like when I had your nipples in my mouth? You tasted so good."

"Is this phone sex?" Sue's voice sounded soft, but she didn't object. "Because I've never done this before."

"Me either, but I'll give anything a shot once. It might take the edge off, if you know what I mean." He prayed she knew what he meant.

"I . . . don't know how."

He gave a small laugh. "I don't think there's hard and fast rules. If we're actually having phone sex . . ." He waited for her to object but she didn't. "We each do the work but pretend it's the other person. We sort of talk each other through it."

When there was silence on the other end of the line, he

took a deep breath and moved forward. "Where's your hand now?"

She hesitated. "On the bed."

"Could you slip it inside your panties? You are wearing panties, aren't you?"

"Yes."

"What color are they?"

He heard her shuffle and imagined her raising her pajama bottoms to check.

"White."

He imagined the white panties she'd been wearing the day he'd stormed into her bedroom, and it made him harden even further. He groaned. "Slip your hand inside your panties, Sue. All the way in. Where it feels good."

He pushed his own hand inside his boxers. "Are you touching yourself?" There was a silence. "Sue? Where's your hand?"

"It's . . . there."

"Where 'there'?" His dick throbbed, and he wrapped his fist around it.

"Do I have to talk dirty, too?"

He chuckled. "I think it helps." Another long pause. "Do you want me to tell you where my hand is?"

"I guess." Her voice was wispy.

"It's wrapped around my dick. Which is harder than iron now. Because I'm imagining you touching yourself, imagining that it's you touching me. I'm throbbing. So hot. Only one thing would feel better." He took a deep breath and moved his hand up and down. "If I were inside you. Inside . . . where your hand is now." He closed his eyes and wondered how she would taste, how her fingers would taste after tonight . . .

"Are you wet?" he asked. "Tell me how you feel."

"I feel . . . embarrassed." Then she snickered. "I'm sorry. I lied. I'm not touching myself."

Feeling like a fool, he jerked his hand from his pants. "Damn," he growled. "Take a chance on me."

"I can't." The playfulness in her tone had vanished.

"Why? We're crazy about each other."

"I know, but—"

"I'm not your ex." Frustration built in Jason's chest. He cared about her more than he'd ever cared about anyone. Hell, he cared more than he even wanted to care.

"I know," she said. There was a long pause. "But I was hurt, Jason."

"We've all been hurt, Sue. But we don't stop living."

"No. But maybe if I'd been more careful before I let myself care about Collin then I would have seen his issues."

Jason raked a hand over his face. "You can't punish yourself because someone else is screwed up. You can't punish other people for Collin's mistake of not being honest with you." He squeezed his eyes shut. "You can't go around thinking the worst of me because of what that asshole did."

"I don't think the worse of you! As a matter of fact, I wish I didn't like you. I wish you didn't make me laugh or make me feel safe. I wish you were mean to little old ladies bearing cucumbers. I wish I didn't want to make love to you. But I do want to."

"Then do it."

"I can't. Not yet." And she hung up.

"Shit!" Jason stood. Clutching his phone, he let out a deep breath. He wanted to go to her, but instead he headed to the bathroom for another shower. This time he'd have to finish the job himself. Cold water wasn't going to work.

And then he realized his frustration wasn't all sexual. He wanted so much more than sex; he wanted . . . Sue's trust. Her approval. He wanted Christmases—or at least the possibility of Christmases. *I don't believe you were a bad kid,* he remembered her saying. Now he wanted her to believe he wasn't a bad man. That he was worth taking a risk on. But, damn, he was tired of having to prove himself.

As he stepped into Sue's study on the way to the bathroom, Mama jumped out of her box. She gave him a hopeful look. "I'm not in the mood," he muttered to the cat. "Besides, why is it that you think I'm a good person but no one else does?"

The feline froze, and her golden gaze shot to the window. Jason followed it. For a split second he could swear he saw a shadow.

Realizing he held his phone, he hit redial and moved to the window. He saw nothing, but . . .

By the time the phone rang, he'd made it to the living room.

"Okay, you win." Sue's voice flowed through the line. "But I can't do phone sex. If I'm going to do this, I want the real deal."

His breath caught at her words—or was it at the shadow he saw move past the living room window? "Get out of the bedroom!" he shouted. He grabbed his gun from on top of the television. "Get out!" He ran down the hall, shoving open her door.

Sue stood, her phone still in her hands. The shadow was now at her window, and Jason's heart stopped when it raised a hand and pointed something that looked like a gun.

"Get down!"

He dove across the room, praying he got to her before the bullet.

CHAPTER TWENTY-SIX

Jason landed on top of her, pulling Sue behind the bed. "Are you shot? Sue? Are you hurting anywhere?"

"No." Her word came out so low that he barely heard.

The knot of pain in his chest started to unfurl, but his knuckles throbbed. Somehow, during the fall, he'd managed to place his hand behind her head to cushion it. "You sure you're okay?" He turned her face to his.

She nodded, but even in the semidarkness he saw the panic in her eyes and remembered she'd just agreed to have sex with him. Damn. "You have lousy timing, sweetheart."

"Did . . . someone just shoot at us?" Her voice shook.

"Yeah." He rested his forehead against hers. "Don't move, okay?" He started to pull back.

"Don't you move, either." She clutched her arms around him.

"I'll be fine." He pulled away, poked his head up, and aimed his gun. When he saw only the broken bedroom window, he ran to the opening just in time to see a figure leaping over Sue's side fence. He jumped through, feeling a sliver of glass cut into his heel. He ran to the fence, pulled himself up, and saw a car squeal away. He couldn't be sure, but it looked like a Saturn.

Cursing, he hurried back to Sue and found her balled up beside the bed with the phone pressed to her ear. She jumped up when she saw him. "I called 911." She dropped the phone and threw herself against him.

"There's glass." He picked her up and started out of the bedroom.

"They said not to leave the phone." Her words came out hiccupping.

"Don't worry." He laid her down on the sofa. Remembering the sound of the bullet, fear shot again to his gut. The bastard could have killed her. Terror squeezed the air out of his lungs. "Are you sure you're okay?" Holding his gun in one hand, he moved his other hand over her.

"I'm fine."

He gazed into her tear-streaked face. Her nose ran; her lips trembled. She was the most beautiful thing he'd ever seen. He cupped her cheek in his palm. "I'm going to kill that bastard."

Officer Tomas and a couple of other uniformed officers from Hoke's Bluff showed up five minutes after Jason carried Sue into the living room. They filled out the paperwork, dusted for fingerprints, and dug the .38 slug from the wall of Sue's bedroom. Sue hardly talked. She sat on the sofa, biting her lips.

Jason hurried Tomas and company out of the house, promising the cop he'd bring Sue by tomorrow if there were more questions. Then he found another piece of plywood in her garage and hammered it over her bedroom window. The whole house was beginning to look like this. Then he swept up the glass and changed her bedsheets.

The mundane details taken care of, Jason's attention shifted solely to Sue, who still sat in a ball on her sofa, her cat curled beside her. She looked exhausted, but he could tell by the way her gaze kept moving to her bedroom that she wasn't going to be able to sleep there tonight. For that reason, Jason led her to his car fifteen minutes later. The fact that she didn't complain about leaving, hadn't asked to change out of her pajamas or pack some clothes—he'd done the latter for her—told him a lot about her mental state.

"Where are we going?" she finally asked, standing like a sleepwalker by his car.

He got her inside, then crawled behind the wheel. Glancing over at her, he thought about taking her to Chase's. But what if the bastard had once followed Sue there? His own place was an hour away, but . . .

He reached over and belted her in. "We're going to Maggie's."

She hesitated. "Your mother's? At this hour?"

"She runs a B&B and lives in the guest house. We'll just grab a room."

"What about Hitchcock? And Mama and the kittens?"

"They'll be okay. I put out some fresh water and chow. I don't think your stalker's after them."

Backing out of the driveway, he kept his eyes peeled for cars. Part of him was wishing that the freak would show back up while he was mad enough to shoot first and ask questions later.

Sue exited the car, following Jason to a door where he fit a key. Only then did she realize she'd left home wearing pajamas. "Jeez!"

"What?"

"I didn't change my clothes."

"It's the middle of the night. You're fine."

"Oh God!" she gasped.

He flinched. "What?"

"What if . . . what if that freak goes back? The cats are all alone, and—"

"There's a patrol car scheduled to be driving by every few minutes. Plus, the guy's not going to go back tonight. He knows the cops will be around."

She relaxed a bit. Jason's words rang true. She trusted him with her life.

Those words flittered through Sue's dazed mind, reminding her: Jason had probably just saved her life. She curled her arms around herself, feeling chilled to the bone.

Her gaze shifted. They were currently standing before an old Victorian with a wraparound porch. The sign in front read: Victorian Inn. It was one of the top B&Bs in the area. Sue had read about it in the paper, and now she remembered the name was on Jason's list of favorite websites.

He opened the door. Moving to the front reception area, he grabbed a key, wrote a note, and left it on the old Victorian desk. "Come on." He took Sue's hand.

She followed him up the stairs and waited while he unlocked another door. Inside, he turned on the lights.

"It's lovely." In spite of her panic, she actually appreciated her surroundings. The room had an antique four-poster. The full-size bed, covered in a down comforter and beautiful quilts, bracketed the back wall. The room's decorations were in line with Victorian style but not overdone.

"The bed and breakfast is Maggie's passion." Jason shut the door. "Our bathroom's in here."

Sue peeked into the large bath, decorated to fit the Victorian theme, but in addition to the claw-foot tub that sat in one corner, a two-man Jacuzzi waited in the opposite.

A moment later, she stopped thinking about decoration and wrapped her arms around her middle. Someone had tried to kill her. Actually tried to kill her. Actually taken a shot at her. They weren't just throwing rocks and rats anymore.

"Would you like me to run you a bath? It might relax you," Jason suggested.

"No." Sue turned to the bed, suddenly unsure of the sleeping arrangements. Okay, she'd agreed to have sex with him in a moment of weakness, but—

"All I want to do is hold you tonight," he said, as if he'd read her mind. He pulled her against him. "You believe me, don't you?"

She nodded, and he moved her to the bed and pulled back the covers. Still dressed in her pajamas, she kicked off her sandals and climbed into lavender-scented sheets.

She watched Jason pull off his shoes and remove his shirt and gun harness. He laid the gun on the bedside table and unzipped his jeans. Sue thought about turning her head, but the casual manner in which he undressed made it comfortable to watch. When he was wearing only boxers, he sat down on the edge of the bed and pulled one foot up into his lap.

Sue suddenly remembered he'd been cut. "It's not bleeding, is it?"

"Nah, it's fine. Barely a scratch." He lay back and pulled her close. "*You* okay?" He pressed his lips to her cheek.

"Yeah." She pillowed her head on his chest.

"Ready for lights out?"

"Please."

The rich darkness brought a sense of belonging, and the tension slowly leaked out of her as she soaked up his warmth, his strength. She trusted him.

"This feels . . . good," he said. His words echoed her sentiment.

She listened to his heartbeat for a while. "Thank you," she finally said.

"You don't have to thank me. Go to sleep." He kissed the top of her head. It was a sweet kind of kiss that hinted at a lot of emotion but nothing sexual. Her heart twinged at the possibility that Jason Dodd really cared about her.

But did that make him safe?

The Thursday morning sun sneaked into the corners of her eyelids, and the scent of coffee teased her nose. Sue wiggled her fingers against the mattress and realized . . . she wasn't touching the mattress.

Instantly coming awake, she remembered where she was and upon whom she was sleeping. Her head lay pillowed on his chest, his hand still rested on her hip. Their positions hadn't changed from last night. Except, she now had her leg thrown over the top of his.

She shifted. Okay, his thigh wasn't the only thing her leg rested on. There was also his . . . pencil.

She started to move her leg and stopped. Oh goodness, but he had an amazing pencil. Inching her leg up, feeling it with the side of her knee, she recognized again how it was a nice, extra-large pencil. Perfect for . . .

She bit down on her lip and recalled him pointing out that she was allowing her fear to stop her from experiencing something wonderful. She had to admit, this felt pretty wonderful.

Life doesn't come with guarantees. We take risks. His words played in her head. And she *did* want guarantees, but was that realistic? Things happened. People died of colds, men realized they had lesbian women trapped inside their bodies . . . Maybe she just needed to take a leap of faith. But could she do that?

She moved her leg up his thigh one more time.

"Do that again and we're going to have a mess on our hands."

An unexpected giggle slipped from her lips.

"You think it's funny?" Jason flipped her over, finding his place on top of her. His pencil, lead up, found its natural spot between her legs. They both froze, their gazes joined. Only two pieces of cotton separated them from being one.

As he lowered his lips, she slapped a hand over her mouth. "Morning breath," she mumbled through her palm.

He nuzzled her neck and rolled off her. "You're killing me."

Standing, she started toward the bathroom. She saw him slip on his jeans and heard him ask, "You want some coffee?"

"Love some." She paused. "Can I take a bath?"

He nodded. "Go for it. I'll get you coffee and make sure Maggie found my note."

Not long after he left, Sue sank into the claw-foot tub

with lots of tickling bubbles. She had just rested her head back when the door creaked open and Jason returned— and walked right into the bathroom.

"Coffee," he announced.

Sue curled up in a ball. "Jason!"

"What?" He set the mug on a small table beside the tub.

"I'm naked. Do you mind?" She fluffed the bubbles over her body.

"I don't mind at all," he replied, giving her a wolfish grin. "Need your back washed?"

"No."

"Your front?"

She pulled her knees closer to her chest.

His grin widened. "It's a big tub. Want some company?" As he asked, his baritone voice dropped an octave.

She hesitated, so very tempted to say yes, but . . . "Isn't your mom downstairs?"

"Would you hate me if I lied and said she wasn't?"

"You should probably visit with her."

"Killjoy." He leaned over and kissed her. "When you're ready, follow your nose to the kitchen. Maggie can't wait to meet you."

After she finished soaking, Sue dressed in the jeans and T-shirt that Jason had packed for her and made her way downstairs, finger-combing her damp hair. Reaching the front of the house, she couldn't help but wonder how many women Jason had brought here. *Don't think about that.* Instead, sniffing the air, she did what Jason had suggested and followed her nose. The scent of yeast rising, cinnamon buns, and sizzling bacon led her to the kitchen.

A small, gray-haired woman, pleasantly plump and wearing a white apron over a pale green dress, stood over the stove flipping the bacon. She must have heard Sue's footsteps, because her face widened in a smile.

"You must be Sue." She dropped her fork and, rushing over, drew Sue into a hardy hug.

Sue hugged the woman back. "And you must be Maggie."

"I've heard so much about you," Jason's foster mother said. "I feel as if I already know you."

"You've . . . heard about me?"

"For almost a year. Jason and I share books, and when he told me he actually knew a writer . . . well, I drove him a little crazy with questions. Anyway, he kept me updated on all your books, told me when you were on that cooking show. I used your recipes. Love the pasta salad! And he bought me a copy of all your books and an extra copy for our guest library." Maggie's aged hands moved as she talked. "He used to bring me over those newsletters, but he stopped. He promised to get my books autographed. But now . . ."

Sue wasn't sure what surprised her more, that Maggie spoke faster than she herself did, or that Jason had been talking about her for over a year. "I'd be happy to sign them." Nervous, she looked around the bright, yellow kitchen. "And your home is lovely."

"Thank you! Sit down and let me pour you another cup of coffee. Cream, right?"

"Yes, ma'am." Sue stepped closer to the counter. "But let me serve myself and . . . what can I do to help you?"

Sudden fear hit her. What was she doing? She prayed Maggie wouldn't ask her to whip up an omelet. She could probably make toast. Of course, there was a fifty-fifty chance she'd burn it.

"You just relax," Maggie said, frowning. "Jason told me about last night. I'm so glad he brought you here." She pulled out a chair and motioned for Sue to sit.

Sue sank into the seat, feeling increasingly nervous but unable to pinpoint exactly why.

"I do hope my son has behaved." Maggie placed a different mug of coffee on the table. "I had a little talk with him after . . . after I called the other night."

Oh yeah. That was why. Sue felt her face heat as she remembered the things she'd said to Maggie on the phone.

"Oh, he's been very good. I mean, nice." She stared at the

steam billowing off the antique cup. Maggie had to know that she and Jason had shared the same room. Did she think—

"I see you two have finally met." Jason stood in the door. His sandy blond hair looked a little mussed.

Maggie walked over and kissed her son's cheek. "Did you change that lightbulb?"

"Took care of it," he answered.

"Don't know what I'd do without him." Maggie gave Sue a smile.

Jason glanced at Sue, too. Their eyes met, and a warm glow filled her chest where her heart would have been if it hadn't taken flight somewhere a moment earlier. Then came an inner voice whispering through her head, *I love this man.*

Which was followed by, *No, I can't be in love with him. It's just aftershocks from him saving my life.*

She tried really hard to believe the latter, but she couldn't. Jiminy Cricket, no matter how much she'd fought him, no matter how much she'd tried to put him off, she'd allowed him into her heart, warts and all. It was true. She loved him.

Oh, Hades. She was up to her ears in it now!

If she hadn't already admitted to falling in love with Jason that morning, Sue would have had to admit it later Thursday afternoon. Standing in the middle of the park, she watched him work with a team of ten-year-old foster boys on their soccer skills.

The last few hours had left her amazed at the layers of wonderful she'd found in the man. First, the teasing yet affectionate way he treated Maggie, and now, how he worked with these young boys. On top of all that, he looked so sexy in those shorts that Sue knew she'd be joining the fornicating masses before the night was over.

Jason winked at her. Sue felt as if she were on cloud nine and still climbing.

But for how long? a voice whispered. How long before

she was stamped "day-old bread" and Jason tossed her out for a hot roll? Her heart dropped into her stomach as the question prowled around her head looking for an answer.

"Hi, are you Mr. Jason's girlfriend?" a young voice asked.

Sue looked down at a dark-skinned girl wearing ribbons and pigtails and guessed her to be around seven. "Sort of." She leaned close. "Are you his other girlfriend?"

The girl laughed. "I'm Cara. That's my foster brother in the red shirt. I come to cheer. I'm a cheerleader at school."

"You are?" Sue said. "I used to be a cheerleader, too."

"Do you want to cheer with me?" The child's eyes danced with hope.

"Sure," Sue said. "I might be rusty but I'll try."

For the next twenty minutes, Sue and Cara cheered the boys on. Jason looked up often and smiled, and when practice wound down, Sue made her way over to where he could wrap his arms around her waist and kiss her.

"Do you do practice every week?" she asked.

"Every other week. Since it's volunteering and looks good for HPD, they usually let me off a few minutes early so I can make it. Then on every other Saturdays."

"You are a good man, Jason Dodd," she remarked.

He seemed to soak up the compliment. "Why is that?"

Volunteering to coach. But something warned her he didn't want to be praised for that. "Must be those shorts," she said instead.

"So, you're checking me out?" His smile turned devilish.

Sue reached up on her tiptoes and kissed his cheek. "I'm going to grab a soda." She pointed to the concession stand. "You want one?"

"Yeah." His phone rang, and he answered it, and Sue took off.

"I want it working as soon as possible," Jason said, his eyes on Sue as she went to get the sodas. His cheek still burned where she'd kissed him. Crazy as it was, he remembered her kissing her grandfather on his cheek, remembered wishing for the same kind of affection from her. Something akin to pure joy filled his lungs.

"Yeah, and I'm trying," the electrician said.

Jason had left his key to Sue's door with Maggie, and the bed and breakfast's handyman and electrician were supposed to get together to get her windows fixed and security cameras and light sensors connected. There was no damn way Jason was letting that freak get close to Sue again.

"Get it done tonight and you can add another hundred to the bill," he promised.

"It's not the money," the electrician said.

"Just do it." Jason hung up.

Reaching down, he dropped a soccer ball into his netted bag and watched Sue stop to speak to one of the boys. His chest tightened as he saw her ruffle the sweaty kid's hair—with no hesitation, no prejudices. He knew firsthand how foster kids often got viewed as untouchable, as if they weren't as clean as kids who had real parents. But not by Sue.

Jason had almost canceled today's practice, but at the last minute he'd decided to simply bring Sue with him. Never would he have thought to bring any other woman with him. That would have brought up too many questions. But that was the thing about Sue: He didn't have to explain anything to her. She knew about his less-than-grand past. And he liked her knowing about it, too.

Rubbing a hand over his face, he hoped Sue would agree to stay at Maggie's another night—just in case the electrician didn't get things up and operating.

One of his players, Jose, came over and asked about the next week's practice. They were still talking when Cara came running up. "Where's Miss Sue?" the girl asked.

Jason picked up a soccer ball and slipped it into the crook of his arm. "She went to grab a soda. I saw you teaching her a few cheers."

Cara's smile showed off a missing tooth. "I like her!"

"Me, too," Jason said. More and more, every hour he spent with her.

The girl looked down at her hands and a folded piece of paper she held. "Some boy asked me to give this to her."

Jason looked at it. "What boy?"

Cara glanced over her shoulder. "I didn't know him. He said someone gave it to him and asked him to give it to me, and I was supposed to give it to Sue. Or maybe he said to give it to you."

Jason looked at the concession stand. A crowd stood in line waiting to get refreshments, but he didn't see Sue. He reached for the note and opened it. The ball he held in the crook of his arm dropped to the ground. The three-word message was written in red:

Die, Sue, Die!

"Tommy," he called to an older boy. "Stay with Cara."

He took off for the concession stand, his heart racing, his gaze zipping from side to side. The closer he got, the more frightened he became. He stopped in front of the crowd, his breaths falling short.

She wasn't there.

CHAPTER TWENTY-SEVEN

"Sue?" Jason's panicked voice echoed through the park bathroom. "Damn it, are you in here?"

Sue's shorts and panties hung around her ankles while she half-squatted, her rear held a germ-free inch above the toilet. She'd just gotten a healthy stream going when she heard him. "What?" She lost her healthy stream.

"What are you doing in here?"

A voice with a bold Jersey accent called from the stall to her right, "This is a bathroom, ace. You figure it out."

"What is it?" Sue grabbed for tissue, only to discover that, just her luck, she'd chosen a paperless stall.

"You said you were going to get a soda!" Jason accused.

"You need permission to go to the bathroom?" the Jersey girl asked.

"I got mace if you need it," a voice with a Texas drawl chimed in from the left stall.

"I don't need the mace, but I need some paper," Sue whispered to her left. She wiggled her fingers under the stall.

"Come out," Jason said, and Sue saw his feet standing in front of the stall to the right.

"Get out or I'll call the cops," Jersey girl yelled.

"I've got mace," the woman to Sue's left repeated.

"I just need a few squares!" Sue wiggled her fingers desperately.

"Where are you?" Jason snapped.

"Call them," Left Stall said.

"No, no, I'm here!" Sue spoke up. "Now get out before you get arrested and maced!"

"I work at the abused woman shelter," said Ms. Right Stall.

"I'm not abused," Sue said.

"Well, I'm counting to three and then I'm calling the police."

"I *am* the police," Jason seethed.

Sue turned to the left stall and hissed, "Just a few squares." When her fingers went unnoticed, she pulled back her hand. "Fine."

"All abused women say they're not abused," continued the lady with the Jersey accent. "Does he hit you?"

"Sue?" Jason banged on her stall door. It didn't seem like he was going to take no for an answer.

"No! He doesn't hit me," Sue said. But it didn't seem like her stall neighbors were going to take no for an answer, either.

"Take the mace." A can rolled into her stall.

"I'm calling 911," said the lady to Sue's right.

"Jiminy Cricket!" Sue jerked up her panties and shorts, then pushed open the stall door, hitting Jason in the chest. The panic in his eyes reconfirmed what she'd suspected: Something had happened. Something bad. She supposed she should be grateful he cared so much that he'd follow her into a women's restroom.

He placed a firm grip on her shoulders. "Are you okay?"

She sighed. "My panties aren't fresh anymore, but I'm fine. What is it?"

"Why would I sit in a different booth?"

Sue put her hand out to steady herself as Jason hit the brakes a little fast to stop at a red light. It was evening, and they were on their way to meet her critique group.

They'd butted heads for the past few hours. Sue had told Mary, one of her critique partners, where she'd been headed that day. He'd raked her over the coals for it. She'd reminded him of his spoken belief that Mary wasn't involved. He'd reminded her that Mary might have told Fritz where she was, and he still suspected Fritz. And since they still hadn't gotten Mary on the phone, he didn't like Sue going to meet the group. Sue reminded him that she still didn't think Benny was behind this, and she'd told him she wasn't going to start living like a hermit. He'd reminded her that she should leave the police work to him—and that her safety was more important than her social life. Then they'd both seemed to remember they were running on little sleep and should probably stop reminding each other of things.

Taking a deep breath, Sue tried to explain in a calm manner. "You should sit at another booth because we won't be able to have a normal meeting if you're glaring at everyone."

"I'm not going to glare, but I'm going to ask Mary if she mentioned your whereabouts to anyone, and then I'm going to find out where Mr. Leather Loafers was all day."

"I'll ask," Sue said.

"I want to ask!"

"See, that attitude is why you're going to be sitting at another booth."

Sue leaned her head back. After failing to find the boy who'd given the note to Cara, Jason had been hovering like a mosquito waiting for fresh blood. He'd practically made her stand in the bathroom while he showered.

Not that she hadn't enjoyed the quick glance she'd gotten of his backside.

He'd then spent the rest of the afternoon on the phone trying to reach her editor.

As the image of his backside tickled her mind again, Sue tilted to one side and looked at Jason. Yup, even annoyed, she still felt that gushy in-love feeling she'd felt earlier. "I'll keep the meeting short."

He met her gaze. "Thank you. But I don't trust that Fritz guy. And I don't see why we can't stay at Maggie's another night."

Sue sighed. "I know you don't trust him, but I do. And

if you're going to interrogate anyone, I'd prefer you do it tomorrow, not during our critique meeting. And as for staying at Maggie's, I don't like leaving the cats home alone."

She saw his hands tighten on the steering wheel, and he said, "I want to talk to your friend about where he was today. And I really think the cats will be fine. It wouldn't hurt to just stay one more night . . ."

Sue couldn't help it; she laughed.

"What's funny?"

"We are. Do you realize we just managed to argue about four subjects at the same time? I didn't know anyone could think that many thoughts but me."

He grabbed her hand and squeezed. "That's because we're good together." He shot her a smile. "Besides, I've had practice. Maggie can do six subjects in the same conversation."

Sue smiled. She wasn't sure why knowing she had something in common with Maggie felt good, but it did. Maybe because after seeing the woman and Jason together, she knew how much they cared for each other. Which maybe meant he was capable of caring for her for longer than three months.

They arrived at the diner with plenty of time. Benny was late, so the critique group started with Mary's work. As Frank offered a few suggestions, Sue found her gaze moving to the booth across the room where Jason talked on the phone. He'd done as she asked and not talked about the case with Mary yet. The fact that he'd granted her wish made Sue feel bad about making him sit at another table.

"Sue?" Frank prompted.

"Let her enjoy herself. I don't blame her," Mary said.

"Blame me for what?" Sue asked.

Frank laughed. "I think you're falling for him."

As Jason had instructed, Sue had kept the dialogue about what was happening with her stalker to a minimum. For that reason, none of her friends seemed tense; they likely thought the situation was resolving itself. "I might be falling for him," she admitted and decided at the very least she needed to apologize for whatever he might have said when he'd made his first round of interrogations. "I'm sorry he questioned you the other day. He can be a bear at times."

"He wasn't a bear," Mary said. "If I was five years younger . . ." She grinned. "Oh, heck, I'm only thirty-eight. I may still go after him."

Sue grinned. "Benny called him an arrogant, green-tinted slime bucket."

Frank laughed. "He wasn't rude with me, either. Benny's probably just jealous."

Sue looked at Frank and then Mary, who shook her head in agreement. She said, "You noticed Benny has a crush on me, huh?"

Mary laughed. "Yeah, but don't worry, as soon as he and his wife are back together, you'll be history. The last time he and his wife were separated, he asked *me* out."

"Hey, you almost can't blame the guy" Frank added.

"Because we're gorgeous," Mary teased.

"That, and have you seen his wife?"

"That's terrible," Mary and Sue scolded at the same time.

"He loves her," Mary added.

Sue nodded in total agreement. Then curiosity took hold and she had to ask: "Did you mention to anyone today about me being at the park?"

Mary wrinkled her brow. "Why?"

"Something sort of happened there."

"Oh." The older woman looked concerned. "Well, I did call Frank and Benny to remind them of the meeting. I guess I could have mentioned it, but I don't remember."

"You didn't say Sue was at the park when you called me," Frank said. Then he added, "You don't think Benny is behind this?"

"*I* don't," Sue said and glanced at Jason.

"Seriously, Benny's not going to send you a rat," Frank said. "He might be hitting on you, but he's not that sick."

"That's how I see it," Sue agreed, rolling her pencil between her palms.

"See what?" Benny's voice startled all of them. "Sorry. My wife was late picking up our son after his game."

"Hey!" Guilt made Sue's voice squeaky.

Benny scooted in beside her, put his arm around her, and purposely looked at Jason. "I see your bodyguard came with you."

Sue saw Jason flinch. She moved out of Benny's embrace and, claiming a good ten inches of booth, she placed his manuscript on the table. "We should get started."

Tina, the pregnant waitress, brought Benny his coffee. Sue went over Benny's chapters, pointing out places she felt needed more description. "By the way, you were missing a few pages," she remarked.

"I was?" Benny seemed surprised.

"Mine were all there." Mary handed over her copy of the manuscript.

"I liked everything but the giant gopher," Frank said. "Too cartoonish."

Ten minutes later, after concluding their literary discussion on what might make giant gophers less cartoonish, Benny dropped a dollar—just a dollar, which wouldn't even cover what he'd ordered—on the table. "Thanks for looking at this so fast. I have to run. I told Beth I'd come by and talk."

Sue's breath hitched—in a good way. "So, you and your wife are working on things?"

Benny shrugged. "We've decided to try."

"Good." She fought a smile.

Benny nodded. "But I still don't like that jerk." He motioned vaguely toward Jason. "The only reason he suspects me of anything is because I asked you out, which isn't against the law. Besides, we're just friends."

Sue silently gave thanks that the old Benny was back.

After everyone left, she added a couple of dollars to the tip, then went and scooted into the booth beside Jason. "Can a girl buy you a drink, big guy?"

"Only if you're planning on taking advantage of me later." Grinning, he kissed her mouth and dropped a twenty onto his bill, which was only for coffee. Sue started to motion to get change, but he stopped her. "It's fine. Looks as if the waitress could use it."

Sue fell for him a little more.

On the way home, they stopped off for her regular Thursday night ritual of cookies and hurricanes at her grandparents'. Jason managed to choke down the burnt cookies and spiked Kool-Aid without making a face. He even feigned interest in another ten-minute discussion about roaches and their ability to survive a nuclear holocaust. Yup, Sue was in love. And that made the idea of sleeping with him all the worse. But she was thinking about it the whole ride home.

As they got out of his car, a light went on to illuminate her driveway. Sue's gaze shot up to the new fixture attached to her garage.

"What's that?" She shot a look at Jason.

"I . . . I meant to tell you about that."

"You know, you mean to tell me a lot of things that you don't," she accused.

"Yeah." He frowned. "I had some light sensors and cameras put up."

She let out a gush of air. "Yeah, well, I think you should have told me."

"I know." He pulled her against him. "I was afraid you'd tell me not to do it. So I decided to ask for forgiveness instead of permission."

She shook her head. "I wouldn't have said no, but . . . You can't keep making decisions for me. How much did this cost?"

"You're not paying for it. I am."

"Oh, hell no!" she growled.

He squeezed her tight. "Sue, please. Please don't get mad. You are completely right, I should have told you, but after last night . . . I wouldn't take the chance."

She looked up into his eyes, then into the light and moving camera beside it. She knew his heart had been in the right place; she even appreciated it. To get mad at him now just didn't feel right.

"Fine. But I'm paying for this."

He kissed her, a slow kind of kiss that reminded her she'd agreed to sleep with him. And when he unlocked her front door, Sue felt as if at least six super-sized butterflies were playing bumper cars in her stomach.

He held her by the waist, guiding her inside. "You okay?"

"Fine," she lied and knelt to give Hitchcock his dose of I'm-home affection while she tried to figure out what to do next.

She could go for the black teddy, jump his bones in the entryway. Or run into her bedroom and lock the door. What did a man like Jason want? What did she herself want? She hadn't had sex in so long, and . . .

"Gotta pee!" she blurted. *Oh, that was really sexy.*

She fled to the bathroom. When several minutes later she came out, Jason was putting a DVD into the player.

"What are you doing?" she asked.

"I thought we'd watch a movie. How about *How to Lose a Guy in 10 Days?*" He grinned. "You might find a trick you haven't tried on me."

"Great." She attempted to understand but didn't. She'd assumed Jason would expect sex. That he still wanted her. That he still wanted to make love as much as ever.

And soon she learned she was right.

Before even one way to lose a man had been presented in the film, Sue had figured him out. He hadn't wanted to watch a movie; he'd just wanted to get her relaxed. And it had worked. Everything he tried was successful. The first five minutes, he'd toyed with her hair. Around minute six, he'd started kissing her. Minute eight or maybe nine—she sort of lost track of time—he kissed his way up to her neck. Shortly afterward he had her in his lap, his hands moving up and under her shirt. It was around minute thirteen that he had her flat on her back with her shirt and bra whisked off.

"You are so beautiful," he said, cupping a breast. He lowered his lips to her right nipple and ran his tongue over it. "Tell me what you like, okay?"

"I like *that,*" she managed to say.

She felt him smile against her breast. Then he kissed her mouth again—the kind of kiss he'd given her that night on Lacy's patio, the kind that had her melting in her panties and wanting them removed.

Instinct took over. She pushed him backward and tugged at his shirt. Unfortunately, she lacked his clothes-removal skills and the garment ended up around his neck like a noose. Laughing, he helped her, and his shirt sailed across the room.

Sue fell on top of him, loving the feel of her breasts against his chest. She kissed him with no thoughts of stopping. Then she heard his voice: "Ef ur gona op . . ."

She was on a roll here, didn't he know that? But she pulled back nonetheless. She stared down at him, hands on her hips. "Now who's talking when he should be kissing?"

CHAPTER TWENTY-EIGHT

Jason brushed the hair from Sue's eyes. God, she was beautiful when turned on.

"I just said that if you're planning on stopping, maybe we should call it off now before . . ." He hesitated. "It's been a while, and I'm pretty eager."

"How long has it been for you?" she asked.

"Four months," he replied, wondering if he'd ever get tired of seeing her face. Or of touching her. He moved his hand over her bare back and to her waist. She leaned in and her breasts against his chest felt so damn perfect.

"Four months. Not since . . . I kissed you."

And just like that he knew why no other woman had intrigued him in so long. He'd wanted her. He'd wanted this.

"Four months is nothing." She dove back for another kiss.

He caught her. "How long has it been for you?"

She turned her head to see the clock. Her hair brushed over his chin. "Two years, five months, twenty-six days and . . . four hours, thirty-six minutes and I'm not sure of the seconds."

He laughed. "Then let's not keep you waiting."

He rose, scooped her up in his arms, and carried her to the bedroom. She weighed so little that he could carry her anywhere. And for a long time. She'd definitely have Godiva chocolate in her Christmas stocking. And on Valentine's Day, he'd get her another big box. Even bigger than before.

He laid her down on the white sheets. He ran a finger over her lips, down her breasts, then lower until he came upon the snap of her jeans. His heart thumped in his chest, sending blood rushing between his legs. He tried to undo her jeans, but his hands shook.

Damn, he hadn't been nervous about sex since . . .

Never. Even his first time, in the back of that old Chevy at sixteen, he'd dived in headfirst and let instinct guide him. It probably helped that the girl had been three years older and had enough experience for the both of them. But now he had experience and his instincts were loud and clear— as loud and clear as the deep voice saying he'd better make this good for her.

Hell, he'd better make it great. After waiting two years, five months, twenty-six days, four hours, and thirty-six minutes, Sue would expect a grand performance. She *deserved* a grand performance. And though the show was just getting started, her part in it was already getting his standing ovation.

Finally getting her jeans undone, he slipped them down her slender hips, careful not to remove her panties. In spite of his body's standing ovation and his comment about not keeping her waiting, he intended to do just that. To make it as good as it could get, he needed to last. If he had her completely naked, he'd be too damn tempted to bury himself inside her and enjoy the pot of gold before the rainbow. Tonight was all about the rainbow. She'd see every dad-blasted color known to mankind.

Looking up, he saw her blue eyes were open, staring at him with such tenderness that his hands shook again. He had a feeling that tonight he'd see a few colors he'd never seen before himself.

Leaning over, he pressed his lips to her navel and brought one hand to her knees. Slowly sliding his palm up her thigh, he came within an inch of touching the crotch of her pink silk panties, but then he stopped and moved back down her leg. She moaned and lifted her hips. Pressing closer, he brushed his lips down to the top edge of her panties and trailed his tongue from one hip to the other.

She moaned again and he glanced up. "Licking in private is okay. You told me that, remember?"

His hand started its upward sweep again, moving deeper between her legs. He came even closer to her center. So close that he felt her heat and dampness but didn't touch.

Touching came after teasing. And he had a lot more teasing to do.

Stretching out beside her, he walked his fingers up to her breasts and drew circles around the rose-colored tips. Then, because his erection pressed painfully against his zipper, he removed his jeans but not his boxers.

Before he could stretch out beside her again, Sue pressed her hand against silk boxers, against his arousal. He drew in a hissing breath. The tip of his sex throbbed. Probably moistened his underwear. He caught her hand and pressed her fingers to his chest.

"We're saving that for later," he said.

"No, now." She shifted her hips. "I don't want to wait until later. Please."

He leaned down beside her, kissing the outer curve of her breasts. "I like it when you beg."

"Then I'm begging. I think I've waited long enough." She reached for his boxers again.

He caught her hands, straddled her, and brought both wrists over her head, pinning them to the bed. "You are a bad girl. And bad girls always have to wait a very long time for what they want."

She raised her hips, pressing herself desperately to him, and he had to pull back to keep from exploding.

"Don't you want it?" she asked.

"Yes."

"Then what are you waiting on?"

"Patience, sweetheart. You'll get what you want . . . just as soon as I get what I want."

"What do you want?"

She tried to pull her wrists free, but he tightened his hold on her hands. He was rough enough for her to enjoy the game but careful to make her understand it was only a game. She had more power over him than he had over her.

"I want you to come twice before I ever enter you. I want to taste every sweet inch of you. I want to be the best you've ever had."

"You don't have to work that hard. You've already won the blue ribbon!" She shifted again, growing more desperate. "Touch me, Jason. Please."

He leaned close and breathed into her mouth. "How many have there been?"

"How many what?"

"How many guys have you been with?"

It wasn't a question he'd ever asked, and especially now God knew he prayed no one would ever ask him; he'd lost count years ago. But something told him Sue had a headcount, and he wanted to know it. He needed to know everything about her. Then he wanted to drive every one of those memories from her head. When she thought of sex, she would think of him. Only him. When she needed something, she would need him. Only him. And if that made him possessive, so be it. This was Sue.

"Two," she finally answered.

Holy hell! Her innocence made him grow harder still.

"Now, touch me," she begged.

"Where do you want me to touch you?"

She shifted her hips. "You know where."

He caught her two wrists in his one and moved his hand down over her breasts. "Here?" he asked, raking a nail gently over a nipple and then moving lower past her navel. Over the top of her silk-covered sex he trailed, stopping just before he touched her most sensitive place. "Or here?"

"There," she moaned.

"How do you want to be touched?"

She made a growling sound. "You talk too much."

He laughed. "That's the pot calling the kettle black."

Then he kissed her, and while he didn't slip his fingers inside her panties, he pressed one thigh between her legs.

She took full advantage of his leg and moved against him. And she moved so sweetly, so seductively, he became lost.

The next thing he knew he'd whisked off her panties. He took the time to brush his cheek against the revealed blonde triangle of hair, time to slip his tongue over the soft damp place he'd wanted to visit for what seemed like years. But he'd barely pulled the little nub into his mouth before she cried out.

He couldn't believe she'd come so fast, so he pushed a finger inside her and felt for himself. The sweet tight pulsations proved him wrong.

"You are *fast.*"

While he'd planned to let her suffer longer, his other hand was busy removing his boxers, wanting to feel the slick tightening of her sex. Wanting her body to milk his. The next thing he knew, he was between her thighs. He found the damp opening and buried his tip inside her soft hot flesh. Heaven.

"Damn!" He'd forgotten the condom!

He gritted his teeth and pulled his hips back. Without moving his body, he reached out a hand for the foil package he'd placed on her nightstand before he'd ever put in the movie.

"Please," she begged. Her arms locked around him, her soft thighs circling his waist. She pushed upward, taking several inches of him back inside her. A deep moan left his throat as her still pulsing flesh wrapped around him.

"Wait." He managed to pull out again, hoping against hope. "Are you on the pill or patch?"

She shook her head, so he opened the foil package with his teeth and within seconds had sheathed and buried himself back inside her.

He bit the inside of his cheek, thinking the pain would help him last, and he hoped like hell she wouldn't last too long. He sure as hell wouldn't.

Placing her hands on his shoulders, she used him as a lever to lift herself higher. Before he knew what was happening, she'd found her way atop him. He lay back, watching her move, watching the way her breasts swayed, and watching her watch him, and he couldn't remember anyone ever watching him so intently as they fucked.

And just like that, he realized they weren't fucking. This was so much more. So much better.

Reaching up, he placed his hands on her hips, only to touch, not to slow or alter her pace. She had the perfect rhythm, easing her hips up and down, her hair shimmering around her shoulders, her eyes on fire with passion. On fire for him.

Her palms rested on his chest as she supported herself, raising herself up slightly then coming down on him, taking him deeper. And deeper still. She let out a deep gush of air. Her palms on his chest curled into fists. He felt her nails leave their mark, but she could have pierced his heart for all he cared; nothing had ever felt this right, this perfect.

The muscles in her core pulsed tight around him again. Massaging him. The power of his climax was earthshaking. Pleasure took him.

"Perfect."

His breath hitched; then just like that he felt it happen all over again. He'd never had a double, wasn't even sure men could have them, but damn if it wasn't happening.

Sue dropped onto him. He wrapped his arms around her, pushed his head back into the mattress, hips upward, and let go. Let go of his fears. Of his doubts. But not of Sue. Never Sue.

She felt the powerful throbbing release of his climax deep inside her, and Sue's own started all over again. Powerful jolts of pleasure continued to pulse through her entire body. She moaned, cried out Jason's name, and finally opened her eyes.

The moment she felt her lashes flutter against his chest,

every doubt, every question she'd entertained about the wisdom of letting this happen fell on her like a pile of bad, ugly rocks. She loved Jason Dodd. Madly. Completely. And now that she'd made love to him, she wasn't sure she could let him go.

But Jason Dodd didn't do commitment. Jason Dodd was going to rip her heart out and shred it into tiny little pieces.

She held her breath and prayed the mattress monster would crawl out from under her bed and drag her away. It didn't matter how frightening or dark the place might be; it wouldn't be as scary as this place was right now.

Yup. No doubt about it. She loved Jason Dodd. Madly. Completely. She'd just had over-the-handlebars, no-pedal-brakes sex. And while she hadn't landed on her face, she'd taken a direct hit on her heart. The repercussions were very likely going to be fatal.

He was addictive. But he was only temporary.

His record relationship was three months. In three months, how hard would it be to watch him go? To lose him? For there was no question about it, loving him was like a powerful drug, and breaking the habit was going to break her heart. Maybe even her spirit. It would be even worse than it had been with Collin.

Did they make patches or gum to help kick the Jason Dodd habit? Was there a support group she could join? Maybe she needed to buy herself a couple dozen ficus trees.

"That was amazing." His words jolted her, reminded her that she loved Jason Dodd. Madly. Completely. Irrevocably.

Jiminy Cricket, where was the mattress monster when she needed him?

Emotion, both from fear and the beauty of what had just occurred, tightened her chest. Tears formed in Sue's eyes. Her sinuses started to sting. Her nose started to run and moisture trickled down on Jason's bare chest. She rolled off of him and hugged her pillow so tight it would have suffocated if it needed to breathe.

The mattress dipped and swayed. She heard Jason breath-

ing, and she squeezed her eyes shut even tighter as if the
blackness behind her lids could make everything go away.
But his warm naked body pressed against her warm naked
back. Skin to skin.

He brushed some hair from her face.

Staring only into the blackness of her eyelids, she felt
him lean over to look at her.

"Sue? You okay?" His words whispered across her cheek.

She kept her eyes closed but forced her throat open, and
she said the only thing she could. "We're never, *ever,* doing
that again."

Jason couldn't believe Sue's words. "Give me five minutes and I'll make a liar out of you," he promised.

She didn't answer.

"Okay, three minutes."

He pulled her into his arms. Her tears felt hot against his
chest, and his insecurity built at amazing speeds. Had he
done something wrong?

She drew in a shaky breath. "The mattress monster isn't
going to help me, is he?"

"Mattress monster?" What the hell did that mean? Was
she joking? Was crying part of her usual orgasms?

He kissed her shoulder and decided to go with the idea
that she was happy and joking.

"Never again," she repeated.

Wasn't that humor in her tone? It had to be. What they'd
just shared wasn't anything that *anyone* could toss aside.

"Too late, sweetheart. I'm invested." He moved his hand
over her hip, cupping her bottom in his palm. Then, slowly,
he slid his fingers into the sweet moist place between her
legs.

"You're so soft," he moaned. "I've never, ever had sex feel
so . . . perfect."

"Perfect?" She rose up just enough to look into his face.
Shimmering in her misty blue eyes he saw doubt, fear, but
he also saw a woman who'd been satisfied sexually. A wave
of relief shimmered through him.

"Really perfect." Damn, she was beautiful. He might not even need three minutes.

"What do you mean by invested?" She melted into him, a sign that maybe he hadn't done anything wrong. Everyone had a little bit of doubt and fear in the beginning, right?

He chuckled. "I bought a thirty-six pack of condoms." He kissed her, one of those deep kisses that she swore she didn't like but seemed to enjoy.

She hesitated, but he moved his fingers between her legs, softly stroking. Her hips started the slightest shifting motion. He really loved that little motion. It was a motion that said yes.

Reaching up, she ran a hand over his cheek. "Okay." She leaned in, her mouth a breath away from his. "But only until you run out of condoms."

He dropped his arms from around her, shot up, and snatched his boxers from the floor.

"What . . . are you doing?" she asked.

He looked over his shoulder. "Getting dressed. I'm going to buy more condoms. Thirty-five more times isn't going to cut it."

She laughed.

He laughed.

But God help him, he wasn't joking. He wondered about making two Christmases with Sue. Falling back into bed, he pulled her against him.

CHAPTER TWENTY-NINE

They had made love most of the night and pretty much all day long. Jason hadn't stopped smiling. He couldn't help it. Not even when Chase kept giving him the eye.

Jason and Chase sat in Chase's Isuzu Rodeo outside of Kathy's mobile home while Sue, Kathy, and Lacy had their Friday girls' night out. The men had been banned from inside the trailer, but the girls had agreed to being watched from the car. That was as good as they all figured it was going to get.

While Chase listened to his iPod, Jason scanned again the file he'd made for Sue's case. He studied the notes about the stolen Saturn. The car hadn't been found, so it was still a loose end. Jason tapped his pen against the file, getting that feeling again—the feeling that he was missing something right before his eyes.

His gaze went to the name of the Cucumber Lady, AKA the Cadillac driver whom he hadn't dealt with yet. While she was unrelated to Sue's case, he felt compelled to do something about her before she injured herself or someone else. Tomorrow. He planned to stop off and talk to her tomorrow about using a taxi or limo service. Yeah, he'd go right after he and Sue spent the morning doing what they'd been doing for the past twenty-four hours.

Another wry smile whispered across his face as he

looked toward the trailer. He hadn't been away from her for more than an hour, and still he ached for her.

He glanced at Chase. "What are they doing in there?"

Chase stared at his iPod. "If it's the same as usual? Drinking Jack Daniels and talking."

Jason frowned. "Talking about what?"

Chase still didn't look at him. "Chances are, Kathy's verbally castrating the last man who made a pass at her. Lacy's probably telling them how cute my nieces are, and I'd bet my left nut that Sue's telling them about all the sex you two have had."

When Jason didn't say anything, Chase gifted him with a shit-eating grin. "Hey, you two are glowing like walking nightlights. The word *sex* flashes from your eyes every few minutes. Admit it!"

Jason smiled and popped a cinnamon ball into his mouth so he wouldn't be tempted to brag. Kissing and telling had already gotten him into trouble with Sue once.

Chase shook his head. "You've been attracted to her for over a year. To be honest, I don't understand what took you so long."

Jason talked around the candy. "It could be that your wife told me she'd castrate me and grind the leftover parts into sausage if I hurt her friend."

Chase's right brow arched. "And you know she means it?"

"Yup." Jason flipped the cinnamon ball to the top of his tongue.

Chase studied him. "So, this is that serious, huh?"

The candy went back into Jason's cheek. The word *serious* vibrated in his chest. "What do you mean?"

"I mean, a man doesn't risk his Jimmy Dean being ground into . . . well, Jimmy Dean for just any woman."

Jason glanced away, shifted in his seat. It wasn't his Jimmy Dean he worried about.

Pushing that thought back, he eyed Chase. "Sue said they've been meeting for years."

"I told you about it. It's the Divorced, Desperate, and Delicious club."

"Yeah, but what do they *do*?"

"Sue didn't tell you?" Chase laughed. "They talk—mostly about sex. Multiple orgasms, favorite positions. Tonight I'm told they're discussing sex and food. I'm dropping by the grocery store on my way home. I'd suggest you do, too."

"Right." Jason chuckled, not believing.

Chase stared at him. "No, I'm serious. You know that they were all abiding by some 'men are dogs' law of celibacy. They didn't have sex so they met once a week and talked about it. Of course, I—woman-charmer that I am—rescued Lacy, but they still meet."

Jason was feeling pretty damn good that Chase wasn't the group's only savior, but he kept his tongue wrapped around his cinnamon ball. He wasn't going to give his friend the benefit of the whole truth, knowing for sure that he and Sue were sleeping together. Not yet.

Chase laughed. "They even give away awards for the 'Most Horny' every week. For the person who needs it most." When Jason smirked he added, "I swear to God, I'm not joking."

"Well, Sue's out of that race." Jason was unable to keep the smugness out of his voice. Then he realized he'd spilled his guts, and he frowned. *Damn.*

Chase thumped the steering wheel with his palm. "I love it when I'm right! Come on, give me details."

Jason frowned. "I don't think so."

Chase scratched his jaw and studied him. "Okay." Silence, and then: "I'm praying Lacy wins the Horny award. That bed at my sister's was the noisiest thing I've ever heard, and after my niece walked in on us in the shower, Lacy cut me off completely. And she was so eager to get here tonight she wouldn't give me fifteen minutes to ease the burden, if you know what I mean. A man can only take so much."

"You got my sympathy." Jason looked back at the file.

"Aah, come on, just a few details," Chase begged.

Jason didn't even look up.

"Just tell me how you got Sue to break her vow of celibacy. What special 'Dodd' trick did you use?"

"I put in a movie." Realizing he was talking again, and that his candy was gone, he popped another into his mouth. More silence.

"Hot shit," Chase said. "This is serious." He nudged Jason with an elbow. "You've always given me details. Good ones, too."

Jason shrugged.

"So, how serious is it?"

Jason frowned. "I said I like her."

" 'Like?' " Chase repeated. "A man likes French toast, likes ketchup with his fries. You don't just 'like' this girl. Not one you don't want to talk about. When a man doesn't want to give details, that usually means it's damn special. So spill your guts. How special is it?"

The question struck a raw nerve. "Back off, okay?" Jason snapped.

"What does that mean?"

"It means back off!" Jason slapped the file on the dashboard. "What is it with you married guys? You're so freaking miserable, not getting any of your own, you want me to tell you about my sex life so you can get your jollies."

Chase eyed Jason as if he'd grown a second head. "Whoa! First off, I'm not miserable, and with the exception of this last week I've probably had more sex this last year than you've had in seven."

Jason pushed his head back into the neck rest and tried to understand his sudden anger. No good explanation came, but a question did. "So, if marriage is such a paradise, why do most people end up divorced? Why do they run around screwing everybody else when they've got 'the one' at home? Do you know how many married women I've turned down over the years?"

Chase flinched. "A good marriage *is* a paradise, and I would never cheat on Lacy."

"But you want to, right?" Jason knew he should probably drop it, but he couldn't. "You're going to tell me you don't look at other women and think you want some?"

"Hell, yeah, I look, and if she's really hot I might even want! I mean, a good piece of ass is great. But what I have with Lacy is . . . a good piece of ass with a hell of a lot more." From the look on Chase's face, Jason knew his friend was about to go into one of his long speeches. Chase was good at long speeches. "As for why there are so many divorces . . . Two reasons. The couple was wrong for each other to start with, or they forget. And it's the 'forgetting' divorces that are sad."

Chase ran his hand over the wheel. "Remember Detective Watson when he was going through his divorce? He got caught screwing the next door neighbor. He forgot."

Jason dropped his file in his lap. "Okay, I'll bite. What *exactly* did Watson forget?"

Chase held up his right arm. "See this? It's just a freaking arm attached to my body. How often do you look down at your arm and think, 'I'm a lucky bastard to have a right arm'? You don't, do you? You take it for granted. It's there. It works."

Jason stared at him. "And what you said is supposed to make sense?"

Chase laughed. "That's what a wife is. She's your right arm. Only, some married people forget what their right arm does. It's part of you, it makes you happy. People like Watson, they do something stupid and they lose their right arms. Then they go through the rest of their lives crippled." He ran his left hand over his right elbow like a lover. "I'll *never* forget how important this arm is."

And as crazy as it sounded, Jason understood. Or at least he thought he did.

"So, because you lost your first wife you appreciate Lacy, is that what you're saying?"

"No. I lost my parents. That's why I appreciated Sarah. But I lost her, too, and I wanted to die. But by some miracle, I found another right arm, and now I know what it's like to do without it. I love Lacy. I love every freaking thing about her. I'm not going to do anything that would risk me losing her."

Jason rolled down the car window and stared out. He'd never had a wife. Hell, he'd never had anyone that amounted to much of a parent, either. Except Maggie, and she hadn't come into his life until . . . later. And with her own marital disaster, she hadn't exactly been a good example when relationships came into play. Maybe that's why the whole marriage thing didn't appeal. Frankly, he didn't even know why he'd let Chase go on like he had. Jason Dodd was a one-day-at-a-time kind of guy. He didn't worry about the future. He just didn't.

He opened up his file again. That was what he needed to be thinking about, not—

"So what do you really have?" Chase asked.

"I said I liked her! Fuck! Can't you let it go?"

"Chill." His friend held up his hands. "I'm talking about the case. What the hell is wrong with you?"

Jason took a few breaths before he answered. "It's this." He shook the file. "The answer is in here somewhere. I just can't put my finger on it."

Pushing everything else from his mind, Jason went over the entire situation with Chase, focusing his frustration onto the conundrum.

"So you think it's the Benny Fritz guy," Chase said.

"Yeah, I'm leaning that way. I went by to see him twice yesterday to ask about where he was when Sue got the note at the park but never caught him at home. When I finally got him on his cell, he gave me the name of someone who'd vouch that he was at some coffee shop, but now I can't seem to reach them." Jason ran a hand over his face. "I dropped the note I got at the park and the card from the flowers at the lab for handwriting analysis, but with their backlog, who knows how soon they'll have that back to me."

Chase nodded. "Did anything come back on the bullet they pulled from Sue's wall?"

"Not yet. Hoke's Bluff is running those tests. I'm dealing with a whole bureaucratic mess."

"Have you spoken with Sarge? Maybe he could get Hoke's Bluff to let go and—"

"I tried. And was told to be careful not to step on too many toes. He said he'd make some calls but that I'd probably have to let things go through their natural channels."

"Fuck natural channels," Chase said.

"My thoughts exactly." Jason sighed. "I did find out that Fritz isn't listed as owning a gun. Not that he couldn't have gotten one off the street."

Chase tapped his hands on the steering wheel again. "You don't think the foot doctor's wife is playing you? Maybe she hired someone. Or the second nurse—"

"I don't think so, but maybe. But fuck, I'm tired of maybes."

Chase leaned back in his seat. "How about the agent? You're backing off on her, too?"

Jason gave another sigh of frustration. "She couldn't be doing it herself. She was in New Jersey when most things went down. And it's more than a PR stunt now. There hasn't been any useful publicity since the first incident." He bent the edge of the file and then flipped it back up. "There's still the cover artist, but now that we know the jerk broke into her computer files, it doesn't have to be someone who's read her manuscript. Frankly I think I'm wasting my time chasing the out-of-town leads."

"Sue's ex?" Chase asked. "You checked him out?"

Jason got a flashback of being kissed. Oh yeah, he'd checked the guy out. Unintentionally. "Sue's pretty adamant about not dragging him into this."

"You know women never suspect their ex-husbands. If I remember right, Sue said he was some computer dweeb. He would have the know-how to break into her computer."

"I know," Jason agreed. "I'm not completely ruling him out."

"Have they found the stolen Saturn that followed you yet?"

Jason shook his head. "I called this afternoon, and so far it's no-go. I even spoke to the guy who took the report on the Saturn to see if I could get information. I got shit instead. He couldn't put his hands on the files. Can you believe that?"

A car passed, and both Chase and Jason got quiet.

"Anyway," Jason continued after a moment, "he was supposed to call me back and didn't. I hate not being on the inside of this case."

"I know," Chase said.

Jason glanced back at the file. "The answer's here. I'm just not seeing it. I feel as if I'm too close to it."

Chase chuckled. "Well, sleeping with the victim is pretty damn close."

"Oh, right. Stupid me. You slept with Lacy while you were on the freaking run from the whole police department. You are *not* one to point fingers," Jason snapped.

"It was a joke," Chase said. "Damn, but you've got a chip on your shoulder."

Jason closed his eyes. "Sorry. I want this guy caught."

"Yeah." Silence filled the car.

"You know," Chase remarked, "I remember a homicide detective who said when he was stumped, he read the file backward." He held up his hand. "I know it sounds crazy but he said he looked at each word. Repetitions, words with similar meanings. Sometimes the truth jumped out at him."

Jason scanned the file again, backward this time. He read his list of suspects: the agent, the cover artist, the ex-husband . . . He moved to the background on Fritz; then, frowning, he looked at the information about the Saturn and the notes he'd taken down that night. *Car lent to a friend, a down-on-his-luck artist.* Jason flipped back to his original list of suspects.

"Shit," Jason said. "You're right. I might have found something."

CHAPTER THIRTY

"You found something? What?" Chase asked.

"The word 'artist.' It's here twice. The guy who supposedly borrowed the Saturn. The owner's wife said he was a down-on-his-luck artist. Then Sue mentioned she didn't like the guy who did her cover art, a Michael Braxton." Jason paused to let his mind wrap around the idea. "The man put Sue on the cover. The publisher said it was a coincidence, but I think the guy is obsessed with her. I finally got contact info on the man but I haven't had any luck contacting him. Still, I didn't look at him seriously because he's in New York. But . . ."

A new realization hit and burned. "Fuck! The editor said he'd contracted out, which means he might not even live in New York. Why didn't I put this together earlier?"

"Because I wasn't here to help you." Chase smiled. "Hey, I'm good."

Jason jumped out of the car. Then he stuck his head back through the window. "Can you take Sue home with you? I'm going to go over and interview the owners of the Saturn."

Chase frowned. "It's sex and food night, and my wife's probably going to win the Most Horny award!"

"I just need—"

"Go," Chase muttered. "But you owe me, damn it."

Sue slipped her peach-colored sandals off her feet and let them fall under Kathy's table. Her toes were feeling pinched again. *Toes and heart,* she thought. Her heart hadn't stopped feeling pinched since she and Jason made love.

"So, what do you think?" Kathy looked at her.

It took Sue a second to remember what they'd been talking about. "Strawberries, yes. Maybe whipped cream. But syrup? Think of the sheets!" Sue sipped her liquid courage named Jack Daniels and let it burn down her throat. Her gaze slipped back to Lacy, who studied her with a give-it-up stare. Loyal Lacy could give pretty mean give-it-up stares, too.

"Did Kathy tell you about Jason's kittens?" Sue asked. "There's one calico and . . ." As long as she talked, she didn't have to think. Thinking could be detrimental to her mental health.

Lacy and Kathy turned to each other. Sue quit talking.

Her heart pinched again, so she recommenced chattering. "Do either of you want a kitten? I'm only giving them to people I know. Oh, and did you guys read the article on feng shui in today's paper? Remember that lady we met at one of your parties, Lacy? Didn't she do feng shui?"

"You mean, one of Jason Dodd's play-toys?" Lacy's eyebrow arched.

Shit! The feng shui chick had been one of Jason's long line of women? Sue held up her glass and attempted a diversion. "To friendship!"

They all downed their glasses with a big gulp.

As Sue waited for the burning in her throat to pass, she wondered if someone, somewhere, would someday say, "Did you hear about that mystery author?" Someone else would say, "Yeah, wasn't she one of Jason's Dodd's bang toys?" Sue felt her throat grow tight.

"Yup, I think Ms. Feng Shui was Jason's girlfriend," Kathy agreed.

A change of subject was needed. Fast. "Wasn't it pretty weather today?" Sue had never been good at fast subject changes.

Instead of answering her question, Lacy looked at Kathy

and posed another. "So, what is your analysis? Is it as bad as we think?"

"Analysis of what?" Sue asked.

They ignored Sue's question. Then Kathy gave Sue an up and down glance. "I told you, she's been kissing toad butt." Kathy puckered her lips and made smacking sounds.

"I haven't kissed a toad's butt!" Sue jiggled her glass and watched the whiskey do laps.

It was tough. She hadn't spilled her guts yet. Normally she was the first to spill, for she told Kathy and Lacy everything. Well, she hadn't told them about her ex and his lesbian trapped inside; that had been her personal secret. Until she'd told Jason. But now the whole being in love with Jason thing just felt . . . too scary to share. Even scarier than the truth about her divorce. Because if she talked about Jason, the rose-colored glasses she'd managed to put on after they'd made love would fall off. She didn't want to lose them because then she'd see again how badly she'd screwed up. And how bad was that?

Bad. She still loved Jason Dodd. Madly. Completely.

The glasses slipped. She was in love with a man who was so afraid of commitment that he hadn't named or checked the gender of his cat. *And don't forget, he thinks women go stale,* an internal voice whispered. Sue wasn't sure if it was her head or heart. But it wasn't her hormones. No, that little voice hadn't spoken since last night. It was probably off somewhere smoking cigarettes after the six orgasms.

Six.

Six wonderful, beautiful orgasms.

Four of which had required condoms.

Which meant she still had thirty-two of his climaxes left before she turned the lights out on this little shindig.

Or before she learned she was wrong. And by wrong, she meant that she would learn she wasn't just another of Jason's flavors of the week, or month, or however long it took before a girl got moldy.

And she was totally serious about the condom schedule.

Jason didn't know it, but when the condoms were gone, if she wasn't sure about what was really happening between them, well, he'd be history. She had to have some rules, a game plan, a method to her madness. This was it. If a pack of thirty-six condoms didn't take a relationship forward, nothing would.

The buzz from her last sip of JD was wearing off, and she became painfully aware of the silence. Girls' nights out were never silent. Never.

She looked up at her two best friends. Concern filled their bloodshot eyes. How much Jack Daniels had they drunk? Sue picked up the bottle.

"I think we're going to have to beat it out of her," Lacy said. "Get me the flyswatter."

"Please," Sue said. "We came here to talk about sex and food. Not about my having sex with Jason."

They both screamed.

"What?" Sue asked.

"You just admitted it!" Lacy said. "You had sex with Jason!"

"Oh, Lordie!" Kathy clutched her heart. "First Lacy, and now you. You both know what that means? I win the Most Horny award from here on out!" She sighed in mock sadness.

"Not so quick," Lacy interrupted. "I've had a very slow week. And, oh, I gotta tell you about Chase's nieces."

"*You* had a slow week?" Kathy asked. "My vibrator gave up the ghost, and I haven't had the courage to go buy another one."

"Isn't this your second?" Lacy teased.

Kathy shot an elbow into her ribs. "I'm making funeral arrangements and a wreath. I thought maybe you guys could come over one day next week and we could give it a proper burial in my backyard."

Lacy and Kathy both laughed, and then they looked at Sue. Their smiles flatlined.

"What's wrong?" Lacy asked.

Sue blinked the watery sheen from her vision and drew

in a shaky breath. "Kathy's vibrator died," she said. "I always cry at funerals."

"Oh, please. Spill it." Kathy grabbed the Jack Daniels bottle.

Sue blinked a few actual tears from her eyes. "Jason kissed my ex-husband," she confessed.

Then she confessed about the lesbian living in her ex-husband's body.

Then she confessed that she loved Jason Dodd. Madly. Completely.

And with the confession came a whole lot of tears and snot. It wasn't pretty.

Jason had gone to the precinct hoping to get a copy of the report, but the report hadn't been completed, and the only thing he'd been able to dig up was the address of the owners of the Saturn.

"I'm trying to explain something here." Jason watched the Andrewses, the owners of the stolen gold Saturn, take verbal swings at each other.

"I told you that asshole still had our car," Kay Andrews snarled at her husband. "I can't believe you were stupid enough to loan it to him."

"I'm not saying the guy did it," Jason repeated. Not that he expected them to listen, when they seemed only focused on hurting each other. "I just need some—"

"He was my best friend through high school," Mr. Andrews snapped. "Just because *you* don't have any friends . . ."

"I would if you didn't freaking run them off," his wife fired back.

"If you mean Lilly, she came at me with a frying pan!" The man glanced at Jason. "Wouldn't you run her off?"

"Maybe," Jason admitted, then shut up. He remembered Kathy showing up at Sue's and the wart comments. And Lacy's anti-Jason campaign. Were all girlfriends bad on relationships?

The husband continued, "Tell her I'm not crazy for saying that bitch can't come back to my house."

Not willing to get involved, Jason shrugged, then watched the pair throw verbal daggers at one another.

Now here was one fine example of the institution of marriage, Jason thought.

"Excuse me," Jason said after having heard enough. "All I need is some information. What is the guy's *name*? Does he have any other family in town? If I remember correctly, I heard the guy just moved back into town. Do you know where he moved from?"

"I know where he wanted to move to," the wife snapped. "He thought he could just stay here."

"Yeah, and after I told him he could, I had to tell him he couldn't because my wife is—"

"Your wife is tired of your deadbeat friends." She fled the room, and Jason decided he wouldn't miss her. The husband looked just as relieved.

"Sorry," he said. "She has PMS. She's not normally a bitch."

Jason nodded but didn't waste any more time. "What's this guy's—"

"My wife doesn't like him because he was my best man at my first wedding. Yeah, he's a little strange sometimes, and yes, he's a bit of a moocher. But, I feel sorry for him. His parents died a few years back, and I don't think the guy has any family that amounts to much. But Mike's a nice—"

"Mike?" Jason remembered Michael Braxton was the name of the artist. "What's your friend's *last* name?"

It was eleven when he knocked on Chase's door. Chase opened it, and Jason shoved a bag into his hands.

"What's this?" his friend asked.

"Supplies." Jason grinned at the confusion on his friend's face. "An apology for my being a jerk."

"You're always a jerk." Chase looked in the bag. "Wow! Champagne, whipped cream, chocolate syrup, M&M's, and . . ." He reached into the bag and pulled out the other item. "A MoonPie?" His brows knitted together.

"Get creative," Jason said.

Chase stared at the MoonPie for a second. "I'm gonna have to give this one some thought."

Jason laughed.

Chase dropped the MoonPie. "Maybe you should take them home with you."

"I've got a stash in the car."

Chase shook his head, then turned to business. "What did you find out tonight about the artist?"

"I think he's the same guy that borrowed the Saturn. The friend who was driving the car when it got stolen just moved back into town from . . . New York. And get this. The guy's name is Mike Brighten. The cover artist goes by Michael Braxton."

"A little pen and ink and a driver's license or a Social Security card can be altered," Chase agreed. "Did you ever find him?"

"He's conveniently out of pocket." Jason frowned and stepped into the entryway. Lacy's ugly dog, Fabio, who had a bad habit of nipping at his pant leg, came around the corner. "Where's Sue?"

What was left of Chase's smile vanished. "In the study with Lacy," he whispered. "She doesn't seem too happy."

"Who? Sue doesn't?" Jason—and the dog now attached to his pant leg—took a step.

"Yeah. When I drove her and Lacy back here tonight, she had that puffy look, as if she'd been crying."

Jason's stomach clenched. "What happened?"

"All I know is that Lacy apologized in advance for having to kill you. I couldn't get anything else out of her because Sue was around."

"No!" Jason took a deep gulp of frustration. "We've been fine!" He met Chase's gaze. "What could be wrong?"

He didn't wait for his friend to answer. Taking off for the study, he dragged the dog with him. Worried more than he wanted to admit, he knocked but didn't wait to be invited inside.

"Who—?" Lacy frowned when she saw him.

Jason's gaze bypassed her. Sue sat on the floor, barefoot, her sandals beside her. One of Lacy's cats lay curled up in her lap. She wasn't crying, but her nose was red. Red from crying. Damn.

"What's wrong?" he blurted.

Sue shook her head. "Nothing." Nudging the orange cat from her lap, she stood and proceeded to straighten her dress that didn't need straightening. Hell, the dress looked great on her. Perfect. She was perfect.

"You sure?" he asked.

"Positive." She went back to readjusting clothes—a sure sign that she'd just lied to him. He'd learned from Maggie that straightening perfectly straight clothes was the same as wiping clean countertops. Something had Sue in knots. And her knots were beginning to form in his gut as well.

"Nothing's wrong," she repeated, fidgeting. "Chase said you got a lead on the cover artist. Did you find out anything?"

Chase walked into the room and went straight for his wife. Like Legos with super-charged magnets, the two of them couldn't be in the same room and not linked together.

Jason's gaze shot back to Sue's puffy eyes. He decided to pocket his questions for later and remembering her question, he explained what he'd uncovered. He finished by saying, "I've got Danny coming over tomorrow while I chase down a few leads."

"Okay." Sue snatched up her sandals and looked at Lacy. "We should go. You two have to be exhausted. Thanks for . . . *everything.*" A lot of meaning went into that last word.

Jason watched the two women communicate with those secret looks that passed between females. What the hell did Sue have to say to Lacy that she didn't want him to hear?

Then Lacy's gaze slapped into him. Jason didn't speak the female nonverbal language, but he'd have to be deaf and blind not to recognize the woman's scorn.

"What?" he asked.

"We should go," Sue piped up. "They're tired."

Lacy glanced at her friend. "I'm not tired." Her eyes shifted back to Jason. "But I've got an urge to make sausage." The threat was clear, and Jason eyed Chase in hopes he could hold back his wife.

Sue reached for her purse. "I didn't know you made your own sausage."

"Yeah, I do." Lacy continued to stare at Jason.

Chase chuckled, but he did wrap his arm around his angry wife as if to hold her back—just in case she came after Jason's Jimmy Dean.

Sue moved closer. Jason ignored Lacy and kissed Sue, something he should have done when he first walked in. Not kissing hello had been one of the prior complaints by a past girlfriend, and on the drive over he'd replayed every complaint any woman had ever made against him and made a vow that he wouldn't make those same mistakes with Sue.

It had nothing to do with Chase's right arm talk. He didn't want marriage; he just wanted to make Sue happy. She needed him. And if he could do things right, she'd need him for a long, long time.

Maybe even longer than that.

"You ready to go?" he asked. He knew he was.

CHAPTER THIRTY-ONE

Three days later, flowers in hand, Jason pulled out of a florist's parking lot and drove back to Hoke's Bluff. Back to Sue.

He wasn't any closer to solving the case, but neither had anything happened since they'd received the note in the park. The sensor lights he'd had installed at Sue's hadn't even flashed. Jason had even gone out there to make sure they were working. They were. But while he knew he should be happy the freak had backed off, Jason couldn't help but wonder if this wasn't the calm before the storm. Everything he knew of stalkers said they didn't just give up.

He'd spent the past few days looking for Brighten or Braxton, who he suspected were one and the same. Kay Andrews, the Saturn's owner, wasn't too off base about the guy being a deadbeat. Jason had visited at least four of the guy's old friends, only to discover that good ol' Mike had stopped by and was told by all four of the guys' wives that he couldn't hang his hat there either. Jason wanted to believe he was on the right track, especially since both Mikes had seemed to fall off the end of the world. But he'd feel a lot better if the New York cops would get off their asses and send him some info. It seemed getting information from the NYPD was about as easy as milking a bull.

Between searching for leads, he'd confronted Mrs. Roberts, the Cucumber Lady, about retiring the pink Cadil-

lac. Jason had given her a name of a limo service. She'd resisted at first.

"What if they don't show up when I need them?"

"They will show up."

"Sometimes they don't."

He finally won her over by pointing out that she, a lady
of such class, should be chauffeured around instead of driving herself. And she did have class. She lived in one of the
most upscale Houston neighborhoods. So she obviously
had the money. Before he was able to get away, she asked
him in for a snack. He'd endured a whole hour of looking
at her family photos along with pie and coffee. Images of
family holidays, family vacations. A whole world of things
Jason knew nothing about. When Jason asked about her
daughter who'd appeared in all the shots, Mrs. Roberts got
quiet and told him her daughter had died of cancer when
she was twenty.

The woman had walked him out to his car and before
leaving she'd added, "You will come back again, right? And
bring that sweet wife of yours."

Wife?

He didn't know why he hadn't corrected her. He'd simply
nodded and gotten away while the getting was good.

Sooner or later, Jason would learn not to get so involved
in the lives of everyday citizens.

Or not.

As he drove, he thought about the last few evenings with
Sue. The nights had been spent reading, going out to eat,
and, his favorite activity, having sex. The best sex of his entire life. Sue had also started asking him for help on her
new book. Which felt good. Real good. What didn't feel
good was knowing he'd never gotten to the bottom of what
was bothering her that night at Chase's. Sometimes he'd
caught her staring into space. Something was buzzing
around in that head of hers.

Nope, that didn't feel good at all.

In the past, Jason wouldn't have worried about stuff like

that. If it hadn't affected the sex, he pretty much hadn't given it a second thought. Not true this time.

He hadn't quite defined what made Sue different. She was just . . . better. Everything was better. The sex. The company. The way she smelled. The way she made him laugh. The way he made her laugh. The sex.

Nor did he worry about her stumbling across a piece of his past or her asking questions he couldn't answer. She already knew his past.

And then there was the sex.

Oh yeah, the sex. The girl was every man's fantasy. But she didn't belong to every man. She belonged to him. Just him.

The night they'd come home from Chase's, they'd drunk the champagne he'd bought, fed each other strawberries, and had a heck of a time with the whipped cream and M&M's. And the MoonPie fantasy had turned out better than he'd ever dreamed. He hoped Chase had figured it out; if not, his friend had missed out on the best part. Just thinking about it now had Jason reaching down to readjust things in his jeans.

He'd barely had to explain the MoonPie to Sue. She'd even added her own spin.

Yup, with Sue the sex was definitely better.

A smile worked its way to his lips as he turned in to Sue's subdivision, and he wondered about the topic for next week's girls' night discussion. The "different positions" one might be fun. A couple of positions he'd like to try with Sue sprang to mind. Something else sprang up, too. It required another adjustment of his crotch. No wonder Chase had such a damn good marriage.

Jason's mind flipped to the arguing couple who'd owned the Saturn, and he wondered if Chase was right about unhappy marriages. Perhaps the Andrewses just hadn't been meant to get married. Then he wondered why the hell he was even thinking about it.

Pulling into Sue's drive, he waved good-bye to Ricky, a retired cop he'd asked to watch over Sue while he was out and about. After Danny's comment about Sue, Jason had decided he wanted someone different to play bodyguard. Plain and simple, Sue's body was too damn important to be guarded by anyone who'd even think about trying to steal her away. Ricky, sixty, retired, and a grandfather, was the perfect candidate. Ricky also preferred to watch the house from his car, and since Sue was complaining about being behind on her writing it felt like the perfect setup.

As Jason picked up his files, a picture of Michael Brighten, provided by Saturn owners, slipped out. Jason stared at the image, feeling his frustration return and prick at the lining of his stomach. If this guy was responsible—and his gut said he was—Jason wanted him behind bars as soon as possible.

The investigation into the man's past had left Jason a little leery. The man fit the profile of a serial killer: a loner, abused as a child, his only trouble with the law was a charge of animal cruelty that had never made it to court.

Not that Jason usually paid much attention to such profiles. Because lose the animal cruelty charge and he himself could be considered right up there with the worst of them.

Slipping the photo back into the file, Jason dropped it in the backseat of his car and decided to shelve the case and think instead about the sexy woman who waited for him inside. Climbing out of his Mustang, he reached back in for the flowers.

As he got to the porch, the sensor lights came on. They hadn't done much since the freak hadn't returned, but he was still glad he'd gotten them. A woman living alone needed all the protection—

But Sue wasn't living alone anymore. She had him.

Jason fit his key into Sue's door and called out, "I'm"— *home*—"here!" This wasn't his home, but he was living in the now, living for the moment. That's what he was doing. And it was great. Couldn't get better.

Liar.

He shut the door, acknowledging the reason for the needling thoughts that threatened to burst his bubble of happiness. It was Sue's unfocused stares. It was knowing that as soon as he found Mike Brighten/Braxton he would no longer have a reason to come home to her every day. Oh, he didn't doubt she'd still need him sexually. But face it: You didn't have to live with someone to be lovers.

As a matter of fact, it was one of Jason's big no-nos.

He'd never lived with anyone. Seldom stayed the entire night, in fact. Sue, of course, had been different.

But she'd needed him to stay. What was going to happen when she didn't?

He tossed the question aside. He was living for today, not worrying about tomorrow.

"In here," Sue called from her study.

Jason walked into that room and handed her the three red roses he'd picked up from the florist. "For my lady and favorite author." He dropped a kiss on her mouth.

When they came up for air, he passed a finger over her lips. "I finished your book today. You had me all the way to the end. I liked the twist of having the villain frame the other suspect."

"You really liked it?" she asked, and he heard so much in that question. His opinion mattered to her. He really liked mattering.

"Hell, yeah, I liked it. I'm in awe of your talent, woman."

After several more deep kisses, he followed her into the kitchen. When she stepped in front of him, he saw she wore those Daisy Duke shorts that had driven him crazy when he'd first come to stay here. She leaned over to get a vase from the cabinet.

With her bottom hoisted high, she looked back. "You better be careful," she said.

"Of what?" His eyes stayed glued on her behind. "It's you who should be careful. You know how I feel about those shorts."

Her grin hit him below the belt—in a good way. Oh, she feigned innocence, but the spark of sass in her eyes gave her away.

She blinked. "Don't you know what red roses mean?"

The question floated around his head. He knew he'd come back to it later, and he probably wouldn't be happy where the question took him, but his other head was doing the thinking.

"I know what these shorts mean." He picked her up and set her on the counter. "Tell me you didn't remember that I told you those shorts drove me crazy."

He moved his hands up her legs and under the frayed hem, expecting to feel her silk underwear. Instead he found something softer than silk. He went hard as a rock.

"Oh, you are a bad girl. You're not wearing panties."

Sue smiled, looking a bit bashful and a lot precious. "It was just a little surprise. That, and . . ." She reached behind her on the counter and pulled out a MoonPie.

"Well, now *you're* going to get a surprise," he said. "Only it's not going to be little. Actually, it's growing even as I speak."

He had just started unzipping her shorts when his cell phone rang. "I'm getting rid of this thing!" He checked the number. It was Chase. Snapping open the phone he said, "Bad time. Later."

"Don't hang up. It's important."

"So is what I'm about to be doing."

With one hand he continued unzipping Sue's shorts. Tight blonde curls peeked out of the open zipper. He slid a finger inside her shorts . . . and then into her. She was already wet. Meeting her eyes, he ran his tongue over his lips, insinuating exactly what he wanted to do with that wetness. He'd started to close the phone when Chase's next words stopped him.

"They found the Saturn."

Jason's attention refocused. "They did?" He pulled his hand from Sue's shorts and shot her a look of apology.

"Yeah. And we were wrong. That artist isn't behind this."

CHAPTER THIRTY-TWO

"It's not him? How do we know?" Jason asked.

"Under the seat they found a few pages of a manuscript. The name at the top was Benny Fritz."

Jason flinched. "I knew I liked that bastard for this!"

"He's here for questioning on the stolen car," Chase said. "He's demanding a lawyer. But before Danny picked him up, he went to see Fritz's wife. She copped to her husband having her parents' .38. Isn't that a match to the slug they pulled out of Sue's wall?"

"That piece of shit! I want to see him!" Jason said.

"I thought you would. But you'd better hurry."

Jason hung up and looked at Sue. She wasn't going to like hearing this. "I'm sorry," he said.

Her eyes were wide. "They caught him?"

"Yeah, but it's not Michael Brighten. It's Benny Fritz."

Sue looked stunned. Then her mouth thinned into a line he'd grown to understand was her stubborn expression. "Jason, I told you, he didn't do this."

"They found the Saturn, and inside were pages of his manuscript. And his wife admitted to him having a .38 that belongs to her parents."

Sue looked confused, then shook her head. "Lots of people have guns. And . . ."

Not believing was easier, Jason knew, but she had to accept this. "If that's not enough proof, he's screaming for a lawyer. If he wasn't guilty, Sue, why would he need a lawyer?"

"Maybe because everyone thinks he's guilty." Sue jumped off the counter and zipped her shorts. "I'm coming with you."

"Not this time." And never in those shorts. They were for his eyes only. "Sorry, but I've let you come between me and this guy once already. I'm going to deal with it my way now."

She wasn't happy when he left.

He wasn't happy about her not being happy, but he had to go.

Jason was walking into the station when his cell rang. "Jason Dodd."

"Told you they wouldn't come! No show! No show! And I've got a hair appointment."

It took Jason a second to recognize Mrs. Roberts's voice. "Did you call them?"

"Yup. They said they'd be here ten minutes ago."

He didn't have time for this, but he'd brought this all on himself. "I tell you what, I think I still have their number. Let me give them a call."

He hung up, went through his previous calls until he found their number. A quick conversation to the limo service had him reassured that the driver was on his way to pick up Mrs. Roberts.

He had just hung up when he met Chase at the front desk, and they went in to see Fritz together. They never played good cop/bad cop; they usually both came across as assholes. This was one of those times. Both he and Chase cared too much about Sue.

A few minutes into the interview, Jason tilted back in his chair and watched Fritz squirm. The leather-loafer wearing weasel wasn't so cocky now.

"What happened?" he pushed. "Sue turning you down really chapped your ass?"

Fritz scowled. "I've asked for a lawyer and haven't gotten one."

"Phones are tied up right now," Chase answered, standing in the corner.

"But don't worry," Jason said. "You'll get your lawyer. Of course, it's not going to do any good. We found the car you stole. Inside were a few pages of some terrible sci-fi novel."

Fritz looked shocked.

Jason watched the man squirm for a bit, then said, "Cut the crap and just own up to it."

"Own up to something I didn't do? I don't think so," Fritz snapped.

"Your wife went to find the gun you used." Chase paced the room. "A simple test and we're going to know it was your slug we dug out of Sue's wall."

"That test is going to prove that both of you bozos are idiots. Why the hell would I try to hurt Sue when I like her? And I haven't seen that gun in ages. My wife keeps it in a shoe box in her closet."

"Jealousy is a pretty powerful motive," Chase said. "It busted your chops that Sue had moved on."

Jason added, "And your manuscript pages just got up and walked into that Saturn, huh?" He crossed his arms. "Now that's good science fiction!"

Fritz's expression was desperate. "Someone is framing me. Setting me up. It happens in fiction and in real life!"

A cold chill ran down Jason's spine. *It happens in fiction and in real life.* What was it he'd said to Sue just this afternoon—that he really liked how one suspect had framed someone else? In Sue's book, it had been when the cop went to question the first suspect that the villain went after the heroine.

Fuck!

Jason leapt from his chair and ran out of the room. Barely out the door, he jerked his cell phone from his pocket. His hands shook as he hit Sue's number. His heart pumped as he waited for her to answer.

"What is it?" Chase asked, stepping out behind him.

" 'It happens in fiction,' " he repeated Benny Fritz's words. "Shit! Why didn't I see this? It's what happens in Sue's book. The real murderer frames someone else. As soon as the detective lets down his guard, the guy goes for the heroine. Answer, damn it! She's not answering." He stared at Chase and raked a hand through his hair.

Suddenly, his friend's words popped into his brain: *Jealousy is a pretty powerful motive.* He swore again and said, "Wait! I totally screwed up. Put an APB out on that man's wife."

Chase's eyes grew round. "Fritz's? You think she's—"

"Yeah. She has motive: jealousy. And she had . . ." Jason remembered the woman hadn't turned the gun in yet. *"She has the gun."*

He took off down the hall, calling over his shoulder for Chase to get the closest cop car in the area over to Sue's.

Sue let the spray of the shower's hot water hit the back of her neck where she wore her tension like a yoke. She'd tried to write, but her doubts about Benny kept her from getting words on paper.

Not that this tension had only begun this afternoon. For days now, Sue had tried to get Jason to give her some kind of hint of what was really going on between them. What was going to happen when he caught the stalker, when he didn't have to stay here to protect her? Would he pack up his things and leave? They were down to sixteen condoms and counting.

She knew she was head over heels in love with him. She also knew that every day those feelings were growing, working deeper into her heart, into her soul, into the very essence of her spirit and life. And speaking of lives, she'd already plotted out hers and Jason's. Like a book, she had the chapters all laid out, and they included *cases* of condoms, an engagement ring, a small outdoor wedding, a couple of kids, and if Hitchcock and Mama could accept it, maybe even a dog thrown into the picture.

Of course, that depended on how many of Jason's kittens she could give up. She even loved the man's cats.

Yup, she had the story of their lives outlined, all figured out. She couldn't help it; plotting and outlining was what she did. But was her plot simply fiction when she should be looking at facts? If only he would tell her what he felt.

Not once had the word *relationship* been mentioned. And they were going through the condoms like potato chips. He hadn't promised, or even pretended, that they were more than just passing time while he protected her.

Oh, mercy! She was truly in line for another heartbreak.

Sue had just stepped out of the shower when she heard the doorbell. She grabbed her white terrycloth robe and tied the belt around her waist. Hurrying to the door, dripping wet, water collecting around her feet, she looked out the side window and saw a policeman. He had his back turned, so Sue couldn't tell if it was Officer Martin or one of the officers who'd come the other night.

As she went to unlock the bolt, her foot slipped on the slick tile and she nearly fell. She barely caught herself on the knob and only opened the door partway. "May I help you?" she asked.

"Sue Finley?" The officer, not one she recognized, lowered his gaze to her bathrobe's neckline.

"Yes." She pulled her robe tighter. "Is something wrong?"

"I was asked to check on you."

Check on me? That didn't make sense. Not if Benny was in custody. "I'm fine."

"Do you mind if I come in and look around?"

Suddenly uncomfortable, Sue kept her finger on the door's lock. She knew Jason suspected Benny, but she didn't wholly buy that scenario, and this guy was giving her a creepy vibe. What if he wasn't really a cop? Wouldn't Jason have sent an officer she knew? "I said I was fine."

"Okay. I'm sorry for bothering you. Just doing my job."

She shut the door and turned the lock. Leaning against the wall, she held her breath until she heard the policeman walk away. Then, shaking her head, she called herself paranoid.

The phone rang, but with her heart still pounding she decided to let the answering machine get it. Not that she would be like this forever. It was just that this was the first time she'd been alone since the attempted shooting. Which brought her back to: Would she be alone tomorrow? If Benny was guilty, would Jason stay?

Five minutes later, when she was comfortably plopped on the sofa, her doorbell rang again. Careful not to step in the wet spots, she reminded herself to grab a mop. Peering out the peephole, she saw a FedEx guy on her porch. It wasn't her normal FedEx guy, Hunky, so she hesitated before opening up and studied the figure a little harder. A big box hid the guy's face. But then she saw her publisher's address on the box. She was supposed to have gotten copies of her book yesterday. Tightening her bathrobe belt, Sue opened the door.

The box was pushed into her hands. The weight staggered her, and her foot skidded on the wet tile. The box hit the floor about the same time as she landed with a thump against the wall.

Her arms flailing to catch herself, she'd felt her bathrobe fell open. Now Sue jerked the edges together, cringing to think that the FedEx man had just gotten the Full Monty. When she opened her mouth to complain, her gaze shot to the gun pointed at her and nothing but air squeezed out her throat.

"You think you can just go around tearing apart families?"

Sue recognized the villain's face, even though she'd only met Beth Fritz once. "Uh, you might want to put that down?" she said hopefully.

The woman took another step inside, shut the door, and leveled her gun at Sue's heart. "Die, bitch, die."

Jason swerved his Mustang to miss the truck. "You get him back out there!" he screamed at the lady who'd answered his call at the Hoke's Bluff police department. "Got that? He'd better be freaking sitting with her when I get there!"

Hanging up, he punched Sue's number again, praying she would answer this time. He listened to the unanswered rings. Something was wrong. Fear clawed at his insides. He jerked his car around a delivery truck, the blue light flashing on his dashboard, and laid his palm on his horn as he ran another red light.

There were no police cars at Sue's when he pulled into the drive. He jerked out his gun and thundered onto the porch. His heart slammed against his chest.

"Sue?" he called and ran inside. As his feet hit the tiled entry, he slid forward and went down. His gun skidded across the room. When he looked up, a woman—a large woman dressed in a FedEx outfit—loomed over him.

A .38 was shoved into his nose. His gaze flipped from the woman holding it to Sue. A loose rope hung from her wrists as if the bitch had been in the process of tying her up. The .38 moved to his brow.

Jason swallowed. "You don't want to do this."

"*Want* to?" the woman snarled, her voice truly more male than female. "I never wanted to do this. She stole my husband. He was leaving me. I have to kill her. And now . . . now, you have to die, too."

"No!" Sue screamed.

Mrs. Fritz's gaze flew to Sue. Jason took advantage. He launched himself at the woman, bringing her to the floor. His first instinct was to use as little force as was necessary, but her voice wasn't the only manly thing about her. The woman had strength. She fought her way back on top. Her knee shot up between his legs—a direct hit. Paralyzed by pain, he felt the air hitch in his lungs.

"Fuck you both!" Mrs. Fritz swung her arm around and aimed the gun at Sue.

Jason grabbed the woman's wrist. Holding nothing back, he forced the barrel away from Sue. The woman kneed him again but this time missed her mark.

"Run!" He yelled at Sue, wanting her gone in case a bullet was loosed. He heard Sue's feet slapping against the wood floor, but, damn it, they didn't slap toward the door. "Go!" He fought for control of the gun as the woman's weight pressed him to the floor.

Then he heard Sue's voice: "Freeze, or I swear I'll scatter your brains and worry about cleaning them up later." Sue stood over them, to the back of Mrs. Fritz. She'd found Jason's gun, or she'd found her own.

It didn't matter. All that mattered was the opportunity this offered. The moment Mrs. Fritz's attention wavered, Jason knew what he had to do. Panic continued to bite at his gut as he waited for the right second.

Sue took a step closer, her arm outstretched, apparently pointing the gun at the woman's head. "I swear, I'll do it!"

Mrs. Fritz's gaze shot up. It was Jason's opportunity. He snatched the gun from the woman's hand. He rolled her over, forcing her face into the wooden floor and putting his knee in her back to hold her down. "I don't like to mistreat women," he said. He didn't put his weight onto her, although she probably matched him pound for pound. "But I'll make an exception if you so much as breathe deep. You got that?"

Pain still vibrated in his loins. He looked at Sue and held out his hand for the gun. Then he blinked. Sue stood, hand still raised, armed with a tampon.

"See? It worked." She drew in a deep shaky gulp of air, dropped to her knees, and tears started falling from her big, frightened blue eyes.

CHAPTER THIRTY-THREE

Sue rolled out of bed early the next Sunday morning, tiptoed into the bathroom, and retrieved the condom box from her top drawer.

It had been almost a week since they'd caught Beth Fritz. The woman had confessed she'd been jealous of Sue and believed Sue and Benny were having an affair. In retaliation, she'd decided to kill Sue by using the plotline of Sue's latest work and set up her husband for the murder. She'd sent the rat. She'd stolen the car. She'd taken Benny's manuscript pages and put them in the car so they would suspect him. She had done it all—and all for nothing, because Sue would never have given Benny a second glance, at least sexually.

Benny had admitted he'd carried a bit of a torch for Sue for several months. He'd also told officials that his wife's mental problems had lasted for a couple of years. The doctors hadn't yet put a tag on her illness, but for now Beth was institutionalized and awaiting trial. Sue didn't want her to go to jail, and neither did Benny. He seemed to care. Out of love or loyalty, Sue didn't know which, but he'd been working closely with Beth's doctors and talking to the DA. Sue had heard Jason assure Benny that the woman's mental state would be a factor in the court's decision.

Sue looked in the bathroom mirror at her reflection. She no longer needed a bodyguard, and Jason had yet to leave.

He'd even taken the last week off from work. But there was one problem that remained, and to quantify it, Sue emptied the box and counted. Eight! Eight extra-large condoms were left, and there had not been one mention of love, commitment, or the future. She wasn't asking for a lot, just a sign of what they were doing here. For almost two weeks they'd lived and loved together, but here she stood, not knowing if they were *really* living together, or if they were really in love.

Okay, Sue knew she was in love, but love needed a partner. One-way streets led to Painsville, and Sue had traveled there too many times for her taste.

She fingered the foiled packages. Both time and condoms were running out.

"You okay?"

Sue swung around, panicked. "Fine as frog's hair." She offered him her grandfather's favorite saying because it was the first thing that came to mind.

Jason's brow crinkled, and he stepped closer. "Frog's hair?"

"Just an expression." She placed a hand on his chest, wanting him out of the bathroom before he noticed . . .

Too late. His gaze shifted to the spilled condoms.

"Great idea!" His smile turned seductive as he traced a hand down the front of her dancing-panda pajamas and into her silk panties. Her breath caught as the tip of his index finger massaged just the right spot.

Jason snatched up a condom, picked her up, and carried her to bed. He laid her down and stood beside her.

Seven, Sue thought as she watched him slip his boxers off. They had seven condoms left.

Then she quit thinking about numbers and focused on the man before her. The very naked man before her. He slipped in bed, his body still warm from sleep, and pressed close.

"Any requests?" He unbuttoned her shirt, one button at a time, a kiss between buttons.

"Requests?" Her shirt joined his boxers on the floor.

"You want the top position?" He moved in and flicked his tongue over her nipple. "Bottom?" He moved to the other nipple and gave it the same attention. "Fast?" He swooped off her pajama bottoms; the cotton fabric landed on her dresser. "Slow?" He cupped his hand over her left knee and then eased his fingers between her legs and moved up her thighs. Inch by slow inch.

"Surprise me." She let her legs fall open.

"God, I love it when you do that," he said.

"Do what?" she managed to ask, her attention riveted to the butterfly touches that danced up her legs.

"The way you let your legs fall apart, giving me access to . . . this."

His finger pushed inside her. Her hips rose with her heart rate. The man knew exactly where to touch her. He'd found hot buttons inside her that had never been pushed before.

"Did I get it yet?" His breath swept across her face.

"Oh, yeah," she moaned.

She reached down to take him in her hand, wanting to offer him some pleasure while he created her bliss.

"No." He caught her hand. "First, I service you." He pushed her hand back to the bed. "Just enjoy. I want to watch you. Watch the way your eyes darken when you come. The way your tongue swipes across your bottom lip."

"Do I really do that?"

"Yes."

Sue melted back in her pillow and let him watch. His fingers were magic. Pleasure built. Built. *Built.*

"Make it last. Let me take you higher."

Hearing his voice—deep, husky—brought the orgasm on. The bliss, fireworks of pleasure, came faster than expected. Sue's breath caught, and her muscles clenched and released in joy.

"Look at me," he demanded.

Opening her eyes, she met his hungry gaze. Her heart thudded as if she'd run a marathon, and every muscle in her body received a shot of powerful stress-reducing, feel-great hormone. She stared into his dark blue eyes, and at that moment everything in life felt possible. She could leap tall buildings. She could swim the ocean . . . In the seven-condom time frame, she could convince Jason to love her forever.

A tender smile widened his mouth. "How was it?" He straightened, kneeling on the bed.

"They haven't created a word for it yet. But seventh heaven or bliss comes close." Sue's gaze traveled down his body: wide shoulders, dark blond hair like eagle's wings spreading across his chest, abs that were hard as . . . Her gaze lowered to his sex, standing fully erect and thick. Extra large. And something about knowing he'd gotten that hard by pleasuring her made her want to give back.

"My turn." She sat up and pointed to the foot of the bed. "Now, I service you."

"You don't have to do that," he said, but he'd already stretched out in the exact spot where she pointed. He locked his hands behind his head, his biceps bulging, and his gaze stayed on her every move.

She didn't mind that he watched. As a matter of fact, she wanted him to.

"And how are you going to service me?" His voice came out in a deep, sexy rumble. She loved that rumble. Loved him so much her chest ached.

"Hmm. I'll think of something."

Slowly she brushed a hand over his chest and down, over his belly button. Her fingers moved into the dark curls between his legs before she wrapped her fist around his pulsing shaft. She recalled how his words had fueled her fire, and while she'd failed at phone sex, maybe she could give this a shot.

"How do you like to be held? Tight?" She squeezed the hot length of his male hardness with her palm. "Or with a soft touch?" She loosened her fist around his sex and only with the lightest contact moved up and down.

"Both are rather nice." He raised his hips, moving himself up and down inside her palm.

"Where does it feel the best?" She released him and ran a finger around his bulging tip. "Here?" She stroked another lap around the velvety head. "Or here?" She ran her thumb down the back of his shaft, following a vein.

He inhaled and hissed. "That feels . . . wow!"

She chuckled. " 'Wow?' Surely you can do better. I'm a writer. I need a better word."

He raised his head a bit, and his blue eyes, hot with passion, met hers. "No, 'wow' pretty much says it."

His grin melted something inside her, and she knew as long as he smiled at her like that, her world would be good. No, not good; her world would be perfect.

"Okay, I'll take 'wow.' For now. But let's see if I can't earn another word." She chuckled, then positioned herself between his knees. She leaned forward and let the wispy strands of her hair brush over his sex before she lowered her mouth. Breathing against the tip, she heard him moan.

"You are better than my best wet dream," he said. His hips rose off the bed.

"Really?" She kissed the top of his thigh and ran her hand beneath the soft weight of his balls.

"How are *those* words?" he asked.

"Better, but not quite there." She lifted that neat little package and gently kissed each of its contents.

"Okay, how about you're fucking fantastic?"

She laughed. "Is that why you have this pearly little drop of moisture right here?" She ran her tongue over the tiny opening, tasting him and loving it.

"Sweet heaven." His hips shifted up, then down. "You'd better wrap that baby, because it might explode on you."

She ran her tongue over him again. "Then explode," she said. "Because I don't think they wrap anything in wet dreams."

She drew him into her mouth, then out, swirled her tongue around the head of his sex and heard the sounds coming from his chest. His cock throbbed beneath her tongue, but before the salty taste of his orgasm came, he had her by the shoulders, pulling her up and pushing her down on the bed.

"I don't get to finish?" She pushed her bottom lip out in what she hoped looked like a sexy pout.

"I want to be inside you." He grabbed the condom from her nightstand. In one quick motion he ripped the foil open with his teeth and sheathed himself. "But I sure as hell hope you can come fast."

He covered her body with his. His weight was sweet. His sex, hard and ready, went right to the spot, and faster than a blink he was buried up to her navel. Pushing in. Pulling out. These were the powerful, passionate strokes of a man who knew what he wanted and was taking it. He was taking all she'd been offering.

Each stroke went deeper, was more urgent. She worked at trying to catch up with him but then realized it didn't matter. It would be nice to just watch him, to feel him without being lost in a climax of her own.

But then he pushed his hand between their bodies and found her hot button. Instantly, she was lost.

Lost in the wonder.

Lost in pleasure.

Lost in love.

Seven condoms to go.

That evening Sue stirred some boiling noodles, praying she could fix one edible meal, when Jason stepped into the kitchen after taking a shower.

"Are you going to work tomorrow?" she asked.

"I still have a week's vacation." He moved close, looked over her shoulder. "Wow! You're cooking?"

"Just pasta." *And please let it be good.* "But shouldn't you save that extra time for"—*our honeymoon*—"a rainy day?"

"Tired of me already?" Humor laced his voice, but there was some serious emotion playing in his eyes. Then he blinked, and the emotion disappeared.

"No. I just . . . I don't need a bodyguard now. And Chase misses you at work." She waited for Jason to say he didn't want to go back to work because he would miss her, because he really cared, because what they had was special. She'd take anything, the smallest sign to let her know what he felt, that she was something more than . . . than Ms. Feng Shui.

"You're right. I'll probably go back tomorrow." He grabbed a beer from the fridge, opened it, and took two long gulps while staring at the wall. Finally, he turned around. "Who called while I was showering?"

"Oh, I forgot. It was Benny." She put the spoon on the stove. "He said he appreciated you talking to the DA about Beth."

Jason shrugged, as if it hadn't been a big deal, but Sue knew it was. And it was just another thing she loved about him.

He took another sip of beer. "Let's hope they lock her up long enough to get her head straightened out."

"Yeah." Sue paused. "I do think they love each other. I think people just forget sometimes." *And can go off their rockers.*

"Do they?" Jason said. He sounded distracted and shot off into the living room.

Sue fought her disappointment, moving her gaze back to the steaming pasta on the stove. Just hearing the word *love* sent this man running.

Dinner came out very edible. So why weren't either of them eating? Sue twirled her spaghetti around her fork, sensing impending doom. Jiminy Cricket, was she stale already? She stared forlornly at the rolls sitting untouched in the bread basket.

"You know . . ." Jason pushed his plate away. "I just remembered that I haven't watered the plants in my apartment. Do you think they're dead by now?"

Her stomach clenched. She said, "Depends on the plant."

But a voice inside her head wept. *We still have seven condoms left!*

"I should probably check, huh?" He twisted the bottle of his second beer in his hand. "But if you'd rather I'd stay . . . I mean, it's not easy going through what you did. I could . . . always buy more plants. Plants are cheap, right?"

"Depends on the plant," she repeated calmly, but in reality she felt no calm. Was that the reason he'd stayed—because he thought she was scared? Jeepers, she didn't want him here if that was the case. But, dear Lord, she didn't want him to go, either. Could she pretend to be afraid? Lie? Could she pull off pretending to be afraid for the rest of her life?

No. She wasn't good at pretending. Not at orgasms—although she certainly hadn't had to fake those—and not at pretending someone loved her when he didn't.

And deep inside she heard a voice say, *You deserve better than that.*

And she did deserve better. She deserved someone to love her. But where was that someone? And why couldn't it be Jason?

Catching her breath, she wished someone would catch her heart, because she was certain it was about to fall and break into a million pieces. Maybe two million.

She braved a smile. "I'm a big girl. Besides, I have a whole pack of tampons."

His gaze moved over her, careless, nonchalant. "Yeah. You've got the tampons." He closed his eyes, opened them, and looked at her as if he wanted to say something. Something important. Something that might matter. But then he took another long sip of his beer and looked away.

He helped her with the dishes. The kicker came when he refused dessert. Jason always wanted dessert—or at least he wanted to watch her eat it. Not anymore. She was toast. And was that mold growing on her arm? Maybe not on her arm, but definitely her heart. She had fuzzy stuff sprouting all over that organ. She felt it, too: fuzzy pain. And it was squeezing the life out of her.

By eight that evening he had gathered up most of his things, kissed her, and said he'd see her tomorrow. The vague promise didn't stop Sue from leaking tears the second he walked out. She leaked on the sleeve of her elephant pajamas, on her pillow, and went through a box of tissues. It wasn't until she was bone dry of tears, cuddled up in her bed with Hitchcock at ten o'clock, that Jason called.

"What pajamas are you wearing?" he asked.

She sniffled, praying he wouldn't hear the pain in her voice. He might have left, but her heart hadn't erased him yet. "Elephants."

"I really like elephants. Want to have phone sex?"

"I don't do phone sex, remember?"

"Hmm, I guess I forgot," he said.

What else had he forgotten? Her chest started aching all over again. How long before he'd forget about her? How long before he didn't even remember to call?

Why did you leave? The question rested on the tip of her tongue, but she couldn't ask it. Probably because she didn't want to know the answer.

Probably the same reason she'd never came right out and insisted he tell why he hadn't called her four months ago. Because deep down, she was afraid the answer would be because she just hadn't mattered that much to him.

And if she hadn't matter that much then, how could she know she would matter that much tomorrow?

Did this mean she had trust issues?

Maybe. Okay, yes, she'd admit it. She had trust issues. Sue Finley had major trust issues. But she'd lost too many people she had trusted to always be there for her. How could she not have some trust issues with someone she really didn't trust? Someone who offered no promises.

"How's your plants?"

"Hanging in there."

Silence filled the line.

"You okay?" he asked.

"Tired," she said. *Dying inside.*

"Do you want me to let you go?" he asked, his tone solemn. *Never.* "Probably."

It had been hell. He hadn't slept a wink. His gut hurt. Was this what it felt like to lose an arm?

Jason pulled into Sue's drive and stared at her house as the sun rose. He hadn't lost her, he told himself and gripped the steering wheel so hard his hands hurt. Leaving was the right thing. They were lovers, damn good lovers. So what if she didn't need him in other ways? She needed him for sex. Wasn't that enough?

He waited at least another thirty minutes before he went inside. Letting himself in, he quietly walked to her bedroom. His heart jumped into his throat when he saw her, all warm, cozy, and sleeping. She was so damn beautiful it hurt to look at her.

But look he did. He soaked in her image, the petite curves swathed in cotton elephant-print pajamas, her right ankle tucked under her left, her hair a blonde halo around her head. His heart wanted to scream out words he'd never said, promises he'd never made to anyone. But such an action wasn't him. He couldn't allow himself to want something that badly. He was a one-day-at-a-time kind of guy, not the kind that made promises or expected them. And for that reason, he stopped wanting what he couldn't have and started thinking about what he could.

He stepped out of his Reeboks, stripped his socks off his feet, and pulled his T-shirt over his head. Unsnapping his jeans, he pushed them down and left them in the middle of the floor with his boxers. Then he walked to the bed, gently crawled in beside her, and kissed her cheek.

She woke with a start, placing her hand on his bare chest. Her hand covered the place where his heart pounded the strongest. That heart, he felt sure, was half broken from missing her last night.

She blinked those sleepy blue eyes at him. "What are you . . . doing here?"

He ran a finger down her cheek and continued down to brush his full hand over her breasts. "I thought you might need . . . something."

He had spent two weeks learning how to turn her on slow, how to turn her on fast. Now he needed a speed to match the desperation he felt in his gut. He leaned over to kiss her.

She pulled back, even though her eyes brightened with passion. "I . . . I've got morning breath."

"I love your morning breath." He unbuttoned her pajamas and kissed her again.

He kissed her lips, tasting Sue, savoring what he'd hungered for all night. He moved his kisses to her neck. The way his face fit in that feminine curve had him changing his mind about needing it fast. No, he wanted it slow. He wanted this so good that she felt what he felt, that she knew all the words he couldn't say.

Slowly he dipped his hand into her pajama bottoms, brushing it across her abdomen, feeling her muscles tighten with each pass of his palm. Her hips rose, encouraging him to take his touch lower, but he wasn't ready yet. Catching the waistband, he slipped off her pajamas. Then he shifted his body downward, placing slow damp kisses on her breasts as he went.

When he looked up and saw the moisture on her tightened nipples, his cock grew harder. He flicked his tongue inside her belly button and heard her moan.

"Hmmm, you like that?" He looked up.

"Oh, yes," she murmured, her eyes closed, both hands holding fistfuls of blanket at her sides.

"Do you like *this*?" He moved down, ran his tongue across the top of her pelvis.

"Yes." She ground her thighs together.

"Now don't go trying to keep me out." He slipped his hand between those locked thighs. "Or you might miss what I'm going to do next."

He felt her relax, felt her hips shift in the sweet up and

down motion that told a man a woman was ready. But he wasn't ready. Not yet. He wasn't finished loving her.

"Spread those thighs for me." A shot of lust hit his groin and a sense of power washed over him when she obeyed. "Wider."

Positioning himself between her knees, he leaned in and breathed kisses up her thighs. Staring at the pink moist flesh before him, he felt his arousal become painful.

"Do you know how beautiful you are here?" He ran a finger up her thigh, over the patch of blonde curls, and dipped it inside the wet cleft of her sex. Her hips shot up and her knees came against both sides of his face. He pulled his finger away.

"Don't stop," she muttered. "Please, I need—"

"Relax your legs, baby." Turning his face, he nipped the inside of her right thigh with his teeth. "Open them back up for me."

"Jason." She said his name like a plea.

"You can beg, Sue, but let me apologize now, because I'm going to take my sweet time, and you are going to just have to suffer through it."

Six.

Six condoms left, Sue thought later as she watched Jason dry off from his shower. Still curled up in bed, still reveling in the three orgasms he'd given her, she watched her tan towel move over masculine perfection.

"Keep looking at me like that and I'm going to jump back in that bed with you and crawl between your legs again."

She grinned, emotionally dizzy from first crying her eyes out and then finding him in her bed this morning, and then enjoying his new level of lovemaking. The man was a god.

"Okay. I warned you." He tossed the towel over his shoulder and dove onto the bed.

Sue squealed, rolled off the mattress, and laughed as a very naked Jason chased her across the bedroom. But what kept her from taking him up on his offer was the use of another condom. She had to conserve them, make them last as long as she could.

He made coffee and then scrambled some eggs while she burned some toast. He didn't seem to mind the dark edges; he ate it anyway.

Just as they were about to sit down, his phone rang. Sue watched him take the call.

"No show again." He cut his eyes at Sue and grinned. "Yes, ma'am. I'll do that."

When he hung up, he laughed. "Mrs. Cucumber Lady needs me to call the limo service because her driver is five minutes late."

Sue chuckled. "Why don't you tell her you can't continue to do this?" But even as she said it, she knew Jason wouldn't. He complained a little, but Sue somehow sensed he enjoyed helping the woman.

During breakfast they talked, but for some reason a lighter mood seemed lost and the conversation felt forced. Sue found herself saying dumb things to avoid awkward moments. "Do you believe in UFOs? Did you know that talking to your plants can help keep them healthy?"

Jason helped her clean the kitchen afterward, and she continued to chatter about off-the-wall subjects.

When the dishes were done and she was in the middle of another tangent, he backed her against the wall, putting everything he had into a kiss—his tongue, his hands, his body. But finally he came up for air and said, "I've got to go or I'll be late." He winked at her. "I'll call you tonight." Then he walked out.

Call. He would call her tonight.

Sue pressed her forehead to the dining room window and watched his Mustang drive away. Suddenly alone, she felt the few tears she hadn't shed last night come a-calling. All she could think was: The man had kissed her mindless and then said he'd *call* her. Why did that seem so freaking familiar? It was like four and half months ago.

No, it won't be like that this time. Jason wouldn't do that to her again.

But as much as she wanted to believe that, she knew she'd grown tired of guessing what Jason felt. Deep down she believed he cared, but it was time for them to talk. To really talk. Tonight when he called, they wouldn't be chatting about UFOs.

Sue waited for the call. When he didn't call at six, she went ahead and dressed just in case he showed up for dinner. At seven she decided to go ahead and make herself a frozen meal. She ate in the study while she gave Mama and her kittens some needed petting time. At eight, she called Lacy just to make sure Jason and Chase hadn't gotten caught up with something at work. Chase answered the phone, so Sue hung up.

At nine, Sue opened a bottle of Merlot and sat down with her ficus plant and Hitchcock to talk. (Since Ms. Ficus was doing well, Sue figured she deserved most of the whining time.) By ten, she'd drunk three glasses. And at ten thirty, when the phone rang, Sue and Ms. Ficus had pretty much agreed that all men were car-thieving, adulterating, bank-robbing, cross-dressing, fresh-bread-loving scumbags. She didn't need a man. She had a piece of electrical equipment that took care of any occasional itch. And as long as she didn't have temptation hanging around, she only itched occasionally.

"Hello," she snapped in her best go-to-Hades tone.

"What are you wearing tonight?" The man was truly tone deaf.

She bit down on her lip. She'd sworn to talk to him tonight, but why? Actions spoke louder than words, right? He'd left her, and other than to come back for a quick bumping of uglies, he hadn't given her one sign that she meant a damn thing to him.

"What am I wearing? Let me check? Oh, it's a chastity belt," she answered. "I'm too tired to talk."

"Too tired?"

He sounded hurt, but she didn't care. Okay, that was a lie; she still cared, but one more glass of Merlot should take care of that problem. Who had she been to question her mother's quick-fix methods? They were working. That fuzzy pain in her chest had dulled. She might try staying in bed tomorrow, too. She set her empty glass down and reached for the bottle.

"You okay?" he asked.

"I'm fine. Better than fine. I'm great!" She took a big swig of wine, this one out of the bottle. "So I'll see ya later. Wait. I have a better idea. I'll *talk* to you tomorrow. And *I'll* call *you* next time." She paused for emphasis. "Or not. But you would understand that, wouldn't you?" She hung up and downed another gulp of wine.

The phone rang quickly afterward, but she ignored it and went in search of a pillow to leak on. As she stepped into her bedroom, she mentally imagined a big road sign standing beside her bed.

Welcome to Painsville, it read. *Where people go when love's one-sided.*

So much for her mother's Merlot fix.

At seven the next morning, Melissa called to remind Sue she had a signing Wednesday evening at a bookstore across town. Sue promptly reminded Melissa of the time difference between Texas and New Jersey and hung up.

At eight, Sue's mother called to remind her that they were supposed to get together at her grandparents that evening for an Elvis-meets-the-parents night. Sue reminded her mother that she had never forgotten an appointment, didn't need reminding, and promptly hung up.

At eight fifteen, her grandmother called to remind her that she was supposed to be respectful to her mother and never hang up on her. Sue reminded her grandmother that Peggy Finley was too old to be tattling. This time her hang-up was a little less abrupt.

At nine, her grandfather called to remind her that both her mother and grandmother were a little nutty but that they loved her. Sue reminded her grandfather that she knew the whole fricking family was a few fries short of a Happy Meal, and if he was smart he'd go ahead and make reservations at the nuthouse for the entire crew.

"But I still love everyone." Sue hiccupped and hung up. Then she unplugged her phone. This was her official veg day, and she didn't need any more guilt-inducing interruptions.

And that's when her cell phone rang.

She snatched it up, checked to see who was calling. This was the last straw. It was Jason.

She slung the phone across the room and went to find another pillow to leak on.

CHAPTER THIRTY-FOUR

That evening, Sue pulled up at her grandparents' house at the same time as a pale blue Cadillac sporting a bumper sticker that read, *Elvis has left the building*. Sue had known that sooner or later she'd have to face Bill in a one on one, but later would have been really nice. Later, as in maybe in twenty or thirty years. Moaning, she dropped her head on the steering wheel.

Be nice. Her mom's plea from the earlier phone call still echoed inside Sue's head.

Stepping out of her car, she gave the man a quick inventory, trying to figure out what her mother saw in him. While his clothes didn't scream retro—navy slacks and a short-sleeved, white silk shirt—his haircut and Elvis mannerisms did. He had *I'm the King* written all over him. From the cocky shifting of his shoulders to the loose tilt of the head and the quivering thing he did with his lips. And don't forget the shoes. Blue suede. Her grandfather was either going to croak or Bill would be pinned to velvet like a roach before the night was done.

As Sue got closer, the man shuffled his blue suedes, wiped his palms on his pants, and then pocketed his hands. Sue's steps faltered. As a fidgeter, she recognized a fellow fidgetee. Obviously this Elvis had a case of the nerves. Not very Elvis-like, Sue thought, and continued forward.

Be nice.

"You made it." Sue waved. She met her mother's beau beside his car and feigned a smile.

In all honesty, she had nothing to smile about. Her heart ached so much that she'd considered going to the doctor and asking if it could be removed. The hangover she'd had this morning still had its claws in her. She'd spent a good ten minutes before she came here apologizing to her ficus plant for her behavior last night. Oh, yeah, she'd given her plant an earful. She'd cried and whined about how unfair it was her father had died; how cruel it was that Collin had lied to her all those years. And how stupid she'd been to trust her heart to Jason. How many times had Sue herself been on the receiving end of one of her mother's Merlot quick-fixes? No one deserved that. Not even a plant.

"Hi." The man ducked his head a little, and his pale green eyes met hers. "I . . . I brought fruit." He motioned to the caddie's open door. "A basket for you and your grandparents."

Sue nodded. "That's nice."

"I bought your grandfather . . . a book on bugs. Your mom said he likes roaches." Elvis appeared nervous.

"Yeah," Sue said.

The guy's obvious vulnerability was softening her opinion of him. His attempt to impress her grandparents gave him another point. But considering she used the one to a hundred scale and he had only two points, the man had a heck of a lot of impressing left to do. And she still wasn't going to Graceland.

Sue met Elvis's nervous gaze. "My grandpa has a thing about roaches. He always wanted to be an entomologist."

"Yeah, your mom explained it." He shifted again, pulled his hands from his pockets, and dried them on his pants. When his eyes met hers, Sue knew he had something to say, and she'd bet a monkey's uncle that she wasn't going to like it. "I love your mom," he blurted.

Sue took a small step back, not wanting to have this conversation, but dad-blast it if she didn't admire the man for being blunt. *Three points*. But there were quite a few to go still.

"I just don't think you guys should rush into anything."

The man nodded. "We're not. I asked her to marry me, but we're going to give it some time. I just . . . wanted to get my intentions out in the open."

Sue felt better—not about Elvis's intentions, but about her mother not rushing things. "Good."

Elvis glanced up at the house.

Sue took pity on him. "They're not that bad," she said.

"Oh, I don't imagine they are. But I haven't been brought home to meet the parents in forty years."

Sue ducked down to see the huge fruit baskets in the front seat of his car. "Look at the bright side. If they like you, they'll show you mom's naked baby pictures."

Elvis tilted his head back, a lock of dark hair falling onto his brow and making him look even more like the King. "Your mom said I'd like you."

"I wouldn't believe everything Peggy says." Sue motioned to his car. "You need some help with those baskets?"

"Yes, thank you." He reached in and pulled out a bag and some yellow roses. His gaze met hers. "I brought your grandma flowers. Oh, yeah, I also got you a book." He pulled out a hardcover and handed it to her.

"*101 Ways to Murder Someone*?" Sue's smile was genuine now. "Wow, I've been looking for this! Thank you!" Four points . . . no, the book was worth about ten. It had been out of print for years. Elvis was up to thirteen points! Who would have guessed?

He smiled back, just as genuine. "I figured you would like it. Your mom gave me your books to read. I . . . stayed up all the nights last week finishing them."

Okay, that got him at least another twenty points. But she still wasn't going to Graceland. Nope. No Graceland.

"Thanks." She looked back at the book he'd given her. "I've really been wanting this."

"Good." Elvis pulled out one of the fruit baskets and

handed it to her. He and Sue moved toward the door, their arms loaded with fruit, flowers, and books on roaches and murder.

Sue sat down her basket to ring the doorbell. A dog barked: Goliath. From the corner of her eye, Sue saw Elvis lower the basket to cover his crotch. *Smart man*, she thought and used her own basket similarly. Real smart. Another ten points. The man shuffled his feet again and shot her a desperate look.

And then, somehow, it hit her. She realized why Bill was here, why he was braving her grandparents and the dog and everything that might befall him inside this house: He loved her mother and wasn't afraid to admit it and act upon it. The fruit-selling, Elvis-impersonating Bill Delaney was just crazy enough to fit into this family.

Too bad Jason hadn't been.

Bill cleared his throat. "Any last minute bits of wisdom you might throw my way?"

Sue thought. "Yeah. Never eat the casserole." Goliath barked again. "And Bill?"

"Yeah?" he asked, his gaze locked on the door.

"Welcome to the family."

Jason paced Sue's living room. Where the hell was she, and why hadn't she answered even one of his calls? He'd left over a dozen messages. He needed to see her. Now. Whatever he'd done, he could fix it.

You can't fix this. A voice from his past played in his head. He'd been nine and only on his second foster home. The caseworker had shown up to collect him from school that day. He'd begged her to let him talk to the foster parents before they sent him away. Surely if they knew it was their own son who'd started the fight they would understand, but the caseworker already had Jason's things in her trunk.

Can't fix this. The voice came again in his head. But damn it, he wasn't nine anymore! Sue and he hadn't even fought. He didn't understand.

He didn't understand women, but he did understand pain. He felt plenty of it now. Pain always put him in the worst of moods. This morning he'd yelled at Chase and called their sergeant a presumptuous overweight toad. Oh, he'd called the guy that before, but never to the man's face and definitely not in front of the man's wife. Then Jason had snapped at Maggie when she called to remind him about bringing Sue by to autograph books. At lunch he'd scowled at a waitress because his French fries were lukewarm. He'd wanted them hot, and preferably hot off Sue's plate. He hadn't wanted to be eating alone, but she wouldn't answer his calls so he could ask her to lunch.

He dropped onto Sue's sofa and heard air seep out the bullet hole, giving a sigh of frustration.

As bad a mood as he'd suffered during the morning hours, after lunch he'd quit holding back and really gave the world hell. He'd had another run-in with Chase, one with Danny, and even managed to piss off the teenage attendant at Starbucks. Then Mrs. Roberts called complaining that her limo driver had doubled his price on her. In a pissed off tone, he promised he'd fix it, and then needing someone else to yell at, he took fifteen minutes to drive over to the limo service and almost came to blows with the idiot driver who'd tried to claim the woman had given him a fifty dollar tip. The woman might be nuttier than peanut brittle, but he recognized a lowlife piece of shit when he saw one.

Jason didn't leave until the boss personally gave the driver his walking papers and he got the man's information just in case he could talk the old woman into pressing charges.

And his mood hadn't gotten any better when he arrived at Sue's house and she wasn't home.

The sound of a key turning in the lock alerted him, and he jumped up just as Sue walked in. Seeing her brought a big aching chasm to his chest. He almost couldn't speak, his chest hurt so much.

"Where have you been? Why aren't you answering my calls?"

"What are you doing here?"

She knelt to pet Hitchcock and avoided his eyes. How the hell had they gotten back to the can't-look-you-in-the-eye stage?

"What's going on?" Jason raked a hand over his face.

Sue tilted her chin back. "I wouldn't know. I'm pretty much clueless." Then her blue gaze met his.

Okay, she was going to look at him. But this wasn't the look a man wanted to get. It was the kind of look that provoked one to cover his family jewels.

"You're mad."

"Am I?" she asked.

Mama strolled out of the back room and did a figure-eight around his legs. Hitchcock hissed. Jason ignored both cats and kept his eyes on Sue. In addition to her pissed-off expression, she looked hurt, and tired . . . and wonderful. All he wanted to do was hold her.

"I guess you came for your cats, huh?" Her voice came out squeaky. "Well, I can't stop you from taking them, but I just think since Mama and the kittens are used to being here that you should just leave them for now." Then she blinked. "Oh, Hades, she's your cat not mine. Not that you'd be heartbroken. You haven't even named her."

He moved toward Sue, but she took a step back. The reaction stung. "What the hell is happening here?" he demanded.

She didn't answer, so he continued. "What is it you want? What do you need from me?"

She shook her head. "Funny you should ask that," she said. "Because I've been meaning to ask you the same question. What *is* going on here? What do *you* need, Jason?"

"Me? I . . . I don't need anything. I'm perfectly fine with the way things are. It's you that's acting as if . . . as if we're over." Just saying it sent pain vibrating through his body. How could they be over? They had just gotten started. He'd counted on Christmas, Valentine's Day, and Easter. He'd even done a search last night to see if they made Godiva chocolate bunnies.

"If you don't need anything, then why are you here? Why are you standing in my living room?"

"Because I have to find out what's wrong. You obviously need something or you wouldn't be acting like this." Damn, it hurt to breathe. The thought of losing her stopped his heart. "So just tell me what it is and I'll give it to you."

"It doesn't work like that, Jason." Her chin shot up.

"*What* doesn't work like that? Damn it, Sue, I don't understand any of this. I saw you yesterday morning. We had sex. I thought I made you happy." Fear pushed his frustration up a notch. "You came three times. What? You wanted four? I offered, didn't I?"

She stared up at him, and he saw that unfocused look in her eyes. The same freaking look that had been scaring him for over a week.

"What else could I want from you but sex?" she murmured. She pressed her palms into her eye sockets and shook her head. The next words came out muffled, but he heard them. "I should have walked when I discovered you didn't name your cat. Jeepers! You didn't even know its sex. When will I learn?"

"*What?*" he bellowed. "You've been going on about this forever. What is the big freaking deal about me not naming my cat or knowing her sex?" He tried to catch his breath but instead blurted another obvious statement. "This isn't about my cat! It's about us."

"Go home, Jason," Sue replied.

"Are you mad because I didn't stay Sunday night?"

He saw tears form in her eyes. "Go home," Sue repeated, but there wasn't any conviction in her tone. Sure, her words were clear, but her expression said something different. Sad thing was, he was no damn good at reading expressions.

Can't fix this.

But he had to try.

"Is that it?" he asked. "You were afraid? All you had to do was say so and I'd never have left." He would fix this, damn it!

She folded her arms over her chest. "I'm not afraid."

While he believed her, he could tell from the look in her eyes that he was closer to getting to the truth. And then the truth stared him in the face.

"You want me to move in. Is that it?"

"No. I will not just . . . just live with you until I go stale."

"Just live with me? 'Just,' as in . . . you want more? Is that it? What do you *need*, Sue?" His heart folded over on itself when she didn't answer him. "What is it you want? A ring on your finger? A piece of paper to frame on the wall?" He slapped his hand on a nearby chair. "Why do people do that when . . . when all it takes is another piece of paper to say the first paper meant nothing? People can walk out of your life just like that, Sue. It's just paper."

He paced once across the room and then came back to stand in front of the chair and her. "A freaking birth certificate or a marriage license doesn't mean crap." He hit the chair with his palm again. "When people decide it's over, they walk away and they don't come back. No matter how much you want them to, they just don't."

She turned and faced the wall. Away from him. He was losing her. Losing his right arm. He felt his entire body shake.

The words formed in his head and he couldn't believe it. He was a one-day-at-a-time kind of guy, but she was his right arm. Swallowing, he tossed away everything he'd thought to be true about himself.

"But if that's what you need . . ." He walked over, took her by the elbow, and forced her to look at him. "If that's what you need, let's do it. We'll find a judge and we'll get that damn piece of paper."

She jerked away. Shock and tears covered her face. "No!"

He looked at her and couldn't breathe again. "What? You don't think I'm serious? I'm dead serious. Let's get that piece of paper. You can frame it. Hang it on the wall. Hell, I'll hang it for you."

Her tears were flowing faster now, and her nose was running, getting red. He tried to reach for her, to hold her, to let her leak all over his shirt, but she shook her head. "You can't even name your cat." Then, pivoting on her heel, she stormed down the hall. "Leave!" she yelled over her shoulder, and she slammed her bedroom door.

As he left Sue's house, Jason's heart lay in a mangled mess. Words replayed in his head. *You can't fix this.*

CHAPTER THIRTY-FIVE

Wednesday morning, in a piss-poor mood, Jason got a call from Michael Braxton in New York. He'd just gotten back from Paris on some photo shoot. Michael Brighten, the other missing artist, had surfaced yesterday, as well.

"What the hell is all this about?" Braxton snapped. "I didn't intentionally put her on the cover."

Jason didn't believe him, but since he now knew the man wasn't Sue's stalker, he really didn't care to speak to the guy. Frankly, he wasn't in the mood to speak to anyone.

He'd barely gotten him off the phone when Chase walked in.

"You look like shit again today," Chase remarked. "Woman troubles?"

"Back off," Jason growled. Sitting at his desk, he downed his fourth cup of coffee. It tasted like it was made last week, but he didn't care. Nothing tasted right. Nothing felt right. He was missing his right arm.

Suddenly hearing what his partner said, he snapped his head up. "Did Sue say something?"

"No. It's written on your forehead," Chase replied. "You're miserable. Only a woman can make a man that miserable."

"Tell me something I don't know." Jason tossed his Styrofoam cup in the garbage and stared at yesterday's jelly donut. He hadn't bothered to eat it or throw it away.

"Okay. I'll tell you something you don't know," Chase agreed. He sat down on the edge of Jason's desk. "But you asked for it."

"Spare me," Jason muttered.

Chase ignored him. "Maybe it's time for you to grow up and stop treating women like they're something to play with and toss aside."

Jason heel-kicked his chair back until it made contact with the wall. "Maybe it's time for you to leave my office before I start tossing your ass out."

"Why? Because the truth hurts?" Chase stood.

"You don't know the truth," Jason snapped. "And you sure as hell don't know what I'm feeling."

"Oh, from where I stand the truth seems pretty fucking evident. And I'd bet my right nut that I know what happened. Sue's probably wanting more out of this relationship than you're willing to give. But you love her. Which explains why you've got your head up your ass, because you're hurting, man. So admit it and just—"

"And just what—ask her to marry me?" Jason pounded his fist on the edge of the desk. "Is that what I should do?"

Chase leaned back. "I don't expect you to go that far, but at least talk about the future."

Jason shot up and went to the window. Swallowing his pride, realizing he wasn't mad at Chase but at the situation, he glanced back. "I asked Sue to marry me."

Chase got a surprised smile on his face. "You did? Hot damn!"

Jason pressed both palms into his eyes, pulled them away, then met Chase's eyes. "She refused."

His friend's smile vanished. "Crap. I really didn't see *that* coming."

Jason's throat felt tight. "I didn't see it coming, either."

Chase crossed his arms on his chest. "Wait a minute. Something doesn't feel right. You asked her to marry you, and she flat out said no?"

"She didn't exactly flat out say no . . ." Jason shoved his hands in his jean pockets.

"What exactly did she say?" Chase asked.

"She said . . . she said, 'You didn't even know the sex of your cat and haven't even named it yet.'"

Chase got a blank look. "Huh?"

"Thank you! That's exactly how I felt." Jason pulled his hands out of his pockets. "What the hell does not naming my cat have to do with us getting married? And I mean, damn! I don't know how to tell the sex of a feline. I even looked it up on Google and I still can't tell."

Chase looked as if he might say something amusing, but Jason was on roll.

"And I've tried. I don't get it. I don't understand."

Chase shook his head. "Are we still talking about the sex of a cat?"

"No!" Jason glared at him. "I've tried to make her happy. Tried really hard. I went over all things I'd done wrong with other women and didn't do them with Sue."

Chase sighed. "Wait. I'm lost again. Let's go back to the first issue." He held up a hand. "You got on your knees and asked her to marry you and—"

"I didn't exactly get on my knees," Jason admitted.

"Well, position isn't everything," Chase allowed. "But you told her you loved her, right?"

"Not . . . exactly." Jason's chest ached.

His friend let out a huff. "Before I explain how badly you screwed up, tell me the rest. Exactly what did you say to Sue?"

"I said . . ." He got a distinct feeling Chase was about to say this was all his fault. And God help him, but he wasn't sure he could handle knowing that. "What does it matter what I said? I offered, and she turned me down."

"Offered? You don't 'offer' to marry someone. You ask. Actually, you beg. That's what the whole on-the-knee position is about."

"So I used the wrong word. It's just a freaking word."

"Oh, but words matter. Women need to hear certain things. And Sue's a writer, so words are probably even more important."

The truth started swimming around in Jason's head and gut. He'd screwed up—but if this was all his fault, didn't that mean he could fix it?

"It's like going to third base without touching first or second. Men don't always need those other bases, but women, well . . . you know women, you know what happens if you try to jump bases. Words are like bases to them."

Jason raised his hands in frustration. "Well, I'm royally screwed then. Because I'm not good with words. Or any of that stuff."

"That's because you're a man. None of us are good at this stuff. But if you want to make a woman happy, you gotta at least work on your presentation. Just like we work on first and second bases."

Jason crammed his hands in his pockets and then pulled them out. "You're good at this. You can say things. Things like that missing arm crap. You make it sound profound. I'm not . . . profound."

Chase smiled. "I do sound good, don't I?"

Jason ignored him, because this wasn't funny. And he was still hurting as if someone had taken an ice pick to his heart. "I can't do fancy words." He looked at Chase and admitted something he'd never admitted to anyone. "I'm scared. I feel like I'm back in foster care, about to be tossed out of another home."

Chase's smile vanished. "We're all scared. They're women, and we're just mortal men. But you can do this."

Jason looked at the ceiling; wishing, hoping, fear climbing up his throat. "I'm not so sure. You know how to say the words. You know what I'm good at?" He swallowed. "I'm good at packing up and getting the hell out without looking like I care. That's what I've done all my life." When he glanced back at his partner, sympathy crossed Chase's expression. Jason hated sympathy.

"Look," Chase offered. "You did something right with Sue or she wouldn't have given you the time of day. I know that. And you know that, too."

Did Jason know that?

Chase pointed at him. "And it's not just words. I mean, yeah, there's some words you'll need to say, but I know Sue." He thumped Jason's back. "She's not expecting you to be Romeo. I think she just wants to know that you really want this."

"I do want this," Jason said.

"Go to her. Buy some flowers," Chase suggested. "Do some soul-searching and ask yourself what she really wants. If it's to name the cat, name the freaking cat. And tell her . . . tell her what you just told me. Tell her you're scared." A smile pulled at Chase's mouth. "Women love to know men are scared. It's a power trip for them."

"A power trip," Jason repeated. Right then he realized he'd given Sue the power to hurt him by loving her. This was what he'd wanted to avoid. What he'd been avoiding all his life. But for the life of him, he wasn't sorry. He wasn't sorry that he loved her.

He met Chase's gaze again, suddenly hopeful. "What else do I tell her?"

"The truth," Chase said. "And stop pretending that you don't care."

Jason let out a breath. "What if she turns me down again?"

"What if she doesn't?"

Chase started out of the office. He hadn't gotten past the door when he swung back around. "Oh, yeah. And if you really want to win Sue over, you'll have to stop kissing her ex-husband." Jason raised his eyes and stared. Chase held his gut and laughed. "Yeah, Sue told Lacy about that."

Jason snatched the day-old jelly donut off his desk and

slung it at the door. Chase ducked, but the donut hit another mark.

There, behind Chase, stood the purple-haired old woman, AKA the Cucumber Lady, with helmet hair. "Men!" she growled and eyed the jelly-filled donut glued to her chest. "Pains in the rear, every one of them!"

"I'm . . . sorry." Jason had to bite back a laugh when he saw the laughter in Chase's eyes.

She pointed her finger at Jason. "That high and mighty limo service you recommended didn't show up again."

CHAPTER THIRTY-SIX

Sue parked in front of Maggie's and placed a hand over her nervous stomach. Dressed in her pink suit, makeup perfect, she was ready for her signing and ready to face Jason's mom. Or at least she was pretending she was ready. After her father died, Sue had learned that pretending to be stronger was the first step to actually being stronger. Until she got over Jason, she was pretending she wasn't dying inside.

When Maggie called this morning and mentioned Sue had forgotten to sign her books, Sue had offered to stop by before her actual autographing. Maggie had sounded so delighted that when the reality of what she'd agreed to do set in, Sue hadn't had the heart to cancel. So here she was, at Maggie's house, about to go inside and pretend that everything was hunky dory when in reality there was nothing hunky or dory.

Squaring her shoulders, she stepped up to the porch. Maggie opened the door wearing a smile and a yellow dress the same color as her kitchen. The woman hugged Sue and then drew her out to the back of the bed and breakfast to her private residence.

"Come, sit down and have tea. Or do you have time for tea? I could make it really fast. I have orange or lemon snap. The books are in here." She led Sue into the living room. "I have cookies, too."

Sue forced herself to smile. "I have time for a quick cup. Thank you. I'll take whatever tea is your favorite."

"Good." Maggie walked into the kitchen, and Sue looked around the room, her gaze drawn to all the photos. A knot tightened her throat as she looked at one snapshot of a young Jason mowing the lawn. As Sue's finger passed over the image, her heart clenched.

"Is my boy behaving?" Maggie set two cups on the coffee table. A spicy lemon scent wafted up with the steam.

Sue folded her arms around herself. "He's . . . behaving fine as frog's hair."

"Frog's hair?" Maggie looked at her, and Sue decided she really needed to pitch that saying. It always got the same confused response.

"He's been fine," she clarified, even though it was a big fat lie.

Maggie motioned to the photograph Sue was studying. "You want to see my favorite pictures?"

As painful as Sue knew it would be, she told the truth: "I'd love to."

Maggie walked to the coffee table. She opened up a Bible and pulled out a thin strip of photographs, the kind that were taken in those tiny curtained booths in shopping malls. Images of giggling girlfriends came to Sue's mind. When Jason's mother gazed at the strip of photos, tears filled her eyes. Then she handed them over.

Sue looked down and her breath caught. The sheet of photos held a teenage Jason with Maggie. Yet, neither of them was giggling. Black eyes and bruises marred both faces. Maggie's, however, looked worse.

Sue touched fingers to her lips, hoping to stop them from trembling. Looking up, she asked, "What happened?"

Maggie blinked away tears. "My husband Ralph. He wasn't always bad—not good, mind you, but not always bad. However, he drank, and when he drank he was mean." She folded and unfolded her hands. "He'd been sober for almost three years. Most of our marriage he traveled with his job, and I felt so alone. We hadn't been able to have kids, and I thought if we took in a child it might help us become a family."

Palming the edge of the sofa, Maggie paused before continuing. "The foster care program asked if we'd come and meet Jason. I wanted a younger child, but the day I met that boy I saw something in him. Loneliness, maybe." She hesitated again. "I learned he'd been taken from his mother at eight while she went into a drug treatment program. She was supposed to get him back when she got well. But, she changed her mind."

Even though Sue had pretty much heard this, she hurt for Jason all over again.

"The caseworkers told me Jason was hard to work with, but . . . it was as if everyone had given up on him. I had to try." Maggie sat down on the small melon-colored sofa and motioned for Sue to sit beside her.

Sue dropped down beside Maggie, feeling emotions crawl around her chest. Strongest of all was wonder: How could anyone have given up on Jason?

"They were right about something," Maggie continued. "Jason was a trying young man. I set rules. He'd break them. I set curfews, and he'd not make them. And whenever I'd try to talk to him, he'd look as if he expected me to call someone to come get him." Maggie stared at her hands. "I was tempted a time or two. But I couldn't do it." When the older woman finally looked up, Sue saw in her eyes the same emotion that seemed to be bouncing around Sue's own chest.

Sue felt her eyes begin to water. The question she'd just asked herself, *Who could give up on Jason?* took a lap around her aching heart. Had she not given up on him?

Maggie continued, "Once I took in Jason, Ralph practically never came home. Every six weeks he might show up for a few days. I noticed he was drinking again." She shook her head. "He and Jason hardly even knew each other. And neither of them seemed to want to get to know each other."

Fidgeting with her dress, Maggie went on. "Then, the last time Ralph came home, he . . . he went crazy." She pointed to the picture Sue had forgotten she held.

"All I remember was Ralph coming at me and hitting me. Over and over again. Then Jason ran in, screaming for Ralph to leave me alone. Ralph turned on him. They fought. It was really bad. Finally, Jason threw Ralph out the front door, tossed him his keys, and told him that if he ever came back, he'd kill him."

Maggie placed a hand over her mouth as if to hold back emotion. For Sue it was too late. Tears rolled down her face, smeared her mascara, and totally ruined her makeup—the makeup she'd applied perfectly for her signing. But she didn't care.

"Jason drove me to the hospital. I told the doctor that I'd fallen, but Jason wouldn't hear of it, and he told them the truth. The cop that came to the hospital that night, he somehow made an impression on Jason. They talked for a long time. They kept me in the hospital that night." Bigger tears filled Maggie's eyes. "Jason wouldn't leave me. He said I needed him and he was afraid Ralph would come back. The next day, on the way home, he took me by the dime store and made me get in this booth. He said that every time I thought about taking Ralph back I was going to look at these pictures and see what he'd done to us."

Maggie looked up. "*Us.* He called us an us, as if we were a family." She paused. "After that, Jason was different. Oh, he was still a handful, but I never had to tell him to take out the trash or mow the lawn. He seldom broke curfew or skipped school. It was as if all he'd needed was . . . was . . ."

"To be needed." Sue finished the sentence for Maggie and wondered how she'd missed the truth for all this time. She pulled a tissue from her purse. "He was afraid to love someone, but if they needed him, then that made it okay. Because then they wouldn't leave him."

Just for a second, Sue remembered Jason accusing her of being too independent. And she wondered . . . Had she herself been a little afraid to need him? Had she let her own past keep her from completely opening her heart?

How long could she cling to the anger she secretly felt at her father for dying? How long could she blame Collin for being who he was? Her father hadn't meant to die, and after seeing the pain in Collin's eyes the other night, she should know he would have never chosen his path if he'd had a choice.

"Exactly," Maggie said. She touched Sue's hand. "He's a good man. I know he can be trying sometimes, and I feel partly to blame because I guess I didn't know how to teach him any different. So I just made sure I always needed him, so he would let me love him and so he would love me back. And I know that's not right, but I didn't know how to make him see."

Sue looked down at her pink shoes and wondered if understanding Jason was enough. *Maybe it isn't,* a voice whispered inside her head, *but it's a start.*

And it was time for her to start fresh, too.

Hope chased away the emptiness she'd felt since he'd walked out of her house last night.

She looked at her watch. "Oh, crappers. I'm going to be late to my own autographing. I have to go. Is it okay if I come back and sign books tomorrow?" She would have offered to come by after the signing, but she now had other plans. Very important plans.

Maggie gave a watery smile. "I talked your ear off."

"Oh, please." Sue cupped the older woman's hand in hers. "I can't begin to tell you how much I needed to hear all this."

"Well, I was hoping . . ."

"Keep hoping." Sue gave her a quick hug and dashed out to her car.

As she drove, she considered calling Jason, but she

wanted—needed—to say this right. After the autographing, Jason Dodd was going to hear from her.

She arrived five minutes late, apologizing profusely. The program director led her to the mystery section where a table was set up and a group of unfazed people stood around munching on snacks. At times, Sue swore people came for the spinach dip and not for her books.

"I was beginning to get worried," said a familiar voice.

"Oh, hi." After kissing her mom's cheek, Sue skirted her to take a seat behind the stack of her books. "How did things go with Bill and Grandpa after I left the other night?"

Her mother stepped closer. "Your grandfather gave Bill the third degree. He actually asked him where he saw himself in ten years!"

Sue smiled. "What did Bill say?"

"He said he hoped to still be selling pineapples and moving his hips like Elvis. And that he hoped I'd be with him."

Sue smiled. "Do you love him, Mom?"

Her mother took a deep breath. "He's the King—what do *you* think?" Then Peggy Finley studied Sue's face. "You've been crying."

"It's nothing," Sue said. "Now . . . you're not going to run off and get married too soon?"

"Not too soon." Her mom took her hand. "But you're okay with it now—Bill and me?"

"I'm more than okay with it. I'm thrilled that you're happy." Sue grinned. "Though we're still not discussing sex."

Her mom grinned. "Bill asked me to tell you that he'd really like for you to come to Graceland with us in a couple of months. He wants to celebrate the engagement."

Sue chuckled. "Would it make you happy?"

"Very," her mom said. "I know it's crazy, but he really loves Elvis."

"Can Jason come, too?"

"I think that would be great."

"Then I guess we're going to Graceland."

Her mother kissed her. "Have I told you lately how proud I am of you?"

Sue held up her hand. "You're gonna make me cry again."

"Then I'd better stop." Peggy grinned. "Because you, just like your mother, don't cry pretty."

Sue chuckled just as a lady stepped over and picked up a book. "Hi!" Sue said, turning her attention to being an author.

The lady flipped through the book. "Did you write this?"

"Yes, ma'am," Sue said.

"That's a lot of words." The lady nodded as she spoke.

"Well, I have been accused of being wordy," Sue admitted.

The lady grinned and then handed the book over for an autograph. "I guess if you can write that many words, I should be able to read them. And the spinach dip was great."

"So you came just because of spinach dip?"

"It's good dip," the woman said. "But I do love to read."

Sue flipped open the cover of the book to sign her name.

Thirty minutes later, Sue was still signing and chatting with the crowd. They'd discussed everything from murdering someone by lacing their bedsheets with contact poison to unstopping toilets. Sometimes, Sue worried about the people who read her books.

The line was dwindling, and it was a good thing because she wanted to call Jason and ask him to come over for a black-teddy party. She grabbed another book and glanced up at the next person in line . . . and her heart stopped.

Jason.

In his right hand he had a bouquet of red roses, tucked under his arm was a box of chocolates. But in his other hand was . . . a cat carrier? He stared at her, and she saw a touch of nervousness in his eyes.

He set the carrier on the table and handed her the roses. "For you. And yes, I know what red roses mean. I never answered that question the other day."

She opened her mouth to speak, but he held up his hand to stop her. Cat noises drifted from the carrier, and her gaze shifted downward then back to him.

"Let me finish." He pushed the chocolates in front of her. "You like chocolate, and I really like seeing you get what you like. And . . ." He leaned down, opened the carrier, and reached inside. "I want you to meet Tabitha." He pulled out a tiny red and white kitten wearing a pink bow around her neck.

Sue stared at the little creature, whose eyes were open. It was curling up sweetly in Jason's palm. She bit down on her lip. "Jason, I—"

"Let me finish." He looked at the cat and said proudly, "She's a girl."

Sue felt her sinuses begin to sting as Jason carefully returned the kitten to the carrier.

"This"—he pulled out a gray tabby—"is Tom. He's a boy." The little kitten, wearing a blue bow, let out a pitiful meow. "The vet had to really look at him to be sure. So it's not just me that has a hard time telling the sex."

Okay, Sue was going to leak for real now. She sniffled.

"This is Pistol—another girl. I think she's going to grow up to be a pistol."

One by one he brought out the kittens, and then at last he pulled out Mama. "This is Taco. The first time I saw her, she was eating tacos from my garbage on my apartment patio. Oh, and the vet's certain she's a girl."

Sue wiped her nose with the back of her hand. Someone behind the table dropped a box of tissues in front of her. "Can I talk now?"

"No. Not yet." Jason waved for whoever had provided the tissues to leave. Sue pulled one out and wiped her nose as he turned around and handed the carrier to Chase, who walked away with it. When she looked to her right, she saw Kathy and Lacy standing beside the spinach dip—the mysterious tissue donors, no doubt.

Jason wiped his palms on the front of his jeans. "I'm not good with words."

Sue snatched another tissue, cleaned most of her leakage, stood, and moved around the table to stand in front of him. The man she loved watched her, looking nervous.

"Jason—"

"I'm not done," he interrupted, taking a deep breath. "Where was I?" He paused. "Oh, yeah." He held out his right arm. "You're my right arm. I can't lose my right arm."

"What?" Sue stared at his proffered appendage.

A hand moved nervously over his face. "That sounded so good when Chase said it."

He swallowed, then launched into an explanation: "Sue, I'm scared. You scare me. From the first time I laid eyes on you I've been scared. You were perfect. And then when I kissed you, I knew I had to stay away from you. Because I wanted you too damn much. That's why I didn't call." He inhaled. "I didn't do holidays. Lord knows Maggie tried, but I figured I was too far gone for that stuff. Now all I can think about is decorating a tree with you. I ordered stockings and your Easter basket from the Internet last night. I Googled Christmas tree farms." His voice grew tight. "I want us to cut down our own tree. I want . . . holidays. I want to count on them. I want them with you."

Sue gave her nose another swipe. "Anyone ever tell you that you talk too much?"

He looked heartbroken. "I'm sorry. I wanted to do this right. I wanted—"

"Jason!" She placed a hand on his arm, interrupting. "You *have* done it right."

He touched her face. "I think you're beautiful, even when you're leaking. I think your animal-exercising pajamas are sexy as hell. You make me laugh, and you're the best writer I know." He glanced around and lowered his voice. "You're not stale. You'll never go stale. You're the hottest piece of bread I've ever tasted. And"—he grinned—"what you do with a MoonPie should be outlawed. In some states, I think it is."

Sue laughed.

"Will you marry me?" He sounded so unsure her heart broke.

"Yes."

"Yes," he repeated, as if in awe.

"And do you know why?" she asked.

"Because I'm good in bed?" He tugged her a little closer.

"No. It's because I need you, Jason Dodd. Not just for protection, not just because you make me laugh, not for sex or because you like my writing, but because . . ." She placed her hand over his heart. "Because waking up in the morning doesn't feel right if you're not there. Food doesn't taste good. Not even chocolate. And no one's there to eat my French fries." Sue could swear she saw a bit of mist in his eyes. "I need you because I *love* you, Jason Dodd. And I'm going to love you forever and ever. And maybe a few days after that."

He blinked. "I don't think I can I top that."

"Then why don't you just shut up and kiss me?" She pulled on the collar of his shirt until his face was inches from hers.

"I can do that," he said. "Words I screw up. Kissing I can do." He took her mouth in a soft sweet kiss that only got sweeter.

"Don't you French her," a familiar voice snapped from behind them.

Sue jerked away and stared at the Cucumber Lady from the grocery store. Her gaze shot to Jason and then back to the granny. "What? How?"

"My insurance," Jason whispered. "I brought her to remind you that even if I am a pain in the butt I deserve a second chance."

"You two love each other," the woman said. "I can see it. So marry him and be done with it." She looked around. "And can you get some more spinach dip over here?"

Jason put his arm around Sue and whispered. "I'm kind of afraid I've sort of accidentally adopted her."

Sue laughed. "That's okay. I think she's sweet and just

crazy enough to belong in my family. Which reminds me, I sort of signed you up to go to Graceland with me and my mom and Bill."

Jason smiled. "Maggie will be jealous. She's always wanted to go to the King's place."

"Then why don't we take her with us," Sue offered.

Jason's looked a little shocked by her offer, then he said. "A family vacation." There was almost a longing in his voice when he said it. Then he leaned in. His mouth touched hers.

"Ah, phooey," said Mrs. Cucumber. "Go ahead and French her.

Jason did.

Gemma Halliday

MAYHEM *in* HIGH HEELS

Maddie Springer is finally walking down the aisle with the man of her dreams. And she's got the perfect wedding planner to pull it all off in style. Well, perfect, that is, until the woman winds up dead — murdered in buttercream frosting. Suddenly Maddie's dream wedding melts faster than an ice sculpture at an outdoor buffet. And when her groom-to-be is made the detective in charge of the case, there goes any chance of a honeymoon. Unless, of course, Maddie can find the murderer before her big day.

With the help of her fellow fashionista friends, Maddie vows to unveil the cold-blooded killer. Is it the powerful ex-husband, the hot young boy toy, a secret lover from the past, or a billionaire bridezilla on the warpath? As the wedding day grows closer, tempers flare, old flames return, and Maddie's race to the altar turns into a race against time.

ISBN 13: 978-0-8439-6109-6

To order a book or to request a catalog call:
1-800-481-9191
This book is also available at your local bookstore, or you can check out our Web site **www.dorchesterpub.com** where you can look up your favorite authors, read excerpts, or glance at our discussion forum to see what people have to say about your favorite books.

ELISABETH NAUGHTON

STOLEN FURY

DANGEROUS LIAISONS

Oh, is he handsome. And charming. And sexy as all get out. Dr. Lisa Maxwell isn't the type to go home with a guy she barely knows. But, hey, this is Italy and the red-blooded Rafe Sullivan seems much more enticing than cataloging a bunch of dusty artifacts.

After being fully seduced, Lisa wakes to an empty bed and, worse yet, an empty safe. She's staked her career as an archaeologist on collecting the three Furies, a priceless set of ancient Greek reliefs. Now the one she had is gone. But Lisa won't just get mad. She'll get even.

She tracks Rafe to Florida, and finds the sparks between them blaze hotter than the Miami sun. He may still have her relic, but he'll never find all three without her. And they're not the only ones on the hunt. To beat the other treasure seekers, they'll have to partner up — because suddenly Lisa and Rafe are in a race just to stay alive.

ISBN 13: 978-0-505-52793-6

What's a blonde pirate always looking for, even though it's right behind her?
Her booty.

ANCHORS AWEIGH

Ahoy, mateys! With her grandma wedded and bedded (eeow!) Tressa Jayne Turner is looking forward to the weeklong cruise that follows. Good food. Warm beaches. Romantic sunsets. A swashbuckling ranger-type, Rick Townsend, who shivers her timbers. Nothing can take the wind out of Tressa's sails this time.

Nothing except this *Love Boat*'s the *Titanic*. For one thing, it's a lo-cal cruise. And Tressa's barely got her sea legs before a dastardly murder plot bobs to the surface. Add one whale of a Bermuda love triangle, and Tressa knows just how Captain Jack Sparrow feels when the rum is gone.

Kathleen Bacus

ISBN 13: 978-0-505-52735-6

☐ **YES!**

Sign me up for the Love Spell Book Club and send my
FREE BOOKS! If I choose to stay in the club, I will pay
only $8.50* each month, a savings of $6.48!

NAME: _____

ADDRESS: _____

TELEPHONE: _____

EMAIL: _____

☐ I want to pay by credit card.

☐ **VISA**   ☐ **MasterCard**   ☐ **DISCOVER**

ACCOUNT #: _____

EXPIRATION DATE: _____

SIGNATURE: _____

Mail this page along with $2.00 shipping and handling to:
Love Spell Book Club
PO Box 6640
Wayne, PA 19087
Or fax (must include credit card information) to:
610-995-9274
You can also sign up online at **www.dorchesterpub.com**.
*Plus $2.00 for shipping. Offer open to residents of the U.S. and Canada only.
Canadian residents please call 1-800-481-9191 for pricing information.
under 18, a parent or guardian must sign. Terms, prices and conditions subject to
ange. Subscription subject to acceptance. Dorchester Publishing reserves the right
to reject any order or cancel any subscription.